THIS IS THE STORY of a young Prussian officer and a beautiful French-Jewish girl who meet in Paris and fall in love during the joyful spring of 1932.

AN INFINITY OF MIRRORS tells of these two, and of the twelve incredible years that followed—years of tragedy . . . of hope . . . of human corruption without limit . . . and of human courage without equal.

"SAVAGE AND POWERFUL."
—Chicago Tribune

D1603407

THE CREST IMPRINT ON OUTSTANDING BOOKS IS YOUR
GUARANTEE OF INFORMATIVE AND ENTERTAINING READING

RICHARD CONDON

AN INFINITY OF MIRRORS

FAWCETT PUBLICATIONS, INC., GREENWICH, CONNECTICUT
MEMBER OF AMERICAN BOOK PUBLISHERS COUNCIL, INC.

A CREST REPRINT

A Crest Book published by arrangement with
Random House, Inc.

Copyright © 1964 by Richard Condon.
All rights reserved, including the right to
reproduce this book or portions thereof.

Library of Congress Catalog Card Number: 64-17935

PRINTING HISTORY
Random House edition published September 11, 1964
First printing, May 1964
Second printing, July 1964
Third printing, September 1964

A Literary Guild alternate selection, November 1964
A Doubleday Dollar Book Club selection, January 1965

First Crest printing, September 1965

All characters in this book are fictional and any resemblance
to persons living or dead is purely coincidental.

Mr. Condon is a member of the Author's League of America.

Crest Books are published by Fawcett World Library,
67 West 44th Street, New York, N. Y. 10036
Printed in the United States of America

AUTHOR'S NOTE

The author wishes to acknowledge his gratitude for the expert professional assistance from researchers in many countries, the kindnesses of individual historians and archivists, and the authors of the various published accounts of the period in which this novel has been set. In Germany, the historian Studienassessor Eberhard Jeuthe, his wife Dr. Ursula Jeuthe, and Herr Redakteur Klaus Scheunemann of Frankfurt-am-Main, as well as the Institut fuer Zeitgeschichte in Munich. In France, Marie Dominique Mistler, journalist of the Paris newspaper *L'Aurore*, who undertook both French and Spanish researches, and Geoffrey Bocca of La Colle sur Loup. In England, Margot Pottlitzer, Roland Gant, and the chief librarian of the Wiener Library, Ilse R. Wolff, all of London. In the United States, Charlotte von Ihering, teacher of German at Georgetown University, and Robert Wolfe, Specialist in German Language Documents, National Archives and Records Service, of Washington, D.C.; Virginia Street of New York, and Joseph M. Fox of Random House, New York. In Switzerland, Mr. James Nolan of Lausanne and Reading, Pennsylvania, and Evelyn Condon of Anières. In Austria, Turhan Bey and Countess Wassilko of the Austrian Astrological Society.

The books and references listed below, in alphabetical order by title, made significant contributions to this novel, an acknowledgment which I immediately feel is greatly understated: *A History of the Weimar Republic* by Erich Eyck (Harvard University Press, Cambridge); *Basic Judaism* by Milton Steinberg (Harcourt Brace, N.Y.); *Blood and Banquets* by Bella Fromm (Harper, N.Y.); *Curfew in Paris* by Ninetta Jucker (Hogarth Press, London); *Death and To-morrow* by Peter de Polnay (Secker & Warburg, London); *Dictatorship and Political Police* by E. K. Bramstedt (Oxford University Press, N.Y.); *Eichmann in Jerusalem* by Hannah Arendt (Viking Press, N.Y.); *France, 1940-1955* by Alexander Werth (Holt, N.Y.); *The Germans: An Indictment of My People* by Gudrun Tempel (Random House, N.Y.); *Ger-*

many's *Revolution of Destruction* by Hermann Rauschning (W. Heinemann, London); *Gestapo: Instrument of Tyranny* by Edward Crankshaw (Viking Press, N.Y.); *Hermann Goering* by Roger Manvell and Heinrich Fraenkel (Heinemann, London); *Grand European Expresses* by George Behrend (Allen & Unwin, London); *Great Houses of Europe* edited by Sacheverell Sitwell (Putnam's, N.Y.); *Histoire de la gestapo* by Jacques Delarue (Fayard, Paris); *Hotel Adlon* by Hedda Adlon (Horizon Press, N.Y.); *Human Behavior in the Concentration Camp* by Dr. Elie A. Cohen (Norton, N.Y.); *Insanity Fair* by Douglas Reed (Covici, Friede, N.Y.); *Paris Under the Occupation* by Gérard Walter (Orion Press, New York); *Laval* by Hubert Cole (Heinemann, London); *La vie des français sous l'occupation* by Henri Amouroux (Fayard, Paris); *Cheiro's Language of the Hand* by Cheiro (Jenkins, London); *Jews, God and History* by Max I. Dimont (Simon and Schuster, N.Y.); *Sword and Swastika* by Telford Taylor (Simon and Schuster, N.Y.); *The Dear Monster* by G. R. Halkett (Jonathan Cape, London); *The Destruction of the European Jews* by Raul Hilberg (Quadrangle, N.Y.); *The Development of the German Public Mind* by Freiderich Hertz (Allen & Unwin, London); *The Final Solution* by Gerald Reitlinger (Vallentine, Mitchell, London); *History of the German General Staff* by Walter Goerlitz (Praeger, N.Y.); *The German Generals Talk* by Basil Henry Liddel Hart (Morrow, N.Y.); *The Kersten Memoirs* by Felix Kersten (Macmillan, London); *The Masquerade in Spain* by Charles Foltz, Jr. (Houghton Mifflin, Boston); *The Nemesis of Power* by John W. Wheeler-Bennett (St. Martin's Press, N.Y.); *The Occupation of Enemy Territory* by Gerhard Von Glahn (University of Minnesota Press, Minneapolis); *The Police of Paris* by Philip John Stead (Staples, London); *The Professional Soldier* by Morris Janowitz (Free Press, Glencoe, Illinois); *The Rise and Fall of the Third Reich* by William Shirer (Simon and Schuster, N.Y.); *The SS: Alibi of a Nation* by Gerald Reitlinger (Heinemann, London); *They Fought Alone* by Maurice Buckmaster (Duell, Sloane & Pearce, N.Y.); *The Unpublished Diary of Pierre Laval* (Falcon, London); *The Vichy Regime* by Robert Aron (Macmillan, London); *The Von Hassell Diaries* (Hamish Hamilton, London); *What the Jews Believe* by Rabbi Philip S. Bernstein (Farrar, Straus, & Young, N.Y.); *When France Fell* by Harry J. Greenwall (Wingate, London); *The White Rabbit* by Bruce Marshall (Houghton Mifflin, Boston); *The Wilhelmstrasse* by Paul Seabury (University of California Press, Berkeley).

for RED

"God surrounded me with an infinity of mirrors which repeat my image again and again and again."

The Keeners' Manual

BOOK ONE

1932 = 1938

One

✠

HE SENT HER A MUSIC BOX which played an aria from *Trovatore* while simultaneously emitting Chanel's wonderful new scent. He sang the words to her with his odd, endearing voice:

> "And can I ever forget thee
> Thou shalt see that more enduring
> Love than mine, ne'er had existence
> Triumph over fate securing
> Death shall yield to its resistance."

His voice was very deep and he faulted top notes. But when he sang the aria, he sang it as though he had commissioned this opera from Verdi to give her one small fragment from it and when she tired of that, its days would be ended forever.

He send her three soft pink pearls every day, the pearls of his grandmother, the tragic wife of the greatest hero of his family, one of the greatest generals of the Royal Prussian Army. His grandmother had loved her husband, but because he could only master the art of useless death, she had left him when he had refused to leave the army. Paule had never seen such beautiful pearls. One morning he telephoned and asked her to bring them with her and they walked to the Place Vendôme, where before her eyes a master jeweler in a broadcloth tail coat strung the pearls together and cooed over them.

Veelee clasped the pearls around Paule's throat in the Tuileries before a round and tranquil pool—a clock without

13

numbers, the timeless timepiece which saw children return
to it with their children to float their boats, and then with
their grandchildren. He asked her to marry him, but before
she could reply he sang the aria softly in her ear in soulful
and solemn Italian:

> "Di te, di te scordar me!
> Tu vedrai che amore in terra
> Mai del mio non fù più forte
> Vinse el fato in aspra guerra
> Vincera la stessa morte."

She had known him for six weeks. She was twenty-two
years old; he was thirty-four. She was tall and slender, and
she had the air of a delighted child who had need to amuse
and give pleasure. When they first met at the Italian Embassy
on the fifth day of May, 1932, Paule stood at the center of a
radiance of beautiful women. She was wearing brown, apri-
cot, and salmon: a scarf over the great lapels of that year;
and her soft, dark hair fell down behind her. She was thinking about a musician named Masson, about her father's four
sets of riding boots in four different tones of leather, and of
her father's latest divorce while Dr. Monti explained the
preparation of *Tacchino Ripieno alla Lombardia* to her, when
the tall, blond, handsome man had appeared at her side,
awaiting his introduction. His dark civilian clothes contrasted
with the uniforms in the room: startling epaulets, blood-red
collars with gold crustings, and heavy dress swords.

The Embassy reception was to honor the Bonapartists who
had assembled that morning at the Invalides around the grave
of the Emperor. It was the hundred eleventh anniversary of
the death of Napoleon, and if there were dry eyes in the
room, it was because the Italian Ambassador had been
obliged to invite outsiders due to the extraordinary vigor of
the social calendar that spring. The conversation in the room
was safe and almost entirely devoted to such current events
as the visit of the Emir Feisal, Viceroy of Hedjaz, whose entourage had exhausted three concierges with demands for
more and more facile women. There was every ingredient to
make that spring a great season. The National Lottery had
just been introduced; Malraux had won the Goncourt; Mau-
riac had entered the Academy; Chanel had just launched the
first of the dressmaker perfumes; a Manet exhibition was at

the Orangerie; Baker was at the Casino de Paris; and Paule's father, Paul-Alain Bernheim, the greatest actor of France and one of the four greatest in the world—most certainly including England—was appearing in *Gifron*. Of his performance, François Winikus of *La Revue de Paris* had written:

> He has proved once again that he is a great actor, as in every appearance, onstage and off, he has ever made. He is a regal ornament upon what is the most adorned on earth, Paris. He brings home to us with vast power that today the Frenchman dislikes war, but at the same time he does not wish war to be represented as a shabby and ridiculous thing. Does the author of this piece really believe that war is something which is only crazy and bloody? He seems to forget that the public is dominated by memories of war as a cataclysm which reaches to magnificence. If the author could have avoided showing war as a ridiculous and silly act this would be a much better play.

The tall, blond, handsome man's name was Wilhelm von Rhode. Dr. Monti said he was the military attaché at the German Embassy—except that everyone knew that since the Treaty, Germany did not maintain military attachés. He frightened her when he clicked his heels and bowed, but then he smiled and Paule like him. She liked the smell of him, phermones which communicated before words. He was much taller than Paule, a new sensation for her. His body had power. His eyes were very blue and his hair was dark blond. He had the most wonderful smile: it paid compliments which no words could convey.

Dr. Monti had finished his recipe. Paule recovered. "It sounds heavenly, Dr. Monti," she said. "My father could eat two of those."

"Myself, in my lifetime, I have eaten two hundred. And I can tell you this: there is nothing the French have ever invented . . . in the kitchen"—and he paused to leer—"which can compare with *Tacchino Ripieno alla Lombardia*." He lifted her hand and bent over it, then bowed to von Rhode, and left them.

Von Rhode took a deep breath and stared at Paule.

"When do you speak?" she asked.

"Let us go to dinner."

"But . . . I was to meet my father here."

"At what time?"

"Seven."

He looked at his watch. "Seven thirty-five. Your father has had his chance."

"Oh! There he is. Papa!" The sound made no impression in the maelstrom. Paule took von Rhode by the hand and plunged into the crowd, moving in the general direction of her father, greeting people steadily as she crossed the room but holding to a course which was several points northwest of her father and in the precise direction of the main exit. He was chatting with three awestruck Italian beauties, but she concentrated on making him look up at her, and when he did she yelled jovially, "Franz! Set to!" and he gleamed with delight. Paule pulled von Rhode through to the top of the main staircase and grinned at him. "If I had interrupted my father on his night off, as he stood there trying to decide which of those gorgeous women he would choose, he would have wept," she said.

"I'm very glad you didn't interrupt him."

"Shouldn't a military attaché be in uniform?"

"It's a long story. What does 'Franz! Set to!' mean?"

"It's a family joke. It's Papa's favorite line from all his plays." As they stood close to each other she saw that they were the right height.

"It comes from a perfectly awful play Papa did in London about ten years ago. He was an eighteenth-century fop who had a manservant named Franz to do everything unpleasant for him. He fought Papa's duels, he was bled for him when Papa was ill, he even got married for him, and whenever Papa needed help he would yell, 'Franz! Set to!'"

Paule and Veelee dined lingeringly at Voisin, in the rue St. Honoré, on asparagus, gigot and white beans, cheese, coffee and Calvados, all joined together by Meursault and Julienas. Early in the meal they shifted from French to German and never left it. They lunched together twice that week and dined three times. They saw Yonnel's *Hamlet* at the Comédie, partly to see Yonnel but also to hear Madeleine Renaud sing Ophelia's song in her extraordinarily primitive voice. They had tea every afternoon at Ixe-Madeleine, Sherry, or Chez Ragueneau; they went on a picnic; they rode on the Bateau Mouche. They talked to each other and listened, they looked and they touched, and they fell in love. At night Paule

16

would lie on her stomach, her chin on her pillow, and stare gravely over the west of the city, trying without success to teach herself to understand what was happening. She lived with her father in the flat where she had been born, which covered the entire seventh floor of a large building on the Cours Albert I and viewed the Seine at a point where the river took care to be at its most elegant. Her father had bought the flat to celebrate his first marriage, to Paule's mother, on June 8, 1909. Paule was born on October 13, 1910. Her mother left them forever on February 21, 1916. Her father blamed his first divorce on mixed marriages, inasmuch as Paule's mother had had nothing to do with the theatre. She was the daughter of a colonial planter in the East, her people had been statesmen, and her brother was a concert pianist of the least theatrical sort. Thereafter, with the exception of the stunning vaudeville contortionist, Nicole Pasquet, Bernheim had always married within the theatre, the opera, or the cinema, avoiding dancers because he believed they were interested only in beefsteaks when away from their work, and abjuring civilians.

Paule took tremendous pride in her father. He was a Commander of the Legion of Honor. His prowess as artist, lover, duelist, patriot, wit, gambler, impresario, horseman, husband, feeder, rager, and fashion plate was constantly in the world press. Since her tenth birthday Paule had been in charge of the leather-bound books which held the yellowing daily history of her father's life. Together father and daughter had pored over the books each day when he was not appearing at a matinee performance, so that she would be able to interpret each item precisely in a balanced and exact manner when the time came to write his official biography. Because of the newspaper clippings, she had been taught English, German, Spanish, and Italian; with French, these were the languages of the box-office countries. No one—with the possible exception of her father—understood better than Paule how lucky they were because of his genius, his presence, and his charm.

These were only a few of the things which helped to endow Paule with her sense of great good fortune at having been born a Jew. Each Friday night, from six to six-thirty, while he drank a half-bottle of Moët, her father would polish her pride with rich fabrics from Jewish history. "It is important that you remember, my love, that it was the Jews who rejected the Romans. We fought them in three wars and beat them in two, and when it was all over they offered us citizenship. You see? And when I say wars I mean wars, not battles. We had Hadrian so rattled that he sent a general named Severus all the way from the British front with thirty-five thousand troops, and we tore them apart. And, believe me, not only because they were tired from traveling. Hadrian knew which general to send. That Severus was a very dirty fighter. He burned everything we had and he murdered every noncombatant in his path. They won. They didn't win fairly, but they won. They were the biggest empire in the world and we were so small we couldn't have filled the opera house, but they offered us citizenship and—never forget this, Paule— we turned it down."

Or he would say, "The origins of anti-Semitism are forgotten now, darling girl, but after we gave Saul of Tarsus the basic material from the life of one of our rabbis, Christianity spread across the world. As a matter of fact, by the twelfth century the Jews were the only non-Christians left in the known world and the Church was taking very good care of us because it had wistful hopes about converting us. And it was extremely important to them. After all, they would have a harder time proclaiming Christ's divinity if his own people disclaimed him, wouldn't they? But naturally we wouldn't convert, so to prevent us from infecting the faithful we were excluded from the feudal system until in a brash decree in 1215, Pope Innocent II instituted the yellow badge. It was then the great sprint toward ritual murder began."

More vividly than her own mother, Paule remembered her father's second wife, Evelyn Weissman, one of the great stars of the French theatre. Her presence was so electric that Paule's father had had to dismiss her as a wife, although he kept her as a mistress for three and a half years after the divorce; he was obsessed with the idea that she was more interested in her own electricity than in home-making. Paule was nine at the time of the second divorce. She was a lovely child, tall for her age, and even the caustic realism of her birthday portrait by Felix Valloton, the Swiss, could not conceal the fact that she was exquisitely female with long plaited hair and huge purple eyes which savored the viewer from a long, finely boned face.

All of Bernheim's wives had been kind and loving to her, although some not as convincingly as others. Dame Maria van Slyke, the film star and her father's fourth wife, had been Paule's favorite. Marichu Senegale, the third wife, an Algerian opera star, had been the least sympathetic. She had wept endlessly and in such a strange key after she had gained ninety-one pounds, causing Bernheim to come home less and less frequently. The one thing all wives brought to Paule was information about her father's mistresses, in the hope that Paule would trade information or even come to sympathize more with them than with her father. A man as intensely artistic as Paul-Alain Bernheim had to have mistresses while he had wives; it was a matter of station, nationality, profession, and health. He kept a small apartment on the Avenue Gabriel but he always made it a practice to begin new liaisons at the Hôtel de la Gouache, at Versailles, always in the same three-room apartment. One bedchamber was for the candidate, the other for himself. The furniture in the large room which separated the bedchambers was removed, except for one table which held a gramophone.

Bernheim's custom was to make love from nine in the morning until noon; to lunch from one o'clock until three; to sleep until six in the evening; then to alternate from the lady's bed to his for love-making until ten o'clock in the evening, at which time a light snack and a magnum of champagne was served in the lady's room. After that they would tango to the gramophone records from eleven until three o'clock in the morning. This regimen required his greatest concentration, and he would be unmindful of complaints from other clients of the hotel. At three o'clock they would retire to their separate rooms to sleep until nine the next morning, when the happy schedule would begin all over again until the lady tired. Twice, despite the enormous sums he had spent at the Hôtel de la Gouache, the management permitted a bird to awaken him at an ungodly hour; on both occasions he had had the bird shot.

Paul-Alain Bernheim was dedicated to everything in life, but most of all to pretty women. If a woman was pretty he had to know her better. His method was direct. On the first day he would send a basket of flowers. On the second day he would send baskets of flowers every hour on the hour; florists had dueled over securing or retaining his account. If on the third day there was no response to the dozens of messages concealed beneath the blooms, he would send a fiacre filled with flowers. Then that night he would bribe his way into the woman's house; crouching on the carpet outside her bedroom, he would scratch at the door until elemental curiosity forced her to leave her bed and open it.

"For God's sake, what is it?" one whispered harshly, "who are you? my God, Bernheim! Are you crazy, Bernheim, my husband will kill you, your flowers have already driven him out of his mind why are you here you will ruin my marriage, Bernheim, for God's sake leave, leave now before there is blood!"

Using his stage voice which could break an electric light bulb at thirty feet, he would answer, "Why have you not telephoned me?"

"Ssssshhhh! My God, telephone you, I hardly know you! My God, you must be totally insane, Bernheim, please, please go before he wakes up and turns into a raging tiger—no, oh no, stop that, Bernheim, no."

He was relentless with such women because they had pretended to ignore him and forced ultimate methods. He would reply, "If you do not want me, I prefer a scandal. I demand to see your husband now. I must have you. Let him run me through, but I must have you."

He was not young when he did these things, because it took some years of experience to develop such pragmatic psychology, but his own wives told Paule that the women always appeared the next morning at eight-thirty A.M. at the Hôtel de la Gouache, ready for duty.

On the Friday evening that she was twenty-two, the evening before Paule's life changed forever and a new age began, as on every other Friday evening before, in the third year of his sixth wife, Paule listened intently to her father saying, "The Jews, my dearest, understood the abstract concept of freedom before anyone. Until we evolved this, man was so captured by all of his humanized gods that it was impossible for him to be free. Our one God, an abstract, gives us freedom to do as we will. Our God is not for this Jew or against that Jew. When the time comes, our God is always free to ask for an accounting, for actions good or bad. When Martin Luther turned his back on Rome he made a profound change in the Christian religion by changing man-God relationships to almost the sort of relationship we Jews have with our God. In fact, Martin Luther invited the Jews to become Protestants with him, because he saw that there was no longer any separating chasm between Judaism and Christianity." As her father talked on he gave Paule one more small reason for her serenity. The more human the world became, the higher her adoration soared.

Two

✠

FROM THE TIME of her father's second divorce Paule—who did not think of herself as being gallant—had developed a most gallant and simple basis for refusing to recognize that she might ever be unhappy. She knew that if her father would permit her to stay with him—if it did not come into his head, in some rage, to send her away to the Hôtel Meurice with the others—there could be nothing which might upset her calm or prevent her joy. All during her adolescence, she had been certain that she would never leave her father willingly, and she resigned herself to the fact that she could never marry unless her husband would agree to come and live with them at Cours Albert I. As the young men came to call, as she fell in and out of love, as she reached twenty and passed it, nothing happened to change this resolve. The frequency of her father's divorces, each one emphasizing his loyalty to her, only strengthened the conviction.

As the thought of the meaning of Veelee grew on her, it grew with her dismay. She loved Veelee: that was immutable and it bore with it other requirements. He was a lieutenant-colonel in the German Army. Because of the army he had not had a permanent, fixed residence since the age of nine. She could not imagine the German High Command ordering him into a perpetual billet at Cours Albert I. Putting her father aside while she thought about this business of loving Veelee, she began to understand that Veelee was to all others as a planet is to motes. But she could not leave her father. He had never left her in all of the times he had smashed his life to start all over again; he loved her and he was loyal to her and he needed her. But the thrilling fact of Veelee was stored in her memory to be examined minutely when she lay on her bed staring out into the night. He was the most beautiful man she had ever seen, and his virile good looks were the equal of her father's. They were both the same tree-sized men, very straight, craggy in some places, gnarled in others, and they could both sing off-key exquisitely and with intense devotion.

Paule arranged to have Veelee call at Cours Albert I at all sorts of odd hours, but for any number of reasons her father was never there. It was spring; he was engaged in rehearsals, in a new love affair, in a divorce, in the purchase of cuff links, and in a lawsuit which he hoped would lead to a duel. She was determined not to have to *tell* her father about Veelee. They must meet. Her father must see and weigh and judge, then know as she knew about Veelee. She pronounced his name in the French way with a hint of song at the end of the word; she couldn't say it any other way, and he told her he had written to his sisters in Berlin to say his name was no longer Willi, for Wilhelm, but V*eelee.*

Paul-Alain Bernheim detested Germans. They were the snakes in his paradise. They were the only warning he had ever given to her and he made the warning as regularly as the announcements of the objectives of Adolf Hitler. All during that spring Paule was suspended between the song in Veelee's eyes and her father's thumping resistance to all Germans. Veelee had finally decided to kiss her and she was relieved because it meant that they had passed each other's first tests and could move on to more sophisticated cross-examinations. Other men had kissed her on the day they had met her, but Veelee, with his aria and his fabled pearls, adoring her with his fingertips and from far within his eyes, had seemed to be trying to convey that they must savor all the fragrant fragments of courtship before they moved along, in good time and in more reflective spirit, to the foothills of the mountains of feeling and emotion. She strained to see these peaks, somewhere up ahead of them; in the meanwhile this calm promise was the beginning he sought for them. She felt protected by the crystal shimmer of that security—further still because he approached her so slowly and with such sureness, as in a stately dance, each moment highly polished and arranged for her pleasure.

In mid-June, her father closed his play. He and Paule were seated together on the terrace which faced south on the Seine. Paul-Alain Bernheim was fifty-six years old but looked forty-six. He had starred in twenty-nine plays and had fought twelve duels, but he had begun to murmur that mirrors were not what they had been when he was a young man. On his father's side he had come from a hum of lawyers, on his mother's side from a clink of bankers. They had all been short people, but he stood six feet four inches, with a nose like a dancer's elbow and shoes that could cradle a cat.

"I thought it would be pleasant to go to Deauville just before the season. Do you agree?"

"Oh, yes, I do. But I cannot."

"Why not?"

"There is a man."

"Ah."

"A German."

"A *German?*"

"Yes."

"And you like him?"

"Oh, yes."

"Then ask him to come with us."

"I would in a moment, Papa, but he couldn't accept."

"Why not?"

"Well, he's . . . he's the military attaché at the German Embassy."

"My God, Paule!"

"I have tried so many times to have you meet him, Papa. I want you to know him."

"But I do know him. I have played him. Does he know you are a Jew?"

She shrugged. "He knows I am your daughter."

All Bernheim knew was that they were in trouble. He tightened his control on himself as if this were opening night, because if he blew his lines or overplayed this most important role of his life, he could lose Paule. He knew that he must take everything very, very slowly.

"Girls will be girls," he said with a gallant but wry smile. "I suppose." He pulled the bell rope. "Let us toast your wonderment, for if there is one thing on which I am an authority, it is falling in love." Paule's eyes filled with tears and she dropped her gaze. Clotilde the waitress appeared. Bernheim ordered Moët's 1915 and waved her away. He had never thought so rapidly. He decided that he must divide his objection—that a Jew could not make a life among Germans—into five or six short, pleasant conversations, each of

23

which must be spaced three days apart. Paule was—at least she always had been—very susceptible to his opinions, his wishes, and the conclusions he reached. Though of course, he told himself, that could not be expected to last forever. If he could hold her for these relaxed talks over the next three weeks, he knew everything could be saved. It was a love affair. In the springtime it was necessary to have a love affair. Everyone had love affairs; in fact he had several going himself at the moment. If he did not crowd her, if he permitted her to let him lead her to conclusions which were utterly inescapable, then she might feel that she had reached those conclusions on her own. He would need to spend time with his books. He would want classical allusions, statistics, records, tribal customs of the Germans, past destructions, and every other possible example. Perhaps a German Jew, who carried the German stain, could marry a German. But not a French Jew—and most surely not a French Jew like this lovely child who believed with all of her loving heart that it was an ennobling privilege to be a Jew without ever having been told of the price such inner glory had cost eighty generations before her. He had to reach her; he had to scale the barrier this new emotion had erected between them. He must seduce her into safety, and seduction took time, and patience, and mutual need. Slowly. He must cast merely a shadow over her confidence tonight. At the next talk there should be less joviality, less urbanity, more concern. Then the talk which followed must be statistical and hurtfully new: Austrian, German and Polish anti-Semitism, its ruthlessness. What were Prussians but German-Poles? Expose the record. Tell her about their army and where *they* stood on the subject of Jews. Make her understand that this was history, not opinion. Make her see that centuries of brutality and callous persecution could not be changed by romantic love. She would see it. If he could have his six short talks, well spaced, she would understand all of it. Naturally he would let the affair run its full course as long as there was no question of a marriage. He knew as well as he knew his name that as happy as she might be if she were married to a French anti-Semite, that was how miserable she would become living in Germany with a German who loved her with all his heart.

"Have you been to Prince Nicholas' exhibition?" he asked.

"Yes. Very nice."

24

"Have you seen the American tennis player, Mrs. Moody?"

"Helen Wills she is called."

"Have you been?"

"No."

"André Lugue is back from Hollywood."

"Ah. When?"

"Last week."

"What a voyage! How exhausting it must be."

"I saw Cochet and Borotra this afternoon against Colliers and Gregory at Roland-Garros."

"Who won?"

"I didn't stay."

"Ah."

"There is a delightful exhibition of nudes at the Grand Palais."

"We went to the Montparnasse show at the Salon de Tuileries last night. It seems quite successful."

"We?"

"Veelee and I."

"Veelee? Oh! Yes. Is he a lieutenant?"

"A lieutenant-colonel." She smiled at him. "That is a very high rank in their restricted army for a man of thirty-four."

"Restricted?"

"Their army is restricted to one hundred thousand men."

"Oh. Yes, yes."

"He is a tank officer, actually. They have very few of those because they aren't allowed to have any tanks, you know, according to the Treaty."

"Oh, well. I suppose he can practice in one of the fighter planes they aren't allowed to have either."

"He's about to be posted back to Berlin."

"Marvelous! How soon?"

"On the first of July."

"That will be a wrench. I can tell from your voice that it will be a wrench, although you did a noble job of disguising your expression. Well, never mind. The mails still work and he will have leave."

"He has asked me to marry him and to go to Berlin with him."

"Ah."

Clotilde poured the wine into two tulip-shaped glasses and disappeared. He lifted his glass and smiled at Paule. "To your decision, my darling girl," he said. She nodded faintly. They sipped the wine.

"What have you decided?" her father asked.

"I have not been able to decide."

She could not leave her father. Everything in her mind and body excepting this pulled her toward marrying Veelee. Five wives ago, had she been of age and had Veelee been waiting then, she could have left her father. But by now she had stitched herself to him with steel cables of need and memory and fear. The fear of being sent away to the Hôtel Meurice and being left alone, the memory of the eyes of the wives who had been sent away, the need to stay with him at the center of the whole world. Her existence depended upon the dynamo which was her father. But he did not know that, any of it. As a great actor's daughter, she had taught herself over thirteen years how to keep her desperation masked from him.

"I have the feeling," Bernheim said lightly, "that it is time I asked to be presented to this gentleman of yours."

"His name is Wilhelm von Rhode. His father and his grandfather have each been awarded collars of the Knights of the Order of the Black Eagle—he has explained to me that there is no honor more distinguished in their family profession. They have all been soldiers forever. Will you be free to meet him at dinner tomorrow night? Tonight he is struggling with a monograph which will explain all about the abstract handling of those non-existent tanks."

"Tomorrow? Oh, excellent. Yes. Here?"

"I would rather here, but if you—"

"No, no. Here. Yes. Will you arrange everything you think he might particularly like to eat with Miss Willmott?" He had finished the glass and had immediately poured another. "I am sure he comes from a very, very distinguished family, indeed," Bernheim said, "but it is a different way of life, you know. Beyond a doubt. They have their customs. Their . . . uh . . . food. Their beers. Their approach to life, which the French have always found mysterious and alien—as, no doubt, they find ours." He coughed. "Indeed, many, many of the people of the world find the Germans and their scheme of things to be quite bafflingly foreign."

"We are Latins," Paule said. "Germans are hardly that, but they have different and remarkable qualities."

"To be sure, your Veelee has, or we would not be chatting this way, but I was thinking more of their tendency toward paranoia. There are the three classical symptoms: delusions

26

of grandeur—you know, Orders of the Black Eagles and Frederick the Great and that sort of thing—and you must admit that they do have delusions of grandeur inasmuch as they find it almost impossible to keep themselves from declaring war upon the world."

"That is all over," Paule said. "Veelee explained that to me."

"I see. Yes. Then, there is the second grand symptom—retrospective falsification, meaning belief in only that part of the past one chooses to believe—even if it never happened."

"Do the Germans do that?"

"Yes."

"Can you remember an apt example?"

"There are hundreds."

"One will do, Papa."

"Hm. Yes. Well. In December, 1918—and I remember it well because it was just a month after the Armistice recorded the defeat of German arms—the returning German forces were marched along the Unter den Linden, where German armies have always paced out their triumphs for the populace. They played the same music and waved the same flags that they would have waved if they had just finished sweeping the world before them, and when they reached the Brandenburg Gate the President of the German Provisional Government greeted them. 'I salute you,' Herr Ebert said, 'who return unvanquished from the field of battle.' "

There was a small silence between them while Paule thought about this. She resolved to speak to Veelee about it.

"Even the Germans will acknowledge the third symptom. It forms their politics, their culture, their army, their family relationships. It is the delusion of persecution." He finished the glass and stood up slowly. "But that is enough generalizing," he said smoothly, smiling down at her with all of his enormous charm. "It is almost eleven and I must go out for a few hours. Tomorrow night?"

"Yes, Papa."

"I look forward to it, darling girl."

She stood up and crossed the space between them quickly to throw her arms around his neck. "Oh, Papa," she said. "I love you so."

Three

✠

PAUL-ALAIN BERNHEIM slumped against the wall of the lift, thinking that all of the things which had made him an actor might be the things which would ruin his daughter's life. If he had been a banker he would have seen it as his duty to tell her both sides of the story of being a Jew: the thrilling, unbowed, glorious, unbending side, and also the assaulted, exploited, and outcast side. But he had become an actor, and he had found that his carefully nurtured theatrical pride could not bear to acquaint her with such degraded realities as ghettos and pogroms. Perhaps he had pushed her too far away from him tonight; was he taking her too far and too fast? How he wished that he had more time—but the German was being sent home on July 1st.

A handsome woman, new to the building, got into the lift from the fourth floor, but Bernheim remained slumped against the side of the lift with his hat on. She thought he was drugged. She recognized him and she had heard that actors took drugs.

Bernheim considered that he could tell Paule that the Germans had no perspective about themselves, and that a lack of insight is the worst of all curses. They took history event by event as it happened, and still they could not distinguish between evil and good. They served each event and each master until they could not turn back when their leader urged them forward, because they were unable to remember the meanings they had left behind. Change took the place of choice, but there could never be freedom without self-understanding and there could be no self-understanding without the ability, the hunger, to choose.

Bernheim strode out of the lift ahead of the handsome lady passenger, walked through the main door, and got into his car, a new Delage sport cabriolet which he had won at chemin de fer and which he had decided to give to Carmen

Victoria Lopez-Figueroa, the Mexican poetess, when he next saw her. He turned the car into the rue Freycinet and moved toward the rue de Belloy, changing gear instinctively and thinking that he could hold off speaking about the habitual German attitude toward Jews until he reached talk number four or five, somewhere around June 20th. There would be ample time before July 1st, and of course, when he met the German the following evening he would go to work on him himself. For example, he might invite him to come backstage at the theatre. Perhaps Coco Marquisada would give him a dose of clap. She would do it for him, as a favor. If he really were the grand Prussian officer who flaunted his honor at every turn he certainly wouldn't think of marrying a wonderful girl such as Paule and passing on the clap. Or Olivier Jerrau would be happy to play cards with him. Officers were very sticky about gambling debts because they knew they could be reported, the slimy sons-of-bitches.

Bernheim stopped the car in front of a small house in the rue La Pérouse and hit his horn lightly. There had never been a deluded movement in Germany that the Germans had not rushed to join. None of them seemed to have even the slightest understanding of a single element of politics. The divisive leaders spoke only to each German individually, and that German did not seem able to comprehend that the politician was interested in massed Germans only to gain power. They must feel about dying the way I feel about loving, Bernheim thought, and he shuddered. Since they were unable to retain the memory of the many possible ways to die, they had had to invent that relentless pecking order so that they would not only be able to get permission to die before their time—and, if they were lucky, have the chance to destroy something first or to take a few *Auslaender* with them—but they could die under orders so that no one would be able to blame them for having died in the first place.

A short woman with hands like a bear's paws and each hand covered with diamonds, came out of the small house. Bernheim opened the door to the front seat beside him. The woman had very large eyes, deeply ringed, and a mouth like the slit on a mailbox. "Take off the diamonds," he said as she slammed the door.

"Why?"

"Because it's not very bright to take two hands filled with diamonds on a *partouse* with a lot of strangers."

"Don't worry. If they want these damonds they'll need to take my fingers off. I had them made good and tight. It's better than insurance."

The car turned into the Avenue Kléber from the Avenue des Portugais, then moved purposefully toward the Etoile. "Such tight rings must hurt your fingers," Bernheim said absent-mindedly, thinking of Paule.

"Well, yes. But nobody can get my diamonds."

In a short time their car swung out of the Porte Maillot into the Bois de Boulogne. Bernheim drove sedately along the Allée de Longchamp. One hundred and fifty yards ahead a car was parked in the darkness with its lights on. As they came up Bernheim dipped his headlights twice. The other car repeated the signal. The woman beside Bernheim bit her lip tightly as they came abreast; each car turned on their interior lights separately. A stout man with a mouth which ran diagonally under his button nose sat next to a seamy woman in seedy clothes and with hair like steel wool. Bernheim's thoughts were on his daughter, but his companion stared eagerly into the other car. The fat man stared back at her without expression while the other woman stared wearily ahead.

"Keep going," the woman said to Bernheim. He moved the car smoothly along the road. "We had him two weeks ago," the woman said. "He should be kept out of *partouses*. He never brings his own woman. He picks up whores at the Porte Maillot and everybody else runs the risk of picking up the *peste*."

"Shocking," Bernheim said. Around a turn another illuminated car, a Hotchkiss, was parked, and he pulled in beside them. The interior lights went on and all four occupants stared at each other. "My God," the woman in the other car said, "that's Paul Bernheim, the actor."

Bernheim's passenger wet her lips as she looked at the other driver. "I like him," she said, and then addressed the other driver with roguish impatience. "Well?"

"Take her, take her," the other woman said. "Ai! Paul-Alain Bernheim! No one will believe me."

Both women opened their car doors at the same time. The blond woman walked around the front of the parked car and Paul's passenger walked around its rear. Each sat down in the other's car and closed the door. The woman with the diamond-covered hands said, "Are you nervous, baby? Don't be nervous." Bernheim leaned across to ask if it was to be a three- or four-car *partouse*. The other man still could not speak, but both women repeated the word *four* several times.

Bernheim sent his car forward and the other car followed him, its driver breathing shallowly because his trousers were covered with short fingers and large diamonds. The procession turned right into the Route de Neuilly. "I am crazy about you on the stage, Monsieur Bernheim," the blond woman said.

"Ah, there we are," Bernheim answered. A large Renault Reina Stella, its lights on, was parked near the Route de Madrid in cozy solitude. Bernheim pulled up alongside and leaned across the blond woman, both of them straining to look into the lighted car. The driver, a blue-skinned Senegalese wearing a floppy straw hat and a light-gray suit, was either extremely tall or prodigiously long-waisted. The white woman beside him was inordinately handsome, one of the most beautifully decadent, dissipated women Bernheim had even seen. The Hotchkiss moved ahead and stopped, but neither occupant got out.

"Three cars?" the Negro asked.

"There was talk of trying for four," Bernheim said.

"God, look at him," the woman next to Bernheim said intensely. "What a piece of man." Her hand, as though on an independent mission of its own, dug its fingers into Bernheim's upper thigh. The Senegalese and the wonderfully destroyed woman talked to each other in what seemed to be a dialect, and then the Negro said, "Four would be fine but three is fine, too, and we have three. It's late. My lady says we make it with three cars."

"Oh, Jesus, yes," the blond woman said. Bernheim tapped his horn lightly and the nervous man in the car ahead leaned out and looked back at them. "We have a vote to keep it to three cars," Bernheim called out to him. The head ducked in for a conference: the head of the other woman could not be seen. The blond woman next to Bernheim said, "Oh, honey, let me ride with this black one. I'll make it up to you later. Let me ride with that one." The man ahead of them leaned out again and said in a loud quavering voice, "Three will be fine."

"You want to change cars?" the Senegalese called over to the excited blond.

"I want to change, darling," she said. "This one wants to change." Bernheim wanted to thank her; he could not stop staring at the ravaged-looking woman in the other car.

"We will change cars," the crumbling beauty said in a heavy Hungarian accent. She bit the Negro's earlobe, then got out of the car on the far side. As the women changed cars, Bernheim gave the address of the small house in the rue La Pérouse. When the women were seated, Bernheim hit the horn lightly again. The Hotchkiss took the lead, the Reina Stella was in second place, and Bernheim's car completed the little unit. "I know you," the Hungarian woman said to Paul. "More than six women have told me all about you." She laughed in her throat with appreciative lust.

The procession had doubled back through the Bois. Ahead of them the other two cars had just turned for the exit to the Avenue Foch when there was a loud sound and the Delage listed, then limped. *"Merde!"* Bernheim said softly. "A flat tire!"

The Hungarian woman became indignant. "A flat tire? What are you going to do?"

"I like you," Bernheim said magnanimously. "My suggestion is that we get a taxi and go to my apartment on the Avenue Gabriel."

"No. I could not. I like you too, but with me it must be group sex. It is the only way for me—I am a stone without it. Four years ago we were snowbound in a train in a pass in the Haute Savoie. Seventeen women, twenty-nine men. I was a different woman then. I was married to a Prince and—"

"Which Prince?" Bernheim was as conscious as anyone else of status symbols.

"Passet-Grimetski."

"Oh, yes. He paints on dinner plates?"

"Yes. You know him?"

"I knew him in the war. That is, just after the war when I was waiting to get home. I had made it as far as Brindisi."

"Plon-Plon was in Brindisi?"

"Oh, yes. And very active, too."

"How strange that he never mentioned it. He knows that my great-aunt was from Brindisi."

Bernheim opened the car door slowly, saying, "Well, I'd better start to find us a cab and help you along with some of this group therapy." He smiled at her warmly and, still thinking hard about his series of talks with Paule, he got out of the car in the darkness of the park and was hit by a large Citroën driven by James Cardinal Moran of Ludlow, England, and, according to the subsequent coroner's report, was knocked forty-five feet.

When the English Cardinal and the Hungarian Princess reached Bernheim, he was nearly gone. Cardinal Moran knelt beside him and began to murmur the last rites, knowing it could do the man no harm.

"Franz! Set to!" Bernheim cried loudly and distinctly, and then he died. It was two minutes after twelve in the morning of June 14, 1932.

Four

✠

KILLED BY ENGLISH CARDINAL
ACTOR DIES BLESSING FRANCE
AS PRINCESS WEEPS

* * *

IN BOIS DE BOULOGNE:
GREAT ACTOR DIES
IN ARMS OF
PRIMATE & PRINCESS
FINAL WORDS
"France is Everything!"

* * *

The understandable mistake of an English Cardinal and a Hungarian Princess of the words "Franz! Set to!" to mean *"La France, c'est tout!"* silenced all of Bernheim's enemies at his death, for to minimize a man who had spoken such last words in the presence of two witnesses of such integrity would have provoked a lynching by an emotional populace. Though his lawyer was soon to hand over to his daughter bank cipher numbers and securities from funds and investments held entirely outside France, the national press, on the morning of the death of Paul-Alain Bernheim and for days thereafter, sternly proclaimed him to be "a true Frenchman" and "a great patriot who died as he lived." The Chamber of Deputies grieved that the nation's greatest artist had been struck down and urged all of France into mourning.

The police reached Cours Albert I with the tragic news at seven-twenty the following morning; they had felt that the daughter might as well be allowed to sleep while she could. At seven twenty-five, Lieutenant-Colonel von Rhode's copy of the morning newspaper arrived as he was putting finishing touches on the study he had written the night before. He was absorbed in his text, and the orderly put the newspaper on the table beside him.

The employment of mobile and armored forces in battle will usually mark a decisive phase, and the tanks allotted should therefore be designed to insure or confirm the success of the main attack. Tank brigades or other mechanized forces are not suited for attacking strongly fortified localities and should generally be used to attack the enemy's weakness rather than his strength. Suitable uses may be to strike the enemy on the flank, to attack enemy reserves in movement in order to prevent their intervention in battle, or to attack gun positions, headquarters, or other valuable points in the rear, when results gained are calculated to have decisive influence on the main attack.

A housefly caused von Rhode's glance to fall on the photograph on the front page of the newspaper. It ran on four columns. He took the paper up slowly, unfolding it to read the story which ran below the fold, then read the eulogy heavily bordered in black and boxed on two columns.

One of the most intensely human citizens of the most endearingly human nation on this earth, our France, is gone. Paul-Alain Bernheim lived for the sake of living, not to live "correctly." With human genius for blending

Humanity's whims and self-indulgences with Humanity's aspirations, he cared less about making a mistake or an enemy than he did that one day he would be done with a life in which he had made all the mistakes and all of the enemies humanly possible.

Paul-Alain Bernheim is dead, blessed with humanism. His life was a vivid explosion which assured all who would seek to curb him that there was little enough time given us for living. In that measure of humanism and expanding life, he was France.

Von Rhode grabbed his cap and, yelling for a car, rushed out of the building.

Paule, in a negligee, took the news from the police numbly. Yes, she would identify the body. Yes. Yes. Yes to anything. When they left she turned away blindly from Clotilde and Mme. Citron and walked slowly along the corridor to her father's study, touching the wall for support. She closed the door behind her and stood where all the minutes of her father's life had been crowded into the leather-bound books. Wherever he had gone this time, perhaps to haunt the rooms in the Hôtel Meurice, to which he had consigned all of his loving wives, a part of him was here and she would stay here with it. He had never sent her away with the others, and this room was as far as she could follow him. How could she ever leave this room? How could she step on the cracks in the pavement of time if he were not ahead of her to set the jaunty pace? She took down the first leather-bound book, as if she wanted to read over the minutes of his life again to try to understand what he had left unsaid to her.

In her grief she had left the front door open. Veelee entered and dropped his cap on a chair. Hearing the sobbing, he moved along the corridor and opened the door to the study. He stood behind Paule's chair and put his hands on her shoulders to let his strength flow into her, and as she turned to look up, he lifted her into his arms, touching her hair, murmuring softly. He had the wit to speak in French. She had leaned hard on the protection of only one man all of her life. Now she saw that one man had been replaced with another, and she was able to cut the tie which bound her to her father.

The funeral was a spectacular of grief, and many flash guns. Three independent musical ensembles, totaling forty-six instruments, were commissioned by three anonymous mourners who evidently had the same idea that he would have wanted it that way. Seven ballerinas of an amazing spectrum of ages were at graveside. Actresses of films, opera, music halls, the theatre, radio, carnivals, circuses, pantomimes, and lewd exhibitions mourned in the front line. There were also society leaders, lady scientists, women politicians, mannequins, couturières, Salvation Army lassies, all but one of his wives, a lady wrestler, a lady matador, twenty-three lady painters, four lady sculptors, a car-wash attendant, shopgirls, shoplifters, shoppers, and the shopped; a zoo assistant, two choir girls, a Métro attendant from the terminal at the Bois de Vincennes, four beauty-contest winners, a chambermaid; the mothers of children, the mothers of men, the grandmothers of children and the grandmothers of men; and the general less specialized, female public-at-large which had come from eleven European countries, women perhaps whom he had only pinched or kissed absent-mindedly while passing through his busy life. They attended twenty-eight hundred and seventy strong, plus eleven male friends of the deceased.

The counsel for the departed, Maître Gitlin, read a short service over the coffin at the cemetery.

As required by German Army regulations, Lieutenant-Colonel von Rhode, on applying for permission to marry a foreigner, had no trouble whatsoever in securing approval from the Reichsministerium through his superior officer, General Klarnet, even though the woman was a Jew. This was a tribute to his family's ancient traditions in the military service of his fatherland.

Five

✠

THE LAW OFFICE of Maître Gitlin was in his large apartment, as was the custom, on the ground floor of a building on the Boulevard Malesherbes above the Place St. Augustin. It opened onto a glass-roofed garden containing exotic plants and flowers. The office itself had lawyers' reassurances of leather and mahogany, with tiers of brightly oiled books in rich colors. One glass wall, which was illuminated during the day by sunshine and by floodlights at night to comfort Maître Gitlin, contained eleven gorgeous tropical birds: a hoopoe, a lilac-breasted roller, and emerald cuckoo, an orange dove, and others—all poised in flight or perched alertly, all frozen by taxidermy as brilliant, as unfeeling, and as lacking in significance as the history of lawyers on earth. Maître Gitlin had a gramophone record, activated by a foot pedal beneath his desk, which simulated the yawping and twittering of the stuffed birds.

Maître Gitlin was a rounded man who resembled what the Lord Buddha might have looked like had he practiced law in Judea in 345 B.C. He seemed asleep most of the time, but it was only that his eyes were turned inward. He lived in bachelor comfort, never revealing his right hand's contents to the left. He greeted Paule as his daughter, for he had been her father's lawyer since Bernheim's first contract.

First, Gitlin turned on the bird record because it delighted Paule, then got down to business. "Today is the day of Ste. Florentina," he said, "who received from St. Leander a long and beautiful letter which has been preserved." Paule loved his openings because they revealed what he must think about as he sat in this gay place for most of his days all alone. "Because it is appropriate to your father's will and to its spirit, I will read the opening of the letter. To both of us, your father was St. Leander in a way, and you most certainly have always been the quintessence of Ste. Florentina."

37

"I have? What was she like?"

Maître Gitlin held up his hand. "I am a lawyer. It would be indiscreet to discuss personalities." He took up a book and read: " 'Casting about, for what rich heritage I could leave you, I have thought of all kinds of things, but they have seemed vain to me, and I have put them away from me as one brushes away with the hand importunate flies. Nothing that I have seen under the sun is worthy of you, but I have found, above the skies, an ineffable and mysterious gift which I cannot possibly praise highly enough. Daughter of candidness and innocence, never fly away from the roof where the turtledove, our mother, has placed our young. Rest now on the breast of the Church. I groan at the thought that another might snatch away your crown, you the better part of myself, you my buckler, my cherished gage, holy victim on whom I count to rise from the abyss of my sins.' " The Maître blew his nose. "Lovely letter, isn't it?" he asked.

"I know about Papa's ineffable and mysterious gift."

"What was it?"

"Himself."

"It was more than himself. He made you a Jew, too. But such a unique Jew as has not lived for perhaps seventeen centuries."

Paule was puzzled. "Why?"

"You are like a Christian, born without the sense of original sin," Gitlin said. "Because of your father's ineffable and mysterious gift you cannot understand the weariness and anguish, and perhaps sometimes even the shame, of being a Jew. He instructed you only in the glory."

"Maître, don't believe that. I live—I read and I listen. I know there are certain people who are against . . . but only what Papa said has any meaning."

"So be it. Now, the other part of your inheritance." He riffled at the papers. "The estate provides approximately four hundred and ten thousand dollars in American securities, as valued on June fifteenth, 1932—a low market. There are cash deposits of over one and a half million Swiss francs held in a number account in the Société de Banque Suisse in Geneva. You will have no difficulty remembering the number: it is your birthday run backward—year, month, and day of the month—and it is your father's wish that you reveal the number to no one except your children, and then only through me or other legal counsel. You own the apartment

38

at Cours Albert I and a small apartment on the Avenue Gabriel. Mme. Citron, Miss Willmott, and Clotilde Grellou are to receive ten years' salary, payable as you see fit, to begin when they choose to retire.

"Your father wishes a bronze plaque, in the shape of a gramophone record, to be imbedded in the floor of room number three hundred and three at the Hôtel de la Gouache, at Versailles, on which is to be inscribed the words *La Tristeza No Es Verdad,* your father's personal philosophy and the title of his favorite tango. I will take care of that. His personal jewelry is valued at five hundred forty-three thousand, seven hundred and seventy-seven francs and is to be found in the large, leather-bound record book in his study entitled *Bernheim's Visit to the Rand,* which had been converted into a strongbox. The twelve automobiles, the lodge at Megève, the villa at Cap Ferrat, the small house at Deauville, and the hotel at Biarritz are wholly owned by the Bahama Corporation, registered in the Republic of Panama and now owned by you through the Liechtenstein company, Hirondelle Imports, which has a broad charter, you may be sure. I should like to be permitted to buy the Hispano-Suiza and the Lagonda sports car—not that twelve cars will be too many for you, but because I see the chance for a bargain here. Ah, thank you.

"Now, the formidable production of income from oil holdings in Texas, Colorado, and Venezuela is held in a number account in the Union de Banque Suisse, Nyon branch, canton of Vaud, together with a portfolio of investments in department stores in Japan, England, and Peru, in citrus holdings in South Africa, and a listing of industrial shares which will be presented to you at the bank on recitation of another number which is your birthday recited *forward.* I am obliged to repeat that your father desires that the numbers of your Swiss accounts be repeated to no one but your children, and then only through a lawyer. In the event of your death before issue, the entire estate is to go to the Organization for Rehabilitation and Training. Are there any questions, my dear?"

"But . . . I had no idea that . . . I mean, the way Papa spent his money how can there be so much left?"

"A good question."

"You cannot conceive of the way he spent money, Maître. He did not have a single financial inhibition. There is one tailor—this is not a myth, because I have the letter from his sister—who went into a monastery after Papa took his business to the man's competitor. Why, Teloge, the hatter, sent Papa a pair of stunning sapphire cuff links one Christmas for the sake of his good will."

"Yes, I know," Gitlin said thoughtfully, "but in a forest when a tree is cut another grows in its place. Nature provides. So it was with your father. His fortune—and as you see, it is a considerable fortune—was left to him by—uh—I think, eight grateful women who were extraordinarily devoted to him. It flabbergasted him each time the news of a legacy came to him. He was never able to remember meeting the woman who left him the extensive oil holdings. He had asked me to write a discreet letter to her attorney requesting photographs of her, but when they came he insisted it was all a mistake, that he had never seen the woman before in his life. But the extraordinarily intimate wording of the will which so vividly, even excitingly described the three days she had spent with him at the Hôtel de la Gouache, left no doubt that he did have knowledge of her." Gitlin sighed with wonderment, but recovered himself at once. "As for the rest, he lived on his income of fifty thousand francs a week from his theatrical activities and equities."

"Maître Gitlin—"

"Yes, my dear?"

"I will be married in ten days."

"Married?"

"Yes."

"Isn't it . . . don't you feel that ten days is so soon after—"

"Yes. But . . . Maître Gitlin, I am going to marry Lieutenant-Colonel Wilhelm von Rhode of the German Army. In Berlin. On the second of July."

"The German Army?"

"Yes."

"Did your father know of this?"

"He . . . he knew of the possibility."

Maître Gitlin rubbed his hand hard down his face. "That is terrible news, Paule. I had to say that and I apologize to you now. For years I have sat here and I have thought of the day when I would wish you all the happiness there is. I want to cry, but—please!—I won't cry. I am your father now. Such words as these won't help you, will they? I must help you."

Paule reached across the desk and took his left hand in both of hers, and then bent over and kissed it. Leaning back, she smiled at him serenely, saying, "What you are feeling are old thoughts, from a hundred years ago. He loves me. Can there possibly be anything anti-Semitic about him loving me?"

"You will live in Berlin?" He rubbed his left hand softly. His eyes were grief-stricken.

"Yes. And his family is one of the oldest, most significant . . . Every man in his family for almost a thousand years has been a commander in the Prussian Army. Veelee says what he means, and he means what he says."

"There are other Germans in Germany beyond his family, Paule," Maître Gitlin reproached her gently. "But we will not talk about the probable. For the moment let us face the legal problems of such a marriage."

"But, Maître—" She thought he was embarrassing both of them by attempting to dissuade her. He understood, and smiled at her sadly. "No, no," he said, "I will not try to dissuade you, darling. You love him. He loves you. I want to help you. And this is not just a matter of your estate—it is a matter of the possible safety of your children—"

"Maître!"

"Forgive me. I will rephrase. Make that—of the possible happiness or unhappiness of your children, if any, and since you will live in Germany, perhaps your own happiness as well." He got up and dragged his chair from behind the desk and sat down, taking her hands in his.

"We must think of three things at the outset, Paule. *a,* The question of your nationality after marriage; *b,* the question of your child's nationality; and *c,* the foreseeable financial problems with relation to the German State. Yes? All right. As to the first, from the day of your marriage—unless most specific and somewhat complicated arrangements are made to the contrary—you will be of German nationality without retaining your French nationality. Do you want that?"

"No," she answered in a low voice.

"Then I must go with you to Germany and we will appear at the French Embassy in Berlin to express formally your desire to retain your French nationality. We will then appear before a German registrar with your intended husband, and there a civil marriage ceremony will be performed. In this manner, legally—and the Germans are legal to the point

41

where they will kill you if you question this—you will be a French national and a German national simultaneously. Now, children. Again there are two choices. Not in the same spirit this time because you must consult the father of the child or children, and naturally he is as proud of being a German as you are of being French. It will be a matter of incalculable importance to him that his child be German. Therefore an agreement must be reached before you leave France—and please, please believe me, my darling Paule, this is the only way."

"But what agreement?" She looked ready to weep.

"I will explain the law first. Under the first choice the child will be of German nationality only, without restrictions. Under the second choice, the child may fall under the classification called *sujet mixe* and be of German and French nationalities simultaneously. Both nations will claim the child as a member of their respective nations on behalf of *ius sanguinis*. Germany will claim the child in all countries except France. The French practice differs in that it bestows the *father's* right upon a Frenchwoman who, though being married to a foreigner, has retained her French nationality." Maître Gitlin paused to mop his forehead with a large white silk handkerchief. "Please do not bear this child in Great Britain or the United States, because it will then have a third nationality bestowed upon it by way of the *ius soli* interpretation which is practiced in those countries."

"What am I to do?"

"Today, if possible, you must speak to your fiancé about the possibility of children. You must tell him what is the truth: that you feel the pride in France which you know he feels in Germany, and that, since the child will be a part of both of you, he must have the right to choose his country himself when he reaches majority." He leaned forward and suddenly spoke with great emphasis. "You must do that, Paule. I cannot explain to you what I know about Germany and what I feel about Germans, but I have explained this and you must do it."

She sat very still and looked into his eyes. "It is my husband's country, Maître. It will be our home. I must love it as my own, because of my husband. But if there are children it is right to have it done as you have said."

"Yes."

"It is my husband's country so it will be mine," she said, and her voice trailed off.

Maître Gitlin cleared his throat brusquely. "As to your property. By an act of December 8, 1931, any German citizen in possession of property or fortune of value beyond fifty thousand reichsmarks and liable to German taxation—and this is certainly your case—must pay twenty-five percent of the respective money value of the said property and fortune on leaving the Reich, if the authorities suspect said citizen is leaving for good."

"It isn't likely that will happen."

"With lawyers, as with life, anything can happen." He tapped his cheek with his forefinger. "If this face could only talk, Paule, it could turn your hair white. All you need to do is to agree that we must be prepared. It is an intelligence test. Do you agree?"

She nodded.

"Your husband is an army officer, and that is a particularly hazardous profession in Germany. If you were widowed it seems to me likely that you would wish to return to France." He got up stiffly and walked to the glass door which faced the exotic garden. "Fortunately, you have no traceable property or income. On the day I attend your wedding in Berlin, I shall make arrangements with a Berlin bank to deposit the sum of fifteen hundred reichsmarks each month, a substantial sum which when added to your husband's pay will represent an unusually comfortable income for Germany today. You will have all of your clothes made here, of course, and that will be paid for here. For the rest, the only record will be safely in Nyon and Geneva, and we'll let the monstrous Germans whistle for their twenty-five percent should you ever choose to leave their insatiably destructive country."

Six

✠

VEELEE WAS NOT A STUPID MAN by any means, but he was not a brilliant man either. He had not been sent to France

43

for his wit. The General Staff had selected him and had prepared him because of his knowledge of essential military matters and for his direct, even urgent, persuasive force. The General Staff had well understood the French conceits concerning French lucidity. They reasoned that Veelee would be baited—perhaps subtly, perhaps not—with unforeseeable conversational gambits, so in his defense they had had an expert prepare a gambit which would attack and confuse the French by enraging them, and Veelee had undertaken the assignment to learn this conversation piece by heart. He understood clearly that it was to be used, at his discretion, whenever a French adversary seemed to be becoming uncomfortably critical of German history or of the present German administration.

Veelee, Paule, and Maître Gitlin were on the Nord-Sud Express. The lawyer had begun quite brilliantly to compare France and Germany, however to Germany's detriment. Veelee's well-ordered mind had merely called upon his memory for the special exercise and, seeming to respond directly to Maître Gitlin's subtle insinuations, Veelee began to speak.

"We can thank geography and climate for the high competence of the German Army," Veelee said, as the train moved through the Hercynian range, hurrying across Germany: the fifth largest state in Europe, composed of great plains, plateaus, and several old mountain ranges, a hodgepodge of lakes, moraines, channels and bogs left by the glacier. Veelee's native land touched nine sovereign states and two seas; it was Roman in the south, Slavonic in the center, and Scandinavian in the north. The train was moving across Lüneburg Heath, in the Old Valley zone; Berlin was ahead, and beyond Berlin, on the Northern Drift plains, lay Pomerania, Veelee's ancestral home.

Paule was knitting. She wore a wine silk Russian blouse, buttoned high at the throat, and a high black fox hat which attenuated the long, bony lines of her striking face. Her large eyes held Veelee with astonishment. She had never heard him express such a reflective facet of himself.

"Harsh winters drive our people to their hearths," Veelee said dreamily. "Deep family unity is developed and headed by The Father, a harsh, demanding, uncompromising figure who forms our character and makes us obedient to authority and dependent upon regimentation. The family is the only educational system which forms the character."

Maître Gitlin smoked a cheroot and stared at the shining brass fittings of the train compartment. He was thinking about the caps of the young train shunters at Osnabrück; peaked crowns of forage caps with stiffeners at the extraordinarily high fronts, giving the railroad yards a weirdly military look.

They were on the Nord-Sud Express's regular run from Lisbon to Leningrad. They had left Paris at two-fifteen P.M. on the previous afternoon and they would be in Berlin within the hour, at eight forty-three A.M. Someone rich must have joined the train at Liège because Car 724 with its barber shop, gymnasium, and shower bath had become part of the train. On inquiry Maître Gitlin had learned that it had been built thirty years before for members of the Russian nobility who were hurrying to lose fortunes at Monte Carlo.

"Schools only garnish character," Veelee murmured. "In Germany everything we have we owe to the demands made on us by our fathers, then to the abnegation of the mother to this symbol, then from having the symbol itself prove the merit of the system by bowing to the authority immediately above him. To a child it is confusing at first, but later he sees the unity of authority and the need for it. We are obedient and law-abiding. We allow experts to do our thinking where possible, because this lengthens the step forward for all Germans."

"We have experts in France, too," Maître Gitlin said, "but they don't rule us."

"I didn't really mean they rule us either."

"We are not a subservient nation," Gitlin insisted.

"The English have discipline, too, of course," Veelee said, moving into the second phase of the talk which had been prepared to disconcert Frenchmen. "I know less than nothing about the family-unit side of their education, or about their schools or other adversities, but they seem to pour their obedience into something outside the family. Into the monarchy? No. I think it must be that the diffusion they acquired from colonizing the world from such a tiny island taught them the need for obedience, if only to set an example. They *are* this island, and that has made them homogeneous. In learning to live so densely packed upon such a small island, they compartmentalized themselves into classes which recognized codes of obedience to each other. They are a family of many classes, and their classes fight for each other when they face the world and only fight against each other through their politics. We admire them."

"I take it you do not admire the French?" Maître Gitlin asked.

"If we were weaker we would, of course."

"You are saying it is a question of politics?"

"Germans don't understand politics—and I don't say that as a soldier. We are trained in politics and we know nothing. Politicians, who are rarely trained in our politics, know even less."

"I quite agree with you."

"It is amazing, really. For all the unity we have when we are strongly led, we cannot seem to figure out a way to create leaders who emerge from a unified people. But in time, in good time. That is Hannover out the window. I am a Pomeranian. When I was a boy a conscript from Hesse never spoke about joining the army, but of joining the Prussians. We haven't been a nation long enough, you know."

Gitlin snorted. Paule stared at Veelee with total wonderment, struck with this incredible contribution of intellectualism, in addition to everything else he had.

"Still," Veelee said, "we are better off for it than the French, who understand politics so well that they pimp for it and send it out into the streets to prostitute its meaning, until only the basest Frenchmen are willing to pursue such a career—mongrels and manipulators and the wearily cynical who fondle governments as they shuttle past. It is a kind of perversion."

"Better a perversion for politics than a perversion for war, if I may say so."

"Please!" Paule said. "No more of this. And don't tell me that you two are just fooling."

"Just an abstract discussion, darling." Veelee looked at her and shrugged, and for an instant she had the feeling it was all over his head, too.

"Of course," the Maître said. "The art of conversation is not necessarily dead. That's all, Paule."

"It would be nicer if you practiced on music," Paule said. "Saint-Saëns versus Wagner, or a conversational theme like that."

"We were discussing education, which is even more harmless," Veelee said, moving up his next set of gambits into the firing line, his memory serving him without flaw. "The French attitude toward their politics, I think, is the fault of their basic education—in the family unit, that is, where it counts. The ability to deceive self, then to deceive life, begins with the family unit. The goal of the French family is not obedience but animal gratification and Saturnalian existence. With such goals how can they find unity? Each man's sensual gratification differs from each other's. And that is anti-family—that is the cult of the individual. That is the total service of self and only of self. A family is a group of people, just as a nation is a group of families, and if the group has divisive goals there is no more group. What France needs is a stern and demanding father. Your revolutionary slogan has come to mean Libertinism, Equal Rights to Self-Indulgence, and the cold, anti-social Fraternity of self having intercourse only with self."

In reply Maître Gitlin's voice answered almost too precisely, adding paragoges to the ending of each word, so that the effect was a caricature of precision. "Frenchmen live to live, not to die," he said.

"And I envy that, Maître," Veelee answered. "I even think it is true to an extent—at least to the extent that each country's solution will contrast with the other's because of the basic differences in our education."

"I hope you are right, and for that reason," the Maître said. "Thank God for the difference too, I say." He stood up. "Please excuse me. I must get some air."

Veelee stared at the slammed door of the compartment. "I'm sure I've offended him," he said, not having the slightest idea how he had done it, "but these long train rides are so dull."

Paule continued to stare at Veelee with new, awed eyes. He had revealed a casual brilliance which she had never imagined he possessed. It was to be many years before she could convince herself that he was not an intensely mental man.

·   ·   ·

Lieutenant-Colonel Wilhelm von Rhode, Herr auf Klein-Kusserow und Wusterwitz, had been a part of the German Army since he had entered the cadet school and his first uniform at Berlin-Lichterfelde when he was nine years old. He could have been educated at a grammar school, but old-timers among the senior officers, such as the formidable von Seeckt, all thought the Kadettenanstalt background to be much more stylish.

It was indeed a military school. Even the chaplain wore spurs under his robes and held the rank of captain. Before each meal the Officer of the Day would shout, "Let us— PRAY!" A barracks order read:

> *After the night prayer the Officer of the Day will command: "GO TO SLEEP!" The cadet will undress as quickly as possible, place his clothes in the regulation place, go to bed, place his right arm under his head, left arm over the blanket, and fall asleep immediately.*

A company of one hundred cadets slept in each barracks and the lights burned all night long to protect the younger boys from the older ones and to permit the NCO who cleaned boots to do his work and to beat off older boys. The cadets were always under supervision. There was not a door which could be locked so that a cadet might be alone for the briefest period. Two hundred cadets dined at each session; thirty cadets were assigned to each classroom; ten cadets studied together in each living quarter. In the extraordinary instance of leave being granted to attend a funeral or a wedding, the cadet was required to report at once to the garrison commander nearest his destination. Riding was the only excuse for being out of uniform. Part of the system was to starve the Cadet Corps; cadets were not allowed to receive parcels from home. This tightened disciplinary efficiency; one of the severer penalties was barring the cadet from lunch or dinner.

Veelee never told his father how he hated the Kadettenanstalt because he assumed that his father would expect him to hate it, as his father had hated it. He had twenty-five minutes for recreation each day which he could squander on walks or spending the five marks per month the cadets were allowed for stamps, supplies, and everything else. The Kadettenanstalt was a fortress of unreality which conditioned the future officers for a place in its extension, the palace of unreality which was the German Army. It was an army which honored suicide when circumstances might have marred the community's illusion of what an army officer was and how he lived. Blunders marred that image, and it was the duty of a brave soldier and an honest fellow to kill himself to wash the stain away. If an officer was insulted by an inferior—such as a civilian whom he could not, in any case, challenge to a duel—suicide was the only way out. Veelee was taught when he was eleven years old that if a drunk came around a corner and there was no reason to deduce why he should not become offensive, the officer should cross the street quickly before the drunk could reach him. However, if the officer moved too late and the drunk struck him or cursed him, the officer must either draw his sword and hack the man to pieces on the spot or kill himself. If neither, and the encounter were witnessed, the officer would be cashiered from the army.

By graduating from the Kadettenanstalt into the army, the cadets could grow to men while still remaining boys at their games, and they could predict the contours of their lives. Veelee spent nine years as a cadet. In the fall of 1914 he graduated in the top eleven percent of officer candidates in his class. He passed his examinations for the general certificate for higher education six months earlier than the general rule, partly because of the outbreak of the war and partly because he had volunteered for service at once in order to escape.

Because Veelee was qualified as a cavalry officer, under the mysterious logic of armies he was not assigned to cavalry. He found himself in the renowned Preussisches Jaegerregiment 2, which held the elite of the Prussian Army and was equal, in the service, to the Guards. Eighty percent of the officers in the regiment commanded by Colonel Prince Ernst von Sachsen-Meinigen were of aristocratic stock. It was a regiment of Rangers, part of the Alpine Corps, and within four months of having been posted, Veelee distinguished himself in the Rumanian campaign of 1915 and was promoted from ensign to sub-lieutenant. He was then decorated with the Iron Cross, second and first class, for distinguished service during the battle of Hermannstadt in September, 1916. He was made lieutenant in February, 1918, when he was twenty years old, and posted to the staff of the Marine Corps in Flanders, stationed at Bruges, where he served directly under Captain Wilhelm Keitel of the General Staff. They were assigned to maintain liaison with the navy.

Keitel was a swot, a prodigiously dull and feverishly ambitious grind, sixteen years older than Veelee. He was a plebeian Hanoverian, light on talent, and his awe at being permitted to roam at large among the Prussian aristocracy flagellated his deep sense of inferiority. Keitel seemed to have understood quite early in life that he could never expect to have position and power; all he asked was a chance to stand close to the powerful in photographs. The mountaineering tools for his painful ascent were complete acquiescence to all authority, subservient adulation for all above him in rank, and a shrewdly cultivated German instinct for resentment. However, he was a gorgeous man in uniform, the model figure of soldierly erectness and calm bearing. One day the Fuehrer himself was to say of Keitel that he had the brains of a doorman at a movie palace, and a German ambassador to Italy was to comment that Keitel had the mathematical ability of a milkmaid.

At first, Keitel was almost subservient to his lieutenant, but he decided soon enough that Veelee was much too offhand for his taste—even unappreciative. Worse, Veelee's uncle, Admiral Ludwig von Schroeder, Commander of the Marine Corps, was determined that Rhode should become the youngest captain in the Prussian Army. An admiral's whim is forged of steel, and on August 2, 1918, the promotion came through. Keitel was exasperated beyond endurance because the young man had made no effort to insure that his captain was invited to any of the Admiral's social functions, and Keitel resented it. There was talk. The Admiral had let it be known that his nephew had displayed much "tact" with the navy but that Keitel had been too "straightforward" —the last time in his career that he was to be accused by that word. Keitel remained deeply hurt until Veelee redeemed himself by organizing the retreat of one hundred and seventy thousand marines from Flanders to the Rhine in less than a fortnight, bringing every man to the German bank of the river on the day before the final date specified by the terms of the Armistice. Keitel was proud of Rhode then, because Keitel was decorated for the operation. They were almost friendly for two months—until Veelee was posted to the headquarters of the Supreme Command at Kolberg. Keitel was the senior, but von Rhode was called. It was too much. Rhode had been moved up to where Hindenburg and the power were, and Keitel was left behind.

The peace terms were a brutal shock to the German people. They had been taught to believe that the war had been forced on them, and after defending themselves as best they could and even going so far as to dismiss their Emperor to institute a most undesired republican form of government, they felt that they were entitled to some form of reward, not the calumny of Versailles.

Incredibly, the German Army was to be reduced to a total of ninety-six thousand men, recruited for twelve years, and four thousand officers, serving for twenty-five years. The nation was forbidden to possess military airplanes, tanks, or any offensive weapons. The General Staff was to be dissolved and not reconstituted in any form. Dire restrictions were placed upon fortifications. There were to be no U-boats, and the navy was reduced to the equivalent of a fleet of Maori war canoes. The German Emperor was charged with "a supreme offense against international morality and the sanctity of treaties."

While politicians ranted, the army acted. It established a cadre upon which the future war of justice would be fought. The General Staff was re-established—disguised as the Office of Troops—and it assembled a group of staff officers who would guide a greater army. Secret courses in military science were established at universities. Officer candidates beyond the limit were trained by the Prussian police force. The treaty did not limit the number of non-commissioned officers, so the new army started out with forty-six thousand of these. By 1923 each senior officer in the miniature army was trained to command a division; each junior officer a regiment; each NCO a company; and each private was a reserve NCO.

In 1808 Scharnhorst had instituted reforms which had transformed the Officer Corps of the German Army. Officers were to be elected by the Corps itself, not nominated by the Kaiser, and a Court of Honor would have complete authority over members of the Corps, effectively removing them from the jurisdiction of civilian courts of justice. The Officer Corps became a caste. Its members viewed themselves as knightly servants of the Emperor, not of the nation. The elite within this caste were men of vivid military ability and extraordinary oneness of perspective, and all members of the Corps were encouraged to express themselves freely on any matter to do with the service. This was the code. A captain could differ with a general in the hope that the differences could lead to improved professional excellence. Clausewitz had described the Officer Corps as "a kind of guild with its own laws, ordinances, and customs"; all that it did on its own behalf was held to be good because it maintained the army's immunity from parliamentary control and because nothing could change unless they themselves changed it.

The army had been the family profession of the Rhode-Kusserows since the beginning of the Thirty Years' War in 1618. They were among the leaders of the army which was the state, the religion, and the iron fist that held together the sprawled Hohenzollern possessions. A von Rhode had been the second of Masters of Ordinance in the Prussian Army. There had been two von Rhodes on the General War Commissariat under Friedrich Wilhelm I. The Académie des Nobles produced seven von Rhodes who were Brigade-Majors appointed by the Kaiser, and they had helped to found the communications and intelligence systems to be used by the future General Staff.

Veelee's liaison assignment was with the Freikorps Grenzschutz Ost, which was defending the eastern portion of Pomerania against an invasion by the Polish Army in the late spring of 1919. From June to December, 1919, he was second General Staff Officer of a brigade stationed near Hannover, and from 1920 until October, 1922, he served as instructor at the Cavalry Training College in that city.

At the end of October, 1922, Veelee was transferred to Berlin to undertake two illegal instructional courses for General Staff officers at the College of Engineers in Berlin-Charlottenburg. This was a group of buildings well known to be a civilian college, and to make sure that there could be no misunderstanding, Veelee was issued an official civilian student card and ordered to attend the lectures attired in civilian clothes.

After casual duty, in 1924 Veelee was a captain on the General Staff of Reichswehr Gruppen Kommando 2, in Kassel. In April, 1927, he was transferred to the Troops Office. He became a major in 1930, the year of the terrible agrarian crisis when forty-three estates had to be sold by auction in the Pomeranian county of Schlochau alone, and though he came through it with few debts, many of his friends were ruined. But everything faced ruin in Germany in 1930: the government, the economy, and national morale. The Communists were gaining everywhere in the country and the army told itself that a new way had to be found to do the same things.

In December, 1931, Veelee was detached from active duty as Lieutenant-Colonel and transferred, with the diplomatic rank of Legationsrat, to the German Embassy in Paris.

Veelee and Paule stopped kissing reluctantly when they heard Maître Gitlin at the curtained door of the compartment. Veelee moved into his seat by the window and recommenced his gazing and daydreaming. The Maître looked more jovial.

"Feeling better, Maître?" Paule asked.

He smiled at her and nodded, but he spoke to Veelee. "It has occurred to me, Colonel, that the Germans are beloved of God because they have always given Him so much more to forgive."

Paule grinned at him, and looked at Veelee, who was so handsome that her heart stopped. "Let us say, rather, Maître, that He loves you both equally," she said, "because you have such opposite tastes in sinning."

Seven

✠

IT IS NOT ALWAYS IMPOSSIBLE to remember when the great changes happen, but it is a slippery business. Even if they are understood at the time, the poignant days go from the memory quickly. To see or to understand the moment of unmasking change—that second when the shimmer of childhood vanished, the light stab of pain which presaged death, the glance and chatoyant smile which brought eleven grandchildren—is given only to travelers in lands which they had not remotely imagined.

When the Nord-Sud Express halted at the Friedrichstrasse Station in Berlin, Paule exchanged gossamer for iron. As her feet touched the platform a brown-shirted squad of SA toughs came parading past her in military formation, singing out their words in coarse cadences, *"No more Jews. Death to Jews. Down with Jews. Death to Jews."* They didn't linger; they merely marched up the platform and back again, then continued through the station to another platform, leaving behind them a wake of not disapproving people, some of whom were wearing inane, good-humored grins.

A high, ice-covered, spiked gate seemed to clang shut upon the life behind Paule. "It really happens here then, Veelee?"

"Nonsense. That was an outrage. They were ruffians. There is an election coming up and they were probably paid a few pfennigs to march about and sing their filthy song."

"They are *paid* to say that?"

"Of course."

"And the people who pay them know that Germans will vote their way because the men say such things?"

He stared at her with uncertainty while the crowds churned around them on the platform. "I don't understand it," he said haltingly. "It has something to do with all the unemployment and the fear. I mean to say, really, Paule, it isn't normal."

She was white with astonishment; her first thought was of her father, who had said that it was the Jews who had saved and made and sustained the renaissance of art and letters in Europe after the long dark ages. Jews were her father and Maître Gitlin, Sarah Bernhardt, Proust and Henri Bergson. As soon as she was alone she must find out about these grotesque election slogans which the slack-mouthed young men had sung so happily for tiny amounts of money. Her hands clung to each other so that they would not shake. Veelee had been talking to her, perhaps explaining, but she had not heard him clearly. Now something caught his eye in the crowd. He waved and bellowed, "Gretel!" then cried out with delight as though the impossible had happened, "My sisters are here!"

Maître Gitlin got off the train slowly and finished directing the porters about their baggage. "Are you all right, Paule?" he asked. "You are very pale."

"It's just the excitement," she said.

A tall, gray-eyed, handsome woman came whinnying and charging through the crowd and took Paule in her arms and covered her with kisses. "Oh! You are beautiful!" the woman said. "He never said how beautiful you are."

"Paule, this is my sister Gretel," but before Paule could respond another sister was upon her, squealing with pleasure. Gisele was tiny. She had dark-red hair, smoked cigars after dinner, was passionately committed to Ibsen, Hauptmann, and Shaw—in that order—and had won prizes for her roses. Gretel was tall and slender, four years older than Veelee and two years older than Gisele. She was as blond as Veelee, had his wonderful smile, knew everything that had happened that morning in the German Army as well as all of its regulations, codes, manuals, and shibboleths, never read books, and did thirty-five minutes of calisthenics each morning and evening. Veelee introduced Gretel's husband. He wore the uniform of a full general, had gray moustaches with soaring ends, a monocle, very naughty light-blue eyes, and a laugh like a lumber saw. Then Gisele pulled her husband into view. He was an important figure at the Foreign Office; thin, wore a pince-nez, a magnificent cravat and flashing stickpin, tons of cologne, and an English-cut suit and bowler. Then Paule introduced Maître Gitlin to everyone while Gretel told them she had secured the most wonderful apartment for them in Charlottenburg.

It was a sunny, six-room flat, with high ceilings, on the second floor of a four-story building facing the Friedrich Karl Platz across the Spandauerstrasse from the Schlossgarten. Gretel lived two streets away; Gisele was on the same street, two doors down. Biedermeier abounded in the apartment: chairs and tables with curved underframes and legs, high-backed chairs with smooth wooden plats, gilded swans, cornucopias, griffins, and foliage carved out of birch, pear wood, and grained ash. The rolled horsehair upholstery under flowered calico made Paule happy; her new world also had old-fashioned reassuring comforts. The wallpaper shouted welcome in many shapes of fruits and flowers, and there were draped curtains, multicolored tablecloths and carpets. There were vases filled with flowers from a dozen of Veelee's friends. Paule couldn't wait to get to work and change it all; she decided to spare only the canary, the gramophone, and the prodigious collection of records.

The marriage ceremony went off to Maître Gitlin's sat-

isfaction. Gretel, Gisele, and their husbands were official witnesses, and they all celebrated earnestly at Horcher's afterward. Before he went back to Paris, Maître Gitlin explained to Veelee that Paule's father had left her an income
of fifteen hundred marks a month while she lived outside
France. He did not elaborate on Paule's fortune, nor did Veelee show any interest—he was overwhelmed at their combined riches. His pay was eight hundred marks a month, a
very handsome sum; at a time when the economic crisis had
caused all civilian salaries to be reduced, the income of army
officers remained unchanged.

On her third day in Berlin, while he was still on leave,
Paule and Veelee went to Klein-Kusserow, where the von Rhode
family had lived throughout their recorded history. Klein-
Kusserow had eighty-six souls. The family's second seat in
Pomerania, Wusterwitz, had sixty-seven people. Everything
was clustered around the large wooden main houses. There
was a minister who had a tiny church, a schoolmaster, a black-
smith, a police constable; all the other people were tenants
and farm hands. The crops were turnips, barley, rye, and
potatoes, although Veelee said that as he remembered it
the principal crop was fir trees. He said proudly that Pomeranian cattle could eat food from which goats turned away.
The glacier had left eskers, kettles, marshes, and boulders.
The highest point in the region was three hundred and two
feet—hummocks tufted with green forests. Somewhere between the bogs and the hummock tops the people struggled
to harvest crops from an acid, young, unfriendly soil.

It was summer and barefoot peasant women wearing white
kerchiefs dotted the fields. At harvest time the estate used
seasonal workers from Poland, most of them female, and the
whole countryside of sand dunes, heather, fir trees, and
pastures would present a pattern of white handkerchiefs.
Veelee remembered the Polish girls as being very pretty, and
told Paule that it was the sub-steward's right to choose any
of them as mistresses for the season. The men of the Rhode
family chose their mistresses from among the sub-stewards'
wives, but Veelee had been sent away to learn about the
army at nine, so this was no more than legend to him. "It
is all going now," he told Paule wistfully. "Small farms are
better for agricultural survival in this part of the world. But
my family still clings stubbornly to the last two estates we

56

have, which is why we are quite poor and perhaps why the men of the family have been soldiers in an almost unbroken line. What we did not have the wit to do with a plow we have done most gloriously with a sword."

It was an idyllic honeymoon. Paule felt that they had been lifted into the peace of heaven.

They returned to Berlin on the 27th of July, 1932, and on the 28th Veelee returned to duty. It was three nights before the national elections. The National Socialists had sent their storm troopers into the streets to demonstrate destruction, and the carnage was more appalling than anything Germany had ever seen. In an army staff car Paule and Gretel were being driven through the center of Berlin when the uncomprehensible brutality began all around them. The car could move only at snail's pace through the rioting Brown Shirts. Women were knocked down and kicked, and bricks were flung through shop windows as young men shouted for the death of all Jews; the car moved sedately, as if reviewing the spectacle. Truncheons were used on the aged; children were flung into the gutters and under cars. They made their way to Paule's flat as quickly as they could. Gretel was retching so badly that Paule stretched her out on the tile floor and held her stomach. There was a doctor in the building; he came at once and gave Gretel sedatives.

When the doctor had gone and her sister-in-law had been put to bed, Paule stood at the window of the room and watched the people beneath run back and forth like ants under a threat.

"I cannot believe what I saw. I can't, I can't," Gretel said. "How can you be so calm, Paule?"

"I am a Jew. That makes a difference. You see it as a German and wonder what is happening to your people. I see it as a Jew and I wonder what will happen to me."

"Nothing will happen to you, Paule. You are a von Rhode now."

"Wouldn't you have said that what you saw could not have happened to your people—to your industrious, kind, cheerful, good people?"

Martial law was declared after seventy-five people had been

killed and two hundred and eighty-five had been maimed and shattered. But the force which the German Army, as ordered by General von Rundstedt, had sent out to enforce the state of martial law against four hundred thousand exultant, blood-drunk storm troopers was a lieutenant and twelve men who were ordered to make the "necessary arrests."

For the first time since she had come to Germany, Paule felt dazed and ill. The German Army was Veelee and Veelee was the army. The army was encouraging the murder of Jews in the streets. She pushed the thought down and down into her mind, to suffocate it. Her father was gone. Veelee would understand. All she needed to remember was that she loved Veelee and that he loved her; the fact of these terrible events could not change what she felt for him and needed from him, nor what he felt for her. She began to read the newspapers with the avidity of an opposition editor. She read them all, and she took a morbid fascination in the tiny outrages as well as the massive murders. The Nazis won two hundred and thirty seats in the Reichstag, and though they lacked a majority, they were the largest party represented. On the day of the elections, after three days of rioting throughout the country, she got a long, ebullient, loving, and passionate letter from Veelee at the cavalry school at Wuensdorf. Among other things, he pointed out that the election campaign had made one thing clear: the Nazis were not against the Jews as everyone had supposed. All inside army information—the only reliable information since the newspapers were owned by a pack of Socialists and union radicals—showed that the riots had only been against the Communists and some Catholics. As a German, he felt he should thank God that there was some force which could openly attack the Communists; the army's hands were certainly tied, and the Communists were trying to "eat the very heart out of our country." The essential opposition, of course, had made him proud as a soldier, but most of all it had dispersed the terrible alarm he had first felt that she might be frightened at the threat of what might have seemed like danger. He would be home soon and hold her in his arms.

Paule had two servants. One, who had come as a present

from Gisele, seemed to know how to cook everything everyone in the combined Rhode family liked to eat, from *Westfälisches Gaenschenschwarzsauer* to *Crambamboli*. The other, a charwoman who came in twice a week, Gretel had found. Paule concentrated on her house, on becoming a good German wife, and on learning to think and feel like a German. She read the *Nibelungenlied* because Gretel told her that it had influenced the attitudes of the German Army. She read *Gudrun* because Gisele had said it was her favorite story of the North Sea coasts. She read sixteenth-century Jesuit dramas from which German opera had evolved. She read the works of Christian Weisse, which advocated rational behavior and the art of getting on in a realistically apprehended world; and her mind tottered forward with a small cry of gratitude when Klopstock enforced his credo that feeling must dominate reason; she went on into the rococo abandon of Wieland, turned to the common sense of Lessing as an antidote, then backtracked to Goethe's *Wilhelm Meister*. She avoided Heine because he had been a Jew. The point of her search was to seek the keys to people who not only were not Jews, but who seemed to be able to blind themselves to all of the sensitive things in Jews which Heine represented. She could not make her way through the dialect literature of Hebel, Groth, and Reuter. She had already read Nietzsche and it had made her giggle, but she reread him with the memory of the storm troopers at earnest work all around the army staff car. She felt at home with Stefan George and von Hofmannsthal, though George's work had been used recently to make the Nazis more palatable in German intellectual circles. She would not read Kafka, the Czech whom the Germans adored; she could not afford hopelessness.

The music library of Paule's landlord had every opera known to man, and while she knitted she listened to Beethoven, Gluck, Brahms, Mozart, and Wagner. Abjuring Bach, she played Brahms and Wagner and Wagner and Brahms over and over again until finally she told Veelee that Wagner surely must have been commissioned to provide recruiting music for the Nazi party. But Veelee did not seem to want to understand.

After Paule had studied German culture for seventeen months she was more French than she had been before, and she fancied she could hear her father's raucous laughter roaring at her from a ribald heaven.

From the second day of their arrival in Germany, they had received invitations from the aristocratic society of Berlin and Potsdam for every sort of event: lunches, teas, dinners, balls, hunts, cocktails, and *Kaffeetafeln*. Many of the invitations came from the wives of cavalry officers with whom Veelee had served in the Royal Prussian Army. But Paule's closest friends were Veelee's sisters and their husbands. These warm and loving people had made her a part of the family instantly and, though she was never aware of it, defied any member of German society to consider her in any other light. Gretel was the most intelligent of the von Rhodes, and she had insight and a deft intuition as well. Gisele, forged in the cold furnace of Foreign Office society, was a social automaton who could talk about anything without being indiscreet but could hardly utter a sentence of substance. Still, she had a loving heart and was a generous, pretty woman. Gretel's husband, Generalleutnant Franz Heller, was called Hansel (by the family only) because of his wife's name. He was a bulky, witty man who, whenever he was able to relax in civilian clothes, wore a Scotch tam-o'-shanter with a bright-blue boss to keep drafts from his bald head. He had a roving eye and contributed to Paule's welcome by flirting with her continuously. Gisele's husband, Philip Miles-Meltzer, was a dark, intense man who was absorbed in dress, health, and Mexican cuisine—the last, perhaps, because it was as far removed as possible from his work. He was a Ministerialdirektor at the Foreign Office.

Other entertainment for Paule and Veelee was provided by a shifting population of officers and their wives, a few lawyers, and now and then people of the Berlin theatre and of touring companies of foreign theatre. Nevertheless, Paule was alone a great deal. Veelee was commanding officer of the Kraftfahrabteilung 3, at Wuensdorf, with instructions to turn it into a mobile reconnaissance force. In theory he was supposed to be free to return home five nights a week, because Wuensdorf was a village only twenty-five miles from Berlin. But it was a new command and so many complications arose that Veelee rarely came home more than twice a week.

When she walked through Berlin alone during the days, Paule watched the fear on the Jewish faces. They thought they were carrying expressions of neutrality or boredom, but sudden street sounds and too-loud voices nearby would make their hands tremble as they lit cigarettes. The pressure from above was making everyone uneasy and anxious. Paule, the new Jew in a new world of Jewishness, became more sensitive to everything which had not yet happened. Only horses and dogs in Berlin seemed to be well-adjusted and happy. She watched storm troopers and SS men fondle large, jolly dogs in the Schlossgarten across the square from her house. They would rub their dogs, play with them, croon to them, and gaze down at them with tenderness while the dogs urinated against lampposts. No German dogs were nervous, and the horses were happy—but not the children, not the people, and not the Jews.

Veelee and Paule belonged to the tennis club. They fenced twice a week. They had a small boat, big enough to hold themselves and a basket of food and wine for the laziest kind of floating on the Mugglesee. Only when they had a family party did they entertain at home.

On fine autumn days, when she could not bear to stay in the flat alone, Paule would go for walks. These strolls were seemingly aimless, but she would usually find herself drawn to the Huldschinsky house on the Standartenstrasse, which Captain Roehm, the storm-troop chief, had rented from a Silesian industrialist and for which, her brother-in-law Miles-Meltzer said, Huldschinsky was never paid. The mansion had held art treasures, but now it housed pederasts, cases of champagne stacked in salons, and tables of delicacies which streamed into the house from Kempinsky's restaurant to feed the hairy orgies which Roehm savored and tittered over drunkenly. When Kempinsky sent its enormous bill for a month of Brown Shirts at the trough, it was not paid; and when Kempinsky sent two men to insist on payment, Captain Roehm broke lamps and vases in a drunken rage while he shouted at them that Kempinsky was owned by Jews and did they really think that Roehm would pay a Jew for anything, except with bullets?

Paule would wander around the streets surrounding the house which symbolized the storm troopers of her nightmares, moving slowly and staring up at it, trying to equate what it now represented with the lessons her father had taught her every Friday evening.

Now, operating from within the government, the Nazi

press had new standing. Attacks on Jews began in earnest. At a signal from Goebbels and Streicher, in cities, towns, and villages all over the country, "spontaneous demonstrations" were mounted. They were all the same demonstration, of course. Crowds led by the SA would enter the law courts and drive out all Jewish lawyers, magistrates, and judges; other crowds drove customers out of Jewish department stores. When the press outside Germany reported these incidents, Goebbels held the German Jews for a form of ransom by organizing a general boycott which would last, he swore, until the foreign press made their reports more favorable to the Nazis. This threat was withdrawn at once, but the first racial law, retiring all civil servants who were not of Aryan descent, was passed. The draft of a law prohibiting mixed marriages, which would also make extra-marital relations between Jews and non-Jews a punishable offense, was published. Jews were taken out of their homes in the middle of the night to be manhandled in SA barracks; some were shot "while trying to escape." When Goebbels' newspaper accused Jews of having rioted to prevent the showing of an anti-Semitic film in the west end of Berlin, windows of cafés were smashed by SA toughs and Jews were beaten up in the streets.

Paule pored over every newspaper. The Nazi press used a jargon of its own, triumphantly justified murder, and employed such arcane devices as pornography to attract readers. Everything outside Germany, the papers intoned, was evil and threatening, every German must relearn that fact every day. Only Germany was preserving the right way of life, the good way, the path of national honor and social justice.

Paule could not speak of these things which tormented her. To speak of them would be to recognize them and to demand that Veelee recognize them—which he would not do —which would have led ultimately to leaving Germany, and she could not leave because Veelee could not leave. Gisele maintained her feather-headed, noncommitted composure. Gretel would not, could not, allow the direction of the German path to be shown to her. She shut all things Nazi away from her. Paule waited for Veelee to tell her that he understood and condemned what was happening; to say that until his superiors acted he could do nothing about it; to tell her how clearly he saw that the situation related to them because she was a Jew and he was a German, and because they therefore were both an immortal part of the people who were being killed and beaten and humiliated and destroyed, as well as being a part of those who were killing, beating, humiliating, and destroying.

Paule began to suffer crippling stomach pains. A "safe" doctor—now there were none practicing who were not Aryan and "safe"—a mild and drunken old man whose surgery was in the building, said that these were understandable symptoms, a chronic problem of the times. The doctor gave her sedatives which calmed her muscles. But the medicine could not slow the racing of her mind, and it could not dull the grinding remorse of having to be ashamed of her husband.

Eight

✠

UNEMPLOYMENT KEPT RISING, passing five million. Farmers had been unable to meet their mortgage payments for four months. If there had been a moneyed class to pull down it would have been sent crashing, but the ruling class was in the army and the army waited steadfastly to serve the side which would win. Something had to be done. Hunger and the loss of faith and face had become the fuse for the dynamite of German resentment. As the people stared at the calendar, bloody hands were fumbling in the darkness for a match.

Businessmen contributed three million marks to the Nazi election campaign fund on February 20, 1933, when Goering explained that there might not be another German election for a hundred years. Hitler was Chancellor, but his party had no majority in the Reichstag. Something had to be done. Communist meetings were banned and the Communist press was shut down. Social Democrat rallies were broken up by the SA, and the leading Socialist newspapers were suspended. Fifty-one anti-Nazis were murdered in the pre-election campaign, following Hitler's appointment to the chancellery by President von Hindenburg, when fifty-two thousand SA, SS, and Stahlhelm veterans were authorized "to take over the policing of Berlin at their own discretion with complete indemnity for the use of firearms." The Reichstag was set on fire, and as a result von Hindenburg signed a decree suspending the seven sections of the constitution which had guaranteed individual and civil liberties. Four thousand Communist officials and hundreds of Social Democrats were dragged from their homes to be tortured and murdered. The state radio, controlled by Goebbels, carried unceasing speeches on almost every street corner. Billboards screamed, bonfires made night like day, and those voices of sanity still remaining could not be heard over the din as they pleaded with President von Hindenburg to protect the nation from its oppressors.

Nevertheless, the election of March 5th did not produce a clear majority for the Nazis. In desperation, Hitler made his peace with the army, the monarchists, and the nationalists, so that von Hindenburg signed the Enabling Act, which transferred the powers of Parliament and, with a legal flourish, put the control of the resources of a great state into the hands of street gangs.

Adolf Hitler had become Chancellor of Germany on January 30, 1933. When he addressed his emasculated Reichstag on January 30, 1934, he presented Germany with the list of his unparalleled achievements. He had destroyed the republic, liquidated all political opposition, obliterated state government, smashed labor unions, banished Jews from German public and professional life, destroyed freedom of the press and of speech, subverted the courts, and begun the total corruption of an ancient and honorable people.

On February 22, 1934, Paule and Veelee were invited to a ball given by Vice-Chancellor von Papen at the Prince Friedrich Leopold Palace. They took Hansel and Gretel in their car, entering the palace through ranks of full-dress guards under the lights of newsreel cameras and flashbulbs.

Clutching Paule's arm under his, Hansel said, "Damn these photographers, I can't pinch you."

"A good photograph might teach the young people how to pinch properly," Paule said.

"Let them go to Rome and study, which is what I had to do."

The General wore full-dress uniform with his pounds of medals and climbed the great marble staircase with increasing difficulty. "We eat too much, you know," he groaned. "My liver is as swollen as a football."

"*You* eat too much. Anyway, why don't you wear a corset? Uniforms are made for corsets."

"My corset is what is killing me," Hansel moaned. "How do you think I keep this magnificent figure?"

"No breath for talking, only for climbing."

At the top, where they were received by the von Papens, Hansel was gasping and clinging to Paule's arm for support.

"My dear General," the Vice-Chancellor said, motioning to a footman. "What have you been doing, wrestling a lion?" The footman and Paule took Hansel to a room across from the ballroom and stretched him out on the sofa.

"My tripes are being strangled," Hansel gargled, breathing like a bagpipe.

"We'll get it off," Paule said, beginning to unbutton his tunic.

"No, no, darling. You must fetch Gretel. It's not that I'm shy, you understand, but Gretel is the only one living who knows how to get me out of this rig."

"I'll find her and bring her back," Paule said, and left the room.

"Get me a large whiskey," Hansel ordered the footman.

"Yes, my General."

Paule's stomach pains were intense. The corridor was crowded, but the ballroom even more packed. The massed colors of uniforms, dresses, jewels, epaulettes, medals, sashes, and the great hanging *hakenkreuz* laying on its side within the symbolic sea of blood on the huge flag all smote at her with the noises of music and speech; shrill cries of recognition, strident commands, and the swirling eddies of many perfumes, cigars and the heavy smell of schnapps and sauerkraut steamed out of the brown-shirted men around her. She could never have found Gretel; fortunately she and Veelee were waiting for her anxiously at the doorway.

"Are you all right, darling?" he asked.

"Yes, fine. But Hansel has had some sort of attack—in the middle corset. And he says only you can get it off, Gretel."

"Oh, no! Not again!"

"He really is in pain."

"Well, he should be if he insists on wearing such tight

corsets at his age. And he doesn't need me to get it off. Anybody can get it off—it's built right into the tunic. He wants me to go home and get him another tunic, that's what he wants."

"I'll get it," Veelee said. "I can be back here in twenty minutes." Paule put up her hand, involuntarily, to stay him but no one saw it, and Gretel said, "You are a darling brother. We'll wait right here." Veelee waved and disappeared in the crowd.

Suddenly a friend of Gretel's came rushing through the crowd, whispering hoarsely to people as she moved. "Oh, my God, Gretel," she said. "He's coming up the stairs. The Fuehrer. He's coming up the main staircase right now."

Paule grasped Gretel's wrist tightly. "I feel sick," Gretel said. "I'll count to myself until he passes out of sight. I'll fill my mind with numbers."

"Look at the women!"

The women around them, magnificently gowned and coiffed, were near hysterical paralysis. Postulants waiting for the Host, they stood staring at the largest archway, some thirty feet away. The men with them were at attention; hands gripped thighs and sweated upon trousers. Paule wondered with dread how Veelee would have been standing if he had still been in the room.

Framed by the archway, Hitler entered wearing evening dress, extremely well-tailored. Somehow this shocked Paule; she had expected him to appear in that awful raincoat. Brueckner loomed just behind the Fuehrer, glaring impersonally at the faces in the great room. Staring at Hitler, Paule remembered the words from *Mein Kampf*: *If the Jew triumphs over the peoples of the world, his crown will be the funeral wreath of mankind, so, today, I believe that I am acting in accordance with the mind of the Almighty Creator. In killing Jews, I am fighting for the work of the Lord.* Paule's great eyes grew larger still as she stood, so tall and so very beautiful, staring at him with fright. The Fuehrer began a self-conscious march through the aisle formed by the crowd. He trudged through an awed silence as heavy as sea water. Papen was blocked behind the SS guard; given no other destination, the Fuehrer headed straight for Paule. He had to lift her hand from her side to kiss it. "My dear lady, may I have the pleasure of bidding you good evening?" he asked stiffly. He bent over her gloved hand, and then his

66

head came up and he looked at her, and she felt an enormous thrill go through her as she stared into the pale eyes. "You are having a good time?" he asked.

The dense crowd around them hung on every word. I am a Jew, she wanted to say to him. You have kissed the hand of a Jew. You are talking to a Jew and all of the rulers of Germany are watching you, she wanted to shout at him, but the eyes devoured her and she answered, "Yes, Chancellor. Thank you, Chancellor."

"You are not German, my dear lady?"

"I am French, Excellency." Could her father forgive her if he saw her? He had taught her about the courage and dignity of Jews, and she was too cowardly to say to this pale, bristled, consuming man that she was a Jew. But she was afraid; she had never been so afraid.

Now von Papen had the Fuehrer by the other arm and was pulling him lightly. He bowed to Paule and left, and the crowd moved with him, leaving a wide space around Paule and Gretel.

Nine

✠

PAULE AND VEELEE returned to the flat in high spirits just before one in the morning. They had left Hansel dancing and drinking and eating with Gretel as though he had never had an uncomfortable moment. Veelee was whistling as he opened the door. "I wouldn't have given Hitler credit for having such taste," he said.

"Well, my God, Veelee, the man isn't blind."

He closed the door and walked past her toward the kitchen. "How about a little wine?" he said.

"Bring the Moët," she called after him.

He stuck his head out of the kitchen door. "I'll bring the Schaumwein."

"Bring the Moët! French champagne is the only champagne and you know it and you just tease me."

"Oh, yes. The French champagne."

"And don't change the subject," she shouted. "We were talking about me and Hitler." She dropped her wrap on the chair, she unhooked her dress and let it fall to the floor around her feet. She wriggled out of her brassiere and stepped out of her shoes as she heard a fine, popping sound from the kitchen and Veelee emerged with a bottle of Moët and two glasses.

"Great God in heaven, you are a gorgeous woman," he said huskily.

"That awful Goebbels woman came over to me later and told me how much her Fuehrer had liked me. She wanted to know how she might reach me so that I could come to dinner and maybe lay him before the *sorbet*."

"What did you tell her?"

"I told her I was a Jew."

"Ha!" He poured two glasses of wine and chuckled with delight.

"You should have seen her face."

"Once was enough, thank you. I saw it in 1930."

"She called me a bitch."

"Ach! And what did you do?"

"I kicked her in the ankle. We were standing close in the crowd and I let her have a real bone-cutter."

He rolled back onto the sofa in laughter and she plopped down beside him. "Now you'll never get invited to one of her dinner parties," he said.

Paule pushed him over and stretched out on top of him and kissed him lingeringly. "How I love you, Veelee," she said. "My God, how I love you."

"I love you more."

"Couldn't be."

"I am twice as big as you. My heart holds more." He rolled out from under her and took her in his arms.

"You know, I thought of Papa tonight," Paule said. "When that murderer kissed my hand and I felt so ashamed that I didn't say—"

"Didn't say what, sweetheart?"

"Didn't say to Herr Hitler that he was kissing the hand of a Jew."

"But he would have loved you for it."

"What?"

"Of course—it's a known fact. They make bets on it.

Whenever Hitler is attracted to a woman she is always racially impossible. That's why he's such a confirmed bachelor —he's afraid he'll go and get himself engaged to a Jew."

"Veelee, you devil—"

"No, really. If you had told him he probably would have said, 'Well, don't tell me I did it again?' I mean it." Paule grabbed him again and kissed him, then dropped the shoulder straps of her slip. Her beautiful body contracted and expanded, and her great purple eyes grew dimmer and dimmer as she stared at him. "Oh, Veelee," she moaned. "How I love you, how I love you."

Veelee was asleep on the broad double bed wearing the white silk pajamas which Paule had had made for him at Lanvin. She sat beside the open window wearing his heavy blue robe. She decided that there was nothing she could have done in that ballroom and that her father would have agreed that there was nothing she could have done. But his kiss still burned into the back of her hand like an infection, and more than ever before she felt her Jewishness. She knew that it was time that her husband knew what she had known for many weeks. Shivering in her dread, yet warmed and exultant because of it, she walked to the bed and touched Veelee's shoulder. He stirred and mumbled and his eyes flickered. "I am going to have a baby," she said. He sat up bolt upright, still partly asleep.

"How can you tell so soon?" he asked thickly.

Her eyes widened with mirth, and she pointed her long finger at him and began to giggle helplessly. She tottered and staggered in circles around the room, wailing with laughter and holding her sides. Veelee began to laugh. As she reeled near the bed he grabbed her and pulled her quaking body to the bed. "By God," he said, "if that's how it works I'm going to try for twins."

Veelee returned to Wuensdorf the next morning, leaving Paule in the sun-bathed bed, happy and at peace. Whatever had happened to turn everything around and to rearrange the sliding furniture within her mind was wonderful. She understood clearly now that it made no difference if she did not like most of her exterior life. She had Veelee and he loved her. No harm could reach her or her baby because of Veelee and his mighty German Army. She dressed slowly, then rode to the Zoological Gardens. She walked with the lively crowds to browse through Wertheim's and Tietz's, buying a large jar of calf's-foot jelly, then took a cab to the Vierjahreszeiten Theatre. It was matinee day and Dame Ellie Lewis, the great English character actress who had been her father's favorite from the time she had helped him to get started in the French theatre, was appearing. Paule's only connection with the old carelessness was with such touring players. She studied the newspapers to know if any foreign companies had been booked. Sometimes they would be French actors and old friends. Sometimes they would be English or Italian. All of the stars knew her father. All of them were a link with Paris and with the cheer of the past. She knew that such visits kept her young for Veelee. They reported frivolity and bubbling meaninglessness, and that was what she needed in her life in Germany.

Dame Ellie Lewis was said to be eighty-seven years old. She had a remarkable memory for the distant past. Whenever she played Berlin Paule arrived at her dressing room with a jar of calf's-foot jelly before the first matinee performance, and the old lady would repay her with a new reminiscence about the splendor of Paul-Alain Bernheim.

"You know, Paule," the great lady said, "for years I have been meaning to ask you something very important. My husband is ninety-four now, the poor man, and he dotes upon unraveling secrets."

What a joy it was to hear French spoken again. How could she have forgotten? She must insist that Veelee speak French to her every weekend.

"It was 1921, I think," the old woman said, "and my question is: What was the name of the restaurant because of which your father won the quarter of a million francs from Benoit Lesrois?"

"Restaurant?" Paule's memory wasn't as sharp as Dame Ellie's. "Oh, no! I remember what you mean. It wasn't a restaurant at all."

"Fascinating! Oh, dear me, my husband will be thrilled. We were in at the very beginning of that wager, you see. It started at our restaurant, the old Hotel du Golf. Benoit Lesrois was a gourmet of such caste that he employed two writers to turn out his bon mots about food and wine. Res-

70

taurant proprietors were delighted to have him dine at their establishments—absolutely free, of course, because of the glory his approval could bring."

"Monsieur Lesrois still is a most formidable man," Paule said.

"He was the greatest causist for fine food in all the world. He invented the congressional system of feeding, you know. He organized thirty-nine seemingly not connected feeding and drinking societies, which he designed principally for North Americans who cannot bear to eat well alone. He became an uncommonly rich man because of this."

"He became so pale when he drank."

"He became as white as chalk only when he drank the red wine of Pauillac, *Château du Colombier-Monpelou.*"

"His third wife was called Josette Monpelou."

"Ah."

"Papa admired her."

"Of course. Well, one evening in the Restaurant du Golf your papa had ordered ortolans under white truffles. When they arrived he opened a small tin of something called condensed milk which he poured over the ortolans and truffles, ate it with gusto, then washed it all down with a Montrachet '06—a wonderfully rewarding wine and a long keeper—which he mixed before everyone's eyes with some American soft drink he had brought with him in a grotesquely shaped bottle."

"They sent it to Papa from America."

"My dear, Benoit Lesrois left his chair like a wounded water buffalo and knocked your father off his chair. Your father took up his cane and beat Lesrois out of the restaurant while Smadja, the old *sommelier,* struck feebly at your father with a long, white napkin. There was total chaos in the restaurant, and four soufflés which my husband was cultivating were ruined. Lesrois rushed to his newspaper and at white heat wrote his famous column *"J'accuse!"* and attacked your father, calling him a disgrace to France. Your papa answered with a full-page advertisement which carried only the name Benoit Lesrois followed by three words: *Liberté? Egalité? Fraternité?* Monsieur Lesrois was hissed wherever he went, but your father was hissed wherever he went, too, and it was of far more consequence in his case, because he was an actor.

"A solution had to be found. Your father sent Monsieur

Lesrois a letter which said Lesrois was too fat to be challenged to a duel. And he was a huge man—he looked like Sir Toby Belch, as Jupp played him. Instead of dueling, your father offered to bet Monsieur Lesrois a quarter of a million francs that he could take him to a restaurant that Lesrois would not be able to identify but which he would have to agree was the finest restaurant he had ever patronized. He was so clever, your papa. He returned the quarrel to the stomach and removed it from the area of patriotism which was causing the hissing so disturbing to his performances."

"He never told me they hissed him in the theatre," Paule said in a shocked voice.

"Well, naturally. He was an actor. The very idea of the wager so amused Lesrois that he accepted at once and spread the word all over Paris. He kept laughing heartily right up to the second forkful of food."

"I was there!" Paule said with excitement. "I ate with them! I was the official witness!"

"How delicious of your father to provide a ten-year-old witness."

"Oh, no, Madame. It was Papa's analysis that Monsieur Lesrois could not defile my innocence by denying what had happened."

"But what did happen, child? What was the name of the restaurant?"

Paule giggled with delight. "There was no restaurant. You see, first Papa had had a recording made at Foyot's which reproduced all the sounds in a restaurant at the height of the dinner hour."

"Why?"

"Aha! You will see. Papa fetched Monsieur Lesrois in the big Hispano-Suiza and blindfolded him. The car drove to Cours Albert I. As they got out of the car I was in the main hall with the gramophone and I played the special recording of Foyot's—and do you know what?"

"What?"

"As Monsieur Lesrois, led by Papa, crossed the main hall, he said, 'Sounds like Foyot's to me.' "

"Excellent."

"Papa told Monsieur Lesrois that they would eat in a private dining room where they would be joined by his daughter as a witness. When he took the blindfold off we were in our small dining room where the windows had been

72

masked. Clotilde served the meal wearing only a black leotard, a white lace apron, a black mask and a white lace cap, and Monsieur Lesrois actually sniffed his disapproval."

"He must have thought he was in a bordello."

"I think so too, because he wanted to say something but my being there seemed to stop him. Well, the food began to appear. Monsieur Lesrois just wept quietly while he wolfed the caviar. It was the roe of the yellow-bellied sterlet."

"How in the world did your father ever get it?"

"A Russian Grand Duchess."

"Oh, of course."

"Few foreigners, indeed few people anywhere, have ever tasted it; it had always been reserved for the Russian Imperial Court before the revolution. Monsieur Lesrois kept wolfing it and weeping and saying, 'Where did they get it, Bernheim?' Papa answered, 'The late Tsar liked this little place—he came here a great deal incognito. I suppose he left them a barrel or two of the stuff.'"

"Oh, the poor man. But then, he did go beyond his depth when he offended your papa."

"The *bourride du Midi* came next, with a good Tavel served—inside a ripe watermelon—you know, *la pastèque de la Provençe*. Monsieur Lesrois began to mumble a prayer of thanksgiving at his first taste of the *Salmis de palombe d'Etchalar*. Those were the only words he spoke for the remainder of the meal. He kept his beady little eyes fixed on the kitchen door when his plate was empty. Concentrating utterly, he just ate and wept and wept and ate. After the *gras-double au safran à l'Albigeoise* came the contrast of a *gratin de ris de veau truffé*, and at this, Monsieur Lesrois began to whimper pitiably."

"But who was this great chef, my dear? The knowledge of such food grayed Lesrois overnight you know, and the lines in his face became absolutely harrowing."

"That was the cruel part of Papa's revenge," Paule said sadly. "When the last ice disappeared, Monsieur Lesrois pleaded for the name of the restaurant and the name of the chef, but Papa refused, smiling. Monsieur Lesrois bullied and cajoled, saying he could make the chef the most famous man in France. Papa just smiled, and Clotilde served a ripened meringue layer cake. By the time Monsieur Lesrois was sipping Papa's epic Calvados his face had taken on a desperate, lost expression which I shall never be able to forget. I could see in Monsieur Lesrois' face the knowledge that he would have to fill the time until his death knowing that within Paris there was food such as he had just eaten, but that he would never enjoy again."

Tears filled Dame Ellie's eyes and she dabbed at them with a handkerchief. A boy banged on the dressing-room door and called, "Fifteen minutes."

"And the name of the chef?" she asked. "I will never tell. I won't even tell Alan."

"The chef was Miss Willmott, who had been Papa's English nanny. She is one of the geniuses of our epoch."

"What contours doth justice have," Dame Ellie intoned. "Perhaps it is better, at that, that Monsieur Lesrois never knew that the cook of the greatest meal of his life was an Englishwoman. But justice did not halt right there, you know, my dear. Your wicked papa was repaid for his cruelty. Years later he told me that he had spent the entire wager on flowers for an auto magnate's wife who, in what your father considered to be one of the best-kept secrets of all Paris, he discovered to his bitterness to be a devout Lesbian."

The old woman kissed her goodbye, and Paule picked her way across the debris of the backstage and left the theatre feeling as euphoric as though she were accompanied by her father himself. Gisele was waiting for her at the Adlon, and they had lunch and a refreshing hour of gossip. Gisele had to leave early for a fitting and so she scurried out the Wilhelmstrasse exit. Paule strolled on the Unter den Linden. A parade was making its way down the Charlottenburg Chaussée toward the Brandenburg Gate. Every sort of Berliner was at the curbside as the marching, brown-shirted men came abreast. They were singing lustily, and the drums and brass of a band rang out behind them:

"Zum letzen Mal wird zum Appell geblasen,
zum Kampfe steh'n wir alle schon bereit,
Bald flattern Hitler-Fahnen über allen Strassen,
die Knechtschaft dauert nur noch kurze Zeit;
Bald flattern Hitler-Fahnen über allen Strassen
die Knechtschaft dauert nur noch kurze Zeit."

Paule asked the woman next to her what the occasion was. A storm trooper in front of her turned around. He had very small eyes that seemed to have been pasted to either side

74

of his nose. His mouth was twisted into a sneer. "What kind of a German are you?" he said to Paule. "Horst Wessel died for this country two years ago today."

"Oh, yes. Thank you." The storm trooper turned away. The elation that she had always felt during a parade began to fade. A mass of party flags went by, dozens of black swastikas in white circles laid upon fields of blood. Paule felt someone grab her arm roughly; the storm trooper was shouting at her. "You are too good to salute the flag? Are you a German or are you some kind of filthy Jew?"

Paule felt herself tremble with outrage. She stared into his tiny eyes with flat distaste. "Franz! Set to!" she said and spat into his face. He punched her heavily and instinctively, knocking her backward into the crowd. She lay on her back and saw him rushing to her, his thin lips drawn back from his teeth, his heavy boot raised to kick her face. But miraculously the crowd closed around her, eager hands pulled her to her feet and spun her back and back, hiding her with their bodies. "You filthy Jew! Filthy Jew bitch!" the choked voice screamed after her as she stumbled toward the stone columns and the large lanterns at the doorway to the Adlon.

Ten

✠

THE IMPERIAL GERMAN ARMY begat the Freikorps and the Freikorps begat the Sturm Abteilungen, called the SA, and the SA begat the Schutz Staffeln, called the SS, which begat an eternity of shame for the German people. Arminius, the Cherusci's Fuehrer, became a citizen of Rome in I A.D. then returned to his dripping, northern forest eight years later to overthrow Roman rule. Arminius led his people to worship Hercules in a weapons-decorated shrine deep in the Teutonwald. Almost two millennia later, Heinrich Himmler turned the German tribes to another barbaric, weapons-strewn religion. He called upon his Fuehrer to breathe upon the decrement of Germany and lo! a miracle skulked upon the earth. The prime sullage was processed. The cloacal scum of losers and rejects, of misfits and resenters; the exuviae of Bavarian emotional cripples, Thuringian hysterics, Saxonian eugenic disasters, Hannoverian paranoids, Swabian aberrants, and Viennese come-aparts became the bone and tissue, nerves and spirit of the SS. The rootless, the aimless, the perverted, the monstrous, the off-scourings of feeble haters yearning for chaos. the mental defectives with a knack for brawling, the secretly vicious who demanded punishment, apolitical lay-abouts and louts—these were the SS, the legally constituted maggots which feasted upon the German republic; the quintessence of the Fuehrer's exalted dream of total nihilism.

The SS was founded in 1923 as the Strosstruppe Hitler, a part of the brown-shirted Sturm Abteilungen, a bodyguard improvised by three Munich bravos named Schreck, Maurice, and Heiden. It was disbanded after the craven farce of November 9, 1923, because the party was declared illegal and the Fuehrer was put into prison. The ban on the party was removed in 1925, but the SA was still illegal and party meetings were being broken up by political opponents, so the Fuehrer ordered that the Schutz Staffeln be built up into protection squads of a leader and ten men each.

In 1926, when the SA was made legal again, the SS, now consisting of two hundred and twenty men, faded into the background. But the Fuehrer understood the uses of two of everything, and he presented the SS with the "famous" blood standard; and in 1929, to balance the power of the SA, he named young Heinrich Himmler Reichsfuehrer SS and ordered him "to form this organization into an elite troop of the party, a troop dependable in every circumstance."

The resolute Reichsfuehrer SS was twenty-eight years old, five feet seven and a half inches tall, and weighed one hundred and forty-six pounds. He wore rimless pince-nez, and his dead-white, heavily blue-veined hands were always in repose. He had been a fertilizer salesman and a chicken farmer and his wife's name was Marge. When he took command there were only two hundred and eighty SS, but he built his charge into a state within a state of over five hundred thousand people, uncovered their talents for murder, and stocked the archives with lore concerning astrology, phrenology, rune reading, Japanese Aryans, selective human breeding systems, Genghis Khan parallels, medieval Teutonic-knight rituals, human skull classifications, alchemy, reincarnation, oatmeal and carbonated water production, and certified Valhalla sites for the readily available German dead. The Reichsfuehrer SS was a devotedly inhuman man in his old-fashioned Bavarian way. He was sentimental enough to obtain a post for his old mother's favorite doctor at the Dachau concentration camp. He designed the SS uniform himself, and the Death's Head insignia for the Totenkorps, as a sure-fire recruiting gimmick. He developed personally the "interrogation" system of identical tortures for everyone, rich or poor, so that Germans might not be thought of as sadists. No careless kicks would scatter teeth from the mouths of young Jewish women: only pre-planned, pre-ordered kicks. No floggings during interrogations were ever self-indulgent. Everything was specified in a manual which clearly stated the standard operating procedure: 1. arrest and detention; 2. if a stick or a club were used the beatings were not to exceed twenty-five blows; 3. floggings were permitted only in the presence of a physician; 4. "rigorous examinations"— meaning that forms had to be executed in quintuplicate— insisted that humane, precautionary procedures be followed. These were: *a.* attendance by a physician; *b.* temporary drowning in ice water *must* be followed at once by artificial respiration—so that this could be followed by other temporary drownings; *c.* the same standard equipment, contained in a kit, must be issued to all interrogation teams, no matter where stationed, and would be available upon request. This kit would contain: 1. a testicle crushing machine; 2. an electrical device kit with electrodes to be fastened to hands, feet, breasts, penis, and rectum; 3. an acetylene torch to be administered only if the interrogation was not going well. No individual German interrogator had devised the interrogating methods, nor did he ever exceed them. Interrogators were only following orders.

SS Sturmbannfuehrer Eberhard Drayst had been assigned to interrogations duty for three years before his transfer. He had worked in Munich and Nuremberg, then was shuttled between Berlin and Munich because he was an excellent interrogator. It was good work, he felt; the hours were irregular and an ambitious man had time for a lot of study. For one thing, he had the opportunity to plan how to get the attention of the Reichsfuehrer SS, whom he had met on enlistment but who never appeared at interrogations, and was therefore impossible to impress in person.

Drayst had been observant. He had asked discreet questions. He had studied files of correspondence and newspapers because he was genuinely interested in learning the inner spirit and character of the Reichsfuehrer SS, in finding the hidden integer which would reveal the man. He knew, for example, that the Reichsfuehrer SS was shy, perhaps even timid, almost maidenly sometimes, because of the way he held his feet when he was photographed with the Fuehrer. To Drayst the Reichsfuehrer SS was the most typical, the most average German of them all. His feet were always so respectful in photographs with the Fuehrer. The Reichsmarschall's feet were indifferent and Ribbentrop's feet were actually servile. What a disgusting man! In his heart Drayst knew he could never have found peace working under either the Reichsmarschall or Ribbentrop. The Reichsfuehrer SS was far, far more German than even the Fuehrer, who was too wild, too unsteady, too inspired, to be typically German. But then how could a superman be typical? When Drayst learned that Frau Bormann called the Reichsfuehrer SS "Uncle Heini" he felt that all of his theories had been confirmed. "Uncle Heini" was exactly right. It fit him like paint, because he was the German of Germans. He had studied his life; he moved along its path with care and application; he balanced his meanings scientifically against the various discrepancies which could arise; and above all else, he remained absolutely sane amid a group of leaders who sometimes did not seem to be in full possession of their faculties.

At last Drayst's patience was rewarded. The big break came almost by accident. He had decided some time before to concentrate upon intellectual approaches to the Reichsfuehrer SS—mainly because he was unable to see any other way.

For six weeks a foolish, sick old man had taken up Drayst's time whenever he visited the boarding house which his mother ran in Munich. At first he had avoided the old pest, until it struck him that the old man was offering him a key to the gate which separated him from the attention of the Reichsfuehrer SS. Here, indeed, was fruit for that ever-questing mind. He wrote and rewrote his letter, then boldly addressed it.

        22 February, 1932

I have had the opportunity of investigating certain
new theories held by Wilhelm Rodenkirchen, ostensibly
a crank. It is his conviction that the character of an individual depends on whether he is first born, second
born or third born, et cetera. He has written a paper
on the subject (with my assistance) in which he rather
vaguely characterizes the different types according to
their numerical natal sequence.

Examples: Frederick the Great, Bismarck, Kant, and
Hermann Goering are examples of third-born children.
Haydn and Rembrandt were great fifth-born men. In
this way he rambles on, his characteristics are abstrusely
vague in the manner of popular astrological predictions
one finds in the newspapers.

However, this man has a "gift" to tell, on first sight,
whether a person is first born or later born, a talent
which he documents by numerous incompletely signed
affidavits of the following kind:

"I herewith certify to Herr Rodenkirchen that after an
acquaintance of five minutes (a subway ride from Neu-
kolln to Hermannplatz) he has ascertained that I am a
second-born child.

                              (Signed) Erika K."

"We certify to Herr Rodenkirchen that he told us, after
looking at us for two minutes at the most, that we are a
second-born child each.

                         (Signed) Annemarie W.
                                  Waldemar W."

                Heil Hitler!

                Eberhard Drayst
                SS Sturmbannfuehrer

After he had found the temerity to send in such a report,
Drayst became extremely nervous. He was ignoring channels;
he was by-passing his own chief, General Heydrich, and the
Reichsfuehrer's own bureau chief, General Wolff. He was

taking the chance that he had completely misjudged the Reichsfuehrer SS; he might now be investigated and broken. He suffered through four days of stress and doubt. On the morning of the fifth day he received a reply.

TO: SS Sturmbannfuehrer Eberhard Drayst
    26 February, 1932
    I am greatly interested in the theories of Herr Roden-kirchen regarding the immediate classification of the character of an individual depending on whether he is first born, second born, third born, et cetera. You will forward the paper he has written on this subject (with your assistance) together with a basic curriculum vitae and personality estimate of Herr Rodenkirchen.

                                    Heil Hitler

                                    H. Himmler
            RfSS u. Ch. d.d.Pol.,im R.M.d.I.

After allowing some time to elapse, during which it could be considered that he was conducting intensive research, Drayst wrote more fully.

TO: Reichsfuehrer SS
    · 6 March, 1932
    Enclosed find primary report written by Herr Wilhelm Rodenkirchen (with my assistance) regarding the immediate classification of the character of individuals depending on whether they are first born, second born, third born, et cetera.
    Herr Rodenkirchen, semi-retired, acts as a sub-manager and porter at the Pension Siegfried, this city. He is sixty-five years old and states that he has devoted most of his life to the development and confirmation of his theories.
    He has had some remarkable victories. If, for example, a first born should not seem to conform to the required characteristics, Rodenkirchen has usually ascertained that the respective mother had had a miscarriage previous to that child, so the alleged first born is actually a second-born child.
    I have helped Herr Rodenkirchen by giving him

some intellectual and statistical advice. He has now formulated his ideas in some parts of his paper better than before—but in other parts considerably worse than before. Most readily refutable is his clumsy condemnation of first-born and second-born children of which he considers the first physically and the second morally inferior. This is an impossibility because it would establish that the greater part of the German people today would be inferior in one way or another.

Even so, a good basic idea is behind his work which needs only to be presented properly and to be examined conclusively. Professor P. Hochuli is correct when he says that the hypothesis made by Herr Rodenkirchen could be tested only by the application of exhaustive statistical methods.

Heil Hitler!

Eberhard Drayst
SS Sturmbannfuehrer

This letter marked the turning point in Drayst's career. He was ordered to appear personally before the Riechsfuehrer SS, who commended him on his intellectual diligence, stated that for some time he had been considering the establishment of a Special Projects Office, and that he felt that Drayst was the right German to take charge of it. Drayst was a university man, twenty-five years old; the Reichsfuehrer was himself only thirty-one.

Drayst was detached from active duty with the interrogation teams and was promoted on the spot to the rank of SS Obersturmbannfuehrer. He spent two rewarding years as Section Chief of the Special Projects Office before being transferred to the SS Fuehrerschule as an interrogations instructor. All of his life Drayst was to cherish the correspondence he had exchanged with the Reichsfuehrer SS; he kept it in a transparent, dust-free file on top of his other papers in an unlocked drawer of his desk so that SD investigators might make a note of the relationship.

Some of the correspondence between the two men blazed new trails and opened inquiries which had never before been considered.

TO: Obersturmbannfuehrer Eberhard Drayst
    Chief, Special Projects Office
    27 March, 1932

I was most interested to receive the outline of your proposed research project #2146, which considers the need for investigation of the possibility that all left-handed people may be open or concealed homosexuals, and you have my permission to carry it forward. I would suggest that you administer this through Dr. L. Roth of the Department of Science and Education.

Keep thinking. Victories are carried by the force of arms, but it is the minds of far-seeing Germans who will prepare the way.

Heil Hitler!

H. Himmler
RfSS u. Ch. d.d.Pol.,im R.M.d.I.

TO: RfSS
    11 April, 1932

Relative to the Study Project #2146 to determine homosexuality factors in left-handedness, I have submitted an outline of the project to Dr. L. Roth of the Department of Science and Education, as per your request/order.

I can report that the subject is also being explored by Dr. A. Weiler, Institute of Eugen Fischer-Dahle and one of our finest medical-research minds. By a lucky coincidence, both he and Dr. Youngstein, head of the Psychiatric Department at the Charité, who is also co-operating, are left-handed.

Heil Hitler!

Eberhard Drayst
SS Obersturmbannfuehrer
Chief, Special Projects Office

TO: Obersturmbannfuehrer Eberhard Drayst
    17 April, 1932

I want to remind you of our recent correspondence about left-handedness in humans. I want to put down my thoughts about this topic for you in writing.

Many signs indicate that man in very early times was left-handed. A great amount of early findings (tools) can be mentioned as proof.

This probably changed with the introduction of the shield. It covered the left side of the body in order to protect the heart. Therefore the right hand had to be used more and more and, by and by, man became right-handed although not exclusively right-handed. We know from the *Waltarlied,* which described the fighting between Walther von Aquitanien with Gunther and Hegenin in the ninth century, that man at that time used both hands. Probably only in the last centuries did man become right-handed.

It is my opinion that a child following natural instincts prefers to use his left hand rather than his right. This is a point which I want you to have Dr. Weiler explore. Is this Dr. Abraham Weiler, the Jew? And have him state why this instinct exists in human beings, with copies to Dr. L. Roth of the Department of Science and Education.

We find ourselves led to this question: Could it be assumed that there is better circulation and better development on the left side of the body? I think you will find that Dr. Weiler will bear me out on this. I know Dr. Youngstein will bear me out, and Dr. Roth, of course.

Furthermore, I should like you to find out if it can be assumed that the reason for a stroke could be lack of exercise of the muscles and the nerves of one side of the body, lesser efficiency in the corresponding side of the brain, and the greater tendency to calcification of the arteries of this part of the brain.

Heil Hitler!

H. Himmler
RfSS u. Ch. d.d. Pol., im R.M.d.I.

With this letter the Reichsfuehrer SS placed maximum responsibility and total intellectual confidence in Drayst. Further exchanges, which Drayst valued highly, demonstrated that he had the character to disagree with the Reichsfuehrer. It also demonstrated his growing self-confidence and indicated the degree of give-and-take intimacy which the two men had achieved.

TO: Oberstrumbannfuehrer Eberhard Drayst
    Chief, Special Projects Office
    21 June, 1932

As you know, the storks of northern Europe migrate each year to South Africa. It is known that the natives of South African countries like to eat stork meat. This represents an opportunity for us to influence the Boers with effective propaganda for National Socialism.

Please submit your project report in this regard not later than the 30th June.

Heil Hitler!

H. Himmler
RfSS u. Ch. d.d. Pol., im R.M.d.I.

TO: RfSS
    30 June, 1932

This is the project report on your request/order #3781 for the investigation of the use of migrating storks to influence Boers with effective propaganda for National Socialism.

I have been in constant consultation with Professor Dr. Hjalamar Mattesohn, Chief of the Ornithological Station Rositten, who has presented these objections to the practicality of the idea:

1: It would be necessary for Professor Mattesohn's staff, according to Fräulein Reiter, his statistical expert, to catch at least one thousand storks and attach rings with leaflets around their legs. This would be a very difficult task. Fräulein Reiter also expresses concern over the problems of housing one thousand storks, if they could be captured.

2: Statistically, we would need to grant that there would be little chance that South African natives would shoot down all one thousand storks. This is based on the fact that so many storks keep returning from South Africa each year. Of the storks which were shot down, according to Professor Roland Handschuh, Chief of the Department of Linguistics at Wartburg University, it would be necessary that the leaflets be printed in one or more of the Bantu languages. Dr. Handschuh reports that the number of Bantu languages is still undecided—ranging, according to different authorities, between eighty and one hundred. However, should we determine that the Storkleg Project is to be carried forward he assures me that the principal languages are Swahili, Zulu, Congo, Luba-Lulua, Luganda (or Ganda) and Nyanja.

3: For the Boers it is taboo to shoot down storks; consequently they could not be counted on for this kind of propaganda response, I am advised by Dr. Peter Maas of the Geopolitical Institute.

4: Since storks are very popular in South Africa, the whole action could turn the natives of South Africa unfavorably against the Reich. (Dr. Maas)

Do you wish this project to go forward?

Heil Hitler!

Eberhard Drayst
SS Obersturmbannfuehrer
Chief, Special Projects Office

The Reichsfuehrer SS showed his innate tact by not mentioning the project again. Drayst liked the challenge of intelligence work, interrogations, and raids, but he would always cherish the two years of scholarly tranquility as Special Projects Chief which the Reichsfuehrer's restless, questing mind had made possible.

Eberhard Drayst was born in Munich on May 26, 1906. He had a mother and seven sisters who remained invisible throughout his life. His father was dean of men and assistant manager of the Kullers' Barber College, a commercial institution which graduated a new class each month at economical rates—or in two weeks with expert tutoring provided by Drayst's father or by the chancellor of the college, Dr. Kullers, at extra expense. Kullers was the businessman of the faculty; Drayst's father was more the artist. His father had been appointed Court Barber to Crown Prince Heinrich of Bavaria; the Prince had become little Eberhard's godfather, thus imbuing the lad with a snobbism which time was never to dull.

Because of the royal appointment, the Royal Coat of Arms was displayed at the street-level window of the college and was printed on its diplomas. The student body usually represented all regions of Germany, many Austrian barbering hopefuls, and even young men from as far away as Glasgow. The literature of the college showed that its graduates were working at their trade in Luxor, Egypt, and Erwinna, Pennsylvania, in the United States of America.

Young Drayst himself received a more formal education. He earned his *Abitur* in 1925, then attended the Universities of Frankfurt and Munich, winning his philosophical doctorate with a thesis entitled "On Pagan Roots in Modern Funeral Practices." He had hopes of being invited into the business of his only bachelor uncle, who had the largest undertaking practice in eastern and southern Germany and was known as The Scientist Embalmer. Many people had specified in their wills that they must be embalmed by Herr Dr. Drayst personally.

Drayst knew embalming. On his days off from school and the university his uncle permitted him first to watch the work, then to assist him at it. Drayst was attracted to the stillness and the sublime serenity of the profession, but his father was an ardent militarist who in 1873 had invented and popularized the military haircut known as *"der Buerstenhaarschnitt,"* and in 1906 had designed and disciplined the moustache of Erich von Ludendorff (which was said to have influenced the shape of the moustache of von Hindenburg himself). Drayst's father had been deeply influenced by the prestige with which that experience had endowed him, and he transferred this military ardor to his son.

Drayst's father was anti-Semitic because Dr. Kullers was Jewish; as Drayst's father saw it, Jewish money had made Kullers chancellor. As early as possible Drayst was enrolled in the Deutschvoelkische Jugendschar and the Jungfrontkaempferverband so that he could understand the danger of the Jews. When he was old enough, the boy was enlisted in the Stahlhelm, a hearty nationalist organization. His father also insisted that the lad become a physical-culture instructor; this strengthened him and served him well during the exacting hours of service on SS interrogation teams.

In 1924, when Drayst was eighteen years old, his father

presented him with his own membership card in the Nazi party. In 1930, after he had received his doctorate, his father's connections were strong enough to place him in the navy. He was stationed at Kiel and assigned to work in the military intelligence organization, Abwehr, with the rank of ensign. Drayst was well-adapted to intelligence work, but he made the fundamental mistake of anonymously telephoning the wives of some of his superior officers and making lewd and obscene representations to them. Drayst was apprehended without delay and dishonorably discharged from the service, which ruined him for any chance of distinction in any of the other branches of the German military. It was a blessing that Drayst's father had been killed in a political riot, for the boy could not have faced him. As it was, he even lacked the courage to confront his uncle and ask for his old embalming job.

Drayst drifted into part-time private detective work in Berlin, but on his last case he was beaten up so badly by a love-crazed client who was broken-hearted over the shocking—not to say needlessly lascivious—details on which Drayst had dwelt in a report on the man's wife's infidelities, that he had to leave Berlin in fear of his life. He almost died on the night train to Munich, where he was taken off the train unconscious and removed by ambulance to the hospital near the Central Station. One of the police officials who attended Drayst was an admirer of the Nationalsozialistische Deutsche Arbeiterpartei; having looked into Drayst's background while he was still unconscious, the official recommended him to the Reichsfuehrer SS. Drayst's combination of a university degree, naval experience, Abwehr training, youth, strength, a dishonorable discharge and a police record impressed the Reichsfuehrer, and when the police official showed him Drayst's paid-up party card dated 1924, the Reichsfuehrer saw to it that the lad's hospital bills were overlooked and had the young man summoned as soon as he had recovered.

They had a talk which Drayst was never to forget. The Reichsfuehrer SS became his idol. Drayst was admitted into the SS on July 2, 1932, as a Hauptsturmfuehrer because of his naval record. He was permitted to buy his own boots and black trousers—a privilege of new members of the Corps— and settled into intelligence work. This included reading foreign newspapers in French and English and, three mornings a week, soliciting advertising with two armed, uniformed men, for *Voelkischer Beobachter,* the party newspaper. He also handled indoctrination sessions for new recruits and sought out desirable Corps candidates on the campuses of universities.

The day began with reveille at six o'clock, followed by an hour of physical training before a breakfast of mineral water and oatmeal. After breakfast came weapons training, but three times a week the recruits enjoyed the activity at which Drayst shone: indoctrination lectures. These were broadly based upon such fixed tenets as "Providence has sent Germany the Fuehrer and it is almost amazing that he is never mistaken," and "Jews are the cancer of society and must be removed with surgical ruthlessness." Free discussions were held on the philosophy of racial selection from such textbooks as Dr. Rosenberg's *Myth of the Twentieth Century* and Walter Darré's *Blood and Soil.*

After dinner at midday, the recruits spent four hours drilling on the parade ground; this was followed by scrubbing, plank scouring, pipe claying, and polishing. Then, if the recruit could still stand, he was permitted to leave the barracks providing his well-flattened pockets contained only a modest supply of paper currency, his paybook, his handkerchief creased according to regulation, and one prophylactic. The recruit remained a novice until he had earned the right to take the SS oath.

Drayst composed his character very carefully during this period. He developed the rare gift of attentive listening. He would cross his legs respectfully, perhaps smoke a cigarette, and wear the same amiable expression throughout any conversation; he seemed always intensely interested but was never pushy about it. He was a man of carefully rehearsed emotional gestures. The perimeter of his long, wide face formed a shape like a heraldic shield; and with his thrusting, sharp-ridged nose hurtling out above his heavy bluish lips, his deep, all-wise eyes in sockets like twin anchor ports, he resembled a modern ocean liner seen dead on. His skin had the color of the interior of a Reblochon cheese, and his chin seemed as pointed as the tip of a spade on a playing card. His ears were not much larger than those of a guinea pig, but the bell-clapper lobes hung down on either side of his face like blank tavern signs in the wind. Beneath almost white-blond hair his eyes, more turquoise than blue, were comic eyes, excepting perhaps to a subject under interrogation, for he could flicker them from side to side with horrendous rapidity. He used this device professionally as an instrument of terror. Altogether, Drayst's face gave the impression of having been homemade, run up by an over-enthusiastic hobbyist.

Drayst had good French and fair English. When he spoke French with his odd accent and his high-pitched voice, it sounded like the record of a *chanteuse* being played at the wrong speed, but he had learned to speak it perfectly and with the same thoroughness he brought to everything he did. Drayst polished whatever corner he was inhabiting with such fierce energy and commanding determination that, combined with his face, his slender, supple height, and his chilling lack of expression, even his associates feared, resented, and admired him.

If Drayst had any professional flaw it was his choice of sexual expression, which was linked to adoration of power and which presented a tricky ethical problem for the SS. The pleasure Drayst took in uttering obscene phrases to a distant woman over a telephone had to do with his own power search but nothing to do with the SS. The Reichsfuehrer SS knew about his telephone aberration and dismissed it as a "trick of character." Drayst's work with the interrogation teams always excited him; not that he ever allowed this ecstasy to get out of hand during interrogations beyond, perhaps, a tendency to overemphasize the *anschnauzen* technique. The larger proportion of those interrogated were Jews whose savings, business interests, and collateral property were the interest of the Party, and of course after 1933 there were more and more Jews to be interrogated. Working with women almost sent Drayst into hysterical blindness although, to his credit, he controlled this so well at work that no one ever knew the intensity of his feeling. It was afterward—afterward during the nights when he would lie alone in his room, remembering, sweating, and trying to breathe, he would have to get up, no matter what the hour of the night, put on civilian clothes and go out to find Jewish prostitutes. In Berlin he would move in the shadows of the Wedding district around the Stettiner Bahnhof, or in the Ackerstrasse, or sometimes, needing more variety, a hotel called the Danziger Hof, which was really a brothel.

At the beginning in Berlin, Drayst would find friends in

the hotels around the Friedrichstrasse Bahnhof, and in the so-called *Offizierspensionen* where call-girl syndicates operated. In Munich the number of registered prostitutes was much smaller than in Berlin, about four hundred as compared to six thousand, but the difference was reduced by the *Bueffetmamsells,* the waitresses in the third-class bars. These were a Bavarian institution rather than a German one, and until he was transferred to Berlin, taken off Special Projects, and required to conduct multiple interrogations day and night, the rewards and loving attentions of the girls in the Sendlinger Torplatz had been completely satisfying.

As time went on, Jewish prostitutes became more and more difficult to find, and it became necessary for Drayst to wait later and later in the night to find and overpower Jewish women night workers. He did this because he had to, despite the SS penalty of death by firing squad if he were caught, the supreme penalty provided by the Reichsfuehrer SS to prevent race defilement within the proud corps. Drayst was soon past caring about that. He *had* to do what he did, and as he entered the women in bordellos, in furnished rooms, in alleyways, or behind hoardings he would plead with them to love him. But after a while his lust took a more sophisticated form: he would beg them to forgive him and then—because he had to protect himself from being charged with such a heinous crime even if they could find it in their hearts to forgive him—he would have to strangle them anyway.

Eleven

✠

PAUL-ALAIN VON RHODE-KUSSEROW was born on the twelfth of November, 1934, at 2:46 A.M. in the Krankenhaus Westend in Berlin-Charlottenburg. He was not baptized, though the decision not to do so shocked his Calvinist aunts. His aunts thought the baby was the image of his father. His father thought he looked exactly like Paule. Paule was certain he strongly resembled her own father. His nursemaid, Clotilde Grellou, who had traveled from Paris for the event, agreed with Paule.

Paule was so happy to see Clotilde again that as soon as they were alone she wept in her arms, asking, "How is Paris? How is Paris?"

"Just the same, Madame," Clotilde said. "Terrible weather when I left. Gray and cold." She patted the top of Paule's head. "Please don't cry, Madame. You mustn't be so homesick."

"You'll see, Clotilde," Paule wept. "You'll see."

"Everything is fine at the Cours Albert, Madame. Mme. Citron keeps everything fresh and clean with just one girl, and she does the cooking herself."

"Have you heard from Miss Willmott?"

"She's gone to America, Madame. She always sends us cards on our saint's days."

Clotilde had brought a letter from Maître Gitlin.

2 November, 1934

My dear Paule:

Can you tell me when you might return to Paris for ten days or so? As you may remember, your father had commissioned Rufin Portu to paint your portrait on the occasion of your 23rd birthday, now one year passed. Portu is anxious to start work. He has a frightfully busy schedule, and since he was paid in full at the rates which he commanded twelve years ago—a sum equal to approximately one percent of what he is paid today—he wants to paint you before his prices soar even higher and increase his anguish. Please advise me as soon as you can.

With all my love,

P. Gitlin

Paule answered at once.

15 November, 1934

Dear Maître:

Please relieve Rufin Portu of his obligation. I won't return to Paris for the reason that were I to leave Germany I don't think I could ever bring myself to return. Please do not let that convince you that I am miserable here. I have a wonderful marriage and a beautiful son, but mastering the customs and reactions of a foreign country are quite as difficult as you said they would be. The point is, I am adjusting—I am trying to learn to be German for Veelee and for Paul-Alain, and I will make it. Were I to disturb this progress by dropping myself into the middle of France—but it disturbs my progress even to write of that. Enough to say that you must not expect me, neither must Portu, for whom it would have been such a great honor to sit.

Warmly,

Paule

Clotilde walked the baby sometimes, and made its formula sometimes, and did its laundry sometimes, but mostly Paule did these things. She spent almost every waking hour with Paul-Alain. She had been nervous about going out into the streets alone after being struck by the storm trooper, and because the pressures on Jews had grown greater each day. No one mentioned these things—and possibly because no one could think of how to begin such a conversation. But Gretel and Gisele took turns looking in on Paule every other day and taking her out whenever she consented to go —for shopping excursions or to sit among a bustle of people at the Café Kranzler or the Bender. Eventually, Paule realized how worried they were about her, and by making a painful effort she broke the spell of her fear by inviting both sisters to lunch with her at the Adlon, walking there by herself through the Brandenburg Gate. She strolled along the Unter den Linden, whose linden trees the Nazis had transplanted to widen the avenue for parades. The trees were now closer to the building line, and as they were shorter than the street lights, the avenue was now known to Berliners as Unter den Laternen. Veelee telephoned her every day, sometimes twice a day. He arranged for surprises to be sent to her by mail from shops and by army messengers. But his assignment had become more and more time consuming, and despite his concern he could not get to the city more than twice a week.

At the time of the Weimar Republic, the short thirteen years and a few months from 1919 to 1933, Wuensdorf had been a training college for army athletes and the garrison for a training battalion of infantry. In 1933 the training battalion was turned into a mobile training unit, and hence had more officers and NCO's, as well as six squadrons to a battalion rather than the normal four. Wuensdorf garrisoned two battalions equipped with armored cars and light Panzer I tanks. As a full colonel, Veelee commanded one of the training battalions, a unit comprising fifty-eight armored cars and tanks, with thirty-four officers under his command. His immediate superior was Major General Wilhelm Schneider, Kommandeur der Panzerschule, who in turn was under the command of Lieutenant General Lutz, the Inspekteur der Kraftfahrtruppen. Paule had decorated the three rooms on the first floor of the village pub which were Veelee's quarters when work kept him steadily at Wuensdorf. At the end of each instructional round which turned out newly trained tank men, when all the tests were over and all the reports on officers and men had been written, Veelee would hold a staff blowout at these quarters. A batman stayed in the apartment permanently and there was a driver for his staff car or for his own sports car, which would take him home to Berlin as often as he could get away, but this rarely happened because his days were packed and exhausting. He was responsible for all inspections: officers' field work, their handling of tanks, their drilling of tank crews and gunnery, and the appraisal of their written assignments on tactical problems; the inspection of each unit's organization for combat and the requirements of the supply columns for various types of tanks; the fitness of tanks and armored vehicles and the testing of armor plate. His instructional work consisted of supervising the work of all other instructors and of presiding at the weekly meetings for discussion of Panzer tactics. He also sat in on classes.

Veelee tried to bring two or more of his officers back to his quarters each evening for a relaxed talk about the more difficult tank maneuvers, so that he could judge and note their grasp of their work and their qualities of both leadership and improvisation. In this way he could be sure that his final reports on them were as accurate and fair as possible. Often he would smile with grim humor over the highest rating which could be passed along in a written report on an officer: "This officer is possessed of a sound ambition."

Veelee's days began at nine A.M., when the staff car arrived to drive him to either of his two offices—if it was a day when no particular field exercise was to be held. Veelee was one of the outstanding tank experts of the world. He had had a part in the construction and development of the German tank since 1925 and had been a member of the tank corps during the time when it was necessary for the technicians to test German tanks within the Soviet Union. He had begun in the Kleintraktor, which was nine tons and had one 3.7-cm. cannon; presently he was testing the Panzer II of 9.5 tons and one 2-cm. cannon.

As luck would have it, General Schneider was hospitalized in Berlin with appendicitis when the Fuehrer, with General Guderian, the German tank corps commander, arrived unexpectedly at Wuensdorf one April day in 1934. The instant they left Veelee telephoned the hospital to report the triumph to General Schneider. To his enormous relief General Schneider was suffering postoperative hardships and could not have visitors or accept telephone calls until the following morning. Veelee leaped into his staff car and told the driver to take him home as quickly as possible.

The day of the tank men was at hand at last, and he was eager to tell Paule about it. The Fuehrer's visit was not unexpected; it was just that he had arrived two days early. Tank men had been fighting a running battle with the High Command for survival and growth for over ten years. General von Fritsch had been adamant about tanks. "The armored corps is just a dream," he had said. "Those who claim it has great strategic value are all liars." Categorically, General Beck had made the High Command's objection most clear, saying, "The vehicles' armament will not allow them to salute properly on parade. Besides, you are too fast; how are you going to direct it all without telephone?" "By radio," Guderian had said. "Nonsense!" Beck had retorted. "A radio will never work in a tank!" General von Stuelpnagel had informed Veelee sadly, "Neither of us will live to see German tanks in action."

But now, if the Fuehrer could be swung over to their side a truly mobile, mechanized tactical striking force could be developed. The tank men were convinced of the superiority of their weapon.

Sitting Paule down carefully and pouring a large cognac for each of them, Veelee explained the triumph in which he had played a leading role that day. "Out of the blue," he said excitedly. "For some reason he hates to keep to an advance schedule."

"He knows that if he did someone would shoot him."

"I don't think he has any illusions about his enemies, if that's what you mean. He knows the Communists are waiting for their chance."

"Communists? Hah! They'll have to stand in line just like anybody else."

"Do you want to hear what happened today or not?"

"I'm sorry, Veelee. Yes—please. Forgive me."

"Now listen carefully. The exercise was scheduled for the morning he was supposed to show up, and that couldn't be accelerated. He understood that. So instead of the actual exercise, I conducted him through the plan on the large blackboard in the briefing room. He was fascinated; his eyes were actually glittering. He let me talk on and I could tell that Guderian was very impressed with the Fuehrer's reactions."

"Well? Then what happened?"

"When?"

"After you had finished explaining the exercise to him."

"Paule! That's the whole point! He came to life. He was absolutely vitalized. He began to take over from me, he improvised, he even changed my tactical plan, but he actually seemed to know what he was talking about. I mean, I'm sure he had insisted on a briefing before he came, and of course my plan had been on file at the Ministry for sixty days, but the important thing is, he *understood* it. He was working with tanks and he knew what it was all about. I mean, what would be the sense of trying to impress me, a colonel at a cavalry school?"

"But what did he say?"

"He yelled." Veelee tried to imitate the Fuehrer's voice. " 'The Mobile Force commander must send his motorized infantry brigade ahead and seize that bridgehead on the river!' " Veelee stabbed the air with his forefinger. "He kept hitting the map on the wall and he yelled, 'The tank brigade must follow not later than fourteen hours behind them and harbor in the woods lying behind the bridgehead. Orders for subsequent moves must be given on reaching the harbors.' "

"What's so tremendous about that?"

"Darling, we need this man! If there is ever going to be

95

a Panzerarmee it will be only because we are able to get his support. If we depend on our own High Command we'll be lucky to get bicycles! That's what's so tremendous about the way he said what he said."

"Oh."

"And he followed right up. He grabbed the pointer away from me and he pushed me into a chair and he—"

"He *pushed* you?"

"Oh, what the hell, Paule—he was *excited*. He pounded that map with his hand and he brought that exercise to life for us. He had everybody so hopped up that they almost fell off their chairs just thinking about the promotions that would be falling on us when the big tank expansion program started. God, it was like being at war. His voice tore into us." Unconsciously Veelee began the imitation of the Fuehrer again. " 'You can see that the bridgehead would be occupied without opposition, that the tank brigade would occupy its harbors with only slight difficulty—but, having lost the element of surprise, it would be unable to proceed with the role allotted. Consequently, we must withdraw the whole Mobile Force. Otherwise the enemy's divisional column would be placed across the line of supply of the tank brigade and would cause havoc among the non-fighting vehicles.' " Veelee belted the cognac. "Isn't that amazing?"

"I guess so. But what about Thursday when you take the exercise into the field? The actual operation when each side is trying to win the maneuvers?"

Veelee's eyes left her face, returned again, wavered, then left again. "Everything will happen exactly the way the Fuehrer said it had to happen," he said, stiffly.

Paule was silent for a moment, and then said, "Darling. Veelee, darling."

"Yes, Paule?"

"You did wonderful work today."

"Yes . . . Well, he shook my hand when he'd finished, and his staff people applauded, and he said I was a capable tank officer, and then he left, on the double. Guderian stayed behind for a second, and he grabbed me by the shoulder and said, 'He is now committed to tanks. Keep him that way.' Then Guderian went racing off too. It was an unusual morning." He poured another cognac slowly.

"And you will arrange for it to happen the way the Fuehrer said it should happen?"

"You heard what Guderian said."

"Well, the fact that one exercise is spoiled doesn't mean anything compared to the future of the tank corps, does it, darling?"

Veelee's face was wooden and his eyes were still turned away from her. "Although the conclusions drawn from the exercise will be largely negative, they are nonetheless valuable," he answered.

Paule thought of her child and of all the false courage she had assumed because she knew that the army would protect them against destruction by the Fuehrer. She could not count on the army any longer. It had been corrupted. Veelee had been corrupted. It had happened so swiftly that they had not yet discovered it about themselves, and they had delivered themselves and their fate into the Fuehrer's hands. It must be happening everywhere. The U-boat men were probably just discovering that the Fuehrer understood their problems and would help them against the admirals who wanted only more battleships; infantry commanders were being "understood" in their problems with the air force; and of course the air force was already getting an overwhelming budget of understanding. In the end, every unit of the Wehrmacht would be made to feel that only the Fuehrer really understood its problems, and his price for his understanding and support would be that collectively they would not be able to deny him anything. To the military, their work was the sun and the moon and the stars; to the Fuehrer they were only a few molecules in his hammer.

Twelve

✠

THEY MUST GET AWAY SOON, she told herself every morning as she awoke. The time was coming nearer when Veelee would need to examine his tanks and his world without Jews in the compound of violent men at Wuensdorf. He would have to make a choice; she could see no other way and she thought about nothing else. Before the worst happened she would ask for the protection of his love for her and Paul-Alain and speak of their situation once and for all. They must leave Germany if they were going to survive. They had to emigrate, but where? Not to France. If they went to France Veelee would not feel that he had solved the problem. Where? Though she moved from one solution to another, she was unable to put her anguish into words, to take the action which she knew was their single salvation.

Paule slept less. Whenever she awoke in the night she would run to the baby's room to reassure herself that he was safe. The more concerned she became with safety the lighter she slept. She was pale, there were dark circles under her eyes and the new hollows in her cheeks made her seem more starkly beautiful. Because she was determined not to admit to anyone—not to Veelee, not Gretel, not Gisele, not Clotilde, not to anyone—that she was frightened and ill, her manner became more and more sarcastic about the Fuehrer and his government. No matter where they might be or with whom, she felt compelled to explain to new acquaintances and old friends that she was a Jew.

The unequal civil war in Berlin expanded. The SS, the government, the army, and an increasing number of citizens were massed against the Jewish population consisting of old men, women, children, theatrical producers, dispensing chemists, artists and sculptors, clergymen, milliners, brokers, watchmakers, butchers and sausage makers, furriers, veterinary surgeons, booksellers, teachers, dentists, and sundry other mighty warriors totalling six percent of the national population.

To keep from talking about the only thing on her mind Paule tried to fill the flat with people when Veelee was home. She took on a bewildering brightness at night. They went out a great deal too, and Hansel was able to persuade her to stop volunteering to strangers the information that she was a Jew. "After all," he said, "bears are bears, but they do not roam through the forest setting traps to catch themselves." He suggested that she must teach herself that at present there was a system in Germany which could not last and that she, like everyone else, must live within that system for the time being. She compromised by agreeing that she would not say she was a Jew unless she was asked. "You must have had very poor training at being Jewish," Hansel said. "No other Jews I know carry on the way you do."

Sleep still would not come, and there were so many things to be done. The family were coming for dinner. She was too tired to eat lunch, so she took the baby out in the pram and walked around and around the Schlossgarten. Then she took a hot bath and tried to nap but still sleep would not come. After a long cold shower she felt better and went into the kitchen to consult with the cook about dinner. They would have batter-flake soup because Hans liked that, some eels with cucumber salad because it was one of Miles-Meltzer's favorites, some pork parcels for Gretel, some French beans with pears for Veelee, and a sago bowl for Gisele. The whole family would be happy. So would she be, Paule thought, if she could only get some sleep.

Everyone was on time and in high spirits—particularly Veelee. Hans pinched her and she appreciated that. Miles-Meltzer wore a pearl-gray cummerbund and sapphire studs; his black satin tie was floppy, in the bohemian manner, and he wore brushed-silver spectacles with sapphire linchpins on either side. For the sixth year in a row he had been voted the best-dressed man in northern Europe—which meant the world, he explained, because the British had slipped horribly and there was no one else.

"But why only northern Europe?" Veelee asked over cocktails.

"That should be clear," Miles-Meltzer said. "We don't include the Belgian Congo or America, do we? No, we only include those regions which produce well-dressed men."

"Whoever told you that Englishmen are slipping must be drunk," Hansel said. "Who runs the poll, Ribbentrop?"

When dinner was served it seemed that it would be a tremendous successs and the men told a series of hilarious stories about Goering, the full-time, overtime, any-time grafter, which they exchanged in rapid repartee.

During a pause between Goering stories, prompted by nothing else except his permanent interest in clothes, Miles-Meltzer said, "Herr Ribbentrop told me today that the Reichsfuehrer SS would call me tomorrow and invite me to become an Ehrenfuehrer."

"What's that?" Paule asked.

"It's a sort of sinister idea, but childish, really," Gisele said. "The Germans love uniforms and when the Reichsfuehrer SS saw the picture of Dr. Schacht wearing the uniform of the customs service, with the rank of colonel-general, he lit up with the idea of creating honorary SS colonels."

"Oh. To suborn them. But how did that awful Herr Ribbentrop get into it?"

"Well, we have our own uniform, as you well know," Miles-Meltzer said. "It was the first thing Ribbentrop did when he took over, designing that. Dark blue with little gold buttons, oak leaf clusters and that tiny gold dagger, and so forth. At my grade we have so much spun silver on the things that at the Wilhelmstrasse they call us the men behind the foliage. He is such an idiot, you know. He refers to the Fuehrer as 'the Supreme War Lord.' However, he is presently embarrassed. Out of ninety-two of our higher officials only thirty-three are members of the Party. He said today that 'aesthetic considerations alone' have made him sensitive to the need for more outward evidence of Party spirit in the Foreign Office. He fixed it up with Himmler to invite Weizsaecker and Division Chief Woermann into the honorary SS and now he's after me."

"What are you going to do?" Paule said lightly. "Let's get up a picnic lunch next Sunday and go out and spend the day at the foot of that new statue to Fritsch at Zehlendorf."

"Who's Fritsch?" Gretel asked. Veelee saw the expression behind Paule's eyes and gripped the arms of his chair.

"Fritsch? The pioneer anti-Semite. Dr. Goebbels says it's a wonderful statue, and being in charge of German culture, he should know. The statue shows a Germanic male—like Himmler, I imagine—kneeling on top of a monster, which is the Jewish race." There was silence. Hansel reached for another bottle of wine from the sideboard and began to fill the glasses. "You can't be reading the newspapers," Paule said, addressing everyone with nervous gaiety. "Last week Dr. Rosenberg stepped in and saved German music. He really did. A hundred and seventy years ago that old fool Handel had been silly enough to base his oratorios on the Old Testament, that pack of Jewish lies, but Dr. Rosenberg straightened it all out. Wasn't that wonderful?"

"Let's go to the Kabaret der Komiker," Veelee said.

"Wonderful idea," Gisele answered, and the others agreed with alacrity. As they got into their coats and were going

down the stairs, Paule chided them for never really studying *Mein Kampf*. "Good heavens, what kind of Germans
are you if you don't read *Mein Kampf* every day? I mean to
say, where else can you find wonderful stuff like: 'The Communists are all Jews. Bad working conditions are due to
Jewish capitalists. Shopkeepers are being ruined by Jewish
department stores. Jewish doctors and lawyers take bread from
the mouths of the professions. Jews are everywhere. All
troubles and hardships in life are due to Jews.' You'd be a
very silly man to pass up an opportunity like a chance to
join the SS, Philip, and you are absolutely right. You would
look simply stunning in that uniform."

Paule and Veelee returned to the flat very late. They had not
spoken to each other for hours. Paule had behaved badly at
the Kabaret der Komiker—and not only among members of
the family. They were undressing in the bedroom, each
seated on a side of the large double bed amid the highly
polished, dark-red chairs and furniture.

"You were disgraceful tonight, Paule," Veelee said at last.
She did not answer.

"I didn't care about dinner—that's what a family is for,
to have someone to talk to. What was insulting was that
ridiculous laughter you kept forcing."

"Really?"

"Yes, really. Kurt Unger said his grandmother was seriously ill and you laughed. Peter Witt said the farmers were
nearly starving in some regions and you laughed. When Frau
Krolich said she had changed dentists because one was trying
to put her on the morphine habit, you laughed. When Professor Koch spoke so earnestly about his theories for getting
more work out of the Italians, you laughed. Everything that
was serious or tragic got a cheap, insulting, sarcastic laugh.
Why did you do it?"

"I suppose I did it because I find those things amusing
compared to other things which keep happening in your
country." She forced another false and irritating laugh. "We've
just got to get used to it, that's what everybody keeps telling
me."

"You're talking about the damned Jews again, I suppose?"

"Yes, I am. Damned Jews like your wife and your son."

"You and the boy don't come into that and you know it!

You have the protection of the German Army, no matter what anyone tries to do."

"I hope our protection is a little stronger than your army gave General Schleicher and his wife when they were murdered in their beds by your German government. No one in your protective army protested that, did they? If you ask me, you should start using your influence to see that Paul-Alain gets into the SS so we can have some real protection."

He wheeled around on the bed and struck her heavily across the face with his open hand. Though she was knocked off the bed, he did not get up. She rose slowly and sat on the bed again. He stood up and stared down at her, breathing shallowly, his face drained of blood.

"It's just that I am a mother, Veelee," she said staring at him sadly. "And Paul-Alain is a dirty little Jew, there's no denying that."

"Stop it!"

He ran around the bed and took her by the shoulders and pulled her to him roughly. He was confused that he had hit her, but he was more confused about finding answers to everything she had been saying all that night. He wanted to make her feel safe and to let her know that he would love her forever, but he had not been trained to sort out things like this and they confused him. She looked at him as though she had retreated behind some shield and was watching him through a peephole.

"Listen to me, Paule," he said desperately. "I have tried many times to talk to you about this, but you have always found some way of turning me off as though I were a wireless set. Gretel and Gisele have tried to talk to you too, but you elude us, you slip away into some other place in your mind and there is no following you there. I don't know why. I think about it all the time, but I swear to God I don't know why you won't talk about something which is changing us. If you would only pour out all these things! I am afraid that you are afraid to open the gates because what would race out of you could wash us away. But that could not happen, Paule. Because we love, and we are sure of that, and we will always be sure of that."

Paule began to weep. He let go of her and walked to the window, wringing his powerful hands. When he turned to her again he spoke with anger against everything he was not able to understand. "Paul-Alain is the son of Colonel Wil-

helm von Rhode, Junker auf Klein-Kusserow und Wusterwitz!"
He tapped his chest. "He is the heir to the four hundred
years my family have served this country with their blood.
Do you think a rabble of gutter politicians can bring the
German Army to its knees? My life is in the meaning of the
German Army, and you are my life and the boy is my life."
What was the fault? How was it happening so fast that he
could not see it to understand it and to stop it? Shapes
lurked in the mists of his soldier's mind, but he could not
bring them close enough. He had been trained to strike at
what he could see, but he could not cope with faceless dread.

She held out her arms to him. She pulled him close to her
and kissed his face over and over again. She wept softly, but
she did not speak.

Thirteen

⁜

THE WINTER OF 1935 to the summer of 1937 saw the rein-
troduction of compulsory military service in Germany, the
reoccupation of the Rhineland, the adventure in Spain and
the full rearmament program in violation of the Versailles
Treaty. Also during this time there were passed the Nuremberg Laws, which deprived all German Jews of citizenship, including Paul-Alain.

Keitel, whose son had married the daughter of General
von Blomberg, the Minister of War, was immediately appointed Chief of the Wehrmacht. As a result of the appointment Veelee joked wryly that he expected any day to be
transferred out of tanks into the Chaplain Corps.

Dr. Gross, head of the Political Office of the Party, had
begun his press campaign for the total exclusion of all
Jewish children from the schools.

The second demand for racial thought for a new
straightening out of the school sphere concerns the
racial harmony between teacher, pupil, and curriculum

. . . fruitful education is only possible if the teacher and his pupils show the same racial attitude. The teacher of an alien race has become for us unthinkable; but the demand that the community of the school class itself, with which the instructor has to work, shall present a racial unity is just as essential. From this demand follows that those groups of the population of an alien race still living among us shall be fundamentally separated in the schools from children of our own kind.

In the spring of 1936, in a decree timed to coincide with the spirit of Easter, Dr. Rust, Minister of Education, ordered all Jewish children to leave ordinary elementary schools. Special Jewish schools were to be "established" everywhere. Segregation was the Fuehrer's solution for the future.

Paule forbid herself to think of the day when Paul-Alain would have to go to school. When he was two years old she began to make plans for his education, intending that the school laws should be circumvented. Veelee was unaware of all of this; he never read the newspapers, which he felt were "a lot of political lies." At Wuensdorf no one ever talked about such things anyway. But he was spending more and more time with Paule, and only his exalting sweetness kept her steady. He stayed at Wuensdorf only when necessary, sometimes arriving home at midnight, and Paule tried to teach herself how to live with what she hated in order to keep what she loved.

On a summer morning in 1937, Hansel called Paule and invited her to lunch at the Adlon. "I've had this on my mind for years, my dear," he said, "and I cannot suppress my carnality any longer." She accepted with delight.

A page boy delivered her to Hansel in the lounge between the ballroom and the Raphael gallery. They were seated in the most distinguished corner of the red-leather bar, where the upholstery was worn.

Hansel ordered a half-bottle of champagne. "Paule, you grow more beautiful every day," he said, toasting her.

"Heavens, who wouldn't look well in a carefree, happy-go-lucky country like this?"

"Just so."

"Have you rented the ambassadorial suite for our assignation this afternoon, Hansel?"

"Careful. You will madden me with lust. I would have, you know—indeed, I intended to—but something else has come up."

"Hmm."

"But first, lunch."

They ate carefully. Paule ate sparingly. The General had eel soup, roast wild boar, then—impulsively—tried some of the *Gedaempftes Taubenbruestchen mit Erbsen Franzoesischer Art Pariser Kartoffeln.* He had to do it impulsively, he explained, because his wife was always trying to stop him. When the meal was done and as he was sipping his second Calvados, he fell silent.

"Why are we here, Hansel darling?"

"Because I adore lunching with you."

"No."

"I don't?"

"We haven't lunched together in more than four months, and the last time it was because you wanted me to persuade Veelee to talk to Gretel about taking you off that diet."

"As I get older I get more transparent. You would never catch Miles-Meltzer out like that."

"Why are we here?"

"Well . . . business. The fact is I was talking with our Commander-in-Chief, General von Fritsch, this week. He was a comrade of Veelee's father, and naturally he's very fond of Veelee. He told me that Admiral Canaris, head of the Abwehr, was concerned about certain things, and he asked me to speak to Heinz Guderian—which I did."

"About Veelee?"

"Yes. And in a way about you."

"You mean Jewish things?"

"Not at all."

"What, then?"

"Well, to be frank—and if you and I can't be frank, who can be—Veelee is terribly worried about you. And it shows in his work—that is to say, Guderian believes it keeps him from doing his best."

"But how can that be, Hansel? I assure you, through enormous effort—terrible, terrible effort—I give him nothing to worry about."

Hansel covered her hand with his. "He worries so much that he holds meetings with Gretel and Gisele and Philip and me about how we must rally round. Sometimes he calls the girls from Wuensdorf twice a day for news about you."

"Oh, Hansel!"

"We know how hard all of this barbarism has been for you." He cleared his throat suddenly. "But that is beside the point, isn't it?"

"How I love him, Hansel."

"Splendid. Good thing in families, I always say. But I don't suppose it has occurred to you—after all, you are a civilian from a civilian background—how overlong Veelee —and let me say that Veelee is a very gifted officer—ah . . . how long Veelee has remained at that little training school at Wuensdorf."

"What do you mean?"

"I mean . . . well, he should have been there eighteen months at most, and he's been there almost five years." He knocked back the Calvados.

"But—"

"Guderian says Veelee is more than brilliant, you know. He implies that Veelee could have had a division by now. Yes, I mean it. But he has resisted the idea of any transfer from Wuensdorf—though so far, thank God, this has suited the Bendlerstrasse and the lapse hasn't even been noted on his service record."

"You mean that because of me, Veelee—"

"Yes—and I honor him for it. He loves you that much. He's probably the first von Rhode who didn't love the army more. And he was right, you know. All this strain on you. Less sleep, I should imagine. Damned Nazis and their schemes. So he worries and wants to be near you. To protect you, et cetera and so forth."

"Hansel, I am ashamed. I never knew." Her eyes grew misty.

"Now, Paule, please. Don't weep, for God's sake."

"I shan't."

"Perhaps if you were to call me General Heller we might get through this damnable thing."

"Please go on, Hansel."

"You see, two things have happened. Keitel's position is very much consolidated, and he is presently undertaking a minute examination of all of his old service grudges. He is quite capable of keeping Veelee a colonel for the rest of his life, but fortunately Admiral Canaris needs just such a man as Veelee—in fact, he said he could not do better. It is a most delicate assignment."

"But what do you want me to do?"

"It's quite tricky, actually. Of course Canaris has no idea that Veelee might refuse the post. But if Veelee does refuse then the whole thing must come to the attention of General von Fritsch, and if that happens Guderian won't be able to keep the blinds down and I will be able to be of no help whatsoever. Therefore Guderian, who damned well needs Veelee in his future tank army, asked me point-blank what Veelee would do if he was approached. I told him I would let him know this evening."

"Are you going to Wuensdorf?"

"There is nothing to be decided at Wuensdorf."

"Veelee is there."

"But you are here. Forgive me, oh God, please forgive me, Paule, but it is you who must decide this thing."

"Tell me what I must do, Hansel." She looked down at her hands, tightly gripped together, as she spoke.

"Let me say that I am . . . we are—the army, all of us —are very grateful to you for this."

"Tell me, Hansel."

"All right, love. I have been assigned to Rome for special duty. Gretel is going to Wusterwitz. This would be a good time for you to take Paul-Alain out into the country, into the good fresh air and away from all this intrigue. If you were to tell Veelee that you had decided that you want very much to go with Gretel—"

"Thank you, Hansel darling," was all she could manage to say.

Veelee's favorite dish in all the world was *Gefuellte Kalbsbrust*. Four months before, in a burst of love, Paule had sent the recipe to Maître Gitlin in Paris, requesting that he ask Benoit Lesrois if he would be good enough to consult with the best chefs about how the recipe might be improved. Benoit Lesrois had taken his work seriously because the request had come from Paule, the witness to the greatest meal he had ever eaten in his life; in fact, he hinted that perhaps now that so many years had gone past she might agree to reveal the name of the restaurant in which her father had won the wager. There had been no further word until the recipe had arrived, the day before Paule's lunch with Hansel. The letter to Paule from Lesrois explained that he had eaten fourteen different versions of *Gefuellte Kalbsbrust* while seeking the best recipe and had traveled four hundred and thirty-two kilometers. The recipe had finally been developed to M. Lesroi's satisfaction by Lucien Courau in the rue Surcouf. Lesrois favored a Labastide-de-Levis, from the Gaillac hillsides of Tarn, if young enough, to accompany the dish. If that was not readily available, she could feel secure with a Pfirsichberg of the exposed Mamburg slopes at Turckheim in Alsace.

The recipe had come at such a perfect time that Paule dashed off a note to M. Lesrois telling him all about Miss Willmott and giving her address in America. On her return home after lunch with Hansel, she gave the servants the evening off, rolled up her sleeves and began to prepare *Gefuellte Kalbsbrust, à la française.*

The telephone was ringing as Veelee came in the front door. He moved across the square hall to answer it, yelling, "What's that wonderful smell?"

"Gefuellte Kalbsbrust!" Paule shouted from the kitchen. "And I made it all by myself!"

"What!" He picked up the phone. "Hello? Yes. Very good, I'll be there." He hung up hastily and strode toward the kitchen.

"You made it! The French touch!"

"I don't know what wine to have with it."

"Wine? Are you crazy? With a dish like this? We have beer." He grabbed her and kissed her, then lifted her and whirled her around and kissed her again.

"Who called?"

"What? Oh. Wuensdorf. General Guderian just missed me. He wants to see me at the Bendlerstrasse tomorrow morning."

Paule's throat tightened. "Just routine?"

"Oh, sure. He runs out of tank officers to talk to."

Veelee watched with awe as Paule served the dinner. "It looks like *Gefuellte Kalbsbrust,*" he said. As he tasted it his eyes glazed over and a look of ecstasy spread over his face.

"Paule!"

"Yes, darling?"

"It is magnificent. My God, what did you do to it? How did you do it?"

She shrugged lightly and looked at him helplessly. "I don't understand," she said. "I used Gretel's recipe—I only did what Gretel told me."

He began to eat rapidly. "This is the greatest *Gefuellte Kalbsbrust* I have ever tasted." She filled his plate again, and again. When he finally pushed himself away from the table he was dazed.

She put more beer in front of him. This must be like the end of life, she thought. When he was gone there would be left only a high, blank stone wall. She pushed herself to tell him what she was about to do with both of their lives, because she hoped that he might refuse to leave her for a reason so frivolous as whether he would win another pip on his shoulder in his army. She stared at him trying to erase any sign of sadness from her eyes.

"Veelee?"

"Anything, my beloved." No one who had ever lived, she thought, could smile like Veelee.

"Would you mind if Paul-Alain and I moved to Wusterwitz with Gretel for a while?"

He blinked. He did not answer. She felt her throat tighten. She gripped her hands together tightly, under the table. Perhaps he would refuse to let her go. If he refused they would mean more to him than the army. If he rejected his army, perhaps, in a shorter time than she had ever dared to dream, she could persuade him to leave the army. They might get away. They might be together forever and get away. She made herself speak again. "Hansel is going to Rome and Gretel will be in Wusterwitz alone, and I thought Wusterwitz would be good for the baby and less tense for me."

He looked at her gravely. His right hand slapped the table lightly. "Of course! Why, you won't even know that Berlin is a part of Germany when you are in Wusterwitz. They are our people. There are village Nazis, of course, but they are *our* Nazis. Let them wear their uniforms and have parades, but you are the wife of Colonel von Rhode."

She had heard her life stop. In the course of one afternoon Veelee was being subtracted from her life. "What will you do?" she asked him.

"The same old thing. I'll soldier. They always have ten jobs ready. But, you'll love it at Wusterwitz. It's really beautiful." He shivered. "How exciting those two old houses are to me."

"Perhaps you should go to Wusterwitz and I should go to Wuensdorf." She giggled.

"No more Wuensdorf. I feel it in my experienced old army bones."

"No?"

"I think I might put in for a new assignment when I see Guderian tomorrow. It's been a long time, in a way."

"Where?"

"They'll tell me. So Hansel has been posted to Rome. They swear by old Hansel. He's a clever one, that old Hansel."

Paule nodded and managed a smile. "Yes," she said. "Hansel is a very clever one."

Within eleven days Veelee was reassigned to special duty in Spain. He was assigned to work under the code name of Rabs, as Admiral Canaris's personal representative to General Franco's headquarters. Minister of War Blomberg's representative, Colonel Warlimont, as part of the military mind imitating children at their games, had been in Franco's favor since September, 1936; and Admiral Canaris's representative, who had been with General Franco since Morocco, had recently had the bad fortune to die. The Admiral was most anxious to place another man of skill and background in Spain, a man who could command influence at headquarters by supplying information on the local situation superior to Warlimont's, so that when the Fuehrer asked his questions the Canaris answers, not the Blomberg answers, would be the best answers.

The Admiral's selection of Colonel von Rhode was a calculated risk based upon the Colonel's already proven superiority to Warlimont on the tactics of a war of movement and on the coordination of combined supporting operations. Franco was attacking; therefore Colonel von Rhode would shine in his eyes.

Admiral Canaris was intensely irritated with Faupel, the German ambassador to Franco's headquarters, who was becoming more and more open in his support of General Franco's opponent in the Falange, Manuel Hedilla Larrey. This gaucherie the Admiral called a "typical manifestation" of the Dienststelle Ribbentrop, the surrogate Foreign Office which operated solely on funds from the Adolf Hitler Spende, in direct competition with the legal German Foreign Office.

Colonel von Rhode need not fear inactivity in Spain, Admiral Canaris explained. General Sperrle, commander of the Condor Legion, loathed Ambassador Faupel so much that he refused to receive him, and at the moment things were rather ticklish because General Franco had requested that Faupel be replaced. "Only a man as stupidly wooden as Ribbentrop would have found a man as woodenly stupid as Faupel," the Admiral told Veelee. Von Rhode's primary assignment was to see that Faupel was recalled as soon as possible; then, for reasons the Admiral did not specify, to see that Sperrle was returned to Berlin for reassignment. Veelee said blandly that he was no hand at intrigue; in fact, he had no resources to accommodate intrigue whatsoever. The Admiral replied coldly that all he was expected to do was to supply full information from General Franco's headquarters and that, as always in history, the conspirators would provide their own intrigues.

Veelee babbled along as Paule got him packed, with the baby seated in a high chair to preside over the meeting so that Veelee could punctuate his report with kisses on the baby's cheeks and neck. "It's a wonderful chance, you know, really it is," he said happily. "Thoma's tanks are in the thick of it, and they are coming up against Russian armor regularly now, ever since Guadalajara. Very heavy stuff. Really interesting."

"You just stay sitting in a tent somewhere, I suppose," Paule replied.

"This morning I persuaded Guderian to pass the word to Thoma to take nine of my tank studies into actual combat. Tremendous opportunity. After this, even stone-headed artillerymen like Brauchitsch and Keitel will have to accept tanks and reappraise the whole order of battle."

"I suppose a lot of Spaniards will have to get killed to prove the effectiveness of the nine studies?"

He looked at her blankly. "Russians, also. That's part of the profession. They can kill us, too, you know. Russian armor is much heavier than ours, love, thanks to that God-damn artilleryman Brauchitsch." He helped her close the last bag, then picked up the baby. "Your old father will be a general soon, Paul-Alain, and then we'll go off to Italy like Uncle Hansel and let the workingmen fight the wars." He tossed the baby toward the ceiling and the child gurgled happily. "I hate to hurt your feelings, darling," he said, "but Paul-Alain is the most German-looking baby I ever saw."

Then, before she knew it, he was gone. He kissed her lingeringly, murmured words about writing and about always loving each other—and then he was gone, out of her life. She never saw him again as she saw him standing at the top of the stairs, grinning and waving, his left arm held high. She never saw him like that again.

Fourteen

✠

"THEY STILL TALK ABOUT my grandfather's wedding here," Gretel said, as they drove along the poplar-lined drive through broad meadows toward the two huge houses suspended in time on the side of a hill. "It began with a squadron of mounted postillions sounding the wedding march on hunting horns. Then came the hussars on matched silver horses—I don't think they were matched at all, but that's what happens when stories are retold. We do have signed books showing that ambassadors and special envoys from all the royal houses were here. I suppose the Kaiser came —he usually found a reason to be at our parties, but it's hardly likely that anyone would have the brass to ask him to sign a book."

Paule was so filled with her new surroundings at Wusterwitz and seeing them through Paul-Alain's eyes that she settled peacefully into her new life. Veelee wrote passionate love letters, when he could get them out of Spain by fellow officers who would mail them from Germany. Within a few weeks she had letters postmarked Zwickau, Aurich, Bad Reichenhall and Nagold—which destroyed her conception that all officers came from East Prussia. "The smartest ones come from East Prussia," Gretel said loyally. "They've been at it the longest. The stupidest come from Hannover. Have you ever known any French officers?"

"No, but once Papa played Maréchal Ney, so I know the dress uniforms."

"I adore French officers. I had an affair with a perfect brigadier when we were posted in Paris in 1919—during the business of the Treaty."

"Gretel!"

"Well, I've never known such a perfect lover. He made seduction so easy. I mean, what was the sense of coming to Paris at all if . . . Well, anyway, Hansel was up to his ears with von Seeckt's worries over the Treaty, and our whole staff was in such a flap that—"

"Who was he?"

"He was—" Gretel's jaw dropped. "His name was—" Her face turned bright red. "My God, Paule!"

"Gretel, darling, what is the matter?"

"He said—I mean, he made no effort to hide it, and he was in uniform whenever I came to his flat—he said he was Brigadier Paul Bernheim."

"Papa!"

"Do you have a picture of your father?"

"Oh, yes! Oh, I am sure it was Papa. It must have been Papa!" She unsnapped the locket on the gold chain around her neck which held a picture of Bernheim and one of Veelee and handed it to Gretel. Her sister-in-law had only to glance at it. "It is him! Oh, Paule, he was the only man I have ever known beyond Hansel."

"Goodness, he must have been dashing as a brigadier."

"It had never occurred to me to connect you with him, because you had said that no one in your family was ever in the army."

"Papa frequently did that sort of thing," Paule said. "It was to inspire confidence. If you had been a banker's wife he would have posed as a banker. Why, a great love of his was a scientist, quite famous really, who dealt in the most abstruse sort of work. Papa pored over monographs and pamphlets on her subject, as though he were learning a starring role, and then led her into bed—like that!" She snapped her fingers proudly.

"But—how did you know all this?"

113

"His wives would tell me. They were often lonely, but it was impossible not to feel proud of Papa if you were in the family. And they would tell me stories of his courtship of them, and they would repeat the current gossip about him—which of course always came to them first."

Gretel's cheeks were still pink. "I feel like a girl again just talking about him," she said.

Paule nodded with pride. "The flat, I am sure, was on the Avenue Gabriel?"

"Yes, but he took me to a small hotel in Versailles first." She sighed. "We tangoed for hours late at night—though heaven knows we did not rest much in between."

Paule laughed delightedly and felt young again.

Berlin seemed to be a galaxy away. The months passed from the multicolored northern autumn to the stark black and white of winter. Paul-Alain grew taller and blond and sturdy; he was so much like his father that it astounded both Paule and Gretel. They walked a great deal. Gretel spoke the local dialect flawlessly, but to Paule it sounded like a Mandarin singing in Gaelic. They drank endless cups of coffee. When they went calling they were always invited to have coffee. The ritual was to refuse so that they could be asked again. When the offer was made a third time it had to be accepted, and the cup would be filled again and again until the drinker turned it upside down. Then the process began once more until the cup was turned over a second time and a spoon placed on top of it.

She spent as much time with Paul-Alain as he would allow. He had begun to discover that older boys were allowed to risk their necks jumping from the tops of barns or sliding down the branches of spruce trees higher than houses, so he had to be watched. He played with a huge set of toy soldiers which they had found in his great-grandfather's study and with which the Battle of Waterloo, in which four of his ancestors had participated, could be restaged in detail. Great-grandfather's room was Paul-Alain's favorite place when the weather went wrong. It was a museum of battle flags, swords, rifles, dirks, sabers, cannon balls and bullets. On the shelves were journal upon journal, written in a clear, minute hand, which described war as the greatest game of all.

Listening to the old soldiers in the region was a concomitant pleasure. Had Paul-Alain been six or seven instead of four, he might have attached himself to one of the old ruins who

114

strode about remembering battles and commands, the details of which had been blurred by hundreds of other accounts heard in so many barracks and bars. Wusterwitz was a vast outdoor old soldiers' home, and a vaster young soldier's pasture.

To counteract the influence of the military atmosphere, each Friday night Paule would pass on to her son the lore her father had so carefully told her about the honor and valor of the Jews.

"One thousand years ago there was a great scholar in France called Rashi, whose full name was Rabbi Schlomo Itzhaki. He was born in Troyes, which is not far from Paris, in 1040. He studied in Germany, just as you will study in Germany, then returned to Troyes, where he founded a school of his own. There were ten thousand Gentiles and only one hundred Jews in Troyes, and Rashi's school was attended by Jewish scholars from all over the world. No gulf of hostility separated Jews and Christians in the Middle Ages; Rashi sang the hymns of the Church, he taught the local priests Hebrew melodies, and he translated French lullabies into Hebrew. He told the story of the passages of the Talmud in the language of Troyes of his day with warmth and scholarship; his style had such wit and elegance that it seemed as though the original Hebrew was French. Rashi's children became teachers and his grandchildren became teachers, and when he finished his work it was sung by all the rabbis that the Talmud had at last been completed."

Hansel's aide-de-camp telephoned from the Bendlerstrasse early one afternoon in February and explained carefully that Hansel would arrive at Wusterwitz the following morning. Gretel tried to learn more, though her experience told her this would be impossible. She had thought Hansel was still in Italy, and she sensed trouble because he had not telephoned himself.

Hansel arrived just after lunch on the afternoon of February 4th. Haggard, he tumbled out of the staff car, embraced Gretel and Paule gratefully, and let them lead him into the house so they could close the doors and hear what had happened.

He took off his huge coat, poured himself a stiff whiskey, and stood with his back to the fire. The women did not prompt him; they could feel the trouble like electricity in the air.

"Has the news gotten here yet?"

"Dear Hansel, what news?"

"Hitler has brought down not only his very own von Blomberg but the army's own von Fritsch as well."

"Hansel!"

"And hardly a man—except for Beck, Stuelpnagel, Adam, myself, and a few others—has even so much as protested."

"But *why?*"

Hansel snorted. "Keitel is the new Chief of Staff of something called the Oberkommando der Wehrmacht. Keitel!"

Gretel's face showed her disgust. "You must tell us the whole story, Hansel dear. This is a catastrophe."

"Horrible story." He knocked the whiskey back. "You see, Blomberg and a woman named Erna Gruhn were married last month. It was very quiet, but Hitler and Goering were witnesses. It was hardly reported in the press, von Stuelpnagel tells me. She is far below Blomberg's class, but how far—well, no one dared to guess."

"A scandal?"

"My God, what a scandal. Count Helldorf, the Police President of Berlin, was embarrassed to find certain dossiers of the Frau Feldmarschall's past life. Helldorf is inclined to be a Nazi, no doubt about that, but he was an officer of hussars first, and he still retains a certain devotion to the military tradition. He knew that if Himmler got the dossier he would never stop blackmailing the army. According to regulations, the dossier should have gone to Himmler, but instead Helldorf took it to Blomberg's closest associate—to Blomberg's own relative, Keitel. And can you guess what Keitel did with these dreadfully incriminating papers?"

"He burned them?" Gretel asked tentatively.

"He passed them on to Hermann Goering!" Hansel shouted, his face grown scarlet.

"My God!"

"What is going to happen?" Paule asked. "Keitel hates Veelee."

"It has already happened," Hansel said. "Stuelpnagel called me in Italy and said that playful telephone calls were coming into the Bendlerstrasse from the whores in every restaurant and café up and down the Wilhelmstrasse, and that Goering had seen Hitler. Of course I came directly to Berlin."

"Frau Feldmarschall von Blomberg had been . . . a whore?" Gretel asked with mounting horror.

"Oh, quite active, quite successful. And Hitler, that hypocrite who blandly pretends not to see the mountain of pederasts in the SA, became morally outraged. Blomberg must go, he cried. Everyone knew that Blomberg's only possible successor would be von Fritsch, our Commander in Chief and a representative of the old army—so Himmler at once produced evidence for his Fuehrer that Fritsch was a raving homosexual."

"Fritsch?" Gretel cried. "Preposterous!"

Over a day later Paule realized that perhaps her father had not been Gretel's lone stray moment.

"Of course preposterous," Hansel said, "why, many's the time he and I—but that's neither here nor there. Anyway, they dredged up some male prostitute who lurks in public toilets for the Gestapo. He identified Fritsch as his client and Hitler—the filthy little blackmailer—demanded Fritsch's resignation in return for silence, but of course Fritsch would not resign. He demanded a court-martial, but Hitler would have none of that and our Commander in Chief was sent off on indefinite leave."

Paule watched the outrage of her friends with pity. Here was the end of their fantasy about controlling that pushy little politician. She sensed that Gretel realized what had happened to all of them, but it was obvious that Hansel had not the slightest inkling of the disaster. To him, it seemed to be a shocking matter which might happen once in a century in a gentlemen's club.

"And then what, Hansel?" his wife asked sharply.

"Gretel, I tell you it was like the day five years ago when von Schleicher came back to the Bendlerstrasse after Hitler had discharged him. We all were outraged, of course. The same men even spoke the same pieces. Beck took charge and said we must act at once to sweep this pigsty clean and restore the honor of the army. The very next day was the anniversary of the Kaiser's birthday, but everyone argued that we must not risk civil war, that aside from this rotten little affair of Blomberg and Fritsch, the Austrian corporal still danced to our tune. One of the more shocking things was that Fritsch— I mean, we have all regarded Fritsch as such a strong man, haven't we?—Fritsch fell to pieces. I mean to say, Beck doesn't have the stature; only Fritsch could have rallied all of us.

But even while Beck was pleading with us, even while I myself was moved to stand beside first Beck, then von Stuelpnagel, and finally Adam—even then Fritsch had his pen in his hand and was writing out his resignation from the army."

"Oh, Hansel! What a tragedy!"

The general shrugged. "I was shocked. Then von Brauchitsch said that all of us—including Fritsch—had better remember the oath of loyalty we had taken to the Fuehrer. From Reichenau I would have expected such a thing, but from Brauchitsch?"

"What are you going to do?"

"At least that is clear, my dear. The army has been dishonored, and if it will not defend itself against that little guttersnipe then he deserves to dominate them."

"Them?" Gretel cried. *"Them?"*

"I have resigned from the German Army."

"Hansel. Oh, darling Hans, you are wonderful!" She rushed to him and hugged him.

"This is too big a thing for suicide," he said, his chin thrust over Gretel's shoulder. "I told Fritsch that. I am proud of my country and I am proud of its army, but if every officer —at least every officer of field rank—does not resign before the announcement of these wretched changes, then I will feel shame for the army and dread for my country."

Gretel was an army wife. "We must start with opposition," she said excitedly, "then we can build resistance until we are strong enough for conspiracy."

Paule watched these pathetic children at their games. "Has Veelee resigned?" she asked finally. Her arms trembled and she had to cross them tightly in front of her. This was not part of a game; she had heard Hitler and she believed him. He wanted to kill her and her son.

"I don't know if the news has reached Spain yet," Hansel said slowly.

"Of course it has," Gretel said, without thinking. "They must have known as fast as you in Italy."

"Do you think Veelee has resigned?" Paule asked tensely.

"Well, he's rather out of the combat area, so to speak," Hansel said. "He's doing quite delicate work of a diplomatic and intelligence nature, as it were."

"What has that got to do with his honor?" Paule asked. "If he and all other officers resign, there will be no Hitler. When there is no Hitler, a sane government can run the country and the officers can return to their posts. Even if he was sent to South Africa or the Antarctic, he is still an army officer. If Hansel has resigned, then Veelee must resign."

"But it is a matter of personal choice, isn't it, dear?" Gretel said. "I mean, they can't all be expected to resign. You heard what Brauchitsch said about the oath."

"What oath? Hitler is a criminal. Would Brauchitsch or Veelee honor their oath to a criminal?"

"For some it is more complicated," Hansel said hastily. "What Brauchitsch said after Hitler made him Army Chief of Staff—"

"Brauchitsch?" Gretel exploded. "My God, how much is there left which you haven't told us yet?"

"Brauchitsch said, 'Why should I take action against Hitler? The people elected him, and the workers and all other Germans are perfectly satisfied with his successful policy.' "

Paule said, "Velee must resign." Her voice broke. "He must. This our last chance. Our last chance." She walked out of the room.

"Don't you believe it, darling," Hansel called after her. "Hitler's good luck can't last forever. We'll get him eventually. Rome wasn't destroyed in one day."

Paule waited for a letter from Veelee through eight days of discussion and debate in his great-grandfather's houses. Hansel, who kept in close touch with the Bendlerstrasse, was dismayed at first that his resignation did not seem to have had the tiniest effect. Brauchitsch agreed with Hitler to relieve sixteen high-ranking generals of their commands. Forty-four others were transferred to different duties. Hitler named himself War Minister and Supreme Commander of the Armed Forces. Keitel became Hitler's *Lakaitl,* and the iron-brained Ribbentrop became Foreign Minister. "There are only three groups left now," Gretel said. "Nazis, non-Nazis, and anti-Nazis."

"What is Veelee?" Paule asked.

"Veelee is a tank commander," Hansel told her, "so he is non-Nazi."

"Why?"

"Well, he certainly isn't Nazi. And since Hitler has shown that he values tanks very highly, how could Veelee be anti-Nazi?"

When the letter from Veelee finally arrived, delayed because of the difficulty of getting it out of Spain, Paule went to her room and saw no one except Paul-Alain and Clotilde for two days. When Gretel pleaded to know what was happening, Clotilde could only say sadly, "She doesn't talk at all, Madame. She just keeps writing, then tearing it up, then writing again."

"What is she writing?"

"I think it is a letter to her husband."

Dearest Willi:

I have your letter which tells of your "surprise" at the changes made in the army, of Blomberg's effrontery in marrying a prostitute, and of Hitler's charges against General von Fritsch. You express the usual professional anxieties over Keitel's ascension and you remember Brauchitsch with reserved regard and you write as though this were the sort of intrigue one must expect in a boys' school.

What about your army? What has become of that army which was using the upstart Hitler, which was there to protect your wife and son? Who will protect us from your government now? In all of your large country must we remain in Wusterwitz because it is the only place you can feel that we are safe from your leader?

What about the honor of your army which has been sent to kneel at his feet at the snap of his fingers? Your honor has empty eye sockets, is deaf, and is bred without a sense of smell or taste—it can touch filth and not withdraw in horror. How will your beloved country be saved from the pit of horror which your leader and your army has dug for it? Can you say that——

Paule destroyed this letter too, then solved her quandary by writing to him only we-are-all-fine-and-Paul-Alain-is-such-a-big-boy letters, which she posted to him once a month. She became so silent that her presence among others was oppressive.

In April, when Brauchitsch advised Hansel that his resignation could not be accepted and that he was "suspended" until recall—which would be soon—Hansel wept in his happiness and Gretel beamed like a lighthouse.

Fifteen

✠

HITLER HAD OCCUPIED AUSTRIA in March and was in a for-
giving, expansive mood. The army was very grateful, and
Paule was doomed to listen to army gossip all through the
spring and summer until she could bear it no longer. When
Fritsch, the former Commander in Chief of the German
Army, actually accepted reinstatement by the Fuehrer's
gracious sufferance and, after having had shame and disgrace
lavished on him, humbly accepted a post as Colonel in Chief
of the Twelfth Regiment of Artillery, Paule could tolerate
army prattle no longer. She told Gretel she must return to
Berlin because she had to begin to think about a school
for Paul-Alain and thanked her with all her heart for her
loving kindness. The two women wept together. Paule pointed
out that, after all, Gisele and Philip were back in Berlin and
that by now she was quite German enough to be able to take
care of herself, so Hansel and Gretel bid her Godspeed and
she returned to the flat in Charlottenburg.

Paule wanted to demand that Veelee make a choice between his wife and son, and his passive non-Nazism, but she
could not for the same reason that she had prayed night after
night when her father was about to leave a wife. She was
inside a family, her own family, and if she resisted too strongly
she might find herself alone. She could not find the strength
to overcome that fear.

The horror began again on the morning of the second day
of her return to the city. The bell rang and the loathesome
block warden was slouching against the frame of the door
when she opened it. He brushed past her into the large sunny
parlor and sat down. "Are you pregnant, Frau von Rhode?"
he asked. He spoke in a Saxon dialect whose intonations, even
in normal conversation, were those of a highly insulted person
complaining strenuously. In the uniform of his office the block

warden had the right to enter any flat at any time and to ask whatever questions he felt necessary.

"No, Herr Waegel."

"The Fuehrer looks for more good Germans, Frau von Rhode. But your husband has not been home for some time, hey? It is better not being pregnant, hey?"

"Yes, Herr Waegel."

"Are you a subscriber to *Der Stuermer?*"

"No, Herr Waegel."

"Then how can we be sure that you know that Jews are our burden and scourge, Frau von Rhode?"

"Our Fuehrer tells us that, Herr Waegel."

"You are a Jew, are you not, Frau von Rhode?"

"Yes, Herr Waegel."

"This is a nice flat. A big flat for one woman and a baby and two servants. You have a wireless set. How much did you give to Winter Relief, Frau von Rhode?"

"My husband, Colonel Wilhelm von Rhode, Herr auf Klein-Kusserow und Wusterwitz, makes the contributions to Winter Relief for us, Herr Waegel."

"I am sure he is generous. He is a German soldier. He understands honor. He knows his duty."

"He understands, Herr Waegel. He knows."

"Still, one must not create a bad impression, Frau Colonel von Rhode." He got up and shuffled to the door. "Heil Hitler."

That one must not create a bad impression underscored everything everyone did in Berlin, Paule thought. The Fuehrer had issued a special decree proclaiming that no one could be forced to subscribe to the Party newspaper. But it made a bad impression if one did not. There was no law that one must do thus and so, but almost anything might happen if one did not.

"I said Heil Hitler, Frau von Rhode." The block warden was still waiting in the open doorway.

"Heil Hitler, Herr Waegel," Paule replied with spirit.

The flat faced the back of the SS Fuehrerschule, the advanced training college for SS officers at #1 Schlossstrasse. Paule was aware of the diffident and very correct young SS men when she walked with Paul-Alain in the Schlossgarten. But she was even more conscious of the almost continual presence

122

of a particular SS Obersturmbannfuehrer. Whenever she walked in the park he would come striding along and greet her heartily. Once he lifted Paul-Alain for a drink at the water fountain, and he tipped his cap pleasantly to Paule before walking away.

One morning as she sat in the mid-October sun and the cold air, watching Paul-Alain as he played with other children at the swings, the SS Obersturmbannfuehrer appeared from out of nowhere and asked permission to sit beside her. She did not answer, but moved over on the bench to make plenty of room.

"We pass each other so often," the SS Obersturmbannfuehrer said pleasantly, "that I feel we are neighbors." Paule did not answer. "I am SS Obersturmbannfuehrer Eberhard Drayst," he said.

"How do you do?" Paule said without looking up.

"And you are Frau von Rhode?" he said.

"I am Frau Colonel Wilhelm von Rhode."

"I know. I have become so interested in seeing you in this park that I took the liberty of calling for your dossier."

"How delicately you put it."

He chuckled. "I learn that your husband is in Spain, that your father was the great French actor Paul-Alain Bernheim, that one of your brothers-in-law rejected the Fuehrer at the time of the disgraceful Blomberg-Fritsch incident, and that another brother-in-law is a factor in our Foreign Office. You are a Jew." He paused. She turned slowly to look at him and he smiled brilliantly, his eyes crinkling. "You have a most interesting dossier. Most of them are quite dull, you know."

"Perhaps it is better to be dull?"

"It is best to be a beautiful Jew like you, Frau Colonel von Rhode."

She stood up instantly and called Paul-Alain. When he looked up wonderingly she called him more sharply, and he trotted to her side and they left the park at once. She almost ran to assuage the fear rising within her, thinking vaguely that she could not come back to the Schlossgarten again, yet knowing that no matter where she went he would move in his dainty and deliberate way to find her. When they reached the flat she removed from the bureau Veelee's service pistol which he had taught her how to fire. She loaded the magazine, then placed the gun in the small, shallow drawer of the table beside the front door. That afternoon she ordered chain locks for

the front and back doors, and she would not hear the lock-
smith's protests that he could not possibly come to install
them until the next day. She went to his shop and said she
would wait there until closing time if necessary, but that the
locks had to be on her doors before evening. Grumbling, the
man went with her, and the locks were installed.

Paule and Clotilde went over the food supply, made a list
to augment it and the provisions were in the apartment before
noon the next day. Explaining to Clotilde that times were
much too tense for either of them to go out in the evenings
without escort, she drilled the maid over and over again to
be sure that the chain locks were fastened if she were in the
apartment alone. If for any peculiar reason Paule were called
away, Clotilde must not, under any circumstances, unchain
the doors unless she heard Paule's voice—and *only* Paule's
voice—ask her to open up.

Paule heard no more from SS Obersturmbannfuehrer
Drayst, nor did she see him again on the street, but she did
not relax her guard.

Sixteen

✠

ON NOVEMBER 7TH, at about eleven P.M., word came that
Gisele had been stricken with appendicitis. A call had gone
out for blood donors; Miles-Meltzer was the wrong type,
but Paule's blood matched Gisele's.

She reached the hospital at eleven-forty P.M., and she and
Philip sat in a waiting room waiting for her to be summoned
for the transfusion. Philip was deeply frightened. He had not
shaved since early morning, and the dark bristles on his
cheeks, over the dazzling finery and under the specially
shaped silver spectacles, made him seem almost shabby. He
did not speak for a long time but merely sat with his hands
clenched in front of him, his forearms dangling between his
legs as though concealing the attitude of prayer. All at once
Paule heard his controlled, attentively educated voice. He

spoke in English, something he had never done before with her.

"One of our junior counselors at our Paris Embassy was murdered today. I am quite sure it is going to make trouble. It would be best if you stayed close to home next week, Paule."

"Why, Philip?"

"The killer was a Jew. A boy, seventeen years old. He was crazed, we think, by what had happened to his parents. Dreadful affair all around. Poland issued a new law which took its citizenship away from Poles who had been resident abroad for a long time. Straight away our government packed all Polish Jews into trains and sent them off to the Polish frontier, because they were stateless." He sighed. "We kept their possessions except the clothes they wore. They were warned not to take food, and they were thrown out of the trains at the frontier, then driven through the swamps into Poland. Sleepy children, men of eighty, pregnant women— five or six thousand people. The Poles would not let them in —because of the new law, you see. They are still out there in that swamp in this terrible winter. Many have died in the last twelve days. The boy's parents—the killer's parents— are out there."

"Oh, Philip, what a world this has become."

"Yes. And I have been sitting here since they told me Gisele might have peritonitis and I have been explaining with great care to myself that such a thing as Gisele being stricken has no connection with the acts of the government I serve."

Paule kissed his hand. "It would be rank superstition to think any other way," she said.

At that moment a nurse appeared and asked Paule to go with her. She went into the operating room and lay down beside the unconscious Gisele at one-five A.M. The transfusion was done quickly and in half an hour she was back in the waiting room with Philip. In a few minutes the doctor came out and said that Gisele would be fine, and after Philip had wept in Paule's arms she said that she was worried about Paul-Alain and must go.

"Be careful, Paule, please."

"I am always careful now."

"Not that they will do anything tonight. They never move that fast, because they pause for the propaganda effect."

"I will be barricaded in the flat if trouble starts."

Philip walked with her to the lift, thanking her again and again and pleading with her to let him take her home—he could take the same taxi directly back to the hospital. But she wouldn't hear of it; they would be bringing Gisele to her room soon and he must be there if she needed him. Philip gave her address to the driver, then warned her again to stay indoors until he called her. "The *Schwarze Korps,* the SS newspaper, said a very odd thing last week," he said. "They said that the Jews in Germany would be hostages against attacks by world Jewry. This could be a start for such a policy."

Paule kissed him good night, got into the cab; and started for the Friedrich Karl Platz.

Seventeen

✠

WHILE PAULE WAS AT THE HOSPITAL, Dr. Goebbels was telling a group of party leaders that riots had been started successfully in the Kurhessen and Magdeburg-Anhalt districts to protest the assassination in the Paris Embassy by international Jewry that afternoon. He explained carefully that upon his suggestion the Fuehrer had decided that in the event the riots spread spontaneously throughout the Reich, they were not to be discouraged. Dr. Goebbels then dismissed the party leaders so that they could get the spontaneous riots organized as quickly as possible.

SA formations were used to burn down every synagogue in the Reich; to loot, destroy, arrest, torture, and murder all Jews encountered. Dr. Goebbels notified neither Himmler nor Goering of his plan. However, at eleven-fourteen P.M., SS Obersturmbannfuehrer Eberhard Drayst, who had just completed a disturbing interrogation of two Jewish women at police headquarters in the Koenigsallee, and who had gone to the offices of *Der Angriff,* Dr. Goebbels' newspaper, to file his information for propaganda use, learned the news of Dr. Goebbels' actions and immediately telephoned the news to his superior. SS Gruppenfuehrer Wolff located the Reichsfuehrer SS at twelve-three A.M., and Himmler arrived at Prince Albrechtstrasse at one-four A.M., ordered his full force into the streets, dressed as civilians, "to prevent large-scale looting," and then dictated the following memorandum:

The order for this pogrom was given by the Propaganda Directorate and I suspect that Goebbels, in his craving for power—which I had noticed long ago—and also in his empty-headedness, started this action at just the time when foreign political situations are very grave. I have talked to the Fuehrer from my residence about these decisions and I have the distinct impression that he knew nothing about these events.

Next the Reichsfuehrer SS dictated a personal commendation to be placed in the service folder of SS Obersturmbannfuehrer Drayst, for his alertness in interpreting the significance of his information.

But Himmler filed a milder reaction to Goebbel's strike than other government officials. The rioting, which was as spontaneous as jewelry by Fabergé, began precisely at two-five A.M. throughout Germany. When Economic Minister Funk learned what was happening at two twenty-nine A.M., he telephoned Dr. Goebbels and said, "Are you crazy, Goebbels? One has to be ashamed to be a German. We are losing our whole prestige abroad. Day and night I am trying to conserve our national wealth and you throw it out the window. If this whole business does not stop immediately you can have the whole filthy mess."

The Reichsmarschall was on a train when the demonstration began. He got the news at the Berlin railroad station, promptly went into a tantrum, and drove directly to the Fuehrer. Goebbels was irresponsible, he said; the effect of such a pogrom among influential people would be disastrous.

While blood was choking the gutters of German cities, Goebbels was summoned to Hitler's residence. After screaming at the Reichsmarschall to stay out of such matters, Goebbels improvised brilliantly by explaining that the Luftwaffe needed planes, that planes took money, and that therefore he had organized the demonstrations because the Jews would be willing to pay a large fine after this night's work.

The Fuehrer agreed, and a fine of one billion reichsmarks was imposed on the German Jewish community.

The taxi pulled away from the Kreuzberg district, the Hill of the Cross, that Calvary which surrounded Gestapo headquarters so grotesquely, and moved down the Buelowstrasse and along the Kliestrasse toward the Kurfürstendamm. Paule thought she could hear screaming and the shattering of glass. People were running. The taxi stopped and the driver got out to try to find out what was happening. As Paule leaned out of the window to hear he grabbed a young man by the arm. "They are killing Jews!" the man gasped. "The SA are breaking everything, and the SS are killing everybody. They are going crazy. Let go! Let go!"

Paule heard the yelling above them and she and the two men looked up. Two men were pushing a struggling man out of a fifth-floor window. "Out, Jew! Out!" they were shouting, but their faces had the calm, determined expression of youths wrestling for a gold medal. The man came down, sliding through the air on a terrible scream. The driver and the young man scattered, and the body fell with a huge sound on the pavement and lay still, leaking rapidly. Only one of the men above stayed to watch it hit.

When Paule uncovered her eyes, the taxi driver had vanished. The taxi engine purred on with mechanical unconcern. As she screamed, a platoon of men on the run rounded the corner sixty feet ahead of her. Every ten feet or so they stopped and fired bursts from their guns into store windows. Tumbling out of the cab, Paule fell on her hands and knees, ripping her dress and tearing holes in her knees and stockings. Frantically, she climbed into the driver's seat of the taxi, not bothering to close the door, and moved the car forward. It was the first time she had driven a car in six years, and it lurched, it struck a running man and bowled him over. While his companions shouted at her, while two of them shot at her, the car fled wildly into the Buelowstrasse.

All around her the smashing and ruining was underway. Men were ripping books in half and slashing paintings in front of a bookstore. The contents of every kind of shop seemed to have been thrown out into the streets by one set of maniacs while another set hacked at them with axe and sledge hammer. She swung the car wildly down another street. No one paid any attention to her; they were already in hell, already doing what they would need to do for the rest of eternity, she thought. They were sightless in their wildness, but someday the axes and hammers must fall upon themselves.

A synagogue was in flames in the Grunewaldstrasse. She crossed the intersection at full speed, unaware that she was still screaming. The taxi came to a rolling stop just past the Stadtpark in the Martin Luther Strasse; one of the bullets had hit the gas tank. The street was deserted. Just ahead of her was the Friedenau S-Bahn and she walked toward it, stumbling and hysterical. She had to get home. She had to be with Paul-Alain. What were they doing to Paul-Alain?

There were few people in sight as she bought her ticket, and they seemed unaware of the chaos so close by. She huddled in the corner of the last car and pretended to be asleep, trying to concentrate on not thinking about the SS men dragging her little boy to the window of the flat and shouting, "Out, Jew! Out!" as they threw him into the street.

Paule left the S-Bahn at the Bahnhof West End and walked as quickly as she could along the Spandauerstrasse. Then, though her knees were bleeding badly, she began to run, at first in a trot, but soon, as she turned the corner into the Friedrich Karl Platz, headlong, her breath coming out of her lungs like live steam. She unlocked the door carefully before she put on the landing lights above her. But before she could reach the switch, still gasping for breath, a hand closed over her mouth and another entered her bodice and slid down to grip her right breast. She tried to struggle, but hands wheeled her around and backed her along the short hall toward the recess under the stairs. As she was dragged past Herr Waegel's door, it opened, and a bar of light fell upon the face and uniform of her attacker. It was Obersturmbannfuehrer Drayst, that man from the Schlossgarten. Desperately she jerked her head back and managed to bite the hand over her mouth. While Drayst cursed, she screamed, "Herr Waegel! Thank God, thank God." Herr Waegel only grinned at her, nodded to Drayst, and closed his door.

She was flung backward into the recess and slammed against the wall. In an instant he was upon her, and she could feel the horror of his hand under her dress, fumbling with her clothes. His heavy shoulder pinned her to the wall and his broken voice babbled at her. "Oh, you sweet Jew, don't fight me, let me take you, how I love you say how you love me you Jew you beautiful Jew let me let me." His fingers were inside her and his other hand was fighting to open his trousers when she kicked her knee upward with all her strength. Then the other knee, and he doubled up with a scream and rolled across the floor as she leaped over him and ran down along the short hall and up the stairs.

When she looked down from the first landing, Drayst was getting to his feet. His face, a ruin stamped with enormous pain, was looking up at her, and he came up the stairs after her as she missed a step and fell, sliding downward. She got to her feet and started up the stairs again, screaming wildly. At the first landing the door of one of the apartments was opened and a large man stood in it in nightdress with a woman behind him. "Herr Gehman," Paule shouted, "help me, please help me." The man started forward in bewilderment, but halted after three steps. Staring down the staircase, he began to back away. His wife looked down at Drayst, then pulled her husband backward into the apartment, and slammed the door.

As Drayst, crablike, pulled himself up by the bannister to the top of the stairs, Paule ran up the next flight. He moved slowly after her. All doors had closed and the landing was in darkness again. She pounded on the door to the flat. There was no sound inside. When she looked over the railing he was still coming, though now he was crawling. She beat on the door with both of her fists and screamed, "Clotilde! Please! Please! Open the door!" Now Drayst was at the landing, pulling himself toward her, gripping the balustrade, his eyes empty and his mouth working spasmodically. Then the chain bolt snicked, the door opened, and she fell into the entrance hall, rolling to one side so that Clotilde could slam the door shut. "Is the baby all right?" she asked hoarsely.

"Yes, Madame."

Paule moved to the drawer of the entrance table and took out the gun. As Drayst's weight thudded against the other side of the threshold, she threw off the safety, shouted "Franz! Set to!" and fired all eight shots through the door. Then she fainted.

Eighteen

✠

MILES-MELTZER REACHED THE FLAT in thirty-five minutes. He saw the trail of blood on the stairs and the carpets of the landing, and he stared with sick apprehension at the bullet-shattered door. He pounded and shouted at the same time, "Paule! Open the door. Paule, dear. It's Philip." Finally he heard the sound of slow footsteps. She opened the door, then closed it behind him and put the chain in place.

"They called me at the hospital, and told me what was happening."

"How many Jews are dead?"

"I don't know. The Foreign Office says the SS has rounded up eighteen thousand for concentration camps."

"Now they know."

"Were you hurt?"

"We are leaving, Philip. We are leaving Germany. We are leaving Veelee. I want a diplomatic passport for Paul-Alain and Clotilde and me. Can you do it?"

"Of course."

"May we have them by eighty-thirty tomorrow morning— this morning?"

"You will have them." He looked at her with anguish. "I could get a signal to Veelee in Burgos."

"No."

"He can be here by tomorrow night."

"I will write to him and explain everything, Philip."

He took her hands and kissed them. "I am glad you are going, you know," he said. "Each time we have said this is only temporary. But this time it is the beginning of the end for us. You will leave on the Nord-Sud?"

"Yes."

"Very well. I will be here at eight-twenty with a car and the papers and a truck for your baggage." He clicked his heels and bowed.

"God bless you, Philip."

After he left Paule went to Veelee's study, sat down at his desk, found paper and a pen, and began to write.

9 November, 1938

Dear Willi:

I have stayed six years and I have tried so hard, but now Paul-Alain and I will leave Germany this morning. Philip has been very kind and is arranging for diplomatic passports so that we may escape. The pogroms are sweeping your country as I write this.

Last night, as, I watched your countrymen murdering Jews like me and your son, I realized that when I had pleaded with you to see what was happening to your country and implored you to take us away, I had been committing a selfish mistake. To remain with you, I was setting us apart from other Jews. You are a part of the monster—you are as much a part of it as Streicher. You are a different claw, but you are the German Army and the deaths and horrors it has condoned. I know that this will make it clear that our marriage is over. I never want to see you again. I will leave your grandmother's pearls with Philip and I will join her memory in your family.

I tried so hard, Willi, but now I am ashamed that I was too cowardly to leave you before this barbaric night as I am ashamed to be your wife.

Goodbye.

Paule

As she sealed the envelope her eyes were hard and dry.

BOOK TWO

1940 = 1944

One

✠

THE FIRST TWO TRUCKLOADS of German troops entered the
Porte de la Villette at five thirty-five A.M. on June 14, 1940.
German footsoldiers moved along the rue de Flandre in the
direction of the Gare du Nord and the Gare de l'Est, with the
Arc de Triomphe and the Eiffel Tower as their objectives.
French newspapers had told their readers that the German
Army was dressed in paper uniforms and carried dummy
rifles; now Parisians stepped forward to finger the woolen
uniforms and admire the cameras which every German
seemed to carry.

The Occupation divided itself into two parts: the Kriegs-
verwaltungchef and the Oberkriegsverwaltungsrat under the
Militaerbefehlshaber in Frankreich. These agencies controlled
all military and administrative powers in France, and they
supervised all branches of the French economy from two
separate headquarters: the Military, based at the Hôtel
Majestic on Avenue Kléber, and the Administrative, based
at the Palais Bourbon.

The Military policed the demarcation line between the occupied and unoccupied zones. It was responsible for the upkeep of roads, railroads, bridges, and other engineering requirements. It also was in charge of propaganda, and
throughout the occupation the army was successful in barring Dr. Goebbels' Ministry of Propaganda from France.
The aim of the German Army was to see that the administration of occupied France was carried out by the French
authorities themselves, under German orders. No interference was visible in French domestic politics. No conqueror

still engaged in widespread warfare could free manpower for such work.

The Administrative branch had one division for its offices' administration, another for collaboration with French police, the control of municipal finances and railways, and the supervision of schoolteaching, libraries, records, and museums. It had a Public Economy Division which Aryanized and regulated all industrial and commercial enterprises and controlled all prices, credit, labor, public utilities, and insurance, and supervised all banks.

The City of Paris and its environs were governed by a military commander for Gross-Paris who was directly responsible to the Military Governor.

An Oberkriegsverwaltungsrat attached to City Hall was put in charge of the Paris budget, municipal taxes, public assistances, and pawnshops, the city's public utilities, the Métro, and all markets.

The rate of exchange was fixed at one French franc to each five reichsmarks, and a law was passed that German money must be accepted throughout France.

On July 15, 1940, an order was issued requiring all art treasures whose value exceeded one hundred thousand francs to be reported to the German authorities within thirty days.

The army really believed that they had managed to exclude the SS from France.

On June 14, 1940, at five fifty-nine A.M., SS Standartenfuehrer Eberhard Drayst, temporarily detatched from duty with the Security Police, arrived in Paris with a party of twenty which had been lodged in small military vehicles in the center of von Kuechler's Eighteenth Army.

As the body of the Eighteenth prepared to enter the city, Drayst's specialists hurried along the deserted rue La Fayette and across the empty Avenue de l'Opéra to settle into their pre-selected accommodations at the Hôtel du Louvre. Because they all wore regulation GFP uniforms of the Wehrmacht military police, the army was not aware that Drayst's group had accompanied the Eighteenth into France. The Fuehrer had solemnly agreed with the General Staff that the SS was to be barred from the West at the time that the SS had simultaneously occupied Austria, Czechoslovakia, and Poland with the army. The criminal conduct of the SS in

Poland had so shocked the world that the military believed that the Fuehrer had at last seen the monstrous black corps in its true light.

It was to offset this tactical disadvantage that the Reichs-fuehrer SS ordered General Heydrich to organize a task force to establish a foothold for the SS in France. Because of his distinguished record, his ability to speak French, and his charm, SS Colonel Drayst was selected to head this independent special mission.

The Drayst unit had a quiet dinner at the Hôtel du Louvre. On the morning of June 15th, still wearing his GFP uniform, SS Lieutenant Gutwillig went to the French Prefecture of Police and requisitioned all French police files indicating the whereabouts of Austrian and German émigrés, all political personalities known to be hostile to the Occupation, and all Jews.

All members of the Sonderkommando were outstanding men, and all except two were the personal choices of SS Colonel Drayst. The exceptions were the Gestapo commander, SS Captain Sperrena, a veteran police officer with eyes like brass carpet tacks, who had been chosen by General Mueller, and Captain Joachin Strasse of Section IV4b of the Gestapo, the Jewish Affairs Section, who had been assigned to France by SS Lieutenant-Colonel Eichmann. Strasse was a top Jewish expert. He had been in charge of the first deportation of Jews from Stettin in February, 1940, when he took thirteen hundred of them into the Lublin area of Poland after they had voluntarily signed a general waiver giving up everything they owned. It had been a political test to see whether the Jews would be willing to walk to their own doom under their own power; to see what the general reaction of their neighbors would be when they discovered all those Jews gone in the morning; and to see how a foreign government would respond when they were suddenly presented with so many Jewish refugees. Everything had turned out very satisfactorily. There was no need for anxiety; the population at large, throughout the world, could not have cared less.

Drayst had two good men from the Waffen SS, Schwartz and Lazar, to do what Heydrich called "the hard details." They were weapons and demolition experts whose gear included burglary tools and anti-personnel mines. They remained together at all times, as though to keep a careful watch on each other, and their conversations consisted largely of technical discussions of the merits of various guns, grenades, gas capsules, mortars, and other equipment.

SS Captain Wilhelm Gohrmann was Drayst's specialist in civilian police management, and SS Lieutenants Gutwillig and Megrau were college lads who handled the SD Ausland Section and the Economics Section respectively. They were both twenty-six years old and had been with the SD since 1935, but both had been at the university working for their degrees until early in 1940.

Each member of the task force represented some category of the complex files the Gestapo had maintained on all activities of the French police since 1935. The SS had been very thorough. For each section of files—administrative, criminal, cultural, political, religious, economic, and artistic —maintained by the French police, a corresponding section in Berlin had been created. After five years of day-and-night duty, filing and memorizing wholesale information bought from French agents, the SS men assigned to Paris knew intimately the regional psychology, the habits,. and all there was to know about the private lives, financial holdings, inner convictions, personal peculiarities, and all other facets of character of all important personalities in France.

SS Colonel Drayst had spent the first eight months of 1939 in Paris, polishing his French, studying the press, meeting and evaluating political agents and informers. Drayst had become an important figure; he had been awarded the Iron Cross second class, in peacetime, for his wounds and for his heroism against the only pocket of armed resistance during the Jewish uprising in Berlin on November 9, 1938.

On the third day of the occupation, Colonel Drayst reported, most unexpectedly, to Dr. Sowa, director of the army's military police, to offer his credentials as an SS officer and to ask that his unit be placed under full army control. He apologized most engagingly for the presence of his little SS unit by explaining earnestly that he and his little staff were there on the track of German and Austrian exiles, Communists, Jews, and Freemasons. If it should turn out that any arrests were required, he would most certainly ask for army cooperation. Dr. Sowa was so flattered by Drayst's manner that, convinced the SS had learned its lesson, he gave his grudging approval. After all, Drayst's unit had only twenty men against twenty-five hundred GFP's—and that twenty-five hundred was about to become six thousand. Dr. Sowa could not foresee that when the SS, SD, and Gestapo became fully operative in France within a very short time, the GFP would almost entirely disappear—twenty-three out of its twenty-five groups would be disbanded and the men sent to the Eastern front.

A second unit of twenty SS joined the Sonderkommando in July, and a third arrived in August. Among them they spoke eleven languages, and they included a wine seller who could talk wine for hours the way the English could discuss the weather; a divorced countess who was an expert on the French aristocracy; and one female schoolteacher from the Sudetenland who was put in charge of charwomen and all wastepaper. Her name was Fräulein Levinthal and she developed an uncanny gift for suppressing any scrap of information which might escape to the world at large.

The jurisdiction of the SS eventually stretched to twelve cities in provincial France. Though this enraged the army, they could not help but admire the way Drayst showed such enormous and detailed respect for all regulations which they imposed upon him. He did everything with correctness. There was none of the former, eastern SS brutality.

Not that Drayst did not have operational troubles. So much time was being wasted by placating the army that Colonel Drayst telephoned General Heydrich again and urgently recommended that he be provided with a "cover" officer of sufficient rank to put the SS on an equal negotiating footing with the army and other potential friction points. Within ten days Drayst was provided with the services of SS Brigadefuehrer Johannus Koltrastt, whose SS rank was the equivalent of major-general. Theoretically, Koltrastt was in charge of all SS, SD, and Gestapo operations for Northern France and Belgium, but Drayst ran the show and Koltrastt was a stooge.

Luckily, Koltrastt was used to being a stooge. He was a pink-skinned, small-boned, white-moustached, forty-seven-year-old fixer who dreaded responsibility, whose daughter was General Heydrich's mistress, and who was further related to the General through a grandson. He had been the first SS leader in Berlin eleven years before; his previous job had been at the city garbage dump, where he had been an "engineer." To welcome him to Paris—and to annoy the army—

General Heydrich personally addressed a mass meeting of French police officers.

Koltrastt's job was to wear his uniform and insignia smartly for negotiations with the army and the representatives of the Jewish Affairs Office of the Vichy Government, to act as the representative of the Chief of Police of the Sûreté Française, and to handle liaison work with Herr Abetz, the German "ambassador" to France (it was felt that the title of *Gauleiter* would not have gone down well with the French people). Koltrastt moved into a splendid building at 57 Boulevard Lannes, spent half of his time in France, half in Belgium, and three quarters of his waking hours in the bars and the *boîtes* of both.

Colonel Drayst was the Befehlshaber der Sicherheitsdienst. His offices and residence were in a palatial building at 72-84 Avenue Foch which was furnished with everything that systematic looting could provide. Altogether there were six Gestapo sections under Drayst's command. One of these was called Gestapo-France, because it was manned entirely by a French staff headed by Henri Chamberlin, a former mess orderly of the Paris Prefecture of Police, who had been interned in 1939 for his pro-German activities. He had been enlisted by the Drayst unit at the start, first as an informer, later as an interrogations leader. Under the name Lafont, he and an ex-police inspector named Bony picked for their underlings criminals serving sentences. These men were marvelously well-suited as interrogators, imaginatively departing from the standard Gestapo methods of torture. They were enthusiastic because some of them received reprieves of as high as twenty-seven years at hard labor, and because their new work provided them with a special identity card licensing them to carry and use arms.

Only SS Captain Strasse, Chief of the Jewish Affairs Section, lived and worked apart from the other members of Drayst's unit. Just as Colonel Drayst was not accountable to General Koltrastt, Captain Strasse, although a Gestapo officer, was not under the authority of Drayst. Strasse reported only to SS Lieutenant-Colonel Eichmann in Berlin, who in turn reported to General Mueller, chief of the Gestapo.

The SS and police tribunals were installed at Boulevard Flandrin in the sixteenth arrondissement. Captain Strasse decided which of those arrested were to be tried and which were to be deported without trial. The routine of arrest, interrogation, and trial was precise. Interrogations took place within ten days after arrest. The luckier ones—those not held for interrogation—were diverted to the internment camp at St. Denis.

Gestapo agents spoke very correct French, but many of them spent a great deal of time explaining that their accents were Alsatian or even Baltic. This hard core was augmented by an organized force of twelve thousand French informers who were paid for each arrest and who ranged in cast from prostitutes, to concierges, to members of the upper classes who could use the extra money. The third line of information came from the usual resources of the French police.

The Gestapo preferred to make arrests early in the morning. The Santé and the Cherche-Midi prisons held thirty-four hundred prisoners and were always filled. All prisoners had the right to counsel, but only from a reserve of attorneys who had been approved by the Gestapo, and the advocate could speak to his client only on the day of trial. To maintain an appearance of impartiality, the judges usually dismissed prisoners falsely accused, but then remanded them immediately to prison as a security measure.

Aside from the SD, SS and the Gestapo, there were six other rival German intelligence organizations operating in France. The Bureau Ribbentrop was unofficial, but it commanded extensive facilities. Ernest Bohle's Auslandorganisation was the official overseas secret service apparatus. Dr. Rosenberg's Aussenpolitisches Amt tried desperately to keep up with the others. The Reichsmarschall's Air Force Research Office conducted extensive and mindless wire tapping which, bureaucratically burgeoning, ultimately impelled its zealous technicians to tap the lines of the Reichsmarschall, as well as those of the Fuehrer himself. (All of the tens of millions of telephone conversations held during the twelve years of the Thousand Year Reich were transcribed in duplicate and filed by a corps of librarians for easy reference if blackmail or betrayal were needed.) Military intelligence was under the direction of Admiral Canaris, and lastly, in addition to his unofficial bureau, Foreign Secretary von Ribbentrop, who was capable of being confused even by a picture book, maintained an official intelligence service so that he might receive contrasting assortments of intricate information daily.

Behind all of these, moving like a black cat in the night and striking to maim and to kill, was Colonel Drayst's SD, which eventually would consume all of its competitors. The chain of command flowed out of Berlin from the Reichsfuehrer SS to General Heydrich to General Mueller, Gestapo chief, to Colonel Drayst or, if Jews were involved, from Mueller to Eichmann to Strasse.

Late in 1941, Strasse had a scene with the Jewish Affairs Agency of Vichy, which had been fighting stubbornly against giving up French Jews for extermination, insisting that Strasse take foreign-born or stateless Jews of which, they maintained, there were plenty available in France. Strasse finally agreed, but when he set out to round up a trainload of Jews for extermination at Auschwitz, he discovered that he had only one hundred and fifty prisoners to ship, and he was sick over the trouble this was going to make for him in Berlin. As usual when he was in trouble, he went to Drayst with the problem and sat in the Colonel's office while a call was put through to Eichmann. Normally Captain Strasse was chalk-pale with a face like a cartoon rodent, but when Drayst picked up the receiver Strasse seemed green, and under his arms large, dark wet circles of perspiration had soaked through his tunic.

"Hello?" Drayst said. "Is that Eichmann?"

"This is Eichmann. Is that Strasse?"

"No. This is Drayst."

"Is that Paris? They told me I was talking to Paris."

"This is Paris. This is the BdS in Paris."

"Ah . . . Drayst! Hello. How are you, Drayst?"

"The same to you, Eichmann."

"Where is Strasse?"

"Strasse has urgent business with the French. We have bad news here."

"Bad news?"

"The train which was due to leave on the second had to be canceled."

"Canceled? Strasse canceled a train? Why?"

"He had no choice. I can bear him out on this." Drayst looked across the desk at Strasse, who nodded with sick gratitude. The Colonel knew about the problems of coordinating departures and arrivals, the difficulties of wangling rolling stock from the Ministry of Transport at a time when the Wehrmacht was constantly demanding priority, and above all, the necessity of having the trains filled to capacity with Jews so that no train would be wasted.

"Why? I don't follow this, Drayst. He knows the problems. I don't follow it and I don't like it at all. How could Strasse cancel a train?"

"They could only get one hundred and fifty Jews in Bordeaux and there was no time to find others to fill the train."

"Then Strasse has let us down—again. This is a disgrace. There is also a question of prestige here, Drayst, you know. The French go too far with us."

"But Eichmann, only one hundred and fifty Jews—"

"Does Strasse realize even dimly the length of time we had to negotiate here with the Minister of Transport in order to get this train for him? We do our job here one hundred percent, and then Strasse claims he can't get Jews. Is this a comedy? I don't know what to say, Drayst."

"It is better, believe me, Eichmann, to store the one hundred and fifty Jews here at Drancy than to waste a train."

"It's a disgrace. I must speak with Strasse."

"He is with the French. He is so angry that he has told them he may take the matter to Ambassador Abetz."

"I certainly don't want to have to report this matter to General Mueller, but the blame for Strasse's failure must fall directly on his own shoulders. He forces me to consider whether it would not be better to do without France altogether as an evacuation center."

When Eichmann had hung up Drayst put the telephone down and said, "Listen, why not put them on the train and fake the bill of lading a little?"

"I would do that in a minute," Strasse said. "But then they wouldn't get the same count at Auschwitz. This morning I was going to put them on the train and burn it to the ground, but then I'd get in even more trouble for losing a few rotten railroad cars."

"Well, be sure to call Eichmann before Monday. Heil Hitler!"

Strasse got up. His face was bitter, partly because of fatigue. Captain Strasse had one very peculiar obsession: a compulsion to own and operate night clubs. During the day he worked on the final solution to the Jewish problem, but at night he supervised eleven night clubs which he had commandeered from Jews. Most of the time he was wandering around in a daze of fatigue; the night before, for instance, the barman in his rue Lapin club had not shown up for duty and he had been obliged to work the shift himself until closing time. "Heil Hitler," he said, and shuffled wearily out of the room, as Fräulein Nortnung, the Colonel's secretary, called, "I have Charles Grimaux on the line, Colonel Drayst."

"Put him on." Drayst waited and stared out the window at the Musée d'Ennery. "Hello, Grimaux? How are you? Fine. Fine . . . Sunday evening?" He pulled an engagement book toward him. "Hm. I think so . . . The astrologer? Marvelous. Yes, I am free, Grimaux. Excellent. My very best to Mme. Grimaux. How nice . . . Ah, yes—there is one little thing, yes. Might you invite another guest? . . . Ah, how very kind of you. It is Frau General Paule von Rhode, the wife of—ach, you know her differently here. Here she is Paule Bernheim, the daughter of your great actor. Please don't mention my name . . . Yes, yes, that is the one. The mistress of the Duke of Miral."

Two

✠

JOSÉ ZORRA, DUKE OF MIRAL, had great length, elbows like *puyas*, stylish thinness, and a close-cropped gray moustache. At fifty-one, his voice contained the quality of intent consideration, that element of self-sacrifice which is the essence of good manners. Gentleness came naturally to him. He smelled of lemons because of Hanford's Vitalizing Lotion which was shipped to him from a gentlemen's hairdresser in Jermyn Street, London; this was one result of a British education. He spoke German with a true Hannoverian accent—the result of still more education, in Germany. He preferred France to both countries, the English to the people of the three countries, and German music, German tenacity, and *Trockenbeeren Auslese* to anything similar in England or France. He pitied all countries because they could not be Spain, but he concealed this deepest love of his beneath a patient deference and consideration for others. He had studied women and art until, as the years had moved imperceptibly and now seemed as thin as shadows, he had become an addict of grace and a world authority on painting in general and on Spanish and Flemish masters in particular.

The Duke of Miral found himself once again in Paris in the winter of 1941 as the single member of an extraordinary delegation from the Spanish government, after he had completed successful, if delayed, exchanges of art between France and Spain. The Spanish had taken the initiative in arranging for the first exchange. The talks had started, most informally, when Murillo's Immaculate Conception was exhibited in the Louvre at the end of 1940. It was tentatively suggested that perhaps this was the most famous painting to cross the Pyrenees following the looting of Spanish art treasures by the French forces in 1808—it had been liberated by Maréchal Soult in Seville—and that its return could effect the greatest good will between the two countries. Unofficially, and because the French evidently had listened attentively to the first suggestion, the Spaniards next suggested that the pre-Iberic bust called Woman of Eliche might also be included, and that it certainly would be worthwhile to think about returning the crowns of the Visigoth kings which were then on exhibition at the Musée de Cluny.

The discussions rose to higher levels. The French cabinet at Vichy agreed to these proposals—providing there was an exchange. The Department of Ancient Oriental Art at the Louvre began to collect the art claimed by Spain. A plenipotentiary was named and an agreement was reached: France would return the Murillo, the bust, and the six gold crowns from the Quarrazar treasure; Spain would give to France the Velázquez portrait of Marie Anne of Austria, El Greco's Adoration of the Shepherds and his St. Benoist, (or two other Grecos of equal importance and quality), and a lengthwise section of the actual tent of François I, used at *Camp du drap d'or,* which was in the Royal Armory of the Royal Palace of Madrid. This tent, a gift of the Sultan Suleiman to François I, had been taken from him by the Spanish on the battlefield at Pavia, in 1525, and had followed François into captivity.

The agreement was signed on December 27, 1940, and the French were so pleased with the bargain that they acted somewhat incautiously. Two weeks before the signing, the

Murillo was sent to Madrid, and the other objects arrived in Spain only six weeks after the signing. The fact was that the French wanted Generalissimo Franco to visit Marshal Pétain as he crossed France on his way to meet Mussolini. Marshal Pétain had not made a really strong impression upon the Generalissimo when he had been the French Ambassador to Spain, so it was especially important that there be no outstanding sources of friction—such as slowness in returning the art objects—between the two governments.

Unfortunately, the agreement on the exchange had never been ratified by the respective governments of the two men who had signed it, and with the desired art now in hand, the Spanish government took the position that the signing of the agreement had only expressed the most unofficial wishes of two individuals. This created a crisis in the French government at Vichy which caused the resignation of the Minister of Foreign Affairs.

Clearly it was necessary that negotiations begin all over again lest honor be smirched or even lost. New representatives from France and Spain renewed the talks, the Duke of Miral leading the Spanish delegation, and by April, 1941, it seemed that a solution was in sight. France needed only to agree to a compromise over two points on which the Spaniards would not yield. Before Miral would recommend ratification he insisted that Spain must have the forty missing documents of the Siramancas Archives which had been stolen by Napoleon's generals in 1809; further, he flatly refused to surrender the piece of tent of François I, even though it had been part of the original agreement which those "two individuals" had seen fit to reach.

The French agreed to give up their claim to the entrance section of the lengthwise piece of tent of François I, and some other areas of it near the entrance, for the excellent reason that this tent was the last trace of one of France's worst military defeats and, all things considered, it would be illogical to display it in a gallery of a French museum.

The bargaining continued until the middle of June. Instead of the piece of tent, the Duke of Miral proposed to give a tapestry called The Brawl at the Inn, whose cartoon had been drawn by Goya, but France could not accept this because it simply was not comparable, either in age or in historical importance. Countering, the French raised the question that if by any chance they were to waive their rights and interest in the piece of tent, would the Spanish give them one Greco of major importance—such as the portrait of the humanist Covarrubias, for example? At last, the Spanish team accepted the French proposals and counterproposals; when they received the forty missing documents from the Siramancas Archives, they even gave France nineteen sketches from the story of Artenice, for good measure. The signing of the agreement took place in Madrid, on June 27, 1941, and was immediately ratified by both countries.

Miral's government was pleased once more with his accomplishments. In November, 1941, because in the past Miral had enjoyed a close association with the Reichsmarschall in the First World War, when Miral had covered the conflict for his family's newspapers and the Reichsmarschall had been thinner and a hero, and because the Spanish Ambassador to Berlin had confirmed the Reichsmarschall's fond recollection of Miral as a willing sharer of women and wine, and because the Reichsmarschall had a connoisseur's regard for Miral's authority on painting, the Spanish government dispatched Miral on an extraordinary mission-of-one. He was to return to his sometime residence in Paris to open delicate discussions which might lead to the return of two exemplar paintings by Velázquez and Goya which had been hanging in the Louvre since they had been taken from Spain by the French in 1810. These items were of far too much value to be discussed successfully with the French government directly, but they might possibly be regained from the French by the Germans, who in turn would hand them over to the Spanish.

This was possible because Rosenberg's unit, whose objective was nothing more or less than to loot France of as much of its fine art as it could lay its hands on, was engaged day and night in filling and refilling the Musée de Jeu de Paume with great, privately owned art collections which were the property of French Jews and which had been seized by special arrangement with the Vichy authorities. All of these acquisitions were entirely legal, because the Fuehrer was a stickler for legality; payments for all works of art were deposited with the Vichy Commission for Jewish Affairs—though it is true that the payments were at grievously lowered evaluations. Art is beauty and beauty is truth; by the war's end twenty-six thousand railroad cars, according to efficient German statistics, had left France, Italy, Belgium, and Holland for Germany, all filled with truth and beauty.

Miral's house stood on the steeply raked bluff over the Quai de Passy, just above the soft river. Talking into a telephone, Miral sat in a dazzlingly baroque room of eight-legged tabourets, gilt table harps, brightly colored chandeliers, fluted pedestals, and painted ceilings—the whole a gay hiccup by d'Orbais. He had arrived twenty minutes before from Le Bourget and Madrid, and had been met at the airport by a Luftwaffe escort commanded by a Colonel Heneker. The Colonel had conveyed the best wishes and respects of the Reichsmarschall, which indicated that the Reichsmarschall did not intend to discourage the Spanish hopes for Miral's mission. A second gesture of hospitality was the Luftwaffe car and driver which were placed at Miral's disposal, complete with a bottomless source of petrol. The final miracle was the working telephone, impossible to come by, already installed in his house; this was, as Colonel Heneker put it, a token of regard.

As soon as the German departed, the Duke tested the telephone by calling the working telephone which had been installed sometime before in the apartment of Madame von Rhode.

"Paule? Pepe."

"No!"

"I am here."

"Oh, Pepe. How wonderful."

"Am I to see you tonight?" They spoke in German to make things simpler for the censors.

"Of course. Oh, yes."

"Ah."

"Where are you calling from?"

He raised his voice slightly so that the censor might register it clearly. "The Reichsmarschall has been kind enough to install a telephone in my house."

"They gave you a telephone? My God, what are you going to be doing in Paris?"

"That will be all we will say at the moment. I called because I had to be sure about tonight. To be so near you and not see you immediately would be like dying of a bleeding wound."

"You are so dear, Pepe."

"And tomorrow?"

"I cannot. Tomorrow is Paul-Alain's seventh birthday, and much celebrating is called for."

"I have a little surprise for him. And the night after that?"

"I have been invited to the Grimaux'. Would that amuse you?"

"Grimaux?"

"The new kind of Frenchman. Very close to the SS and suddenly very rich."

"Ah, that Grimaux. Yes, that would amuse me very much. I am told that Dr. Martin Kroner Schute is in Paris for just a few days, and it would be interesting if I just happened to run into him at the Grimaux'. How is it that you are going to such a place?"

"Curiosity. Boredom. They have succeeded in luring Europe's greatest astrologer and they seem to be using that to invite just about everyone they don't know. Who is Dr. Schute?"

"The art adviser to the Reichsmarschall. It's a splendid arrangement all around. Shall I come for you at eight this evening?"

"Sooner if you can. I have missed you."

"How I long to see you, Paule." The Duke hung up the telephone and stared across the room assembling all of her beauty within his mind. He thought of how Euclid had cheated posterity by making the concept of space everything and the concept of time nothing. Newton had "proved" that time flowed uniformly—as though there could be anything uniform between the measurement of the centuries during which he had loved this woman and the light years of speed by which his life was carrying him away from her. He would be an old man while she was still young and beautiful. St. Augustine had said: "Before the sound begins we cannot measure the time it is going to take, nor after it has sounded can we measure the time it has taken, for it is then no more. Can we measure it then in the present, while it is being sounded? This will not be possible as the present is without duration." How could there be time for him to find the truth she represented, or her magic, which glimmered and then concealed itself? How could she find him; how could he show himself? How could he know what his life meant until he had lived it and then could say, "I am a particle of the love that is felt for you"? He felt that he and Paule were

like figures facing and reflecting each other endlessly in an
infinity of mirrors, which were the past and the future.

Three

✠

FROM CHILDHOOD Paule had been frightened that she might be
left alone. Now she discovered that the fright was over and
that she might have ended it at any time by walking away
from dread and leaving it behind her. On the 11th of November, 1938, twenty hours after leaving Berlin forever, she
held Paul-Alain in her arms, and stared out of the train window at the outskirts of Paris. She was marveling at the death
of her fear. She was free; she would never set foot in Germany
again. That exalted her, but she would never see Veelee
again and she could not think about that. As the train rolled
into the Gare Austerlitz she felt transmigrated to another life.
She was free of the helplessness which her marriage had
become but most of all she was free of the lifelong fear of
being left behind, alone.

She and Paul-Alain raced through the halls and galleries
and terraces at Cours Albert I with Clotilde and Mme. Citron
running along behind them weeping. Each time they came to
another side of the house they would troop out to overlook
the beautiful city and Paule would point out the landmarks
to her son. Over and over again Mme. Citron said that he
certainly was a big boy. Paul-Alain had never seen such a
big apartment. He said that he never wanted to leave it and
that they could play all kinds of games with closets and
fireplaces and long, open windows like these. When one of
the maids rushed in with two cablegrams, one stamped from
Burgos and the other from Berlin, Paule tore them in half,
said there would be no reply, thank you, and threw the pieces
into the fire.

While her son napped Paule called three old friends and
was invited out for three nights running. She called Maître
Gitlin and asked him to take her out to dinner. She called

Rufin Portu and made arrangements to begin the sittings for her portrait, five years late, because her father had wanted it. She called a coiffeuse, two couturiers, an interior decorator, a toy store, and an employment agency. That afternoon she had her lustrous, long black hair cut short and dyed blond. She ordered eleven new dresses and suits; flowers for six rooms of the flat; a toy boat and a bicycle; and hired a *chef de cuisine* to begin work the following Monday. The next day she started to redecorate the apartment, and she installed Paul-Alain in her old room and moved herself into her father's enormous, mirrored plantation of a bedroom.

While she was dining with Maître Gitlin, a young stage director who had been an apprentice under her father stopped at their table, and after expressing his pleasure at her return, asked if he might call her. She said that she would be in touch with him as soon as she got settled, and she took his number.

As they explored the soufflé Maître Gitlin expressed what was on his legal mind.

"Now, do you want me to begin divorce proceedings?"

"No."

"Shall I seek a legal separation?"

"No, thank you, Maître."

"Shall I petition to have a French court appoint you the legal guardian of your child?"

"No. Paul-Alain is with me and that is enough. His father has been hurt enough."

"Will you reconcile?"

"I don't see how we could. He doesn't even understand why we have separated. It is a frustrating thing to have your marriage turned to stone by politicians."

When Paule was alone at Cours Albert that night, she sat wrapped in furs on the eastern terrace, facing the hill of Montmartre, and began to think with her body again. She could feel herself shedding the anxiety about being a Jew in Germany. Her fear was moving away with the speed of a planet. She had earned the right to stay sane, and the only price seemed to be loneliness.

At a quarter to one she telephoned the young stage director who had stopped to chat with them that evening. Germany was a place of the dead, but not Paris, she thought joyously and lustfully. When she heard his voice she said that if he was alone she would like to visit him. She slept with him

151

that night, the next, and the night after that. Then she moved on to another man.

The young director was not the second man Paule had ever been to bed with, but he was the first since she had met her husband, the first man since her husband had gone off to Spain sixteen months before; he was the first warm, quick, clean body she had held in her legs and arms since she had felt that filth in the alcove in Berlin. After him, they came to her or she went to them in endless procession. As she drowned herself in sex she would think of the ancient Teutonic concept of hell—an underground place called Niflheim, an icy cavern of freezing pain through all eternity—and as she consumed more and more men she thought joyfully that she was punishing Veelee in a way that would leave the deepest wound, so that he could become disgusted with her and they could be free of one another forever.

The blind abandon of her nights was tempered by the cleansing and healing serenity of her days with Paul-Alain. She never brought men home, and she never stayed with them after dawn. She rose with Paul-Alain, dressed him, petted him, played with him, loved him, and lived for him. They spent their days at the merry-go-round, on the seesaws, and at the puppet shows of the Tuileries and Luxembourg gardens. They sailed boats and rode the donkeys along the Champs-Elysées between the Concorde and the Rond-Point; they fed milk out of nursing bottles to little piglets and gave carrots to little goats in the Jardin d'Acclimatation; they rode the small train and tasted the delights of the Cirque Medrano. They knew every zoo and they strolled together happily, complimenting the flowers on their beauty in the Jardins des Plantes. They went to the seashore in the summer and they skiied in the winter, and together they drew applause on figure skates. She taught Paul-Alain to count, to read, and to write before he went to school.

Like her father before her, every Friday night Paule told her son the ancient stories from the proud history of the Jews. "When the Greeks came to the Near East after Alexander the Great, they brought with them their philosophies of pleasure, which the Jews saw only as a threat of national suicide. We wanted nothing to do with their views on morals and art, but their philosophers fascinated us. We tinkered with the ancient Greek philosophies and debated them back and forth among us, subtly changing them until the Greeks became attentive to all our changes and took the renovated philosophies back to Greece. Thus we provided the world with a Jewish cloak called Christianity, and in exchange we found ourselves wearing a Greek robe called Talmudism."

Paul-Alain had his grandfather's great gifts. He could throw the whole household into convulsions of laughter when he entertained them with his imitations of the world he saw every day. Like his grandfather he was a great eater, and he never grew tired of the story of the trick played on Lesrois. He made it a point to tell people that he was a German and that his father was a colonel in the German Army. Paule made sure that he knew all of the von Rhode family tales of glory and prowess, of the historic battles they had led and won, of the great horses they had mastered and the medals they had been awarded, but she always thought of him as a French boy. They spoke French throughout the day but talked in German every evening until his bedtime. Paul-Alain was his mother's universe, her garden, her song, her food, and her meaning.

In March, 1940, Rufin Portu telephoned Paule. She had had a standard, short-term affair with Portu during the Christmas season of 1938. Portu was impersonal about everything except his work. In painting her she had become a part of his work and he had made love to her much as the librettist of *Aïda* would have made love to Amneris—not to the actress who was playing Amneris. Then, after the portrait had been finished, Portu undertook to paint a likeness of the daughter of a purple chieftain from Lake Chad, and, as always, he extended the art of his art, and Paule had found another man.

"Paule?"

"Yes."

"Rufin."

"Who?"

"Rufin Portu. Can you come by for a drink this afternoon?"

"Why?"

"Isn't a surprise better than a reason?"

"No."

"Well . . . Now don't be angry."

"Now there are two whys. Why should I be angry?"

"I am not procuring you for someone."

"Why not?"

"Paule, listen. There is this man. He knows painting—I mean it. Have I ever said that? He knows the problems and he knows the results. So I like him. He saw a photograph of your portrait and said, 'I have to meet that woman.' I said, 'Well, maybe, perhaps.' I didn't say yes, of course. You know? He squatted and stared at the picture. I have it in half-size, in black and white, and it is very good for black and white. I thought that he was just posing, and I didn't say anything. But he stared at it for so long that I asked him why. I suppose that I was waiting for him to say that it was a wonderful painting, which of course I like to hear. But he said, 'Why is the hair blond?' 'Why not?' I said. 'She is not intended to be blond,' he said. 'You have found the wounds behind her mask,' he said. 'If we could retrace the way and collect all this woman's tears, we could swim in them,' he said."

"Who is he, Portu?"

"My countryman, José Zorra, Duke of Miral. Good bones, wonderful nose, very silent eyes like a manager of matadors."

"Anything else?"

"Yes, yes. But I have said enough."

"Not what he said about me. About him."

"How can a man tell a woman about a man? Come to my house and see him. Observe his tailoring. Guess his age, which I would put at about fifty. Feel the texture of his hand when he greets you. Eat with him, hear him talk. Then, if the signals are good, sleep with him, and count a few more minutes saved from the moments after you are dead."

Miral was waiting in Portu's high-ceilinged studio in the rue Lavoisier. Against the baseboards there stood brightly colored portraits and scrapbooks of photographs of portraits. Paule had dressed carefully in a white wool suit and a white wool cape trimmed with silver fox. Portu introduced them, excused himself to make a drink, and never came back.

Paule could feel Miral's eyes on her like warm hands. She leaned into his silence, and they sat, facing each other, but not speaking, for many minutes.

Finally he spoke, mocking her gently. "Well? Tell me about despair."

154

"Mine, your Grace, or yours?"

"If you could tell me about someone else's despair you would not be desperate."

"If I am desperate it is because I know others' desperation. I lived in Germany for six years."

"I see."

"Why have you decided I am desperate, your Grace?"

"Why did you dye your hair such a color?"

"You say that as though I were more villainous than desperate."

"Villainy is a state of grace. It believes in its own deeds for their own sake. Consider the lives of the saints, each of them struck down by their most terrible egos. That is villainy. To create a state of mind which pursues the abstract until it burns or stones one to death—that must be villainy in God's sight. For the saints were his creatures and forbidden to take vengeance against themselves. Vengeance was His, He saith."

"Do you say now that I am desperate because I am a villain, and that I am a villain because I take vengeance upon myself by dyeing my hair?"

"Something like that."

"You don't like blondes?"

"I adore blondes. My late wife was a blonde. Incredible and very beautiful. But I would not have liked it if she had dyed her hair green."

They dined late. He started by amusing her, became fascinating, then learned, then protectively prescient. He had a long memory, a good mind, a jauntily egotistical manner, and could make her laugh.

As they strolled along the Avenue Marceau toward Cours Albert I the street light fell at an angle upon the silver of his bared head, as he walked hat in hand. The effect of this image on her was gone instantly, but it had been there long enough to save her and she never forgot it. He was like her father. She thought she saw a sanctuary.

Four

✠

THE VICHY GOVERNMENT gave to the Germans first four hundred million, then five hundred million francs a day to pay for the costs of the Occupation. Paris was now a provincial German city, it pleased the Fuehrer to say. German country boys were brought to the Eiffel Tower every day on excursion buses. The elevators were not running but their cameras weren't heavy, and from dawn until night they climbed up and down. Below the tower the Champ de Mars was a carpet of Algerian nut peddlers and pimps; where green grass had grown there now grew orange peels, candy papers, and army-issue contraceptives. At curfew five-man patrols, armed with carbines and walking in the middle of the streets, succeeded each other at short intervals. Indomitable fishermen still sat motionless along the quais. Swastikas on a field of blood flew from all public monuments. The twelve thousand French policemen still on duty had been retaught to control traffic with stiff, mechanical, Teutonic hand signals.

In 1939 France had used three million tons of gasoline. In 1941 fifty thousand tons were available for all official and civilian use. Doctors used bicycles or gasogene cars driven by gas distilled from charcoal burning in a huge stove on a trailer behind the vehicle. The Paris bus system broke down in October, 1940. Of the two hundred and sixty thousand buses and trucks, one hundred and five thousand were destroyed or diverted to the Germans. A few gasogene buses, whose gigantic stoves on their roofs made them resemble triple deckers, were in use. Over two and a half million Métro tickets were sold each working day in 1941, an increase of fifty-four percent over 1940. Horse-drawn fiacres were available, but they were perilously expensive and there were too few of them even for the new-rich class which had appeared almost simultaneously with the Germans. Almost eleven million bicycle licenses were issued in 1942, and so many gangs of thieves were at work that people would carry their bicycles up many flights of stairs whenever they visited. The brothels opened at three P.M. Military bands, consisting mostly of tubas, splayed oompahs into the Place de l'Opéra, in the Tuileries, in front of Notre Dame. Actors and actresses seemed to be the only civilians who still drove cars, a fact not entirely appreciated by the public.

A new bourgeoisie was being born, the result of a plan within a plan within a plan which had been painstakingly evolved in drab Berlin buildings many years before. Hard-eyed people were buying real estate cheaply from soft-eyed, frightened people. With the hard cash coming to them, farmers and butchers and dairymen bought hotels and châteaux, large wine stocks, great restaurants, and fashionable health resorts. The Bourse operated almost normally; the only restriction was that all stocks and shares had to be left in the safekeeping of the central stock-certificate bank. There was much speculation in gold and in foreign bank notes. The *louis d'or*, worth twenty francs in 1939, was worth six thousand francs in 1944. Small-time money-lenders, notaries, and contractors who had been hod carriers before the war staggered under the weight of the profits of building the Fuehrer's Atlantic Wall. Night-club owners, pimps, black-market restaurateurs, and brothel keepers catered eagerly to the German trade, moved up the financial ladder rung by rung, and buried their gains behind a cousin's barn out in the country.

Vichy floundered from one bit of reckless mindlessness to the next. To ingratiate themselves with their new hosts, the French government dismissed and discredited Jewish doctors, teachers, architects, artists, and professors because the German design insisted upon the elimination of intellectuals—who, after all, only criticized things. Almost at once Vichy lost its power of independent thought; just as quickly it moved vigorously to eradicate any independent thinking by the French people, hopefully to replace it with a mystique of obedience.

"What is a Gaullist?" Claire Grimaux asked with sincere interest. "I go all over Paris constantly and I have never met one."

Almost all of the guests at the evening reception given by

Charles and Claire Grimaux arrived in their own cars.

Grimaux was forty-one and adored intrigue. Like Goering, he was a man of pretentious but frequently endearing charm. He had an ingenuous stutter to his speech and a slight cast in one eye which won sympathy. In spite of the stutter he spoke very rapidly, in imitation of certain American business executives whom he had admired when he met them in prison in the years before the war. His beautiful new wife, Claire, was twenty-six; before the war she had been a film star and the mistress of a high churchman. Grimaux had been convicted twelve years before for having issued a quantity of checks without funds. Upon his release from prison he had come to Paris from his native Clermont-Ferrand and, by dint of a prison education which had instructed him in the procurement of false papers, had been able to change his name. The German police organization had selected him from its exhaustive files; contrary to his impression, no one had lost sight of him for long.

When Grimaux was established in his new identity as a serious but most available businessman, he published a newspaper for which friends on the Quai d'Orsay—who were also friends of the German cause—were able to obtain a subsidy of twenty-five thousand francs a month. When the Occupation began and he had been favored with an interview with Colonel Drayst, Grimaux changed the name of his newspaper and the subsidy for its publication was increased to one hundred and eighty-three thousand francs a month. His conscientiousness in merchandising the German ideal, in spite of the increasing harshness of the German occupation, had been rewarded with a codirectorship in yet another newspaper with still another subsidy.

The Grimaux were delighted to see Paule again, though they had never seen her before, and they were absolutely thrilled to receive a genuine Spanish duke. Mme. Grimaux whirled them off to meet the other guests, a special wartime congregation elite only by reason of money. They came from everywhere: Dominican diplomats, Hungarian espionage agents, three thrilled Americans accompanied by two jaded Swiss mistresses, three Japanese policemen on a professional exchange, many pro-German Parisians, and assorted Nazi industrialists, and members of the German Army and SS. Grimaux actually served pink champagne because it impressed the Germans. The caviar was excellent. Most of the conversational noises in the salon came from the pro-German Parisians who, moved by the ideal of order and one Europe, were talking earnestly to uniformed Germans about the chances of obtaining a larger supply of petrol—though oddly enough, the prettier women seemed to talk about nothing but obtaining bulkier industrial authorizations.

Paule and Miral met a former *faiseuse d'anges* who was now the favorite couturière. They met seven actresses and four actors from the Comédie Française. They met General Koltrastt, who was very drunk, and the affable Captain Sperrena. An Italian infantry general remembered Paule's father with exquisite emotion, and Prince Marcelin de Fontoyon was ecstatic over the silver lace of her dress and the Peruvian silver ornaments in her hair. "Silver lace under a face means good gold bars in some safe place," the Prince said. "I am perhaps the most abjectly sentimental man you have ever met where money is concerned. It's not a royal quality, I suppose—though I've never known a royal who wasn't swept away by money's charm—but there you are."

The Prince had been an early and easy target of the German parallel police organization. He had an expensive narcotics habit and lived quite desperately until the Occupation delivered him. Now he was the dowsing rod which the SD used to tap French economic resources. He was a bagman for Koltrastt, Drayst, and Sperrena, and one of the pillars of the SS financial structure in France. Through him, enormous fortunes were transferred from business partner to business partner, with the SS always sharing. The Prince's title had great appeal to the new ruling class. With SS assistance he learned how to divine the true make-up of corporations, how stock issues had been divided, and the several unseen means by which corporate control of a company could be obtained. Through the Prince, Drayst had become a very, very rich man, and in turn, the Prince earned enough to corner half the narcotics in France if he had wished to. Because he seemed so innocuous, and because he frequently was able to trade some surprising information himself, merchants were delighted to tell him which firms were actually controlled by Jews and to give accurate estimates of the probable fruits of confiscation. Women well-placed in the upper berths of politics, who frequently found themselves short of money because of gambling reverses or the expense of keeping young men who were hard enough to find, would sell him information about the extra-legal business affiliations of the statesmen they served from the flats of their backs.

Paule and the Duke also met Charles Piocher, who, in direct partnership with the SS, controlled twenty-seven percent of the black market of Occupied France. Piocher was a stocky, violent-looking man, with a shock of black hair and a very red face, whose voice was harsher and twenty decibels louder than anyone else's, and who had two gold teeth which glittered wealthily in his mouth.

Piocher's dossier had been thoroughly examined in Berlin in April, 1940. It showed that Piocher had spent a total of six years for theft and assault in various *nha-pha,* the prisons of Indo-China, at Thai-Mouyen and Lai Chau; and in Poulo-Condore in Cochin China. He spoke Tonkinese, Chinese, and Cambodian. There was reason to believe that he placed no value on human life. He had been deported to Paris in 1937 and had been arrested for living off the earnings of prostitutes—in contravention of Article 334 of the law of April 13, 1936—his sole profession until Colonel Drayst had found him and had moved him into the black market. He had enormous strength as a result of the hard-labor regimens of the *nha-pha,* and an insensate temper, which was a help in a profession in which he had to beat up farmers and field hands and keep a gaggle of amateur competitors constantly in line.

"To think that we go back together all the way to Salamanca!" Martin Kroner Schute said to the Duke of Miral, including Paule in the conversation as they stood apart from the other guests in the corner of the large room. "That is not so terribly long in time, but in terms of history—ach! It was the summer of 1936, Frau General, and what a time that was. On the last day of summer Generalissimo Franco was made head of the Provisional Government, and at that moment, Salamanca became the capital of Spain. Germans, Americans, Rumanians, Italians, French, and British filled the place to the attics. What a mix-up! The Japanese mission actually accused us of stealing their papers! There were farces everywhere! A French captain caught an Italian colonel in bed with his wife and shot him dead. Then, because I happened to be passing by in the hotel corridor, he asked me to help him down the backstairs with the body. 'Throw him down the stairs,' I said. 'What's the difference? Go in and comfort your wife,' I said. There was a crazy Rumanian major from the Iron Guard in the hotel. Ach! He was overjoyed about the shooting, because he had been ordered to bring back to Bucharest the body of a Rumanian hero who had fallen in the cause of Spanish fascism, and this was his chance because it wasn't likely he would get a body any other way. So he made a deal with the French captain and while they carried the body off to the Rumanian's room, I went in and comforted the captain's wife. Ach! What a summer! All over the north of Spain the Falangists were fighting in the streets with the Carlists—and they were supposed to be on the same side, I think. We had our Condor legion there, and they were allowed to fly in their own prostitutes from Hamburg.

"At that time, as always, my job was in the service of the Reichsmarschall. I have been advising him on all art matters since 1934—though I can assure you, Frau von Rhode, that I am by no means an exalted expert like our Duke here. Salamanca was really my first big field trip. In those days, of course, it was still possible to move Spanish art out of the country, which is one thing we can say for the Republicans—I am only making my little joke, of course. Well, as you can imagine, the first thing I did on arriving in Salamanca was to look for this man right here. I found him having tea at the Grand Hotel—I have a fantastic memory— with two of the most exquisite Filipino women. They were so beautiful that even now, such a long time afterward, I can feel excited as I talk about them. Rosa and Fernanda. Wonderful little women. So tiny. Feet like little pork chops. We talked about the Reichsmarschall—you remember, your Grace?—and the times you had enjoyed with him at Mulhausen. He often speaks of them when I bring it up. I was so pleased—even may I say thrilled, sir—that you remembered those days that I cabled at once, and let me say the Reichsmarschall was flattered—yes, totally flattered—that you had remembered him so kindly. That shows what a remarkable sort of man he is.

"Of course, you were a part of a great saga of the Reichsmarschall's life. He shot down twenty-two Allied planes, and he was awarded the Iron Cross, second and first class, the Zaehring Lion with Swords, the Karl Friedrich Order, the Hohenzollern Medal with Swords, and then, on May something, 1918, he was given the *Pour le Mérite,* the absolute highest of the high. Now, of course, he lives only for art.

Today he has become so absorbed in art collecting that he often forgets the affairs of the Luftwaffe for weeks on end. Isn't that fabulous? Eh? With a war on? Do you realize that his collection amounts to over fifteen hundred works of art, valued at over one hundred and sixty million dollars? (I use the dollar because it is neutral and stable—although who knows, eh, your Grace?)

"When I first began to serve the Reichsmarschall, I found his taste already formed. However, I have been able to develop and extend it, and the masterpieces we have acquired together have greatly increased in range and number. *Heh-heh-heh-heh*—I should think so. In Paris alone, some thirty-eight thousand houses owned by Jews have been sealed up, and the Einsatzstab Rosenberg has catalogued over twenty thousand works of art. Some of it is remarkably fine stuff, you know. There are over five thousand paintings, almost twenty-five hundred pieces of antique furniture, and a rewarding number of the Gobelin tapestries, which are so beloved by the Reichsmarschall. *Heh-heh-heh-heh-heh*. Which reminds me. You must look in at the basement of the Palais de Chaillot. It is filled to the top with pianos. Bechsteins, Pleyels, Steinways—all taken from Jews. What a musical people they must be.

"But to return to my point. What the Reichsmarschall has done for German art can hardly be calculated, and yet only six days ago General Stuelpnagel, our military governor here, wrote a bitter letter to Field Marshal von Brauchitsch to complain against the Einsatzstab Rosenberg. Luckily, the Reichsmarschall acted quickly and no harm was done. I ask you, why does this General Stuelpnagel do this? What does a soldier know about art? I will modify that statement. The Reichsmarschall is a simple soldier, yes, but he is extraordinary and aesthetic, and he is the only soldier who knows anything about art—and I say that as an expert. I would say the same thing even if they tortured me." Dr. Schute blew his nose and simultaneously held his other palm aloft to keep anyone from interrupting him. "It is his fitness of things. A sense. His breeding tables have enormous length. I have seen his genealogical tables, and he is related to Charlemagne, Frederick the Great, and St. Elizabeth of Thüringen. So who can blame him if he takes a slightly spectacular view of history? How should a man act who is next in succession for the leadership of the most powerful nation on earth and who has his own private army of twenty-two infantry divisions? Like some little householder? No! He is a big man. He weighs three hundred and ten pounds as of this week, and this is majestic, my friends. You should hear . . ."

When word was passed into Colonel Drayst's private meeting with Mme. Selahettin that Frau General von Rhode had arrived, he did not leave at once because he could not tear himself away from this woman who was the first real genius of palmistry and astrology that he had ever encountered. She was a short, slight woman with white bobbed hair and heavy bangs, and if one were to see her walking across a park in her strange high-soled shoes, Drayst thought he might guess that she was, say, an Irish bookseller. But her dossier showed that she was half-Egyptian and half-Bavarian, and her hands were incredibly psychodynamic—as she had pointed out herself. She had bright eyes and a ready smile, and nothing about her was in the usual seer's tradition. She was a part-time gnome from a children's book, she spoke German with a Swabian accent, and she was the most famous fortuneteller in Europe. A year before she had been unknown, yet now there were hundreds of leaders who would not make a move without her. According to Himmler, she had never made a mistake about the past or the future. Like all great and wonderful phenomena, she had one weakness: she could not function anywhere but in Paris. Mme. Selahettin could have lived at the side of the Fuehrer, and she had sobbed bitterly when she had confessed that as much as she would have liked to serve the German cause in the Reich, her powers left her the moment she left Paris.

The Reichsfuehrer SS was able to explain this phenomenon: it was due to an intersection of magnetic fields peculiar to that part of the world. He had asked Dr. L. Roth of the Institute of Science and Education to make measurements of spatial conduits and the lines of magnetic power supply as they came directly into Paris from the various transfixing and transversing points in outer space, and Dr. Roth had confirmed the Reichsfuehrer's suspicions. Thereafter Mme. Selahettin charted the Fuehrer's zodiacal anticipations through Luftwaffe couriers, advising him on moves and warning him of upcoming dangers. The Reichsfuehrer SS had twice journeyed specially to Paris for consultations with her, and he had personally pronounced her the most remarkably gifted seer who had ever come to his attention. By her advice he had become extremely careful about his teeth. Selahettin had been thoroughly investigated by multiple SD and Gestapo teams, and there was no doubt that she was absolutely genuine.

"I cannot see you before next week?" Colonel Drayst asked with chagrin.

"To cast your horoscope I need to work day and night, dear Colonel Drayst, doing nothing else. You are a leader and must be served."

"A leader? Greatness?"

"Yes, greatness. It is in your palm, and it will be confirmed by your stars." She closed her eyes and leaned back in her chair. "Your right and left hands hold the total physical reincarnations of the lines, stars, and triangles in the hands of Napoleon I, Emperor of France."

"Ach!"

"Your tasseled lines, grilles, trident and spearhead, and the islands on your hands proclaim as loudly as the voice of heaven that you are singled out to gain great riches and power. You will rule with compassion and justice, for that is your nature—your right hand, in these points, matches the right hand of the philosopher, Socrates, and the left hand that of St. Paul, he who was Saul of Tarsus."

What a marvelous woman, Drayst thought dizzily. She held up the two black prints she had made of his hands. "When we meet on Saturday I will bring you reproductions of the hands of Napoleon and Socrates and St. Paul, and you will begin to understand your greatness—which of course must be guided and channeled at first."

"At my office on the Avenue Foch?"

"At two o'clock."

Drayst thanked her warmly. "I have a question, Mme. Selahettin," he said. "There is a woman in the room out there. Will I ever possess her?"

"Not at first. There will be, or there has been, a struggle."

"Yes!"

"You must not press her yet. The decision has not yet been frozen into the sea of time."

Suddenly Drayst lusted to see that beautiful Jewish face. He left the room abruptly, eager to see the panic and fear

164

in her eyes when she saw him moving toward her, after she thought she had killed him.

Five

MIRAL HAD AT LAST MANAGED to halt Dr. Schute's torrent of conversation and was speaking to him in the far corner of the room. Paule was standing alone, and she did not see Drayst until he was almost upon her. She almost screamed. The color left her face, and her great, purple eyes showed all the terror he had prayed to see there. "How extremely wonderful to see you again, Frau von Rhode," he said softly. As he took her elbow and pulled her easily down upon a sofa, Paule imagined she could see Herr Waegel, the block warden, smiling as he shut the door to cover them with darkness.

"You did not know I was in France? No? But I am the BdS. Yes, I arrived with the first troops. I have known you were here, of course, and I have been waiting for a graceful opportunity to talk to you." He made a boyish pout. "But you have become so deathly pale. Do you think you see a ghost? Did you think you had killed me with your little pistol?" He laughed generously, showing his pointed white teeth. "At that, you nearly killed me with your little knee." She moved away from him along the sofa, until she was out of reach of his hand. He held it up; the palm was deeply puckered at the center, as dimpled as if he had been crucified. "The stigmata bestowed by your little bullet," he said jovially in carefully accented French. "So you did not miss me completely." She caught her lower lip between her teeth. Her eyes glittered, never leaving his face, and there were beads of sweat on her forehead.

"You know, perhaps, that Dr. Globke has decreed that to obtain a marriage license Czech brides of German soldiers may now furnish photographs of themselves in bathing suits and no longer have to be photographed entirely nude. But I don't agree with that, Frau von Rhode. With you, everything you do excites me. I read about you at night from your file that I have had built up here. I have a wonderful Paris file on you. I have photographs of you in bed with many men." She drew back, but he held her forearm, then withdrew his hand. "Yes. Yes, I do. They show you doing wonderful things. We have very good photographers, you know. So many men, Frau von Rhode! You ran wild for a year after you left your husband, eh? I am not judging you. It was good for me. I like it—it was a natural thing. I want you that way. That is how I see you every night. Yes. There are so many things I want you to do with me when you are ready." His blue eyes seemed polished. "What I would give to rip that dress off you and take you here and now."

Paule stood up and swayed unsteadily. Miral saw her and crossed the room.

"Are you all right, Paule?"

"Yes. May we go now?"

"At once."

Grimaux rushed to them at the door, motioning frantically to his wife, and Miral bade them good night as he helped Paule into her wrap.

The Luftwaffe car was waiting. "To my flat, please, Pepe. I must see Paul-Alain. I am so frightened. I haven't felt this way since Berlin."

"I understand. I will let you get a full night's sleep."

"No, Pepe. I want you near me tonight. You must help me to drive this fear away."

Six

✠

CHARLES PIOCHER had left the Grimaux reception forty minutes before Selahettin departed, and he was waiting for her in the concealed room behind her fireplace. She had been driven to her door by General Koltrastt, who wished to ask about the future prospects of his grandson.

"A good night for you, love?" Piocher spoke in English with the sound lower-class accent of a British Army barracks.

"Rather, yes. Drayst asked me to bring his horoscope to his office next Saturday at two o'clock. Is that enough time for you?"

"Plenty of time."

"Did you have a good night?" Her accent was very North Foreland School and Girton College.

"Four trains full of plane parts will move through Strasbourg toward Nancy Thursday night, Dr. Egger Haus happened to say. Up they go. I also picked up a vague clue about Drayst. Very saucy, really."

"If you could see that man's palm—and I don't mean the one with the hole in it. It has every vicious mark a hand could have—including a broken lifeline turning sharply toward the thumb, which means violent death according to all the books they made me read before they sent me here."

"Did he buy your package?"

"Indeed, yes—though I did have a feeling I had gone too far when I told him his hands were replicas of Napoleon's."

"What did he say?"

"He merely sat up straighter and swallowed hard." Selahettin began to arrange books in stacks on the table in front of her. "You know, Drayst's horoscopes may be the slimiest I'll ever do. The man has a closed Trigon between Neptune, the Moon, and Uranus, and Venus is in his twelfth house in conjunction with Mars. That means very little libido but lots of mortido."

"So long as he's healthy."

"Oh, he's blooming. He's a devout pervert, Charles—I'm not sure what sort, but I suspect the criminal, hack-'em-up type. Pluto is very, very closely in conjunction with his Saturn. Pitilessness. He certainly would not stop at murder."

"Murder? He's a full colonel in the bloody SS. Some scoop."

"Oh, Charles, I mean for sexual expression."

"Lamb, for all we know they may recruit chaps like Drayst by their horror scopes. You'll want his file, I expect?"

"The entire file, please. And will you ask them to make me two handprints similar to these, but to print them as

167

halftones as though they were photographs taken from some old book? The prints should be of a hand of Socrates and a hand of Saul of Tarsus, with Drayst's markings on them. Also, they should check his fingerprints to see if he has a criminal record."

"Where would they get handprints like those?"

"I'm sure I don't know, Charles. They're the experts." She fitted a cigarette into a long holder. "Have them use De Gaulle's."

"Anything else?"

"No, thank you."

"If the weather holds I'll have it all back here Thursday night. Time enough for you?"

"Splendid."

"What do you know about a woman called Frau General von Rhode?"

"Not a thing."

"Can you run it down tomorrow?"

"Definitely. I have Claire Grimaux tomorrow. She'd tell anybody anything."

He shook his head in amazement. "If you could have seen what Drayst was saying to Frau General von Rhode . . ."

"Seen?"

"I read his lips. Bloody little libido, as you said, and an awful lot of bloody mortido."

"You see? There actually may be something to astrology," Selahettin said.

"I've got to find out more about him and her."

"I could use the flutter light on Saturday."

"You think he'll hold still?"

"Hah!"

"But surely he'll know you're using it to hypnotize him?"

"I shall tell him the flutter light is a psychic antenna for reaching the spirit world. When I let him know what it did for the Reichsfuehrer SS he'll go under like an anchor."

"That's it, then. Thank you, love. I must be off."

"Good night, Charles."

Piocher left through the sliding door on the far side of the room, and Selahettin pulled out a pad of blank zodiacal charts and began to lay down Drayst's horoscope. She was as bored as a midnight bookkeeper; she found fortunetelling very dull. She had given up her practice of psychiatry in 1939 when the faculty of the German university which had trained her had been sent off to an extermination camp. She had felt badly enough about it to ask a few discreet questions and, because she had attended the right schools, and because her father was a peer, she had been accepted by The Old Firm. Its people had taught her palmistry, astrology, numerology, and sand reading. She had been drilled and tricked and pushed very hard, because she was the first qualified candidate who seemed to fit the cover, and whatever they taught her she was able to enrich with a few dozen psychological ploys of her own. She had arrived in Paris from Munich, with Egyptian papers, in the fall of 1939, nine months before France fell and, despite the fact that she spoke abominable French, within fourteen months she was the rage of Paris. Of course, The Old Firm and her family did have a few splendid connections to start her off nicely.

Piocher went home across the river to the seventeenth arrondissement, where he lived with Fräulein Nortnung, Colonel Drayst's secretary. This love match had been arranged by the authorities on both sides. The Gestapo thought they had planted Fräulein Nortnung on Piocher, whom they wanted under surveillance at all times because he represented such a large source of income for various officers. The Old Firm, on the other hand, was delighted by the alliance because Fräulein Nortnung was quite soft in the head about Piocher and would procure anything he needed from Colonel Drayst's files. Aside from being a loving companion, Fräulein Nortnung was as strong as an ox, and after a day's work for the BdS she would hurry home to do Piocher's bookkeeping, count his cash, and answer the telephone. She had a very good head for business.

Piocher had a way with women. He was an average-looking man, but he'd always had his share of loving friends and took it for granted. He was sent to Paris in 1937 by The Old Firm because of his knowledge of the dialects of the French-Asiatic colonies. He had known the *nha-pha* since childhood; his grandfather had been prison governor at Poulo-Condore. He had entered France at Marseilles from Saigon and had reported to the police on his first day in France. His language facility to one side—though it was of considerable importance—Piocher had been chosen as the British agent for this assignment because he was a brutal man who had been a sergeant-major in the Irish Guards for twenty-one of his twenty-six years of army service. He was forty-one years old and he had been a hard soldier since he was fifteen.

Piocher's orders were clear and effective; as it turned out, The Old Firm knew as much about pimping as they did about astrology. Piocher was on detached duty from the British Army but remained on army pay to protect his pension rights. He was told to set himself up as a pimp in Montmartre and to handle the women exactly as he had handled troops. In a month he had twelve women working for him, though it had been necessary for him to murder two rival pimps to gain acceptance and respect in the *milieu*. When the Occupation broke up his business—because most of his women had left him to go south in 1940, driven by fear of the German invasion—his newer enterprises quickly established him with the Gestapo. Early in 1940, he had branched out into narcotics as a wholesaler. This provided him with capital, and when the Germans set official, artificial prices on all commodities, he had the cash to move in quickly and to establish himself in the black market, which had sprung up overnight.

Within weeks, soldiers of all ranks in the German Army, which had an endless source of supplies, plunged into the black market. But to make really big money meant weeding out the amateurs and small operators so that the fewest possible traders could operate at the wholesale level. The SS accomplished this with ruthless effectiveness, and in exchange for benefits of partnership it gave strong protection, sure transportation, and all necessary signed permits to purchase anything whatsoever. "Unapproved" traders were thrown into prison or sent off to labor camps. By November, 1940, the French wholesale black market had been largely stabilized.

Piocher's textile business alone grossed tens of millions of francs. His meat-and-grocery supply, because of the regularity and speed of his deliveries to restaurants, made a daily profit of seven hundred thousand francs. Since business was on a cash basis, and there was no safe place to keep that much money, Piocher had to buy buildings, paintings, and real estate, in addition to adding weekly to a small burlap sack of diamonds.

Communication between consumer and supplier was remarkable. There was no advertising nor telephoning; yet everyone seemed to know when and where and what could be bought, and at what price. Petrol would be exchanged for coffee, coffee for shoes, shoes for wine, and the wine barrels would go back to the vintner filled with bacon or potatoes. Tailors sold eggs; jewelers sold artichokes. Goods had to be carried in small parcels; a train full of people might bring three tons of corn into Paris.

Approximately twenty-seven percent of everything bought or sold at the wholesale level was funneled through Piocher, and he operated his businesses as he had been ordered to do —like any British sergeant-major. His effectiveness and enormous success gave him an entree to the highest levels of the command of the German Army, and unwittingly the SS provided him with information almost daily which, together with other snippets of information, aided the Allied military command, sabotaged the economy of the occupied territories, and frustrated long-range German plans.

Piocher punished short-weighters with relentless public beatings across the length of Les Halles, and disciplined and marked thieves by shredding their cheeks to ribbons with a knife. Openly he shot to death two men who had moved into his territory in Lille. He dominated all the black markets of Europe the way he had run armies, and he was as punitive with SS and Wehrmacht mistakes as he was with anyone else's. He was a sergeant-major in His Majesty's Army and there would be no nonsense from anyone.

By December, 1942, Piocher had amassed twelve million seven hundred thousand francs in cash, plus jewels, real estate, paintings, and miscellaneous property—all to the embarrassment of the British government. If he tried to discuss the matter with The Old Firm he was silenced. No one was ready to talk about what should be done with money like that. Just the thought of future intra-Ministry arguments over the disposition of the money made many people ill. Certainly Piocher knew it wasn't his money. His army base pay, twelve shillings a day, was piling up in London, and though his present scale of living was more that of an emperor than a sergeant-major, those shillings were more real to him than the bushels of thousand-franc notes in his bedroom.

Piocher left a message at the drop in the rue des Bourdonnais to be transmitted by his radio operator to London

171

sometime before dawn. Then he went home to Fräulein Nortnung, who threw off the blankets and wiggled her pink toes at him. Piocher's women would no more have asked where he had been than a green recruit would have asked a lieutenant-general where he had slept the night before.

"They are shipping too bloody much to Germany," Piocher said in a brisk shout, "and it's all coming out of my frigging pockets."

"Ja, Carlie," Fräulein Nortnung said.

"I want you up an hour early in the morning," he said, undressing with despatch. "We've got to get things organized."

"Ja, Carlie."

Piocher stood naked beside the bed and smiled down at her. "You've got nipples on you tonight like a pair of thumbs," he said affectionately. "Move over."

A Lysander aircraft brought the Drayst dossier and the handprints of Napoleon, Socrates, and St. Paul to a pasture near Fenton-Dormer on Tuesday night. The package was sent along to Paris at once in a bale of lettuce, and Piocher picked it up at Les Halles.

On Saturday, Selahettin was able to astound Colonel Drayst as they went over his horoscope together. She told him that it was so remarkable that she would do for him what she had done for the Reichsfuehrer SS. The Colonel was deeply grateful, though he had no idea what she meant.

Selahettin mounted the flutter light, with its spinning, gleaming aluminum disc, on the desk directly in front of Drayst and ordered him to stare into it and concentrate. She talked to him soothingly, and he went under in four minutes. When she brought him out of his trance she told him that the magnetic forces were unpropitious. They would try again in six months. They would see.

Selahettin met Piocher that night.

"He tried to rape her during the pogroms in Berlin in '38. She shot him. He is literally and clinically insane about her—that is my opinion as a psychiatrist, Charles. He has raped many Jewish girls and he has strangled three, but she is the most beautiful and desirable Jew he has ever seen, and also she is the wife of an old-line army general. The army makes him feel inferior, he says; the army is always looking down on the SS. She is the compensator. He says that he must have her, and while he has her he must kill her."

Seven

✠

HIS SUPERIORS at the Bendlerstrasse were relieved when Veelee's Jewish wife left him. His anxieties solved, he was now the model of a professional officer. Too driving perhaps, too silent, even dour, but the world was forcing Germany into war once again and a serious attitude was commendable.

Hansel had written twice to Paule in Paris, but he got no reply. Gretel wrote her sister-in-law eleven letters and Gisele five, but Paule did not reply. Once Hansel had mentioned Paule's name in Veelee's presence, but the savagery of von Rhode's response had silenced him instantly.

After the political meetings with the British, French, and Mussolini in 1938, Guderian had been made Commander in Chief of all Wehrmacht Mobile Forces. When he offered Veelee the post as Chief of the General Staff of the Sixteenth Army Corps, formed by the First, Third, Fourth and Fifth Panzer divisions and the Eighth Panzer brigade at Sagan, under the command of General Hoepner, Veelee accepted like a shot. The Sixteenth Corps was the first of its kind in the Wehrmacht and, the embryo of the future, mighty Panzerarmee.

In August, 1939, when war was declared, Veelee was transferred to the Tenth Army under General Walther von Reichenau. Reichenau, a Nazi, was the most political of the generals, and he seemed to feel the need to compensate for this in the eyes of the Officer Corps. His military behavior so resembled Errol Flynn in mid-film that everyone was slightly dazed. He swashbuckled as though he were following the orders of a general staff of lady novelists, and while neither Veelee nor most of his fellow officers approved, they were impressed by Reichenau's ability to become so operatically

Italian just because war had been declared. Once the man had even swum a river at the head of his troops.

During the Polish campaign—which made the eyes of all tank officers shine self-righteously after their nineteen-year fight with the mossbacks to employ mobile force—the Tenth attacked out of an area that reached from Kreuzberg to Gleiwitz in Upper Silesia. The Eighth was on its left flank and the Fourteenth on its right. Though the roads were bad, during the first days of the campaign they moved forward at an incredible rate of speed each day, and the hot summer dust lay around them in choking clouds. Then resistance stiffened momentarily. Veelee was awarded the Iron Cross, second and first class, for distinguished service in reinforcing and supplying an infantry battalion which had been cut off after capturing a village. The battalion had suffered heavy losses and was about to surrender when Veelee attacked with a rashly collected force of three tanks and one armored car after intercepting a radio message to the divisional staff. The division had replied that it would be impossible to send relief, but Veelee launched a cross-country raid and scattered the Polish force encircling the battalion. Of course Reichenau was pleased by this kind of initiative, and after awarding Veelee his decorations he sent him off to see the Fuehrer, who had stationed himself in the village of Praha to watch the siege of Warsaw.

Veelee found his Commander in Chief in a church tower, the command post of an artillery battalion, an instant before noon on September 22nd. As Keitel introduced him to the Fuehrer with cold disapproval, and as the Fuehrer began to shake his hand, the huge bells in the clocktower immediately overhead began to ring out the twelve strikes of the hour. Because speech was impossible, the two men were forced to freeze into a most unnatural tableau, each shaking the other's hand, each standing awkwardly bent forward as though life had stopped the instant they had touched, each smiling so broadly and showing so many teeth that after the seventh bong they appeared to be snarling at each other in an uncannily skillful taxidermist's display. At each new bong, each man would roll his eyes upward toward the bells imploringly, and the resounding *boinnnnggg* and *BONGGG* seemed to vibrate their bodies. At the moment of the last bong, just as the Fuehrer was about to greet and congratulate his brave officer, Keitel shoved between the two men a written message which announced that General von Fritsch had been killed in action at about ten o'clock that morning.

The Fuehrer was very pleased. "Good riddance," he said, and, diverted by the blessed silence and the refreshing news, he turned away from Veelee and walked to the railing of the tower to observe the progress of the siege once more. Veelee stared with horror at the back of the Fuehrer's head. He could not believe what he had heard. Fritsch was the army.

"Fritsch could never find the nerve to shoot himself," the Fuehrer chuckled, "so he probably stepped in front of a bullet during the attack. What a fool he was!" Veelee turned away. He was ashamed. As he stumbled down the spiral staircase from the tower he at last understood Paule's warnings. He had become the lickspittle of an Austrian *canaille*—he and the whole German Army.

The next morning, at five minutes to six, Veelee pistol-whipped an SS Sturmbannfuehrer in the main square of a Polish village. In front of an SS company of men and the people of the town, he knocked the man backward over the hood of a car which carried a banner with the rhymed slogan: *"Wir Ziehen Nach Polen Um Juden Zu Versohlen!"* Eleven men and women of the town lay face down on the street with the backs of their heads caved in. When the angry mumbling of the SS men behind him rose in volume Veelee turned and told the remaining officer to form them in a single rank. Then he walked slowly toward the line, standing at attention, eyes front, and as he came to them he took his glove off, picked up three stones and dropped them into the gauntlet. Working slowly and methodically, Colonel Wilhelm von Rhode, Junker auf Klein-Kusserow und Wusterwitz, slashed the face of each man in the line with forehand and backhand strikes of his loaded glove. When he reached the officer at the end of the line he shook the stones from his glove, put it on slowly and carefully, hawked from deep within his throat and spat into the officer's face. The line of men remained at attention except for one who fell to his knees and then toppled forward on his face.

In company with hundreds of other official army eyewitness reports on the conduct of the SS, Veelee filed a protest about this incident. Outrages ranged from rape to the official filming in color of the sacking and destruction of a Polish town and its people by gun, club, fire, and explosives—all presented with music and narration as the men of the town were told to lie down naked on top of one another, forming a huge pile of bodies while the women and the children of the village looked on and oil was poured over the pile and set on fire. Reports of such incidents came in from every sector to General Blaskowitz, the army commander and military governor at Krakow. Blaskowitz poured his distilled denunciations of the SS on Keitel, on the Reichsfuehrer SS, and upon the Fuehrer himself as mass murder succeeded hopeless disgrace, until, in March, 1940, the offended Fuehrer screamed at Keitel, "Make me rid of this reactionary!" The final, bitter protest from Blaskowitz concerned a minor Party official who, reeling drunk, had ordered a Polish prison to be opened and then had shot five whores to death and clubbed two others into fornicating with him in the open, mud-soft prison yard.

In January, 1940, Veelee was promoted to Major General and put in command of the Fifth Panzer Division of the Sixteenth Army Corps, which was composed of two tank divisions and one mechanized infantry division ready for battle in the west.

In the Belgian campaign Veelee was awarded a Knight's Cross—one of only eight thousand two hundred and thirty awarded in the six years of war waged by a force of ten million one hundred and three thousand Germans.

Parachutists had penetrated the upper galleries of the fort at Eben Emael but could make no further progress. On the morning of May 11, 1940, Veelee raced ahead of a vanguard of tanks and armored cars across the only two intact bridges to the north, surrounded the fortress, and led his men in hand-to-hand fighting through its underground tunnels until the twelve hundred Belgian defenders surrendered.

On September 2, 1940, Veelee became Chief of the General Staff of Reichenau's Sixth Army. His headquarters were in Normandy, ninety-one miles from Paris, and though he ordered a telephone installed in the apartment at Cours Albert I, he did not call. He had drawn within himself and he avoided other officers except in the line of duty. He corresponded with his sisters, with Hansel, and with his army sponsor, General Heinrich von Stuelpnagel. Once he dined with Miles-Meltzer in Bruges. Every week he wrote to Paul-Alain in German.

My dear Son:

 The war continues. The excitement of our sweep has ended, and now we must pay attention to the thousand details of daily routine to secure what we have won. You have had a unique view of this war, being a German who lives in Paris temporarily and who finds himself occupied, as it were, by his own people. I hope the telephone which I had installed in your flat is a convenience for your mother. I thought that it could be useful in the event that you needed me urgently.

 I am well, and I always keep busy. I would like to be able to see you and to play with you and your boats in the park, which you tell me about. I know that park very well. It is a beautiful park and since I want very much to have a picture of you and your boats, I am going to request that someone in military headquarters in Paris telephone your mother and arrange to have some photographs taken. Please look directly into the camera and smile or not, as it pleases you. Please greet your mother for me.

With love and devotion,
Your Father

Veelee's news of home came mostly through Hansel, who could easily pass such information through army channels from general to general. A super-specialist, Hansel was still at the Bendlerstrasse, where he belonged if things were to continue to prosper.

24 January 1941

My dear Willi:

 This time he is all out to bring down the upper classes, the intellectuals, the educated, and the cultivated. I don't understand how we could have fooled ourselves that he ever had any program beyond his hope for the destruction of the world. I heard him speak today—a bad carbon copy of his best work, I would say.

 We are groping onward here. We haven't had a soldier worth a damn to run things since Beck resigned, indignant and unbending. Keitel is completely incapable of understanding things and I have long since ceased to look to him for help. He might have risen as high as major with any other government in power, but with these unmentionables he is now Chief of the High Command of all the armed services. If I hear Brauchitsch say once more, "I am a soldier and it is my duty to obey," I shall send for my father's old dress sword and run him through.

Professor Dr. Ernest Gold, the only man since Wagner whose music soothes Hitler, tells me that the Fuehrer now takes his shoes off during arguments with Jodl and Warlimont and continually hurls them at the walls until his point has been made. This calls for considerable running around the room by the Fuehrer and the generals, and Gold feels that if rubber shoes were used the rebounds might be better.

Miles-Meltzer tells me that because one SS man was killed a week ago in the old city in Warsaw, five hundred Polish intellectuals were selected at random from lists of lawyers, teachers, doctors, writers, et cetera, and were murdered. The looting in Poland, judging by the Reichsmarschall alone, has been prodigious. Hans Frank and the SS do their level best to keep up with him, but of course it isn't possible.

Here is a joke: an indoctrination takes place in a half-filled sewer in Dusseldorf. "Who have we to thank for the night fighters?" The crowd answers, "Hermann Goering!" Then: "For the whole air force?" "Hermann Goering!" Then: "Upon whose orders did Hermann Goering do all this?" "On the orders of the Fuehrer!" "And where would we be if it were not for Hermann Goering and the Fuehrer?" "IN OUR BEDS???"

Gretel and Gisele are well. Gretel talks French in her sleep, and you may take it on good authority that very soon it will be even more dangerous to talk Russian.

Keep warm and sleep well,
Hansel

Veelee refused home leave. He was transferred to North Africa in April, 1941, and put in command of the Fifth Light Mobile Division, one of the two German armored divisions which made up Rommel's Afrika Korps.

General von Rhode was wounded for the first time in Africa, with second-degree burns of the waist and legs, when his tank was hit by an anti-tank shell. He was out of action

178

for forty-two days. In October, 1941, he was awarded the Order of St. Mauritius and St. Lazarus by the Italian government for preventing the capture of the entire staff of an Italian division by a British commando unit. Veelee shrugged the episode off as an accident. He had left the Italians' perimeter to hunt gazelle, and on his way back he had nearly blundered into the British transport hiding in a wadi near the camp. He killed the two soldiers left in charge, then destroyed one of the British cars with the guns of the other, and thus raised the alarm for the Italians to defend themselves from the surprise attack.

In January, 1942, General von Rhode was transferred to the command of the Twenty-first Panzer Division. He was en route to Rommel's headquarters for his orders when his car was attacked by three British dive bombers. The driver was killed instantly, and the car moving at more than seventy miles an hour, bucketed off the road into a stone kilometer marker which sent it high into the air. The crash severed Veelee's left arm above the elbow, crushed his ribs at the right side of his spine, and destroyed the sight of his right eye. He was flown unconscious to a rear-area hospital in Munich that night.

The series of operations on Veelee were completed on February 27, 1942. He had lost his left arm, the sight of his right eye, had suffered unascertainable brain damage, and the muscles of the right side of his face had been completely paralyzed.

Eight

✠

ADVERTISEMENTS normal for the spring of 1942 appeared in the newspapers of Paris.

You are eating less!
Strengthen yourself with QUINTONINE!

Workers! Leave now for Germany!
More Opportunities! Bigger Pay!

Lissac must not be confused with Isaac, that particularly Jewish name. No matter how many rumors you may hear, our house is completely exempt from Jewish elements. Shop Now!

Das Haus fuer Geschenke mit den gesten Namen
Pierre Auber, Frères

Juwelen—SCHMUCK—*Uhren*—BRILLANTEN—*Rubinen*

SECRETARY, *24, very loyal, not Jewish.*
Write Delamoindre, 36 rue de Nation.

ARYAN MAN *looks for job, veteran salesman.*
Vaudier, 51 rue Pavois-Leval.

MECHANICAL DENTISTS ARE URGENTLY REQUIRED IN GERMANY. ALL INQUIRIES MUST BE MADE TO GERMAN EMPLOYMENT BUREAU, 72 AVENUE DE SAXE, LYON. DO NOT DELAY. WRITE NOW!

In the winter of 1941-42 both men and women wore their hair long for warmth, and shoes were so old that people preferred to walk barefoot when it rained, or made new shoes out of wood. Women's shoulder lines were very square and the men's very sloping. The women wore high roll-neck sweaters, very short *plissé* skirts and, as compensation, elaborate hats trimmed with feathers and flowers. Men's suit material was so shoddy that jackets and trousers shrank to half-size after a shower.

Europe was on German time; when it was five P.M. by the sun in Paris, the clocks said it was seven P.M.

In the whole of France, all but seventy-nine motion-picture theatres were reserved for German armed forces. The most popular film shown was *Les Visiteurs du Soir*, which portrayed a feast in which eleven servants brought in immense silver platters of roast suckling pig, venison, peacock, and swan. Thanks in part to a severe lack of hard liquor and wine, the French became avid sport fans, some even going so far as to participate. Novels of espionage, stories of the war of 1914-18 and—because one of its heroes was called Israel—

Pilote de guerre by Saint-Exupéry, were among the thousands of books censored or forbidden.

The new rich and the officers of the Wehrmacht and SS went to Lapérouse, Tour d'Argent, Drouant, or Lucas-Carton. These restaurants served their clients the very best food because they paid a tax of ten percent to Secours National. At Lucas-Carton one was likely to dine next to uniformed Gestapo officers fresh from interrogations in the rue des Saussaies. At a time when the average monthly salary for a Frenchman was approximately three thousand francs, *asperges sauce hollandaise* cost fifty-five francs at Tour d'Argent. Fouquet's and Le Colisée seemed to attract German officers of the rank of colonel and upward. Black-market operators ate with them openly, cheek by jowl. At Chez Carrere, where it was made clear that the clientele did not wish to have to look at uniforms, Germans were forced to dress in civilian clothes or be cut cold.

Others ate differently as the Occupation went on:

ATTENTION
EATERS OF CATS!
CERTAIN PEOPLE HAVE NOT HESITATED
TO CAPTURE AND STEW CATS TO FEED
THEIR FAMILIES. THIS IS HIGHLY
DANGEROUS. CATS EAT RATS WHICH
CARRY THE MOST DANGEROUS GERMS
AND CAN BE FATALLY POISONOUS.
TAKE CARE!

Crows sold for ten francs, and the number of pigeons in the Place Pierre-Lafitte in Bordeaux dropped from five thousand to eighty-nine. Food was the universal obsession. Unoccupied France had no seeds, no sugar, no coal, and no grain; Occupied France had no wine, oil, or soap. Special cards entitling the holder to extra rations were issued to aid manual laborers; but the bureaucracy also included billiard-table manufacturers, but not the makers of umbrellas; canning workers at fish factories, but not those who canned vegetables; and those who made eyes for toy dolls, but not watchmakers. The production of food had been virtually halted; eighty thousand peasants had been killed and seven hundred thousand were prisoners of the Germans.

The Wehrmacht buying office employed over two hundred people to procure such shipments to Germany as ten tons of playing cards, one hundred and seventy-six tons of frying pans, and thirty-four tons of shoe polish. The simple purchase of cabbage created hostility from all of one's neighbors. There was not enough food, there was not enough room, and the pressure of everyday life generated unexpected antagonisms.

And yet never was so much money spent in France. Savings came out of woolen socks to be squandered. People who had never smoked bought cigarettes frantically in the black market; alcoholism increased even though liquor was ten times more expensive than before the war, and almost impossible to obtain. Women who had put away half a million francs after ten years of hard work were dressed by the best couturiers and went to theatres and restaurants where they had never been before. Dairy keepers and grocers were so fawned upon that they became arbiters of the public taste: they made or ruined plays, destroyed or established the reputations of restaurants. Everywhere shortages created status and catered to the worst in human behavior.

For the young in heart there were several dozen brothels that were better heated than the cinema palaces. Some had been there for a hundred years; others, newly established by the Wehrmacht, imported girls from German farms. There were bordellos for soldiers, for warrant officers, and for officers above field rank. At the Platzkommandatur fuer Gross-Paris in the Place de l'Opéra, a uniformed young lady at the information desk kept an official file of all brothels German soldiers were allowed to visit. By regulation, soldiers had to leave all brothels through the back door, where a German Army doctor administered an injection against VD. There were brothels for civilian workers, and special brothels for the tourists from all over the new Europe of which the favorite was the house with the double, gold-plated bathtub in the Chaussée d'Antin. There were houses which displayed placards in two languages forbidding Germans to enter at all. The tallest whorehouse was the nine-story building in the rue Chabanais which had reopened for business at three P.M. on the day of the arrival of the German Army in Paris. The most populated house was in the rue des Renaudes, near the Ternes. The girls at the Sphynx on the Boulevard Edgar-Quinet in Montparnasse were often paid by army generals in blank permits.

But there were also whores outside the *maisons closes*. These were the men who wrote the daily newspapers. Their hygiene was assured by the Presse-Gruppe of the Propaganda-Abteilung, and their abortions were performed either by the Kommandostab at the Hotel Majestic or by Dr. Goebbels' ministry far off in Berlin. Their lewd exhibitions were the daily press conferences at which the news was explained to all editors, and those books, films, personalities, and events best avoided were singled out. Interdiction was simplified by forbidding the publication of anything pertaining to Austria, Czechoslovakia, England, Poland, the United States, and Yugoslavia. Whenever the Propaganda-Abteilung suspected the strength of the management of a newspaper they took it over and published the journal themselves; at one point there were fifty-one such publications, with a total daily circulation of just over three million. Labor was shipped to the brutal labor camps in Germany by the hundreds of thousands. It is doubtful that any of them were comforted by the admonitions from his pulpit of the Bishop of Lisle, who urged France to submit willingly to forced labor in Germany, not so much as a patriotic duty but as a form of national penance and to hinder the spread of Communism.

Some intellectuals took comfort in recalling the absorption of the Franks by the Gauls. No doubt freedom was desirable, but would not freedom at this moment simply mean disorder? "What kind of a country is this?" asked Alfred Fabre-Luce, a Frenchman filled with the greatness of the Fuehrer. "With a constantly falling birth rate, with minds fuddled with drink, with an army which committed suicide, how could such a country stand up to Germany? Inexorably, Europe is coming into being—forever excluding England."

Nine

✠

WHEN ADMIRAL CANARIS came to see him in the rest hospital in Pomerania, Veelee could not have felt more surprise if Winston Churchill had strolled into the room. The Admiral was small and serious, and on that afternoon somewhat diffuse. They chatted about Hansel and about General Stuelpnagel, and then Canaris said, "Speaking of Stuelpnagel, I think I can anticipate your next assignment, General."

Veelee sat up even straighter.

"I've just been through to Paris," the Admiral continued, "and I must say that Stuelpnagel was very firm about having you on his staff."

"Me? He requested me? You are very good to tell me that, sir. Frankly—" He shrugged. "Well, I was sure I was about to be assigned to the Home Army."

"Germany needs your experience, General—and your traditions."

"What is the job, sir? They can hardly need a tank commander in Paris."

"Signals. A lively command."

Veelee's voice grew softer and happier. "My son is in Paris."

"Has it been a long time since you have seen him?"

"Four years. But he's only seven, so they are four big years."

"Well then, I envy you, General."

"My wife is there, too, but I have changed a little since they last saw me."

"Change is nothing. It is when life does not change that there must be concern."

"They'll get used to the arm easily enough," Veelee said with certainty. "I have already. But this face is something else again."

"There is a trick you might use."

"I'll take any ideas you have, sir."

"Remembering pictures of your father and grandfather, perhaps a monocle wouldn't be such a bad idea, you know."

"A monocle over a socket? I like that. Conspicuous waste. Real ostentation. I could prop it in there, even if the muscles don't work."

"It would add a glittering sort of a deception, really."

"It would, wouldn't it? And very old school."

There was a pause, and then Canaris said, "Von Stuelpnagel showed me your letter some time ago—the one about your meeting with the Fuehrer at Praha. Hope you don't mind."

"I was rather upset."

"It must have been a shocking moment for you."

"I hope the letter didn't embarrass you, sir. Officially, I mean."

"Not at all. I travel a bit, you know. Quite a few of our friends concur with your feelings."

"Then why hasn't anything been done?"

"It will be done."

Veelee took a deep breath. "I hope I may be included in such plans, whenever or wherever they may happen, sir, and may they happen the day after I walk out of here."

The little Admiral stood up. "Have faith," he said. Veelee started to rise, but the dizziness still came over him when he moved. "Here," the Admiral said, "I have just remembered something—the reason I am here today." As he smiled at Veelee in a winning and a conspirational manner, his hand went into his side pocket and came out again. "I just happen to have a monocle of Fritsch's."

Veelee was against the Fuehrer on what really amounted to social grounds. The propriety of the German Army had been offended by that vulgar and murderous man. His objections did not recognize the moral putrescence with which the Fuehrer had infected Germany, making it a stink of rotten death in the nostrils of the world; nor had he the knowledge to assess what the Fuehrer had done to destroy the country physically, its precious institutions, the minds of its youth and its capacity to grow taller and straighter. Veelee had not been trained to think at all, only to act in the framework of the German Army. Since the Fuehrer had offended that army, he must be punished and then preferably banished into death.

Neither Veelee, nor the Admiral, nor anyone else in the old-line German military establishment could ever have understood that they could never succeed in bringing the Fuehrer down because they were hunting him in the wrong dimension, in a wholly different forest.

Hansel was on home leave, and he came to see Veelee with the news that he had been taken out of the Bendlerstrasse and given an army corps in the center of the Eastern front.

"We might as well be led by a blind traffic policeman," he said as he settled down in an armchair in the hospital room. "Say! I like the effect of that monocle. I'd never guess that you have only one eye. You know, as one of my young men said, the Fuehrer has a superb grasp of military deployment and logistics up to the level of a regiment—well, perhaps a company. He certainly falters when he begins to play with a whole division, he is totally lost when it comes to directing the movements of a corps, and blacks out utterly when he tries to figure out what one does with an army. Therefore, if you consider that this pill-happy maniac is shuttling army *groups* in and out and back and forth, you may have some remote, shadowy idea of the havoc he is manufacturing and of the German blood he is pumping into the ground."

"Why hasn't he been shot?"

"What did you say?"

"Why hasn't he been arrested and shot? We happen to surround him with three army groups and a full reserve."

"There are plans, you know, Veelee. Is it entirely safe to talk here?"

Veelee nodded.

"Well, he's the luckiest swine you can imagine. Twice it was agreed that he should be killed on a fixed date, and twice he changed his plans at the last moment. Not only that—he looks us in the eye and says that he knows we will try to kill him and that changing his plans is what has kept him alive for so long."

"But even we must have a few fanatics!"

"On the whole . . . no."

"No one will drive into his bodyguard with a heavy tank and finish him?"

"Oh, of course," Hansel said, mildly and patiently. "The real problem is that we have no leaders. The field marshals keep saying they are bound to the Fuehrer by that oath of allegiance—which in most cases means they are merely frightened silly of him, because no reasonable man seeing the Fuehrer every day could take the oath seriously any longer. As for the others, they are like panicked horses in a burning barn. They want action, but each one wants to charge off in a different direction and there is no one leader strong enough to hold them in line." He shook his head sadly. "By God, if Seeckt were still here—"

"Seeckt! What of the young men—the majors, the colonels? To hell with the generals. Why don't the young men act?"

"It's our system, Veelee. They will act—I *know* they will act—but because of the chain of command they must be convinced that we have failed, that we cannot move. Time robbed us, you know. Beck could have taken charge of this execution, but he is sick and old now. Hammerstein is dead. And someone has to be in command, Veelee—that is the way we are. You know that."

"Tell them something from me, Hansel. I respectfully recommend that they assign a sound staff colonel to procure a tank and a crew. No more bother with decisions from field marshals. The tank will go through any building to find him and blow him into the sky. With three days of staff work and three minutes of action, we could all try to become sane again."

When Gretel and Gisele came to the hospital they burst into tears when they saw Veelee. He fumbled in the drawer of the night table and took out his monocle and waved it jauntily. "Belonged to von Fritsch," he said, fitting it carefully into the hollow of his face. "What you don't know," he said, "is that the edges of this thing have been covered with glue."

"You look exactly like Grandfather," Gisele said.

"Like Grandfather when Grandfather was laid out in his casket," Gretel said.

"They start me on the sun lamp tomorrow," he told them.

"I'll look like Baldur von Schirach before they're through with me."

"Oh, Veelee," Gisele said, "I hope not."

"This hospital smells worse than any I have ever been in," Gretel said.

"Just today, perhaps," Veelee said. "We are very full."

As they sat at the end of the bed he realized that they did not look well either. Their faces were sallow and puffy from too much starch and too little of anything else. Gisele had developed a tic at the left corner of her mouth which twitched incessantly. Miles-Meltzer had been killed in a bombing attack on Hamburg.

"You are being posted to Paris, Veelee?" Gretel asked.

He grinned. "You probably know my hotel." Only one side of his face moved with the grin, and he noticed that they both looked away for an instant. He would have to learn not to smile when he saw his son again.

"Hah!" Gretel said with delight. "I do—the Royal Monceau. You have a two-room apartment on the quiet, court side."

"Gretel, you know more about the army than Keitel."

"My God, Veelee, I hope so."

"Will you see Paule in Paris, Veelee?" Gisele asked.

"Of course he'll see Paule, you goose."

"I don't know," Veelee said.

"But you will want to see Paul-Alain?"

"Yes."

"When you see Paul-Alain you will have to see Paule. There is no other way."

"All right."

As the two sisters went down the hospital corridor they were depressed and silent. Not until they left the building did Gretel speak. "My God, he looks awful. Why didn't Hansel prepare us?"

"We saw him at a low point, Gretel. He'll get better from now on."

"Do you think I should write to Paule and prepare her?"

"Yes." Gisele sighed heavily. "If only she would answer. If only we knew that she got the letters."

"She was very sad."

"But you could write to her through Clotilde, as you always do."

"But should I this time? I suppose he will want to surprise her."

"Men are mad for surprises. Only men like surprises. To give them, not to get them."

They began the long walk to the train, in the hope that it would be running.

On April 2, 1942, Major-General Wilhelm von Rhode was named Nachrichtenfuehrer beim Militaerbefehlshaber in Frankreich, commander of the Signal Corps installation under Colonel-General Karl Heinrich von Stuelpnagel, Military Governor of France. He was responsible for all wireless and telephone communication in Occupied France, the courier service of the German forces in the country, the maintenance of permanent broadcasting installations and mobile transmitters, and the defense of all telephone lines against attacks from commando and resistance units. From the hospital Veelee had been routed to Paris through the Fuehrer's headquarters at Rastenburg, in East Prussia, for ten days under General Fellgiebel, whose command was then the most complicated communications center in the world. Veelee was still quite weak and most of the time he had great difficulty in concentrating, but his lifetime of soldiering, his monocle, and his frozen face carried him through.

Veelee had two offices. The first was at the Hôtel Majestic on the Avenue Kléber, in the headquarters of the Military Governor; the other was at the headquarters of the Commander of Gross-Paris, at the Hôtel Meurice in the rue de Rivoli. As usual, Gretel's information was impeccable, and he was assigned quiet rooms on the court side of the Royal Monceau.

Veelee walked past Cours Albert I on his first evening in Paris, but he did not telephone Paule until the third day, a Saturday morning. He had not heard her voice for five years.

When Clotilde answered the phone Veelee tried to disguise his voice; Clotilde was a weeper. "Mme. von Rhode, please."

"Who is calling, please?"

"This is the office of the Military Governor."

"General von Rhode! It is you! Oh, how good to hear your voice again, sir." Clotilde began to weep. "Frau General Heller wrote to me to say you would be here. Oh, when you see Paul-Alain! He is so handsome! And such a good boy.

Madame will be so happy—" There was a pause, and then he heard Paule's voice.

"Veelee?" Her voice trembled.

"Why can't my sister mind her own—"

"Never mind. It doesn't matter. Are you in Paris?"

"Yes."

"Please come now; Paul-Alain will be home from school in ten minutes."

"Thank you. That is very kind of you."

Veelee was perspiring heavily when he put the telephone down. He leaned back in his chair to rest, and then after a few minutes he walked slowly to the lavatory and washed his face carefully. He looked up slowly into the mirror and stared for a long time at his ruined face. Stiffly, he reached into the pocket of his tunic, removed the monocle and fixed it deeply into his right eye socket. The heavy gold leaves denoting his rank gleamed on the scarlet collar tabs of his gray tunic. The campaign ribbons across his left breast carried the emerald ribbon of the Italian Cross of St. Mauritius and St. Lazarus, two tabs of the Bronze Medal for wounds in action, four silver decorations for having been awarded the Iron Cross twice—both second and first class—in each World War, the gold and white of the Knight's Cross; and a tiny gold eagle on a royal-blue ribbon symbolizing twenty-five years of military service.

Veelee pulled on his black beret with its silver Death's Head pin as he re-entered the office, and an orderly held out his white silk scarf and his gray leather overcoat. A car was waiting for him in the porte-cochère. He patted the empty left sleeve of his coat and, sitting stiffly erect, told the driver where to go. The monocle glittered over his limp cheek and his chin was high.

Clotilde, Mme. Citron, the two chambermaids, M. Deboucoux-Piccolet, the *chef de cuisine*, the two scullery maids, Paule's personal maid, and Paule were all standing in the hall when Paul-Alain opened the front door to let his father in. Mme. Citron had pleaded that everyone be on hand to greet the General, and Paule had agreed because it would postpone for a moment longer that first instant when they had to be alone.

A very broad, tall, blond man stood in the door, his monocle glaring at them balefully.

"General von Rhode! Your arm!" Clotilde cried out. Paule

turned and rebuked her silently, then turned again, saw the right side of his face and walked to him and kissed him on the right cheek. "Welcome to France, my General," she said. She took his hand, led him forward, introduced him to the staff, thanked them, and dismissed them.

After a pause Paul-Alain asked about each one of his father's medals and decorations, and Veelee said, "I am going to take you to the park and tell you all about them," but he did not look at Paule.

"He must be back at one o'clock for lunch," Paule said.

"Will you be here for lunch, Papa?"

When Veelee did not answer, Paule said, "Of course your Papa will be here for lunch." Clotilde was lurking in the doorway, and Paule sent her to fetch Paul-Alain's hat and coat.

"What happened to your arm, Papa?"

"I left it in North Africa."

"In a battle?"

"I was riding in a car when a plane flew in and shot at the car, and we had a most spectacular smash-up."

"That is the same as a battle."

"The effect was quite the same," Veelee said as Clotilde returned with the boy's hat and coat.

To Paul-Alain's chagrin he was taken off to nap after lunch. Paule and Veelee sat on the south terrace. It was a rare April day for Paris, neither rainy nor cold. Paule spoke lightly of the weather, of her luck in having such a cook, and of how frantic the black market made their existence, and as she talked she mourned the changes in his face.

Just as unobtrusively, he mourned the changes which had come into hers. "Paul-Alain is a fine boy," he said finally, interrupting her. He spoke in German.

"He is a fine boy," she answered, in German.

"He behaves well and he is not silly."

"Oh, he can be quite silly."

"I am grateful to you for his attitude toward me. When I reread your last letter to me this morning, I began to fear all over again that you would not have been able to keep from infecting him with the bitterness you felt toward me."

"I feel no bitterness now, Veelee."

"That letter shocked me. I haven't seen anything in the

same way since the first time I read it. I—I couldn't comprehend what had happened—why you had changed and how you could change. It was sudden and cruel, because the letter of four days before had been the usual news-filled, loving letter. I didn't know what to do . . . I sent you a cablegram, but of course you didn't answer. Then, when I saw Miles-Meltzer seven months later he told me about that night and the bullet holes in the door and the terrible harm which had been done to you, but by that time I had settled so deeply into despair of you that I could not climb out again. I wanted to talk with you as we are talking now, but the war came and everything's changed, and now it's too late for what might have been."

"They are still killing Jews, Veelee. Only now it isn't just Jews—it's everybody. Are you doing anything about it?"

His head pounded. Her voice sounded very distant and then very close, and he was thinking of what they had lost.

"Do you have another man now, Paule?"

"Yes."

He had seated her to his left. At lunch she had noticed the care with which he had placed her, so that though his empty sleeve faced her, his slackened cheek could not be seen, and now she suddenly remembered him as he had looked ten years before, the morning her father had died.

He seemed to read her mind. "There are many worse off than I," he said. "On both sides. This sort of thing is a privilege of my profession. Your hair seems shorter."

"When I came back to Paris I had it cut short. The first year it was dyed blond."

"You thought you could make yourself over?"

"I suppose so, Veelee."

"And now the wounds from Germany are healed? Now you can permit yourself to look—"

"Not quite. But we do the best we can."

"And now you can relax about being a Jew again."

"Hardly. Paris is occupied by your countrymen, after all. They are killing Jews every day. I have lost all joy in being a Jew."

"It is not the obvious changes that matter, is it?" Veelee asked gently after a long silence. "My arm, my eye, my face —they are nothing. My profession is all I have. I don't look at it as only a practice of violence, as you must see it. It is an intricate trade involving many skills which are hard to learn."

"Such as obeying orders. Any orders whatsoever if they are issued by anyone above you."

"We all do what we have been taught, you know, Paule. Even your father, the freest of free souls, obeyed his training. But we were talking about loss. We live apart in another country, but that is not what breaks our hearts, is it? It is the loss of the innocence of what we had. And so it is with my profession. In the olden days of my family, it was a gallant profession and it required faith and honor. Now there is no faith and no honor. No arm, no eye, no face, no wife, no son, no place—all of it a waste, my dear. And waste is the greatest sin of all."

She stared at him sadly. "My profession, we might say, was to be your wife. I have been thinking about it for five years, and I suppose that any one of my father's wives might have happily exchanged my adversities for those my father gave them. I see that men must test women, as some women must test their men. My father tested them with his great weaknesses and you tested me with yours. As a German with faith and honor who could not dare to recognize what was happening to his country, you had to test me— and I failed you. I broke and ran, out of self-pity. I failed you."

"It was a privilege of your profession," he answered her, staring into her eyes. His voice shook and his hand grasped at the arm of the chair convulsively, and he stood up with an effort. "I must go now."

"Veelee, perhaps if we try—"

"Let's not add to the waste, my dear. You have this lover you speak of, and we have been talking, don't you see, about a different woman, and certainly, about a different man." He clicked his heels, made his military bow, and walked across the terrace, through the study, and out the door of the apartment.

Ten

✠

FRÄULEIN NORTNUNG, personal secretary to SS Colonel
Drayst, was feeling nervous because SS Captain Meisters and
his friend, SS Staff-Sergeant Heim, of the SD post at Lille,
had been executed that morning on the order of the Reichsfuehrer SS. Captain Meisters and Sergeant Heim had withheld
foreign currency, to the amount of four hundred thousand
reichsmarks, from the security funds entrusted to them, and
they had used the money to procure a life of luxury for
themselves and others. In so doing, the order for their execution had read, they had transformed a sacred public office into a private commercial enterprise. The executions
bothered Fräulein Nortnung because, with the help of
Charles Piocher, she had gradually developed a sort of ware-
housing business, which, though it might not have been legal,
was extremely profitable. In fact, she had already bought at
a bargain price through her brother-in-law, a very good Swiss
lawyer, a wonderful resort hotel in the Ticino canton of
Switzerland. But of course, she had never permitted her ware-
housing business to interfere with her work for the SS. After
all, in a certain sense the black market *was* her work. Certainly Colonel Drayst had enormous interests in the black
market. She also happened to represent unofficially Fräulein
Lorenz, a very sweet person and special secretary to the
Reichsfuehrer SS. The things she had to find and ship back
to the Prinz Albrechtstrasse could not exactly be done officially.

Yes, of course her case was different. Why, for one thing,
she only warehoused her own property. One warehouse had
furs—broadtails, sealskins, some sable and Persian lamb—
and it should all be very saleable merchandise because there
was going to be very little fuel in the coming winter. The
second warehouse had coffee, canned meats, tobacco, textiles,
leather goods, liquor, wine, and excellent confectionery.

Charles Piocher had found her a reliable and talented Jewish convict whom she had been able to have released in her custody because she was always doing favors for the Gestapo, and he managed both of the warehouses for her very honestly, because he was so scared of Carlie.

Fräulein Nortnung had sent three silver foxes and three blue foxes each to General Wolff and General Mueller as a token of her admiration for them and for the wonderful things they were doing. A cat could look at a king, she had said in her note to General Mueller, the head of the Gestapo, and his personal secretary had written her a very, very sweet thank you note, because General Mueller did not believe in signing anything himself. Sometimes she worried about employing a Jewish convict, but if Charles Piocher had found him it must be all right. They all took their hats off to Carlie.

Still, the execution of Captain Meisters and Sergeant Heim made her nervous, and when Captain Strasse came a little early for his ten-o'clock appointment with Colonel Drayst, she decided to ask him about it.

"Did you hear about the executions this morning, Captain Strasse?"

"I heard."

"Does that frighten you?"

"Why should it frighten me?"

"The night clubs."

"So?"

"It's illegal to do outside business, and besides, you employ Jews."

"Who says it is illegal? I run my night clubs on my own time. Who understands the taste of the German public in Paris as well as I do? I have Jews because they know their business, thus giving my German public greater value."

"But the executions—"

"Ach! They were killed because of some homosexual mess —the order was a cover-up. The Reichsfuehrer SS hates a scandal of any kind. He is a nut on honor—you know that. Besides, you are practically assigned to Paris to deal in the black market for the Reichsfuehrer SS alone, so why should he object if you happen to have two warehouses to store goods so that he can be served efficiently when he asks for something?"

"That's just what I was thinking."

"You hear from Fräulein Lorenz every day. What do they need today, for example?"

Fräulein Nortnung shuffled through the papers on the top of her desk. "She is so sweet, that Fräulein Lorenz. Today she would like a gym suit for the four-year-old godson of the Reichsfuehrer SS, and a swim suit for his fourteen-year-old daughter. The last one was too small—she must have a forty-two. They liked the Lodenstoff material very much, and she wants six hundred more yards of it for the Reichsfuehrer SS. He also needs some antique silverware, a dinner service for eighty, and can we find for Fräulein Bergquist, the beautiful Swedish journalist, a Bessarabian housemaid." She looked up. "Why Bessarabian, I wonder?"

"I am not sure, but I think there are no Jews in Bessarabia."

"Also, the Reichsfuehrer SS needs twelve dozen silver frames, postcard size, one foal-fur coat—Fräulein Lorenz adds, this is so cute, also, can you please send one of these along to me—then forty pounds of floor wax, sixty pounds of bacon, lard, and smoked meat in equal portions—and that's all for today." She sighed like a lunch whistle. "My God, think what the order every day from the Reichsmarschall must be!"

Captain Strasse shrugged. "So don't worry about executions this morning," he said. "That's war," he added.

Fräulein Nortnung's telephone buzzed, and she picked it up. "Yes, sir," she said and hung up. "He's ready for you now, Captain Strasse," she said. "And thank you very much for your reassurances."

"Heil Hitler!"

"Heil Hitler! Oh, Captain, one moment, please. Colonel Drayst asked me to type up this police card and give it to you to discuss with him."

Strasse was feeling more exhausted than ever, but freer and endlessly euphoric. Through a very good friend who was the nephew of Fräulein Manzialy, the Fuehrer's vegetarian cook at the Wolfsschanze, he had been able to buy a large supply of the special pills which Professor Morell prescribed for the Fuehrer to keep him so full of zest and optimism. The pills were absolutely wonderful, but it was necessary to take them without interruption because otherwise they left a person feeling desperate and almost suicidal, and suicide was the last thing he needed. He grinned happily to himself. He was in love with a beautiful girl who was as fascinated by the night-club business as he was. If he had searched the world he could not have found a girl more wonderful than Yoka, nor one more exactly suited to his future life. She was really a night person, Yoka; she wouldn't live any other way. She slept until six in the afternoon, lunched at nine, started work at eleven, finished at seven A.M. and went to bed at nine or ten. She was like an artist. There were so many restrictions in life, she said, that the least she could do to fight it was to refuse to live in the same way other people lived. What a wonderful girl!

The only flaw was his own schedule. His Gestapo work took so much time, and there was no way to duck it. As his extermination quota went up, the work became more demanding still, requiring his entire concentration from eight in the morning until six in the evening. He could not have kept going if it weren't for Professor Morell's pills. His eyes burned all the time.

He had never been in love before—mainly because no one had ever liked him. Yoka was crazy for him; she would do anything for him. She wouldn't even take presents from him —she just wanted to be with him. She was Dutch and therefore a good ice-skater, and she was a good cook and almost as good a housekeeper as a German. Also, she thought that all he did was run the eleven night clubs. She had never seen him in his uniform. She actually hated the Gestapo. She didn't like Germans, even—in fact, she hated Germans. She thought he was Danish, and she was crazy about the way he wore a beret. Well, what the hell, the war would be over soon and he could burn the God-damn uniform. She thought that he had to live with his dying mother, a sweet, little, sick old Danish lady.

Dr. Morell's pills sometimes gave Strasse long lapses of memory—not that he didn't feel well, just a little tired, but marvelous—and sometimes he wished he could take such a big dose of pills that he would lose his memory until the end of the war. Then he would take his discharge right here in Paris, and maybe he would have twenty night clubs by that time, and they could get married and he could finally get a little of the peace and love and comfort that he was entitled to.

He told her that when he wasn't with his mother he was lining up supplies for the clubs. She was ecstatic in her admiration for a man clever enough to own eleven night clubs. They represented everything wonderful to Yoka, just as they did to him. She had never known anyone in Holland who could afford to take her to a night club. Then, after the invasion, there were no night clubs and her parents were killed accidentally in some SS operation and she had come to Paris and gone right to work in Au Toujours Noël.

Strasse knew how she felt; in Luebeck he could never afford to go to night clubs either. Then, after he had gotten his commission with Section IV4b, he had gone to a night club in Berlin and it had changed his whole life. He couldn't really explain it; though he and Yoka had talked about it a lot. But people who might have been weak or mean or nothing at all during the day—people who might not, say, be very nice people really—could walk into a night club and snap their fingers at a waiter and assume a power and a presence. They had a *meaning* in a night club. They even looked cleaner. They looked up to themselves, and that was why he put so much emphasis on service, the most obsequious kind of service, in his clubs.

At least all these things had happened to Strasse when he had gone to that club in Berlin, and so when he was in charge of the interrogation of the fourth Jew the Gestapo had arrested in Paris, on the fifth day after his arrival in the city, and he heard the man admit that he owned a night club in Montmartre, the idea of actually owning a night club had almost exploded inside his head, and he had sent everybody else out of the room.

The man was bleeding from one ear because he had fallen off the high stool where they made him stand, naked, between the artificial drownings. He was a knobby, short, skinny man with blue skin.

"You want to get out of here?" Strasse had asked sympathetically.

"You have the wrong man." He had been saying that over and over again all morning. He was a Jew, and yet he kept saying they had the wrong man.

"That doesn't matter, sir," Strasse had said kindly, "we'll kill you anyway." That kind of talk was against regulations, but he wanted to make his point quickly and see this man's night club. "But if you want to get out to Switzerland or Spain, with real papers and no tricks, then just sign over your night club to me and away you go. I'll even give you five hundred francs."

The man pretended to be confused. "My night club? It's nothing. Chairs and tables in a loft, a few spotlights and a bandstand. No stock. What do you want it for?"

Strasse hadn't even listened to him. "What is the name of the club?"

"El Casino Latino."

What a name! The prisoner on the stool towered overhead, and Strasse reached up and took him by the testicles and squeezed very hard. The man screamed and swayed, and Strasse steadied him on the stool. "Do you want me to have that night club?" he asked. The man nodded. Strasse let go and said, "All right. Good. You can sit down now, sir. I'll go and make up some papers."

Maybe the Casino Latino wasn't much of a club, but it was his first, and he would make it great. He got his supplies through Piocher. Piocher made sure the price was right and even lent him the money to get started. Coal was procurable from the *luxe* hotels accommodating officers. These hotels had worked frantically to get the army business because it was one of the most fabulously profitable in the whole war. The German Army paid them full rates, and kept the hotels open and running when there was no other business to be had. More importantly, these hotels were given purchase-order permits for food, wine, liquor, paint, textiles, wood, and coal. Each hotel was able to buy from five to eight times as much as they needed, and they resold the excess on the black market. Next to such controllers of the black market as Piocher, the operators of the *luxe* hotels earned the great fortunes of the Occupation. When Strasse appeared in his Gestapo uniform to buy coal, the hotels were happy to deliver it at cost. Heated night clubs did all the business to be had in Paris; they were among the few places people could go to keep warm, and there was much more room than in the bordellos.

Strasse's other night clubs were acquired in the same manner—or rather by the same principle, because the method changed. Why wait for night-club owners to be arrested by chance? After assigning his French police to investigate the ownership of all night clubs, he inspected those owned by

Jews for their locations and potential capacity, and when he had made his choice he would have the owners brought in for interrogation. He was always meticulously fair. He had sent only one man to Auschwitz for extermination, and that was because the man had deliberately kicked him in the face with his knee when Strasse had grabbed him by the testicles. The others were given their freedom and exit papers—which of course they could always sell for a good price.

Strasse prided himself on being a fair man, and he was also proud of the strength of his hatred for Jews. He had only to remember the obscene, disgusting pictures of them in *Der Stuermer* to make himself sick. When he talked to Colonel Drayst he wished there was some way to measure how much he hated Jews, because he knew he himself hated them more than even Heydrich or Goering. Maybe he even hated them more than the Fuehrer himself. He had worked very hard to prove this point in Paris. It was a cushy assignment, and Eichmann had called him "you lucky dog." The only trouble was that he was exhausted. Yoka had so much passion for him that he thought she would burn the life out of him, and apart from that he had never been so busy at IV4b. Thank heaven for Professor Morell and the pills.

From the beginning Strasse organized his work carefully, going partly by the book and partly by his own intuition and his hatred. He had offered money and power to the French anti-Semites to set up an Institute for the Study of the Jewish Question and had installed it on the Boulevard Haussmann, in a substantial building he had requisitioned from a Jewish business. Once they were his lodgers, such Frenchmen as Captain Sézille and Darquier de Pellepoix became the most active campaigners for total extermination. In 1941 he had been able to persuade Pucheu, Minister for Home Affairs, to set up a special police department for Jewish problems called PQJ. In addition, he had guided the amateurs at the Propaganda-Staffel in setting up the Young Front Headquarters. This consisted of a hundred young toughs who were given a complete wardrobe of dark shirt, tie, boots, badge, beret, crossbelts, and trousers, and a comfortable clubhouse at 36 Avenue des Champs-Elysées. The lads were used to smash Jewish shops, beat up their owners and, in general, work hand-in-hand with another of his inspirations, the anti-Semitic newspaper, *Le Pilori*.

On the 23rd of June, 1942, the Reichsfuehrer SS had issued an order demanding the evacuation of all Jews in France at the earliest date. The greatest pressures were put upon Strasse. Thank heaven he had completed his model index, entirely cross-filed, of all Jews by alphabet, streets, professions, and nationality. He would be ready in two weeks. But there were so many details to oversee! He even had to straighten out the Commander General of the Army about the proper wording of the directives. The Wehrmacht now understood that they must not refer to transports as being sent "to the East." And the term "deportation" could not be used either, because it recalled the Tsar's infamous deportations to Siberia. In the future, the term would be "sent to do forced labor" and one hundred thousand Jews were the quota from France—with the French government paying for the transportation—and Strasse wanted them to go as quietly as possible. Because he did not want to interfere with the enlistment of genuine French forced labor, his directive to the army provided that in the future all deportations should be called "transplantations." The term was an inspiration; the Jews might even begin to feel secure, to send for their children under eighteen and go more quietly.

Strasse had gone over the disposition of the children carefully with Eichmann, and they had decided that as soon as possible convoys should be dispatched with a ratio of five hundred children to every seven hundred adults.

But every irritation was put in his way. The damned French police had been so negligent in carrying out his orders that a great number of Jews had been registered as Turks, Armenians, and Greeks, and as far as certain police were concerned, the law forbidding Jews to engage in trade seemed to exist only on paper. He even had reason to suspect that certain French police intentionally furnished Jews with opportunities to contravene the law. In his circular letter of the 26th of June to the French prefects of police, Strasse carefully outlined once more his directions for the transplantation of Jews, based on pre-grouping before departure so that each train must have at least one thousand Jews; and it was forbidden for transplantees to take anything with them except ration cards, wedding rings, and—as a sentimental gesture—pets. The railroad cars must be neat and clean on arrival in Poland, and a Jew in each car must be held responsible for this. All lists must be in quadruplicate, and Section IV4b must be notified by telephone at PASsy 54-18, or telegram, of the number of women in each transport, the name of the transport leader, and the nature and quality of the food included.

It was certainly bad luck, Strasse thought, that the greatest Jewish raids coincided with the arrival of hordes of furloughed soldiers as rich and wide-eyed as tourists. For the last ten days he had been getting along on two hours' sleep. Night clubs needed constant supervision, no doubt about it; there were a thousand details to such a profession. Recently he had discovered that his doorman at La Bonne Bouche was actually a leper, and the attendant of the ladies' room at La Petite Tahiti had been doing a brisk abortion business in Strasse's washroom until he had burst in on her in search of the cigarette girl whom he had just learned was selling narcotics to favorite customers.

And the whole problem of his clothes was crazy. He couldn't wear his uniform, partly because of Yoka and partly because the soldiers wouldn't have any fun if an SS officer was standing around. So he would work in his "Danish" civilian clothes, then go home with Yoka, undress, and later get dressed again, then go to his apartment to undress again and change into his uniform. Six times in and out of clothes was exhausting all by itself.

Strasse had organized the big razzias, the biggest raids of his career, to be handled entirely by the French police, under his supervision. It was a model plan and he was proud of it. Drayst had told him that it was a little masterpiece. Twenty-two thousand Jews, one-fifth of the number in Paris, were to be delivered for extermination to the designated Paris transit camps. They had been divided proportionally by arrondissement so that in the future they could be transplanted geographically. Berlin wanted three trains a week, thirteen a month, each carrying one thousand Jews from Paris to Poland. It was a terrible problem to get enough rolling stock, because of the bombings and sabotage. For each shipment he needed ten boxcars or cattle trucks into which one hundred and twenty transplantees could be packed for the sixty-hour journey (the trip usually killed eighteen to twenty-one per car en route).

It might be necessary for the Fuehrer himself to order

the Wehrmacht to release trains. Wherever possible, Strasse did his best to use trains from the Vichy zone, but the French were absolutely impossible about giving up trains. Razzias? Fine. Have all Jews been declared stateless the instant they crossed into the Reich? Fine. But when it came to taking their trains they were impossibly stubborn. He had been forced to take the matter all the way to Laval, who had agreed to release the trains, but only on the condition that Jewish children under sixteen years old from the unoccupied zone would be transplanted in the company of their parents. Fortunately, the question of children in the occupied zone did not interest Laval.

On arrest, the Jews were to be grouped together in the official hall of their arrondissement, then driven to the assembly point at the Vélodrome d'Hiver for removal to the transit camps at Drancy, Compiègne, Pithiviers and Beaune-la-Rolande. Searching for Jews took time, but if the techniques in Strasse's plan were followed one convoy a week could leave each camp, and he would be running four trains a month over his quota.

That morning, before going to Colonel Drayst's office for their ten-o'clock meeting, Strasse had been over the plan for the razzias with his twelve French police inspectors, good men all. Every Jew on every card must be sent to the Vélodrome. Where all the inhabitants of a flat or a house were arrested, the gas, electricity, and water must be turned off. Those pets not taken should be left with the concierge, the keys to the flat must be handed to the concierge or a neighbor, and these persons were to be held responsible for the property. On no account could children be permitted to be left with neighbors.

Strasse was particularly annoyed because the cards were producing Jews almost entirely from the lowest strata. Why had not Jews of high social standing been listed? Someone was making money out of this, he thundered. (He knew it was that Gestapo bastard Sperrena, who would let anyone loose if they paid him enough.) Then an argument had started about the children. He had stood up and beat both fists rhythmically upon the polished table top yelling, "Stop it! Stop it!" And then he'd had to leave the meeting for a few minutes while he took two of Professor Morell's pills. They worked instantly, and because he had felt about two feet taller when he returned, he had disposed of the matter

203

calmly and judiciously. The director of the prefecture and the general delegate of the French police wanted the Jewish children put in homes around Paris. But had they considered the cost in petrol, manpower, and time for such a notion? No, of course not. Naturally, Darquier de Pellepoix, the Vichy Commissar for Jewish Affairs, had agreed with him. Strasse made a counter-proposal: that "an effort be made" to see that the children were not separated from the parents, and that, when necessary, such children be sent to the transit camps at Pithiviers and Beaune-la-Rolande. The police inspectors had objected to this so violently that he could shut them up only by saying that it would be necessary to refer the entire matter to Berlin. But he knew what their decision would be. Kill old Jews and let young Jews grow? Were these people crazy?

Strasse told his inspectors that they must aim for a goal of twenty-five thousand transplantations from France to Poland by September 1st. He was counting on them, he said, and of course they all swore that it would be done.

Eleven

✠

SINCE THE EVENING of the Grimaux reception, over a year before, Colonel Drayst had been telephoning Madame von Rhode at random hours of the day and night to talk obscenely to her and to recapture some of the sense of power and sexuality he had felt as a young ensign at Kiel. This act gave him feelings which he had never been able to set down successfully in his diaries; the closest he had come to capturing its ecstasy was when he had gone deer hunting once: all of the possibilities to destroy with no possible chance of the destruction turning against himself. She never spoke to him, and within a few seconds she would hang up.

Drayst was in no hurry. The delay was exquisitely exciting. He wanted her only once; after that it would be too late for her or anyone else. But the time was getting much closer; attitudes were changing in France and they were changing him. More and more Jews were being interrogated, and when he knew that women were being questioned, he could not stay away. The war inside his head would start and lurch out of his control. When night came with its soothing darkness, he would change his clothes and go out to find them, to weep on their breasts and to beg them for love until he had to kill to keep his sanity. But they were only the symbols of Frau General von Rhode, who lived inside his skin.

It was ten o'clock; Strasse must be waiting outside. He called Fräulein Nortnung and told her to send him in. As the captain entered he held up the police card. "What's this for?" he asked.

God, what an oaf Strasse is, Drayst thought. "First, good morning. Sit down, relax. You work too hard." He was a desperate little murderer, Drayst thought as he smiled; Strasse must drive himself because if he ever stopped he would know what everyone else knows—that he is nothing.

"I'll sit, but I have no time to relax," Strasse said.

"About the card. Listen, Strasse, I want to ask you to do me a favor. A personal favor." Drayst knew that the only way he could get what he wanted from Strasse was to put a price on it.

"I am always happy to oblige," Strasse answered. "That is how life moves along. A favor for you, then a favor for me."

"The big razzias start next Thursday, is that correct?" Strasse nodded. "Well, as you will see, I have filled in a name on that card." Strasse looked down at it casually. "This is my favor, Strasse. You will think I am some kind of romantic milksop, I suppose, but what must be must be, et cetera."

"Romantic?"

"There is a certain lady."

Strasse snorted. He was having a few problems himself, after all.

"I cannot seem to make her know I exist," Drayst continued smoothly. "I want to arrange matters so that she must come to me for an excruciatingly important favor, so that when I grant the favor she will be very, very grateful. Do you follow me?"

Strasse grinned at him. "Drayst, you are a born general. I take my hat off to you and they take their pants off for you." He guffawed and slapped his thigh, then grew serious. "But how do I come into this intrigue?" The conversation put Strasse into high spirits because he needed three new toilets for his clubs, and Drayst had the requisitions for them.

Drayst cleared his throat. "The lady's husband is Stuelpnagel's Nachrichtenfuehrer."

Strasse whistled. "You're a very ambitious man. But I like that—screwing the wives of the army, the haughty bastards."

Drayst smiled. "The favor is that you place that card in your hand in the eighth-arrondissement file of the Jews chosen for Thursday's razzias, so that the police will pick up the lady's son and hold him for a while."

"But the army will swarm all over my police."

"No. The army has representatives at all your meetings, so they won't bother the police. They'll come straight to you, and all I ask you to do—and this is the favor I am asking, because you may feel that I am infringing on your territory —I want you to tell the army that the matter must be referred to me."

"Yes. That could be a serious infringement of my responsibilities."

"Think about it."

Strasse stared at Drayst steadily for a moment and then said, "I need three complete toilets with washstands, cabinets, urinals, tiled walls and floors, wiring—all with complete plumbing and labor—to be installed in three of my places."

"Consider it done. Just give all the details to Fräulein Nortnung."

"That's fine. That's very good. Only tell me one thing. How will you cope with a Prussian major-general whose son has been taken in a razzia?"

Drayst made a steeple with his fingers. "I have thought about that. I will not be here. The wife will be calling the General every half-hour to recover the boy, but when she hears that it is up to me, she will take over." He was not able to conceal a smile. "She will tell him she knew me in Berlin and that the army-SS feud makes things more difficult, and that they must get the boy back at any cost—anyway, she will do it the way women always do such things. Then she will call me—and I will be in."

"How will you handle her? Will you make a flat bargain for a lay before you give the boy back?"

"I don't know. First I must see what sort of a state she is in."

"Just remember that the boy won't be getting any special handling from these French police, believe me. I can't tell them that this whole business is just a gag to help a friend get laid."

"Ach, don't give it a thought. It will be an experience for him. Anyway, he is a Jew."

"Oh, he is a *Jew!* Why didn't you say so in the first place?"

Twelve

✠

VEELEE AND PAUL-ALAIN made an early start on Sunday. They had lunch out of a picnic hamper on a Bateau Mouche, then took a carriage ride through the Bois, because Paul-Alain liked to watch the soldiers salute his father. After the carriage ride they walked slowly back to the Royal Monceau and ate cake and lemon ice in the garden. Then Veelee changed into civilian clothes so he would not have to spend the rest of the day returning salutes, and they went to see a film on the Champs-Elysées.

When he said goodbye to Paul-Alain that evening, Veelee told him that he wouldn't be able to see him for more than a week because he was going on an inspection tour. Paule wasn't at home when they returned to Cours Albert I so she didn't hear this news, and Paul-Alain, being a busy and forgetful child, didn't remember to tell her.

Veelee left the following morning in a light plane from Le Bourget for a detailed inspection of the communications installations along the Atlantic Wall from southern Belgium to the Contentin peninsula. No posts were to be advised in advance of his arrival; he had decided to appear at each irregularly, so that his inspections could not be anticipated. His headquarters in Paris would know only where he had been the day before, but not where he could be reached on any given day.

On Wednesday afternoon, Miral's Luftwaffe driver took Paule's bags from her apartment to the car where Miral, waiting for her, was reading a long report from Dr. Schute. As often seems to happen to children on the occasions of their mothers' departures, Paul-Alain had gotten a stomach ache and been put to bed. Paule wavered between going and staying, but Clotilde and Mme. Citron reassured her. At last, Paule instructed them that if Paul-Alain wasn't better by the following afternoon Clotilde was to call Dr. Sebire. She told herself that she was being overcautious; as a matter of fact, Paul-Alain looked so well that she suspected he was teasing her.

Paule also reminded Clotilde that General von Rhode would be coming as usual on Thursday, the very next day, and again on Sunday, so that if there were any problems she could ask him then or even telephone him at the Royal Monceau or the Majestic. She herself would be back early on Monday morning. Clotilde quite understood everything, but still Paule hovered in the doorway explaining, more to convince herself than Clotilde, that this was her first vacation in ten years, that the sun might help her cough, and that she would be gone only for five days.

Still, her heart had sunk at the actual moment of leaving Paul-Alain; it was the first time that they had ever been separated. Finally she sighed and started toward the front door, still going over details with Clotilde. She did not know the address of this place they would be visiting and undoubtedly it would not have a working telephone, but since General von Rhode and the entire German Army were at Clotilde's disposal it wouldn't matter.

When Paule finally crossed the threshold, she stopped and turned back; clicking across the marble on her heels, beautiful and crisp in a new suit, she returned to Paul-Alain's room.

"I don't know how it happened," she said, "but I didn't kiss you goodbye."

"I thought of it," Paul-Alain said dreamily, "but the front door is such a long way off."

"You know I'd walk straight across France for a goodbye kiss from you," his mother replied, and she lifted him into her arms and held him, kissing him softly again and again.

The *Cie. du Métropolitain* bus, with a police driver, seventeen passengers, and four uniformed police guards stopped in front of the building at Cours Albert I at six-ten A.M. on Thursday morning. The sky was reflecting the soft morning light; it would be a clear, hot summer day. Two policemen got off the bus, a young one with acne and an older man with the eyes of one who had looked at his problems through a tall bottle the night before. He examined a card in his hand as they entered the building. When they had disappeared, a third policeman left the bus and paced up and down nervously. It was the ninth stop they had made since the razzias began at four A.M. "Take it easy, Grosjean," the driver said to him. "It's all in a day's work." Grosjean glared at him.

None of the seventeen passengers in the bus could communicate with each other or with the policemen, except in cases of parents and children. They were all foreign-born Jews who had fled to France for sanctuary and they were gabbling in German, Lithuanian, Italian, and Hungarian, and in dialects of some of those languages. Because they could not speak or understand French there had already been misunderstandings, and these promised to get worse as the day wore on.

Cours Albert I was stately in its elegance. It had once entertained Henri IV at a dinner party given by Nicolas Chabouille. Its plane trees filed along the river bank from the Pont des Invalides to the Pont de l'Alma.

Mme. Citron was startled and indignant when she opened the front door and found the two policemen. She wore a peignoir and her nightcap was askew on her head. "Are you drunk?" she said, thereby offending the older policeman. "Take your hand off that doorbell—there's a sick child here."

The older policeman looked at the card again. "Paul-Alain Rhode-Bernheim."

"What about him?"

"Is he here?"

"Of course he's here. Where else would he be?"

The young man with acne was peering past Mme. Citron at the magnificence of the apartment. The older one shrugged. "Bring him out, please," he said. Both men were feeling ill-tempered because they hated the duty, and because Grosjean —and his talk about principle—had been making it worse for them all morning.

"Bring him out? He is sick. He is a little boy eight years old."

Clotilde heard Mme. Citron as she came rapidly across the entrance hall in a flannel nightgown, without slippers. "What is it, Madame?" she asked.

"These *flicailles* have Paul-Alain confused with some criminal of the same name."

"Listen, Madame," the acned young man said. "Is he a Jew?"

"Yes."

"Then there is no mistake. This is a razzia for Jews."

"My God, his grandfather was Paul-Alain Bernheim!"

"Where was he born?" the young policeman asked.

"In Germany."

"Then get him out here, please. This is taking too much time."

"Please," Clotilde said. "He is a sick little boy. He has been awake most of the night with a fever. Please."

The young man shouldered his way between the two women. "All right, if you won't bring him out we'll take him out. We're only doing our rotten job."

"Where is the boy?" the older one said sharply to Mme. Citron.

"This boy's father is Major-General Wilhelm von Rhode of the General Staff of the Military Governor," Clotilde said angrily, but the older policeman looked at her sadly and said, "It's no use, dear. This is an SS operation. Now do you want to dress the boy or will we?"

Clotilde's eyes filled with tears. "We will dress him," she said firmly. She moved down to Paul-Alain's room, Mme. Citron trailing behind in bewilderment. The young man shouted after them to move quickly, please.

Clotilde asked Mme. Citron to get Paul-Alain ready while she called the General. She went to the telephone in the study, dialed the number of the Royal Monceau and asked for General von Rhode. He was not in. Well, when would he be in? The hotel did not have such information. When she called the Hôtel Majestic the number rang thirty-one times before anyone answered, and when she asked for General von Rhode the voice said that generals did not appear until eight-thirty at the earliest and hung up.

Clotilde ran along the hall to Paul-Alain's room. It still smelled of the paregoric she had given him for his stomach during the night, and she could hear his querulous voice from the bathroom. He was complaining about having been woken, but his voice was dull and apathetic.

"I'll dress him now, Madame," Clotilde said. "You go out and talk to them, please. Offer them a glass of wine and try to take their minds off him." Muttering, Mme. Citron left the bathroom as Clotilde knelt in front of Paul-Alain and nuzzled his soft cheek. "You are going to have a great adventure, Paul-Alain," she said.

"My stomach hurts. I feel dizzy, Clotilde."

"That's the way it is with soldiers and with generals. Often they don't feel well before a battle, but they must be brave all the same."

"A battle?" he asked dully.

She finished dressing him. "Like a battle. You will be playing prisoner-of-war." She wiped his face with a cold, damp cloth. His skin was hot and dry. "In war, these things happen," she said, large tears falling down her cheeks. "They always come for the men, you see, and that is why I cannot go with you. But it will be for only a short time, because the moment I tell your Papa he will land on their backs with both boots and they'll be sorry they ever did such a thing. You'll see."

"Will they let me lie down?"

She fought her tears and her fear and her panic at not being able to save Paul-Alain. She drew him to her tightly. "I know you will be a good boy, Paul-Alain, because you want to make your mother and father proud of you." She stood up and took his hand and they walked down the corridor.

The older policeman scrawled his name and number across a slip of paper, ripped the page off the pad and handed it to Clotilde as a receipt for the merchandise. Then he took Paul-Alain's hand, and in an instant they were gone.

"What are we going to do?" Mme. Citron asked over and over again. "What will we do?"

Clotilde ran to the door and raced into the hall to lean over the balustrade. "Please! Where are you taking him?" she yelled into the stairwell. "Where will he be?"

"None of your business!" the young cop shouted up at her in a fury of conscience. She ran back to the apartment and read the slip of paper. "They are from the commissariat in the rue Clément-Marot," she told Mme. Citron. "I can't read his name, but that is all General von Rhode will need to know."

"What did the General say when you told him?"

"I couldn't reach him. Not until eight-thirty."

"Two hours? Oh, Clotilde, Clotilde. His stomach was so hard and swollen."

Clotilde set her jaw. "I will go to the Hôtel Majestic and wait until he comes there," she said grimly. "That will be the quickest way. Such a little boy! My God, what is happening to France?"

The bus reached the Vélodrome d'Hiver at one twenty-three P.M. with ninety-one passengers. Paul-Alain was sitting on the long back seat between a large, brown man who spoke steadily to everyone in Csano, a Hungarian dialect of Bukovina near the Carpathians, and a despairing Italian woman who wept unceasingly. The air was foul and the summer sun pounded on the roof. The bus had been forced to move slowly, stopping frequently, and it seemed to wait longer and longer while the police assembled its cargo. Shortly before noon Agent Grosjean had ripped off his tunic and cap, flung them on the street and walked off cursing toward the Boulevard Haussmann.

Paul-Alain sat listlessly, battered by the strange sounds and smells all around him. He stared dreamily out of the window as the bus started and stopped, but he did not pay much attention because they did not seem to be going anywhere. Images of shimmering people in soft focus hovered around and above him. He sweated heavily.

At eight-thirty Clotilde approached the barricade guarding the military headquarters at Avenue Kléber. When an armed guard stopped her she said she worked for General von Rhode and that she brought an urgent message for him. He asked for her pass. She did not have a pass, she said, but it was a matter of life and death that she see General von Rhode. The guard said he could not admit her without a pass. Well, would he telephone from the sentry house so that General von Rhode could approve her admission? General von Rhode had not passed the checkpoint that morning, so there was no point in calling him. Then could she see General von Stuelpnagel? Did she have a pass? No, but it was an exceedingly urgent matter concerning General von Rhode's small son. The sentry was sorry, but she would have to have a pass. Would he call General von Stuelpnagel from the sentry house? That would not be possible. How could she reach either General? She must send a written request and the matter would be given fullest attention and a reply issued within five days.

Clotilde walked slowly toward the Etoile, tearing a small handkerchief into small pieces as she walked, staring at the Arc de Triomphe but not seeing it, and trying to decide what to do next. Finally she went to the post office behind the Hôtel Majestic and sent a telegram to General von Rhode, spelling it in German with difficulty. She paid for the telegram, then she walked home as quickly as possible, to wait beside the telephone.

The telegram was delivered to General von Rhode's office within an hour and the duty sergeant placed it on the thin pile on the secretary's bare desk. It remained there unopened, because the secretary had been given leave during the General's absence from Paris and all correspondence was being handled from the General's other office in the Hôtel Meurice.

The Vélodrome d'Hiver had opened in 1910, on the site of the old Galerie des Machines. It was built to be used for bicycle races, but in time, after the craze for six-day bicycle races had passed, the enclosed stadium was used for ice hockey and for political meetings. In 1931, it became the Palais des Sports, though no one referred to it by any other name but the Vélodrome d'Hiver until after the razzias. It had a capacity of twenty thousand people, who sat on stone steps as in an ancient amphitheatre. Since the Occupation the Vélodrome had stood idle, and its facilities had fallen into rusty disrepair. In the agreement to lease the premises to the Germans, the only restrictions the owners made was that no one wearing ordinary shoes be permitted to walk upon the banked board track. This obligation was strictly observed by the Germans who, in their thorough way, made a recording in French, which was to be broadcast over the public-address system whenever the danger threatened.

On the Thursday evening, July 16, 1942, of the first big razzia, when twelve thousand eight hundred and eighty-four Jews, including four thousand fifty-one children under fourteen years of age, most of whom could not understand French because they were refugees from seventeen different nations speaking forty-two dialects, were locked into the arena, the loudspeaker system went wild with outrage. Over and over again the same message poured down upon these bewildered people in a language few of them understood: *"Attention! Attention! Walking on the board track while wearing shoes is strictly forbidden. Attention! Those who walk upon the board track with shoes on will be immediately and severely punished!"* Police, who were extremely resentful of the assignment, were posted with leaded sticks all around the edge of the board track to beat back the people who doggedly kept walking on the boards with shoes.

The Gestapo checkers were more angry with the French police than the Jews when they discovered how miserably the French had failed to meet the minimum requirement of twenty-two thousand ordered by Berlin. Captain Strasse had actually been hoping for twenty-eight thousand. The Gestapo's handling of the Jews became more brutal as the evening wore on and an approximate yield of only thirteen thousand was confirmed, and they did everything but spit upon the police who had let them down.

That was the tactical dispute. A greater, strategic argument between Captain Strasse and the Vichy brass was raging in Strasse's office. The French wanted the children stored in orphanages around Paris. The Germans not only pointed out that there was inadequate space in segregated orphanages, but that they could not tolerate having other children contaminated by Jewish children. The argument was extended to Pierre Laval in Vichy and to SS Captain Dieter Wisliceny, Eichmann's aide in Berlin. The specter which clouded both sides of the argument was transport. When Wisliceny said that the problem had become overwhelming for Franz Novak, the transportation executive, Strasse asked maliciously if the razzias had come as a surprise to Novak. Suddenly Eichmann's voice bellowed into the telephone; Strasse was not to criticize Novak, who had accounted for more Jews than Strasse would in a lifetime. Novak was fighting Ley, the Wehrmacht, the Ministry of Transportation, the Ministry of Agriculture *and* the Reichsmarschall, who was diverting trains for loot which should be carrying Jews instead. If the interference and the criticism continued Eichmann said that he would ask that the matter be brought directly to the attention of the Fuehrer.

Strasse interrupted to ask for an official decision on the French objection to shipping children under sixteen years old to the extermination camps. Wisliceny's voice broke into the conversation to demand hotly how the French could take such a stand when only three weeks ago the Reichsfuehrer SS had honored France with the top priority for the elimination of their Jews only because the Vichy government's legislation had shown such insight into the Jewish problem.

Eichmann cut in again. "Strasse, I must be protected on this—a scandal could come out of this."

Wisliceny said he would like someone to explain to him the difference between a ten-year-old Jew and a forty-year-old Jew. Strasse said he would report the Vichy position as soon as possible. "Heil Hitler!" he shouted, and hung up.

Because they had taken their shoes off, the Quakers' assistance teams were permitted to move the very sick to the infield at the Vélodrome d'Hiver. Most of the internees had brought no food with them, and though the Secours National offered to feed them this was refused by the police until the end of the second day. The Red Cross was authorized to provide medical aid under special conditions. The sick could only be evacuated by permission of the doctor at the prefecture who had to be consulted in each individual case by telephone. When he was told that one child had caught scarlet fever and that two others had measles he replied that the symptoms of the diseases, as described to him, were not clear enough. As a result an epidemic of diphtheria, scarlet fever, and measles broke out in the packed arena.

Due to haste or oversight, the French police and the Gestapo had neglected to check on the water-supply system in the Vélodrome. After the twelve thousand eight hundred and eighty-four had been locked into the stadium, it was discovered that only one faucet worked. It was not until late Friday morning before the matter could be brought to the attention of anyone with the authority to send for a plumber. When the plumbers did arrive it was discovered that the supply of drinking water could not be increased. For the same reasons, there were only six working toilets available for the twelve thousand eight hundred and eighty-four people.

The internees were ordered to sit on the cold stone tiers all around the track. The others packed into a thick ring in the circle outside the board running track, and those who were clearly dying lay on rows of stretchers all over the infield. Paul-Alain, huddled behind a screen of men and women, had seated himself on the floor with his back to the wall in front of the first tier of seats of the arena. His fever was high; the shapes around him seemed to move in slow motion and soft focus, as through a steam of smells, and the inexorable sound of the strident warning from the loudspeakers, repeating over and over its message which pierced his ears and hammered at his nerve ends, produced steady physical pain. *"Attention! Attention! Walking on the board track while wearing shoes is strictly forbidden. Attention! Those who walk upon the board track with shoes on will be immediately and severely punished!"*

Because of the wall at his back, Paul-Alain was able to sleep fitfully. The thousands on the stone tiers had to work to sleep and work to stay awake. They fell over forward; they slumped unconsciously on their neighbors; they got cramps and exchanged body lice.

Only the most experienced among the perpetually persecuted had known enough to insist upon their right to bring food. The Gestapo had expected to move the internees out to the transit camps more quickly, but the argument between Berlin and Vichy was still raging. On Friday afternoon, at one-thirty P.M., the Quakers' teams were allowed to bring in food, but this was no more effective than the one water faucet; the prisoners, particularly the children, were so frantic with thirst that food didn't interest them at all.

On Thursday and Thursday night many of the children had been diverted by the novelty of their surroundings. They had made friends despite the language barriers and organized games in little communities in all parts of the arena. Little girls had made dolls' houses out of luggage or rolled a ball back and forth among friends, and the boys had played football with wadded newspapers. But by Friday the oppression had become too much even for the children. The plumbers

216

worked frantically, as perhaps they had never worked before, from two-thirty in the morning until one o'clock the next afternoon, but the pipes were either rotten or had been ripped out, and when they finished there was still only one faucet to quench the thirst of a long line of never fewer than eleven hundred parched and patient people who filled hats, shoes, and bottles to take back to their families, and then returned to stand in the line again. On Saturday morning, another water source was added when firemen connected a hose to a city hydrant and ran it into the arena. With only six toilets children and sick people could not wait, and small children could neither be washed nor changed.

Thirst in that airless auditorium was a worse pain than hunger and Paul-Alain's sense of heat was magnified by a rising fever. He dreamed of water, but he was aware that he was drinking in a dream and he would cry out and wake up wild-eyed. The sounds all around him had dropped below the level of language. A young policeman had to be clubbed into unconsciousness near the main door when he tried to shoot a Gestapo agent who said that one water tap was good enough for thirteen thousand Jews, and that it was even generous because, after all, they had been expecting twenty-two thousand. Hysterical, shouting, shrieking women walked up and down the stone tiers yelling the names of lost children, unable to ask anyone for help in Ivrit, Yiddish, Tagvy, Lithuanian, Ladino, Lamut, German, and Rumanian in this Babel of despair.

The dying began on Friday evening, at first from scarlet fever, advanced tuberculosis, and pneumonia. Thirty-two were dead by eleven P.M. Friday night, and the bodies lay in the heat for fourteen hours while the sun pounded upon the metal roof of the arena, and the body heat and the breathing of the living halved the available air. After Friday no guard would stay inside the place because of the heat and the stench and the terrible noises which burst from the throats and hearts of the thirteen thousand caged human animals.

The only illumination was a single work light which hung from the ceiling over the infield. The public-address system never ceased its mindless shouting: *"Attention! Attention! Walking on the board track while wearing shoes is strictly forbidden. Attention! Those who walk upon the board track with shoes on will be immediately and severely punished."*

217

One hundred and twenty-six children and adults had died by Saturday afternoon and thirty-one babies were born, alive and dead. The old people prayed over them.

Paul-Alain had departed into his memory. He was reliving those afternoons with his beautiful Mama in the Schlossgarten. He was riding in the open carriage through the Bois with his thrilling Papa, and hundreds and hundreds and hundreds and hundreds of soldiers were saluting. His hands never relaxed their tight grasp upon his lower stomach. His eyes could not have been seeing their surroundings any more because he was continually smiling.

On Saturday the police came in hasty force and herded over four thousand of the people out of the arena. But they refused to allow anybody under sixteen to leave because the matter of their disposition had not yet been settled. Mothers were brutally beaten with leaded batons when they tried to drag their children along with them. Approximately three thousand adults and all four thousand and fifty-one children were left behind in the Vélodrome. Most of the adults were the sick, the mad, and the aged. On Saturday evening the Red Cross was allowed to send in a team of six people, who spoke only German and French among them, to offer to take messages to the outside from the remaining internees. Fifteen volunteers from the Quakers and the Secours National were permitted to move among the heaps of people to look for the ill and, when they found them, to try to decide which ones most needed a doctor. After a horrified survey the three agencies protested to the police, who reported back to Strasse, who finally agreed to allow doctors to go in—providing they were Jewish doctors—because there were sixty-one cases of measles, one hundred and thirty cases of whooping cough, and one hundred and eighty-four cases of scarlet fever, and there was no way to isolate these cases. Late on Saturday night the Jewish doctors received an authorization to evacuate the most gravely ill, but the French police countermanded the order on Gestapo instructions.

While the children watched death after death on one side of them and birth after birth on the other, in the heat of a most arid hell, arrayed on stone shelves, lying among their bodily foulness, the great voice called down from heaven: *"Attention! Attention! Walking on the board track while wearing shoes is strictly forbidden. Attention! Those*

who walk upon the board track with shoes on will be imme-
diately and severely punished."

Paul-Alain was hemmed in by four sisters from Alsace, each one over seventy; by a huddle of eight unrelated children, three with scarlet fever, two with measles and two with whooping cough; and by two stout men in their fifties who sat, starkly mad, facing Paul-Alain, strapped by hand and foot to a heavy wheelbarrow and singing something tonelessly over and over again in a strange dialect. They saw nothing outside their minds, for they had been arrested in a mental hospital at Argenteuil.

The screen of bodies around Paul-Alain prevented the Quakers from finding him until two forty-five A.M., Monday. He had not eaten nor drunk since Thursday, his eyes shone like torches, his clothes were sodden with filth, his skin was red, burning hot and dry, and he whimpered fitfully as he slept clutching his right side.

The doctor knelt beside Paul-Alain for five minutes. "Scarlet fever," he said, looking up at the red-eyed Quaker woman with the crumpled face who had been working without sleep for three days, "and acute appendicitis. It may have burst. His temperature is forty point five and if the evacuation order does not come in an hour I will have to operate on him here." He stood up, lifting the boy, and they walked with him across the board track, each of them wearing shoes, to an empty spot under the dim, hanging light over the infield.

The Red Cross finally got word to its Swiss headquarters, which demanded that the French and Germans look upon the horror in their midst. The evacuation order was given by SS Colonel Drayst at three-ten A.M. on Monday.

Thirteen

✠

PAULE HAD HAD A GLORIOUS HOLIDAY. The weather had been marvelous and, as always, Miral had been a perfect companion. For the third time he had asked her to marry him. He was being recalled to Madrid, she was the only meaningful thing left in his life, and he would prefer to be married in Paris but would settle on a ceremony anywhere.

Paule loved Miral and because she was able to fulfill him, she loved him more. "If there weren't this war," she said as she lay in his arms, "I would marry you tonight."

"Why should the war change that? I'll take you and the boy out of the war." He kissed her temple. "Anywhere you say. Lima—is that far enough away? Buenos Aires?"

"I couldn't go anywhere without Paul-Alain, and Paul-Alain cannot leave Paris because his father has had a far, far worse time than even he knows. The greatest medicine for him is Paul-Alain. His son is what he lives for now." The conflict never left Paule's mind, because she had never been able to resolve it. "Everyone is waiting because of this war, darling. Millions of men are waiting to be civilians and I must wait to be a duchess."

He sighed.

They left the Loire valley at seven o'clock on Monday morning and Paule was back at the Cours Albert I at twenty minutes to ten. She was glowing with sunburn and euphoric with a successful love affair as she slipped her key into the lock and entered the apartment, bursting to see Paul-Alain again.

"MADAME!" Mme. Citron's scream sent Paule into rigidity in the doorway. From every corridor it seemed that footsteps and sobbing were racing toward her. Clotilde reached the entrance hall first, stopped short, and stared haggardly, her face swollen and the color of porridge, her hair uncombed. She was unable to speak, and Mme. Citron and the waitress and the two housemaids silently stood in the other doorways like corpses. Paule stared at each one in turn while a fear greater than any she had ever felt flooded her mind and stopped her heart. She wheeled again to Clotilde.

"What has happened to Paul-Alain?"

"They took him away."

"Who?"

"The police."

"When?"

"Thursday morning."

"Thursday? *Thursday* morning?"

"Yes."

"Where is he now?"

"I don't know, Madame. I don't know, I don't know, I don't know." Clotilde was weeping bitterly.

"But his father—?"

"The General is away. I tried and tried. I went to his hotel, I went to his office. I have telephoned, I have sent a telegram, but—"

"Oh, my God. Oh, my God."

"He was so sick when they took him, Madame," Mme. Citron moaned. "We tried to make them stop—"

"Sick?"

"His little stomach was hot and hard and swollen. He had a fever."

"Who took him? You must know that?" She still stood in the doorway.

"The police gave us a receipt," Clotilde said. "They were from the rue Clément-Marot."

"Did you go there?"

"No, madame, you see—"

"Clotilde, how could you not go there?"

"I told them who Paul-Alain's father was, Madame—"

"We told them who his grandfather was, Madame," Mme. Citron sobbed.

"And they said it was no use because this was the SS. There has been an enormous raid. They have taken thousands and thousands of Jews."

"Weren't they looking for me? Were they looking for me and they took him? Oh, my God, my God."

"No, Madame. They asked only for him, only for him."

"They had his name on a card," Mme. Citron said. "I answered the door and they looked at this card and they asked me for him."

Finally Paule moved. She ran into the main salon, took up the telephone and rattled the hook frantically. "Military Headquarters for France," she said. When the military operator answered she spoke in German in a loud, harsh, parade-ground voice. "This is Frau General von Rhode. Get me General Stuelpnagel. At once!" Waiting, she covered her eyes with her hand and whimpered and then fought for control of herself.

At last, the Military Governor came on the telephone and was greeting her warmly when she interrupted him. "My husband is not in Paris, as you know. I have been out of the city for four days, on a holiday. Yes. Thank you. On Thursday morning the SS had the police arrest my son. He is eight years old." She listened, then gave him her address. Her voice quavered, but she was able to control it. "Thank you. Thank you, General. I shall be waiting on the street in front of the building."

General von Stuelpnagel walked rapidly from his desk to the door of his office and flung it open. "Send a car to Frau General von Rhode and bring her here at once." He gave the address. "Then get me the BdS and send Ernst or Blanke in here on the double. Then send out an alarm to every communications post on the coast ordering General von Rhode to report to me at once." In pain, Stuelpnagel walked back to his desk. Rhode's father had been his great benefactor; Rhode was his friend and protégé, Rhode was the old army. They had killed Jews before his eyes, and they had laughed in his face when he had complained, but it had never come to this. Rhode had given his country almost everything—an arm, a wife, an eye, a face, and now a son who was a child. It had come to this.

The telephone rang. It was Drayst, the BdS.

"Drayst?"

"Good morning, my General."

"On Thursday morning the eight-year-old son of General von Rhode of my staff was taken by the French police in a Jewish raid. His absence was not discovered until a few moments ago. You have one hour to report that child's whereabouts to me or you will be shot." He slammed the telephone back into its cradle.

Blanke came into the room at a half-trot. "Yes, sir."

"General von Rhode's eight-year-old son was taken in the raids last Thursday. Who took him? Where? Where is he now? What is his condition?"

"Where did he live, sir?"

"Cours Albert I."

"Then he would have been taken by one of two of the three commissariats in the eighth arrondissement, sir—either from the rue Cambacérès or from Clément-Marot. In either case he would have been taken to the Vélodrome d'Hiver, the reception center from which the Jews were to have been redistributed to transit camps. However, there has been a disagreement between the French police and the Gestapo in the case of the children. All of the children are still at the Vélodrome d'Hiver."

The Commander's confidential clerk appeared in the doorway. "I have General von Rhode on the field telephone, sir," she said. Stuelpnagel sat down very slowly, wheeled in his chair and picked up the green telephone.

"Rhode?"

"Yes, sir."

"Where are you?"

"Veules-les-Roses, sir."

"Plane with you?"

"Yes, sir."

"Rhode, ten minutes ago your wife telephoned to say that the SS had taken your son—"

"I beg your pardon, sir?"

"Your wife will be in my office almost immediately. I suggest that you return to Paris at once, I shall send Blanke with her when we locate the boy, and Ernst will be standing by to escort you. I have nothing more to report now. Return to Paris immediately." He hung up.

When the confidential clerk ushered Paule in, Stuelpnagel put his arms around her, as a father would. "Now Germans know every shame," he said. Crisply, he turned to Blanke. "Herr Blanke is our specialist," he said. "He believes that he has located your son and he will take you to him now."

Blanke clicked his heels and made a short bow. "Does Madame have a picture of her son?" he asked.

"Yes. Why?"

"Over four thousand children were taken in the raids. Several photographs would be helpful in finding him."

"Four thousand children," General von Stuelpnagel said in a cracking voice. "That is how we make war now."

The staff car shrieked to a stop behind the GFP weapons carrier at the main entrance of the Vélodrome d'Hiver. Six soldiers and one sergeant leaped out, machine rifles at the ready. Blanke tried to help Paule out of the car, but she streaked past him and sprinted across the sidewalk. The military police raced in ahead of her and opened a hole through the two layers of policemen barring the door. Two soldiers pinned the French police to each wall with their rifles and the sergeant pulled open the front door. Paule darted across the short foyer and into the arena. Ten feet inside she stopped, threw back her head and screamed at the top of her lungs, staring with utter horror at the seven thousand internees, smelling the sweat, urine, and feces, smelling and staring at death.

"Jesus! Jesus! Jesus!" Blanke said, his head turning slowly as he tried to see everywhere at once. He pulled Paul-Alain's picture out of his pocket, and as Paule ran forward into the crowd of bodies laid out on stretchers in the infield, Blanke stumbled dazedly forward and began to look as systematically as possible among the crowd.

Veelee had felt almost healed in the dark places of his mind since he had come to Paris and had rediscovered Paul-Alain. The boy had nearly cleansed him of the killing he had done and seen. Lately his mind could retain the things which seemed far more real than the real world. Paul-Alain allowed him to think of the future.

In the hospital Veelee had been afraid that he had lost control of himself forever. He had wept helplessly at the sight of wounded men, and once he had become hysterical upon being introduced to a Colonel Poll, because the man's name sounded the same as Paule's. He had been badly frightened all during the journey to Paris, hardly able to control his conviction that the train was about to separate into its thousands of parts as it raced along the rails. At the Royal Monceau he had slept in a chair with a cocked pistol in his lap, because he had begun to imagine that he was those two British commandos in the desert, and he knew that Rhode was coming slowly over the rise to kill. Veelee had not been able to talk to anyone about these things because he knew that they would send him away from Paris and Paule and Paul-Alain. He had been as steady as steel when General von Stuelpnagel had received him, nodding affably and agreeing to everything, but he was not able to distinguish the words that the General was saying. Before his eyes, von Stuelpnagel's eyes had seemed to fill with tears, and since this was impossible Veelee was sure the war was getting to him.

Every night at six o'clock the General would saunter into Veelee's office and take him across the street to the officers' mess at the Hôtel Raphael and pour two whiskies into him.

Still, Veelee supposed he was doing his work well enough. It was the work of a senior officer in a rear-area command, and that had become instinctive to him years before. After seeing Paule again and noticing the scars and changes in her face he decided she had suffered more than he; he had only endured the mutilation of his body, whereas she had suffered the murder of her hope. They were lost to each other in a billowing cloud of smoke of loss and regret, but they still had what their love had produced, Paul-Alain, to keep them together until somehow all things could heal. Paule loved him still—even he could see that, he told himself— and he loved her more than ever before. His mind and his body were shapeless and purposeless and no longer of much use, but in time their loss would be healed by Paul-Alain.

His son. His Paul-Alain. The best of the goodness of both of them. What a fine boy. His father's friend—his own friend—von Stuelpnagel had given the boy a decoration ribbon he had found in his desk; he had pinned it under the boy's lapel with a great air of secrecy and then had beamed down at Paul-Alain because he was such a fine boy. But now Veelee was becoming confused again because he could not understand what the General had meant about the SS. Were they starting that Youth Movement nonsense in France? Had they taken the boy to some youth camp? Not that it would hurt him—outdoors all the time, cold showers, plain food.

The car was on the main road to Paris from Le Bourget. Ahead of them, coming from Paris, a convoy of trucks was turning off, and as they passed he could see that the trucks were jammed with civilians.

"What's all this?" he asked the driver.

"There have been very big Jewish raids, sir," the driver said. "I think this convoy is taking them to the transit camp at Drancy about a half-mile up that side road."

"Poor devils."

"Pardon, sir?"

"I said it's a rotten way to fight a war."

"Yes, sir."

Veelee reached the Hôtel Majestic at twelve-thirty P.M. to find Stuelpnagel waiting. He was very pale and his square jaw was held firmly outthrust. "The BdS has located the boy," he said immediately.

"Located?" A strange choice of word—one doesn't locate a pupil in a classroom or a boy in a youth camp.

"Rhode, I—"

"What is happening, sir?"

"A car is waiting to take you to fetch your wife so that both of you can—"

"But what has happened to Paul-Alain?" The General saw that Veelee had not yet comprehended what the SS had done. "Rhode, something terrible has happened," he said slowly. "Your son was taken in the widespread Jewish raids which began last Thursday."

"A *Jewish* raid? My boy?"

"We thought he would be found at the Vélodrome d'Hiver, where your wife is now. But early this morning he was removed to the transit camp at Drancy because he has become ill."

Veelee turned away from him and ran for the door. "Rhode, wait!" the General said loudly. "There is no way for me to reach your wife at the Vélodrome. Pick her up and then go to Drancy. Ernst will see to it that you get the boy out instantly, but he'll need his mother—his mother must be there."

As Veelee ran out of the room the horizon inside his head began to tilt again. The long corridor offered blank patches in his vision, and he walked unsteadily to the lift repeating his son's name over and over again within his head. As he came down the steps Ernst took him by the elbow and guided him into the car. He fell as he was getting into the seat, but he pulled himself up at once as Ernst got in beside him and the car roared out into the Avenue Kléber.

Ernst found Blanke and Blanke found Paule. Veelee stood on the board track under the barrage of sound from the loudspeakers, staring dazedly at the carnage all around him. Peering through the murk, he was unable to decide whether he was looking for Paule or Paul-Alain. "Sergeant!" he yelled, and the sergeant who had accompanied Paule came running up.

"Sir!"

"Bring the police officer in charge to me."

"Yes, sir."

Blanke found Paule high up on the stone tiers. Her dress had been soiled where she had vomited, and she was weeping silently and breathing in great shuddering gasps from the exertion of moving up row upon row of the stone steps shouting Paul-Alain's name. She had talked to people in the five languages she knew and showed them Paul-Alain's picture, but they had either stared back at her in bewilderment or had begged her for water.

"We have located the boy, Frau General," Blanke said.

"Thank you, Herr Blanke. Where is he? Take me to him, please."

"He has been moved to Drancy."

"To the transit camp? My God, then we must go. What if they should ship him? What can we do if they ship him before we get there?"

She began to pick her way down the tiers of stone. Blanke overtook her and went ahead of her so that she could support herself on his shoulder as they descended. "Your husband is here," she heard him say, and as she looked down she saw Veelee standing on the board track towering over the police and the soldiers around him, his gray-white hair gleaming like a helmet, immaculate in his black uniform and boots, his left sleeve pinned neatly back, the monocle fixed in his eye. When she came close she saw that his single eye was wild and his face frantic to overtake what he was aware that everyone but him clearly knew. He put his arm around her and she clung to him. "My mind doesn't take this in at all," he said into her ear. "It comes, but then it slips away. It's Paul-Alain, isn't it? But Paul-Alain in such a place as this?"

"He isn't here, my dear," she said. "Come with me. We will find him now." She took him by the hand and led him toward the exit as the loudspeakers screamed, *Attention! Attention! Walking on the board track while wearing shoes is strictly forbidden. Attention! Those who walk upon the board track with shoes on will be immediately and severely punished.*

Suddenly the GFP sergeant stood in front of Veelee. He was holding a gun in the back of a police officer. "The police commander, sir," the sergeant said.

"What about him?"

"You sent for him, sir."

"Ah? Oh, yes." He turned to the police officer. "Turn off that recording," he ordered.

"I cannot," the policeman said. "That record is playing on Gestapo orders."

"Sergeant."

"Sir!"

"Issue axes to your men and destroy this running track."

"Yes, sir." The sergeant saluted as Veelee strode away and got into the waiting car beside Paule.

Drancy, the transit camp from which Jews were shipped to the extermination camps in Poland, sat on a plateau in the northeastern section of Paris. Around it were vacant lots littered with rubbish and a few low cottages and high-chimneyed factories. The camp itself, a mass of dark bulky buildings, took the overall shape of a large horseshoe, and covered approximately eighteen acres. Originally intended to be used as workers' flats, each building had four floors and a staircase whose landings opened into single large rooms which had been designed for twelve beds and into which either sixty adults or one hundred children were now crammed. They slept on planks covered with straw; in the winter, the police tried to steal the planks for firewood. Male internees were separated from female, and then the groups were sorted by the French Physiognomical Police. This was a special squad composed of experts who could spot Jews on sight without needing to check their papers, and could even separate them into social ranks.

The camp's black market, which was controlled by the police, was necessary for survival because each inmate's daily ration was two ladles of soup, a quarter of a pound of bread, and two Jerusalem artichokes. For a price, food parcels could be sent in from the outside for people who could not help getting hungry while they waited to be shipped off to be gassed to death.

The camp was guarded and administered by the French, and the commanding officer was an officer in the French army. The Germans dealt only with such exceptional matters as deportations and hostages, and the internal organization of the camp was left to the prisoners. For three years there were never fewer that five thousand Jews at Drancy; it was a small eddy in which they paused briefly before being whirled off centrifugally into the extermination camps.

Paule and Veelee found Paul-Alain on the second floor of a room in Drancy's great horseshoe, off the landing of *Escalier Zazous.* There were ninety-three other sick and

228

dying children in the room, covered with lice and scabies and sleeping fitfully on urine-soaked straw. Paul-Alain opened his eyes as his mother and father knelt on either side of him, gave a cry of joy, and smiled. As Paule bent over him, murmuring her love for him, he managed to touch her cheek lightly with his hand. Then his hand slipped downward and clutched the lapel of her suit. As it slipped off and fell to the straw, he died.

Fourteen

✠

FRÄULEIN NORTNUNG, as naked as a coin and blonder than beer, her long hair woven in a tightly plaited *schnecken* coiled around her ears, was rubbing her splendid Nordic bosom with a rough towel. The towel felt good but it didn't compare with the way Carlie could use a towel. When she compared Carlie to the men she had left at home, they seemed to have been carved out of liverwurst. She slipped into a pair of white pom-pom mules from Carlie's Marseilles warehouse and, as fine a figure of summertime womanhood as any conceived by Rubens, thundered into the salon of the flat.

It was hardly a typical apartment of the period. Three one-hundred-pound bags of coffee beans took up one corner of the salon; a bundle of new currency notes amounting to six hundred and twelve thousand francs were stacked on a bookshelf under a copy of the memoirs of François Paul de Gondi de Cardinal Retz, for which a general in the Luftwaffe Ground Supply Office had said he would pay extremely well because it was the perfect birthday remembrance for the Reichsmarschall. Along the wall, woolen blankets had been stacked five feet high. Three dozen tins of butter were on the low table in front of the sofa, and on the desk were piled eleven pads of signed Wehrmacht purchase authorizations. The far wall was lined with cartons of Players and Gauloise, amounting to perhaps sixty thousand cigarettes.

Piocher was snarling French gutter argot into the telephone, telling someone that he did not want any advice on what to buy and at what price. How the hell should he know why there was a sudden market for mutton? He didn't care either—get the mutton.

As Piocher hung up, he looked at the spectacularly naked Fräulein Nortnung and smiled at her encouragingly with his atrocious teeth. "I like your hair up like that, *puppchen*."

"It is only for the bath this way, Carlie."

"No more. Keep it up. I like it that way."

"Ja, Carlie."

"What a beautiful ass you have."

She tossed a cushion at him in playful appreciation; had it hit him, he would have been knocked off his chair.

"Well, what was new at the office today?"

The happiness faded from her face and was replaced by an extremely complicated expression of indignation. "What happened today I think I could never believe if I had not been there taking notes on the extension phone so that Colonel Drayst can have his own record if there is a wire tap on us and they try to say we said something else."

"Really? What happened?"

"General von Stuelpnagel, the Military Governor for France, himself called Colonel Drayst. Wehrmacht from the top of his head to his feet. He said straight out, no preliminaries, that Colonel Drayst had one hour to deliver this information or he would be shot. Shot! The BdS!"

"Well!"

"The idea of the Wehrmacht talking to the SS that way. Listen, if Colonel Drayst wanted to he could have General von Stuelpnagel shot. And maybe he will be shot—the Colonel sent that threat straight off to the Reichsfuehrer SS so that he could know which way the winds are blowing here."

"Oh, come off it, *liebchen*."

"It's a matter of SS honor, isn't it? And General von Stuelpnagel is no favorite of the Fuehrer's—everybody knows that."

"Your Occupation would be in some mess if a colonel-general couldn't threaten a lousy colonel."

"About a Jew?"

"What d'you mean, about a Jew?"

"It was a ridiculous thing. He said he would have the BdS shot because of a Jew—not even a grown Jew, a child."

230

"What child?"

"All right, I'll tell you from the beginning. Because up to the time General von Stuelpnagel told Colonel Drayst that he would have him shot, Colonel Drayst felt very sad—personally sad. Over only a Jew. It was a mistake. Believe me, I can tell you he had nothing against the child."

"Whose child?"

"The little son of General von Rhode."

"The Nachrichtenfuehrer?"

"Yes."

"His child is a Jew?"

"The wife is a Jew."

"What happened?"

"The son was picked up in the razzias last week."

"A general's child? The child of a hero like von Rhode? That was naughty. Maybe Colonel Drayst felt personally sad because he knows how the Fuehrer uses war heros in his business. Come here. Don't sit in that draught over there."

"There is no draught, Carlie."

"Come here."

"Oh, Carlie, it is so hot for what you want." She leaped like a hippopotamus and lay down with her head in his lap. "You know, Carlie? You are the only man who never says it's too hot to do it in the summer. Actually, the summers are much cooler in Germany."

He kneaded her right breast as though preparing dough for the oven. "How did Colonel Drayst happen to have a general's child included in a razzia?"

"The BdS is only human."

"Is that so?"

"Don't tease. He is so terribly in love with Frau General von Rhode, a Jew yet, that he can't bear it that she won't have anything to do with him."

"Ah. Pity."

"Yes. So he was destroying himself to think of some way he could make her change her mind. Then he decided that if he could rescue her little son from the razzias she would be so grateful that . . . you know."

"What happened?"

"Well, everything went wrong. The boy was in that place for four days before the parents found out. Evidently they were out of town or something. Then, instead of going through channels, they went to General von Stuelpnagel."

"They got their son back?"

"Oh, they got him back all right. We were able to trace him. We found him for them. But in the meantime he got sick and he died."

"Ah."

"Yes. A terrible thing."

"How old was he?"

"Seven or eight, I think."

Piocher disengaged himself from Fräulein Nortnung in a manner reminiscent of a driver getting out from under an overturned truck. He walked to the large center table, lit a cigarette and chucked on his jacket.

"Where are you going, Carlie?"

"Out."

"But it was so nice, what you were doing."

"Go to bed and get some rest. I'll be back in an hour or two." She pouted as Piocher left the apartment.

Selahettin was in the room behind the hidden door, two pencils stuck in her hair, her left hand gripping her forehead as she pored over the horoscope forms to conform them with the dossiers flown in from London. She was too absorbed to speak, so Piocher sat down quietly, put his feet up on a chair, and picked his teeth absent-mindedly.

After a few minutes Selahettin closed the pad with a slap. "My predictions get wilder every day, Jock. Not that my clients seem to think so."

"Our predictions may be wild, love, but they'll all come true the day the invasion starts."

"Can you have someone send me a case of Jameson's?"

"First thing in the morning." He took a black notebook out of his pocket and made a careful note. "Who goes back to London next?"

"Gant. Tomorrow night, weather permitting."

"I don't want any radio signals on this one, love. Lace it up in the best code and ask Gant to take it home with him. Your client, Drayst, has caused the death of the only child of Major-General Wilhelm von Rhode."

She grunted. He told her what he knew, and though she tried not to show that she was affected, her hands trembled as she lit a cigarette. "That's one of the worst so far, I think," she said judiciously.

"It can be a fine thing for us, love. Could be worth a hundred bombers, this."

"How?"

"Let them tell me from London. But suppose you were the mother of that little boy and I came to you and told you I knew the name of the man who had ordered the death of your only child. What would you do?"

"It wouldn't bring the boy back, Jock."

"Ah, we know that, love."

She ran her thin hand through her hair. "I'm a spinster, Jock, and too gently raised to answer that as it should be answered."

"But what do you think you'd do, love?"

"I would ask for his eyes under my heel," she answered sadly. "And I'd want to see his heart steaming in a gutter."

"That's what I thought. That's what I'd do. And that's what she and her husband will do when the proper time comes."

"When?"

"Send the news to London, love. They'll tell us when."

Fifteen

✠

IN THE SIXTEEN MONTHS that Paule remained alone at Cours Albert I she mourned the loss of her son, but as time evolved her grief for him diminished to make room for anxiety about her husband. Worry for the living lifted her out of the shadows of the life she had arranged for herself. She continued to work on the biography of her father, but with the difference that it became a tribute and an occupation rather than a refuge. She dressed herself again and studied herself in her mirror carefully, for she was convinced that she and Veelee would be together again soon.

She knew now that she would always love Veelee, and she accepted the fact joyfully because it counterbalanced the hatred which had almost capsized her. It was a strong, green, growing hate; if it had been vines it would have covered all of Germany and paralyzed all Germans, crushing the life out of them slowly and agonizingly.

Paule had spent the first months alone in the Cours Albert I, dressed only in a negligee and wandering from her bedroom to her study to lose herself in the work. She had sent all the servants away because of what all of them had not done to find Paul-Alain or to bring her running back to Paris to save him. She had spent the months thinking of how she might kill the children of all the Germans, how she might somehow pour her molten grief upon them as they had upon her. Time had passed, sixteen months had passed, but still she hated. She had narrowed her hope of retaliation down to the policeman who had signed that receipt for the living body of her son, and now she spent all her time hoping that Veelee would come back to her so that he could devote *his* time to finding the man responsible. Then she would act—then they would act together. She was not yet sure how, but some justice would teach that to her; she had the resources and she had the will.

She felt a patronizing disdain for Veelee's method of revenge. They had killed his son; therefore he would kill Hitler. He had explained his concept of the matter to her with some care, then had gone directly to General von Stuelpnagel. Within three days he was on special duty in Berlin as the General's confidential delegate to General Olbricht, coordinator of the assassination plans. This way of thinking was too remote for her, and therefore of no interest. The murders for which Hitler was responsible were so fantastic in number that they only diminished Paul-Alain's murder. If she and Veelee were to repay an eye for an eye by retaliating significantly, then she wanted two men to die—or rather not just to die; she wanted to kill the two men who had taken her son by the hand and led him to death and ordered that he be taken away to die.

Hitler's pervasive corruption had surrounded her. His contempt for moral laws had convinced her that there was no longer any law, moral or civil, criminal or protective. His screamed demonstration that force was the law and that force was on the side of wrong and that wrong was right had entered her pores with the hatred she felt. From Norway to Greece, he had brought this moral change and, in the end, it could be seen that murder was *not* the worst thing he had done; his most transcendent evil was the corruption with which he had contaminated the living.

She had been so sodden with her loss at the funeral that she had not yet begun to think of the things she must do. Veelee had been quicker. The direction he had taken was wrong, she knew, but he had told her his plans in the huge black car right after the funeral. Maître Gitlin, José Zorra de Miral, Clotilde, Mme. Citron, Veelee, and General von Stuelpnagel had come to the ceremony. The rabbi had spoken the final words just as she had requested: "We now put to peace, to join the lengthy civilization of his forefathers, this amiable child who loved with all his heart this world, and who laughed with the joy of being a human and a Jew."

After the funeral, Veelee had driven her to the door of Cours Albert I, as preoccupied as any businessman about to embark on an important trip for his firm. When he had said goodbye to her, she was as absent-minded as he was. She considered him dead; she was certain that neither he nor anyone else would get closer to killing Hitler than to the bullets of his bodyguard, and she forgot about him as soon as she entered the apartment. She did not hear the servants when they spoke to her, and she walked into Paul-Alain's bedroom without removing her hat or gloves. It was just as it had always been: the slate over the bed still said: BON JOUR MAMAN in shaky chalked letters; the toy monkey still hung by its tail from the headboard. She sat on the bed and removed her gloves slowly as she stared at the spiked helmet which had been his grandfather's. Paul-Alain had enjoyed so much marching up and down in it, shouting commands in comical German and making her laugh whenever he wanted. It was then that she began to imagine that vines were growing from the ends of her fingers, moving across Germany, crushing and killing.

Miral telephoned Paule thirty times in the first two days, came to the house four times and forced his way inside the last two times. She would not be found, and as he roamed through the vast apartment looking for her, she moved silently ahead of him on bare feet, her face stained, her hair a tangle, wearing only a negligee, always two rooms ahead of his shouts of her name. He pleaded with her to come away with him while she hated him almost as much as if he were a German for taking her away from her son when she should have been there to save him. On the fifth day the Duke gave up and went away, and she did not think of him again.

Riding back from the cemetery in the huge black Mercedes, while Veelee earnestly explained his simple solution, she had said to him in a very reasonable tone of voice, "I think you should all kill each other. That is your way, after all. Soon your army will want to kill all Germans as the only way to retain their honor. The Germans must be killed, your army will reason, because they voted for Hitler and gave him the power which has destroyed the Fatherland. And the SS will like that too. After all, they are engaged in the supreme task of murdering all Germans anyway, and it is their chance to die themselves in defending their Fuehrer and their loot. And every other German who is not in the Wehrmacht or in the SS knows his duty. Half of them should be lined up on the east of Germany and half on the west in long lines facing each other; then, at a signal from your Fuehrer, who will be seated upon a heap of decomposing children on the ground between them, they will all kill each other. Your Fuehrer will be very proud. It is the final solution for all of you, Veelee."

He had been staring blankly out the window as she spoke. "Yes," he answered. "You are right. I must kill the Fuehrer."

For many months whenever Paule thought of Veelee, she heard the jackboots of the storm troopers who had paraded so many years ago along the platform of the Friedrichstrasse Station calling for the death of all Jews. Over and over again she felt the freezing fear she had felt then, and she could see that across all of those years she had been pulling that fear toward her, hand over hand, until she had found out what had been weighting the awful end of it—her son's corpse. Paul-Alain was gone, forever gone. Dead because he was a Jew—incredibly, incomprehensibly dead because he had been a Jew.

After a long while she was able to concern herself with the happiest days of life, the days when she had been the daughter of the greatest actor in all of France, one of the four greatest actors of the world, most certainly including England. She sat in the study with the thousands of pages of newspaper cuttings and theatre programs and citations and letters and notes and began to write her father's biography, as he had always intended that she do. She stopped

236

bothering to dress. She would get out of bed at odd hours, not knowing the time because she had not wound the clocks nor opened the shutters, and walk to the study to begin her work. In a short time her hair grew gray and she became very thin because she did not think about eating. Clotilde brought her food on a tray but Paule ignored it.

She did not place as much blame upon Clotilde as she did upon José Zorra de Miral because she knew that Clotilde's heart was breaking too, but she could not help thinking that there must have been some way for Clotilde to have found her after Paul-Alain had been taken away. Clotilde had known that they were using a Luftwaffe staff car, and she should have known that it was necessary for the driver to inform the Luftwaffe transportation officer where the car was taking them. She refused to believe that Clotilde was unable to get into the Hôtel Majestic or to reach General von Stuelpnagel in any way. She had not really tried; she was just another servant; they were all alike. Paule had dismissed Mme. Citron and all of the others on the day of the funeral, and when Mme. Citron had tried to object she had slapped her sharply across the face and told her to be out of the house within one hour. Maître Gitlin would give her all necessary information about her pension. It was too much for her to have to see this gabby old woman who had babbled to the police that Paul-Alain lived there. Everyone knew that when police came to one's door in wartime one should deny everything. The police might have gone away and they could have hidden Paul-Alain until she returned to save him, to cherish him, to keep him.

In the spring, Clotilde had gone away. She had remained six months longer than any of the others, but she was deeply ashamed and bitter that Frau General von Rhode accused her, more and more each day, with the same eloquent eyes as her father's. For two months Paule was alone in the huge flat, but she was almost unaware of it. In the summer, Clotilde suddenly reappeared, her chin outthrust, her eyes determined slits. She rang the doorbell again and again but when Paule did not answer it Clotilde waited outside the front door all day. In the evening she heard Paule's slippers sliding across the marble floor and then she had pounded on the door with all her might. When Paule opened the door they stared at one another, and then Frau General von Rhode crumpled forward into Clotilde's arms, sobbing like a child and saying over and over again how happy she was that Clotilde had returned.

Sixteen

✠

On the evening after his talk with General von Stuelpnagel, Veelee was briefed at the Hôtel Lutetia, Paris headquarters of Abwehr, the Wehrmacht's military intelligence organization commanded by Admiral Canaris, whose sympathies provided the plotters with an excellent cover.

When the briefing was over, Veelee asked the officer who had come from Berlin for the meetings with Canaris and von Stuelpnagel to take a walk so that he could give him a message for Berlin. As they circled the Hôtel Lutetia, Veelee explained that it must be conveyed to the leaders of the army's resistance that assassination was the only solution. Because this could not be done without involving so many conspirators of so many shades, he alone, Wilhelm von Rhode, must be chosen to carry out any attempts to be made on the Fuehrer's life. To talk to his shorter companion Veelee bent his head downward and his monocle glittered sinisterly in the purple summer dusk as the two men walked through the tree-lined streets. He spoke rapidly of several methods he had in mind to remove the Fuehrer. Why waste a whole man? Furthermore, he pointed out, he had the rank to gain him entry anywhere.

In 1942 the objectives of the army resistance were based upon "isolated action"; that is, the marshals of the Eastern front would refuse to accept orders from the Fuehrer in his role as Commander in Chief. This nicety would allow them to believe that they were not violating their oath to Hitler, the Supreme Commander of the Armed Forces, but were only refusing to recognize him as Commander in Chief of the army. At that moment, the Home Army under General

238

Beck would seize control of Germany, dissolve the Nazi States, depose Hitler and restore the independence of the army. Thereafter, all officers of the German armed forces could consider themselves honorably released from their oath of allegiance to the Fuehrer, and the true Germany would then be re-established. Unfortunately, the plan began and ended with the marshals in the east, and none of them were having any part of it.

By mid-1943 the leadership of the army resistance had fallen by default to junior officers. The powerful leaders of the army had been eliminated or had eliminated themselves: Colonel-General Hoepner had been publicly cashiered; Guderian had been removed from active command; Reichenau had died; von Witzleben had developed hemorrhoids and had immediately been retired; Beck was on the inactive list; Hammerstein and Franz Heller had rank but no troops. Von Rundstedt had replaced Witzleben as commander in the west, and while he was aware of the conspirators' plans and might even have been sympathetic, he said he was far too old to become involved in such games.

In the east the marshals vacillated for various reasons. Paulus was servile, and von Kuechler was completely deaf to all arguments. Von Bock despised the Fuehrer, but he would not risk his marshal's baton, and Manstein said that he was far too engrossed in the military problem of taking Sebastopol.

The weakest and most opportunistic commander in the east was Field Marshal von Kluge. He was a Hamlet-imitator, Major General Henning von Tresckow, his Chief of Staff, explained to Veelee. Von Tresckow was a Pomeranian; a boyhood friend and neighbor of Veelee's who, like Veelee, had at first embraced the military promises of the Fuehrer enthusiastically. Unlike Veelee and many others, however, von Tresckow had seen his mistake and had moved into opposition, and then into resistance. The atrocities of the Polish campaign had shocked him into awareness of the crime he had been abetting, but he was one of the few who had translated shame into action.

"For two years I have been battling for von Kluge's soul," Tresckow told Veelee. "I dominate him now, but only in a personal way. The moment he is out of my sight he lapses into doglike obedience to the Fuehrer. You can't imagine such vacillating. I tell you, Rhode, each time that I have him nailed to a definite plan of action, when I am absolutely sure I have him, he fades away like smoke in your fist at the most critical moment.

"We have blackmailed him. Oh, yes, I swear to you. As you know, field marshals are paid thirty-six thousand reichsmarks a year, plus an allowance—which is all right for people who want money, but it cannot compare with what has been stolen by Germans who really worship money. So the Fuehrer hands out tips—little gratuities—the way you might give a coin to a men's-room attendant. Yes, look shocked, my dear Rhode, but it is true. And he will say, no income tax on this little tip. Yes! He gave Kluge two hundred and fifty thousand reichsmarks on his birthday—*plus* a permit to spend yet another handsome tip on improvements for Kluge's estate, with a copy of a letter to Speer, the minister in charge of buildings. When I saw that letter I said, 'At last we have the son-of-a-bitch.' I went and waved it in von Kluge's face. I told him I would broadcast the bribe to every man in the Officer Corps of the German Army, and he knew I meant it. But he wasn't in the least embarrassed or humiliated, you know—not at all. He adopted the air of a man who thinks he should at least *pretend* to be embarrassed in the event that I did broadcast it, so he agreed to a meeting with Goerdeler, the civilian politician of the movement. It was a tricky business to get Goerdeler admitted to the area, believe me. We could never have done it without Canaris and Oster.

"The meeting was held in the Smolensk forest and I was there, Rhode. Kluge at last agreed that he would lead a mutiny of the armies in the east at the moment word came from Berlin. Goerdeler was in such high spirits that I thought he'd break out singing. Before Goerdeler could get back to Berlin—you hear me?—*before* Goerdeler got back to Berlin, Kluge sent a letter to Beck, taking it all back, withdrawing, changing his watery mind again."

After the Kluge disappointment Beck appealed personally to Paulus, who was surrounded in Stalingrad, his quarter of a million men condemned to death by the Fuehrer's shrill tantrums for victory at any price. Beck asked Paulus to broadcast an appeal to all the German armies, but though he was far out of the Fuehrer's vengeful reach Paulus' only reaction was a glub of radio messages singing devotion to his Fuehrer.

In all, there were three major resistance groups. The first group, consisting almost exclusively of army men, urged their Fuehrer's arrest, trial, and legal execution. The second group, mainly civilian, wished only to discuss what should be done in the certain event that Germany lost the war, thus eliminating the Fuehrer automatically. The third group, led by junior army officers, pressed for the Fuehrer's earliest assassination. All three groups wished fervently for a "just" peace for Germany, and with the exception of the third group, they were hesitant about ridding Germany of Hitler until they were assured of this.

Veelee shuttled back and forth between von Stuelpnagel's headquarters in Paris and Berlin until the British and American troops landed in North Africa on November 7, 1943. On November 11th, the German Army swept across the Vichy line in France to take up positions on the Mediterranean coast. All of Veelee's time was engaged in extending military communications across France to connect operations with Paris headquarters, through which the Fuehrer, the Bendlerstrasse, and all others concerned could remain in contact. Not until late in February, 1943, did he become available again to the resistance movement.

In the interim, his duty to the army and his sworn duty to the memory of Paul-Alain never left his mind, and always he thought of Paule waiting for him at Cours Albert I to tell her that the Fuehrer was dead and his son had been avenged. The thought of revenge hounded and exhausted him, and the fatigue affected his already unstable mind. He kept telling himself that he should not be worrying about communications: he should be in Germany getting ready for the chance that had to come. Only his reflexes and his thirty-five years of army training, which enabled him to meet implacable demands, kept him going. But he was forever looking over his shoulder toward the time and place where he had to be. When he tried to sleep he dreamed of Paule pleading with him to avenge their son. Some nights she would curse him and on others she would weep inconsolably, begging him to tell her how the boy could rest unless his father found his honor and killed the Fuehrer. Sometimes in the dreams she was his wife, but mostly she was his mother, tall and fragrant, whom he could not re-

241

member having seen after the morning when he had been taken off to enter the army—at the age of nine.

At last, in February, 1943, Veelee was sent again to the Bendlerstrasse to see General Olbricht, chief of the General Army Office and deputy to General Fromm, commander of the Replacement Army. It was planned that the revolt which would secure all German garrisons on the day when the Fuehrer was struck down would spread from this building and insure the seizure of power in Berlin, Cologne, Munich, and Vienna. Beck and Goerdeler, the military and civilian leaders respectively, still counted on Field Marshal von Kluge to assume command of the Eastern front as soon as the Fuehrer's death had been confirmed. Only then could the Field Marshal free himself from his oath to the Fuehrer and of his paralyzing fear of him. After von Kluge had committed himself it was only a matter of hours before all other field commanders, on all fronts, followed his lead.

Veelee was accepted as an invaluable weapon. The setting of the assassination was to be at von Kluge's and Tresckow's headquarters at Army Group Center in Smolensk. Tresckow was in command of the plot and Veelee was to be the executioner. However, provisions were made for a second executioner, because there was an excellent chance that the first would not be at the right spot at the right time because of the shiftiness of the Fuehrer's itinerary. He would be expected on a Monday and arrive on the Friday before or after, and the problem of luring him and his entourage from Rastenburg to Smolensk was formidable. Tresckow had been able to arrange the visit through General Schmundt, the Fuehrer's adjutant, who was innocent of the plot, but with whom Tresckow was on familiar terms.

As always, the arrival date was fixed and canceled many times, but finally a definite date of March 13th was announced.

On the morning of that day Tresckow told von Kluge of their plan. As the Fuehrer left the plane, Major General von Rhode would drive an armored car, all weapons firing into the Fuehrer's guard. Kluge vacillated over the plan and at last only twenty-five minutes before the Fuehrer's arrival, the Field Marshal said that he could not countenance such an act and that no armored car would be made available to the plotters. Thus, they were forced back upon the second plan.

After tireless experimenting, the use of German-made bombs for the alternate assassination plot had been discarded because of the noise of the fuses. The Abwehr was able to secure small British bombs, of the sort used to kill General Heydrich, which had been dropped by enemy planes for underground use. Two of these small bombs were imbedded in a package wrapped to look like two bottles of brandy, and the package was to be planted in the Fuehrer's plane on its return flight to Rastenburg. Veelee was enraged at being cheated out of his right to kill the Fuehrer, but von Tresckow took the cooler view that the second plan was probably better. An exploded plane would look like an accident, and even the semblance of one would avoid the political disadvantages of a murder which could provoke strong SS resistance.

Outwardly Veelee seemed to be in icy control of himself, but within he was consumed. For days he had been chewing combat-fatigue pills. These brought on weeping spells, but he was able to explain this to von Tresckow, who immediately understood. He had wept as he worked over the mechanisms of the small bombs; at the same time he felt great pride that soon he would be able to return to Paule and tell her that they could all rest in peace, because the job was done.

After the Fuehrer's party arrived, there was a gala reception at which Veelee shamelessly flattered the General Army Staff's Colonel Brandt, who was traveling with the Fuehrer's party. Later, over a second cognac, Veelee asked Colonel Brandt if he would be kind enough to take back a little gift of two bottles of brandy to General Stieff, at Rastenburg. Colonel Brandt said he would be delighted. The following morning, Veelee accompanied Brandt to the airfield and entertained him with stories about Keitel in the First World War and, from an imagination he did not know he had, about the lissomeness of the women of Paris. As Brandt boarded the plane, Veelee started the mechanism of the bomb by pulling a piece of string apparently holding the wrapping paper together and gave the package to Brandt with thanks and wishes for a successful journey.

The bomb had no clockwork to advertise itself. A button broke a glass vial, which released a chemical, which melted a wire, which held back a spring, which moved a striker, which hit a detonator, which exploded the bomb. The plane was due to crack over Minsk in thirty minutes. Berlin was notified that the operation had begun. Undoubtedly the first word of the explosion would be radioed in by one of the fighter-plane escorts.

An hour went by, then another half-hour, and there was no word. Two hours and eleven minutes after the bomb's button had been pulled, a routine message brought the news that the Fuehrer's plane had landed safely at Rastenburg. The bomb had never exploded.

At seven-o-five P.M., while von Tresckow watched, listened, and sweated with him, Veelee telephoned Colonel Brandt. "Brandt? Rhode here. I hope you had a delightful trip."

"It was a good trip, thank you, sir."

"I really do hate troubling you like this, Brandt, but I wondered if you'd had the opportunity to give that brandy to Stieff?"

"Well, not actually, old boy, you see—"

"You haven't?" He looked at von Tresckow, who sighed heavily, expelling air like a sea lion. "Oh, marvelous! Twenty minutes after you'd left, a shipment of some perfectly marvelous cognac—I mean the real thing arrived from my wife in Paris, and I do want Stieff to have the best."

"Stieff? What about Brandt?"

"Nothing but the best for Brandt as well. Two of the finest and they'll be yours in the morning. Von Tresckow's aide-de-camp has business at your place and he says he'll be glad to take some packages along."

With fantastic courage, Lieutenant Fabian von Schlabrendorff, aide-de-camp to General von Tresckow and a lawyer in civilian life who had become a lion of the resistance, flew to the Fuehrer's headquarters, calmly exchanged packages, caught a night train to Berlin and dismantled the bomb in his berth. The mechanism had worked almost perfectly; every component had performed exactly as planned except that the detonator had been defective.

Generals Olbricht and Oster, and young Colonel von Stauffenberg invited Veelee to dinner at the Zeughaus after the assassination attempt failed, and General Olbricht thanked him for the extraordinary dedication he had shown. Then he explained carefully that they were going to have to make further plans, which would necessitate some delays, and under the circumstances perhaps—

"Delays? No, no!" Veelee shouted. "There must be no delays. My wife is waiting. The Fuehrer must be killed. My son. We must finish all of this. I want to start over again with her before it is too late. I did it all wrong, all wrong, General. You are young, Stauffenberg, you know what I mean. We haven't had days like that, not since Charlottenburg and Wuensdorf. No, no, before that, even. No delays, absolutely no delays, gentlemen. Let us make new plans here and now, but there must be no talk of delays."

Stauffenberg seemed to take charge. "I do understand, General von Rhode. Not delays in that way—of course not. We were speaking of delays only in that the Fuehrer, as you know, moves so unpredictably. We have had explicit information that he is about to change the base of his operations to the west in order to prepare for the Allied landings."

"To the west?" Veelee examined their expressionless faces. "Yes, yes! He would want to be in the west. That would be his post when the invasion comes."

"Therefore, General," Stauffenberg, himself lacking one eye and most of two hands, said in a firm but gentle voice, "we consider that you would be most useful if you would consent to return to Paris to await the next assignment."

Relief filled Veelee's face. "Thank you, and forgive my stupidity. I should have anticipated such a move. I am so sorry. You know"—and he made a horrible attempt to smile—"I had forgotten about the war, I think. When you spoke of landings I almost had to reconsider, but it is better that I give all my thought to killing the Fuehrer. There are many others to fight the other war. We have this one job and it is my job, only my job." He got up so hastily that he knocked his chair over, but he did not hear it fall. "Thank you and good night. I must not lose any time. You will want me to be there, prepared. It was a lovely dinner. Good luck, gentlemen, and good night." He fixed his monocle in his right eye socket, clicked his heels, bowed and left the room.

The three men sat silently for some time. Finally Olbricht spoke. "He was a great officer."

"He is Germany," Stauffenberg answered. "Broken by tyranny and unable to understand what has happened to him."

Seventeen

✠

COLONEL-GENERAL KARL HEINRICH VON STUELPNAGEL was
a compactly built, kind man and an austere soldier of the
old school. Since 1933 he had been anti-Hitler and anti-
Nazi, and he and General Beck had stood back-to-back in
opposition to the new Germany from its first official days. In
November, 1943, he was fifty-seven years old; on August 30,
1944, he was strangled to death by piano wire, suspended
naked from a meat hook in front of turning motion-picture
cameras in the Ploetzensee, Berlin, prison after confessing
to complicity in the attempt on the Fuehrer's life on July
20, 1944. The motion-picture films of his execution were
projected that evening at Rastenburg for the pleasure of the
Fuehrer.

Despite his Prussian name, von Stuelpnagel was not of the
aristocracy. Through his mother, he was the grandson of a
renowned Bavarian General von der Tann, distinguished in
the Franco-Prussian War. He had not been educated at a
Kadettenanstalt, but after passing his matriculation examinations at the Lessinggymnasium in Frankfurt, and attending
the University of Geneva, he suddenly decided to enter the
Hessische Leibregiment 115. He despised military jargon and
military comportment with his subordinates. He was an easy-
going, considerate gentleman who enjoyed the theatre,
books, music, and good conversation.

At the end of World War I Stuelpnagel had been a captain
of the General Staff, where he was professionally befriended
by Veelee's father, Colonel-General Klaus von Rhode, who
was one of the most perceptive "talent scouts" the General
Staff had ever had. Under this sponsorship von Stuelpnagel
was marked to be moved forward. In February, 1938, he
became Quartermaster General of the General Staff from
which he joined the Zossen Conspiracy, which sought to remove Hitler from office in the autumn of 1939, just

after the Polish campaign. In May, 1940, he was given command of the Second Army Corps.

In July, 1940, Stuelpnagel was assigned to head the German-French committee, which was concerned with resolving questions of the Armistice, when he received a cable from Keitel demanding that he stop aiding and abetting the interests of the French. The Reichsmarschall also accused him of being a captive of the French and demanded that a German Embassy be established in Paris to deal with several acquisitive matters within the interest of the Reichsmarschall. Von Stuelpnagel's labors in directing the committee brought about a most considerable reduction in the payments of four hundred million francs a day which France was forced to pay for the upkeep of the German occupation forces.

In January, 1941, he was transferred to prepare to take over the command of the Seventeenth Army in Russia. When the Russian campaign started, the Seventeenth Army belonged to the Southern Army Group, under the command of Field Marshal von Rundstedt. Working with Kleist's Panzergruppe, Stuelpnagel's Seventeenth Army conquered the Ukraine and captured six hundred and sixty-five thousand Russian prisoners in the Battle of Kiev, on September 10th. After capturing Kharkhov on October 25th, Stuelpnagel began to pass back steady advices to Brauchitsch and the Fuehrer against any attempt at further advances, throwing the Fuehrer into insensate rages. The Russian counter-offensive began at the end of November when the Southern Army Group in general, and Stuelpnagel's Seventeenth Army in particular, began the retreat from their positions.

The Fuehrer relieved von Rundstedt on November 30th and replaced him with Reichenau, and almost at once Reichenau's reports spoke of "this touchy and highly pessimistic intellectual Stuelpnagel." This reached the Fuehrer on the same day as a letter from Stuelpnagel, which seemed unbearable in its irresponsibility, blaming the retreat on slipshod planning which provided no winter clothing and other startling inefficiencies. The Fuehrer wanted to have him cashiered on a parade ground, as an example to the whole decadent Officer Corps, but Rundstedt and Halder pleaded that von Stuelpnagel was the most experienced man in the army for the command of France and the Fuehrer said he would agree to anything if "this irresponsible lunatic is banished from my sight."

Colonel-General Karl Heinrich von Stuelpnagel was Military Governor of France from February, 1942, until the early morning hours of July 21, 1944.

Paule was looking over the clippings covering her father's visit to New York in 1928 with his own classical repertory company, and of his simultaneous liaisons with a visiting European queen and a channel swimmer when she heard the door behind her open. Thinking that it was Clotilde, she said impatiently, "No, no, Clotilde, I'm busy."

"It is I, Stuelpnagel," a voice said. Paule spun around in her chair, her first thought was that her hair was a rats' nest and that all she was wearing was a nightgown and a negligee. Then her mind took its next step, and she gripped her throat with her hands. "Veelee is dead," she whispered.

"No, no, he is not dead," the General answered. "May I sit down?" She nodded, and he seated himself, his face expressionless; had he smiled, even in greeting, she would have been convinced that he was laughing at the way she looked.

Paule pulled the bell rope. "We must have some champagne," she said, feeling foolish even as she spoke, because it could not have been after eleven o'clock in the morning. But almost before she had finished the sentence, Clotilde came through the door with a bottle of champagne and two tall, tulip-shaped glasses.

"What a marvelous idea," the General murmured as Clotilde poured and then left at once. "To the future," he said gravely, lifting his glass.

Paule dipped her glass at him and wondered how to answer. "I have been writing my father's biography," she said apologetically.

"No life could have been more refreshing than his," the General said. He smiled at her with such warmth that she felt open and at ease with him instantly. "I remember him well, you know. One day in the mid-twenties, I traveled almost two hundred miles to see him. What a wonderful actor he was."

"Oh, yes! That is to say, thank you.

"I suppose it is unnecessary to say that I am surprised to

see you, General." She had not left the apartment for sixteen months and she had seen no one but Clotilde. Then all of a sudden the Military Commander for France strolled into her room at eleven A.M. and began to drink champagne, and she felt no more strange than if he had been her lover and she had been used to receiving him every morning. She marveled more when she realized that the last time they had met had been across Paul-Alain's grave, and still she did not reject him.

"I feel badly about that, but I feared that if I telephoned I would not be permitted to talk with you, and after all, I could not pull my rank because this is a most unofficial call."

"About Veelee."

"Yes."

"Is he . . . better?"

"He is a hero. He has given almost all he possesses to Germany. That was his duty, but so few of us have done our duty. It takes greatness, you know."

"And a sort of madness," Paule said.

"That, too. At any rate, for him to continue in his present state of health would be a mistake. To continue effectively, that is. At this time, at this stage, we have him in the wrong work, one might say. The only solution for him is rest, but due to the nature of his zeal, he must not know that he has—ah—been taken out of play. May I?"

"Of course."

The General lifted the wine bottle out of the bucket and filled the two glasses again. "He needs you, Madame, and I need you, because he is my friend and the son of my friend. The only other solution would be a . . . a hospital. He is fixed on doing his duty. Reality and fantasy are interwoven for him, and only you can tell him whether he has done his duty, because its motivation is the tragedy you share. My God, the sad, German world of duty. We seek it to serve it, but always someone else must tell us where it is and what it is."

Tears came to Paule's eyes. "Thank you, General," she answered.

Veelee rang the doorbell at Cours Albert I almost exactly sixteen months after he had left Paule on the summer morning after Paul-Alain's funeral in 1942. Clotilde took him into the study, where Paule was working on her father's book. Paule did not appear surprised that he had returned; she stood up, put her arms around his neck and kissed him briefly before staring into his haggard, broken face. "May I stay here, Paule," he said, "until I can sort everything out?" She nodded, and led him toward the big bedroom.

Eighteen

✠

By May, 1944, Veelee's health was considerably improved. The terrible depressions had left him and he was able to go back to work as Chief of Communications for France.

In May, 1944, the German Army was nervously confused about the Allied intentions. Eighteen days during that month the weather, tides, and sea had been suitable for landings, but nothing had happened. Putting himself in the place of General Eisenhower, Field Marshal von Rundstedt reported to the Fuehrer that no invasion was "immediately imminent." On the 4th of June, the Luftwaffe meteorologist advised that the Channel would be shut down for a fortnight by inclement weather. On the strength of this, the Luftwaffe conserved its remaining resources by temporarily abandoning aerial reconnaissance over southern English harbors, where troops were being piled aboard ships. In addition, the German Navy had withdrawn its craft from the Channel because of high-running seas. It seemed so unlikely that any landings would be attempted that on June 5th Field Marshal Rommel set off by car to spend the night with his family in Wuerttemberg, then to proceed to Berchtesgaden the next day for meetings with the Fuehrer.

Of course, there were the usual reports from agents in England that landings could be expected to be tried between the 6th and the 16th, but there had been hundreds of such warnings since April. On the 6th of June, General Dollmann, commanding the Seventh Army, which guarded all beaches in Normandy, ordered his senior officers to Rennes, one hundred and twenty-five miles to the south, for a map exercise, and relaxed his standing alert over the troops. In the early evening of June 5th, Rundstedt's headquarters learned that London was sending an extraordinary number of coded messages, and that the German radar stations between Cherbourg and Le Havre were being jammed. However, Rundstedt did not consider the situation alarming enough to pass this information on to the Seventh Army, whose position the Allies were then approaching in a thousand ships.

One British and two American airborne divisions landed between Caen and Cherbourg just after one A.M. on June 6, 1944. The general alarm was sounded at one-thirty A.M., but at two-forty A.M. the area commander was advised that von Rundstedt did "not consider this to be a major operation"—mainly because Rundstedt and Rommel had convinced themselves that the real landings would be made up the coast at Pas-de-Calais. The Commander in Chief West continued to be deluded until the afternoon of June 6th.

Professor Morell and the Fuehrer remained calm. The Fuehrer preferred to wait to see what would develop, and went to bed without releasing the tank division for which Rundstedt had been pleading. He awoke at three P.M. on June 6th, took his pills, and issued his first order of the invasion at four fifty-five P.M.

Chief of Staff Western Command emphasizes the desire of the Supreme Command to have the enemy in the bridgehead annihilated by the evening of June 6 since there exists the danger of additional sea- and airborne landings for support . . . The beachhead must be cleaned up by not later than tonight.

Charles Piocher's real work was almost over. The French Resistance, with which he had worked for four years to organize, train, indoctrinate, and arm with the power of England and her Allies, now began its crippling strikes. The Marguerite de Ste. Stephens Group, operating out of Augustus des Pierres, cut all underground telephone and electric-current lines leading to the major garrison and ten-gun battery at Longehommes-Vert, and cut four hundred yards of telegraph wire from the command posts of Pessac-Alouette-Gazinet and Château Laffargue. Nine electrical locomotives were disabled only four hundred yards from the Pessac station, and railway lines were sabotaged between the powder factory and d'Oblinger. The Group Dodo Midi destroyed a motorized convoy of twenty-four trucks, killing one hundred and sixty-two Germans, wounding one hundred and eighty-two, and forcing the convoy to retire to Nonie-Wintour; attacked and seriously damaged the Bordeaux command headquarters; derailed an entire troop train, and destroyed all enemy cables at the Ste. Jeanne d'Ennis center and those between Dax, Pau, and Toulouse. The Group Lefanan cut the main railway line at Château Absinthe; destroyed telephone and telegraph lines, felled forty-six trees across main military highways, and blew up nineteen electric pylons for a total loss of eight hundred and sixty thousand volts. The Rolande-le-Gant Group destroyed two railway bridges; exploded seven pylons, which halted railway traffic for six days; cut seven underground cables at the mouth of the Seine; derailed seven German trains; sabotaged all railway signals in their area; took fifteen hundred gallons of petrol from German stores; put out of commission a thirty-three-ton loading crane and nine steam locomotives; severed all electric cables linking the mines on the right bank of the Seine; and destroyed two V-4 prototypes and sent photographs of them to London via the Spanish route.

Industrial sabotage reached heights to which not even Piocher could have aspired. Production was so dislocated that scores of factories became utterly useless to the Germans. All previously reconnoitered demolitions were carried out. Roads were blown up, telephone and telegraph communications between enemy headquarters were destroyed, the dispatch riders who were then sent out were killed, and fighting troops desperately needed elsewhere had to be deployed to insure communications safety. Piocher had worked well.

On May 26, 1944, Charles Piocher pulled himself out of bed, making no effort not to awaken Fräulein Nortnung, an impossible achievement without sunlight and many bells. He shaved carefully, dressed in striped silk underwear with a matching striped silk shirt, a beige linen suit, a floppy brown fedora, and set out in his Dupont for the von Rhodes' apartment at Cours Albert I. It was five-fifty A.M. when Clotilde answered his insistent ring. Piocher pushed past her and shut the door behind him. "Get the General and his wife out here," he said, "and then bring me some coffee and croissants."

Clotilde was shocked. "We don't get croissants until seven o'clock," she said.

"All right. I'll settle for coffee," Piocher told her, and sauntered into the small salon. He was studying photographs of Veelee at Wuensdorf when Paule and the General entered the room.

"What the hell is this?" Veelee said. He had a coldly murderous look and his hand was jammed into his dressing-gown pocket.

"Why, you're the black-market man!" Paule said in astonishment.

"That's me, love, Charles Piocher. Now sit down. We have a lot to talk about."

Veelee was so baffled that he could not maintain his threatening role. "My dear man, it is six o'clock in the morning." To try to recapture his menacing air, he added, "I have a gun in my pocket."

"I should think so," Piocher answered. "So have I." He sat down with the briskness of an insurance agent closing a deal.

Paule and Veelee sat down slowly and warily.

"What do you want?" she asked.

"Plenty, Madame. But it will seem like nothing. Coffee is on the way."

"Plenty?" Veelee said. "Plenty of what?"

"Let's wait for the coffee."

"No, no."

"Then talk to each other," Piocher said. "I don't do any business until I have coffee." He walked back to the photograph of Veelee at Wuensdorf, then moved crab-fashion to his right to study a picture of Veelee with Keitel at Bruges in 1918.

"This is insufferable," Veelee said, walking to the telephone. "You can do your talking to the military police."

"Say, is that Keitel?" Piocher asked. Veelee picked up the telephone, but Paule moved to his side and put her hand over his. Gently, together, they replaced the receiver in its cradle. "Keitel certainly was gorgeous," Piocher said.

Clotilde came in with a tray and poured coffee for each of them. Piocher sipped his and made a face. "Horrible," he said. "I must be crazy to have breakfast out. This afternoon I'll send you some real coffee." The Rhodes had not picked up their cups.

"Tell us what is on your mind, Monsieur Piocher," Paule said.

"It won't be easy, you understand," Piocher told her, "so I'll be blunt. I want certain military information from the General here—"

"You *what?*"

"I'll put it this way," Piocher said. "I'm not exactly what I seem, except that I seem to be becoming what I am—which is the SOE fella for France."

"SOE?" Paule asked.

"Special Operations Executive. British. At least, I think they're still British—it's been a long time since I looked, and De Gaulle is in London, too."

"Do you mean you are . . . ?" Veelee's jaw had fallen. Paule's eyes began to fill with hope. Something within her heard something that had not been said. She sat tensely. "Let us speak in English to be certain," she said.

"To be certain?" Veelee said in strangled tones. "To be certain of what?"

"Yes, you must be certain, Madame," Piocher answered gravely. "You above all others."

"Sure of what? Damn you! Sure of what?"

"General, sir," Piocher said in Cockney English, "I want you to give me the plan of all telecommunications between Paris and the Channel, plus the plan for all intercommunications between all posts in that military zone."

Veelee took the pistol from his pocket and cocked it, and Paule said hurriedly, "What is it you intend to pay for this, Mr. Piocher?" She pronounced it Pee-o-chur, in the English manner.

"This will hurt, Madame," Piocher said. "But I cannot be delicate. I will give you the name of the man who ordered the French police to arrest your son, and the name of the man who persuaded him to issue the order."

Veelee returned the gun to his pocket and sat down heavily. He and Paule stared at Piocher, but they could not speak. Piocher could not bear the silence, and he rose and walked to the cut-glass decanters on the sideboard and poured himself a drink. "First morning drink I've had since I left the army," he said, and downed it. Then he poured three more and took

254

them to the Rhodes. "Here we are," he said, returning to French. "We may not take the same paths, but I suspect we have the same goals—death to them all." Veelee did not look at his, but merely drank it down and continued to look at Piocher.

"Who are they?" Veelee asked coldly.

"Madame?" Piocher said to Paule.

She leaned forward, her eyes wide and her hands trembling. "If you will give us their names, I will—we will tell you anything." Veelee looked only at Piocher, his expression slowly changing as he realized what was happening.

"It is best to be brief," Piocher said, peering at each of them sympathetically. "I want military information in return for two names."

"Will you help us with what we will need?" Paule asked.

"To the limit of my resources, Madame," Piocher answered as Veelee looked rapidly from face to face, unsure, confused, desperately seeking his duty.

When Piocher had gone, Paule called Clotilde. "I love you, Clotilde," she said. "You are a part of my family as much as —almost as much as Paul-Alain. I want you to go out now and stay away until this evening. When you come back, everything is going to be better again."

"I will pray, Madame."

"You listened to M'sieu Piocher?"

"Yes, Madame." Paule looked squarely at Veelee to be sure that he was listening, and then back to Clotilde.

"What would you do, Clotilde?"

"Kill them, Madame."

Veelee and Paule sat across the room from each other in silence until they heard Clotilde close the front door decisively.

"What is honor, Veelee?" Paule said. She crossed the room and sat beside him on the sofa and put her hand over his only hand. "They took your arm, your son, your eye, and a part of your mind, they've destroyed the country you love, and now they are going to make you into a traitor to their country. But it is only *their* country now—it is no longer the one you hold in your heart."

Veelee turned his head and looked into her face, but he did not speak.

"Honor exists outside of us, does it not?" Paule asked. "Especially so, I should think, in the case of a man and a woman whose son has been murdered like an insect, without honor. Think of the years they taught you about soldiers' honor. Think of the lifetime that I have been taught in various ways about a Jew's honor. Then tell me whether your soldier's honor and my ruined honor have any meaning when we think of Paul-Alain dead. There is honor, and there is honor. What happened to us during the four days it took to murder Paul-Alain will live on forever, and now that we are about to learn the names of the two men who killed him I can tell you, at last, what honor is, Veelee. Honor is not being able to live if those men are to live. Honor is not being willing to live unless we kill those men in the most disgusting manner possible. It has come to this, dearest: you must become a traitor and we must become murderers, or else we lose all honor and all peace forever. That is our only duty now."

"How is it to be done?" Veelee asked. "We must not wait."

She lifted his hand and, her eyes closed, kissed it as though she was swearing upon a sacred sword. "I have thought of the way," she said.

Nineteen

✠

IN JULY, 1944, Paris was the rear area behind the heavy fighting in Normandy and Brittany, and Captain Strasse discovered that this produced a thirty-eight percent increase in the gross volume of his clubs. In a sense, he said to Yoka elatedly, every night was just like New Year's Eve. "I never thought I would be hoping for the war to last forever," he said, "but I certainly can't object to this one any more."

"Just so long as it lasts until every dirty, fucking Boche is dead," Yoka said.

Strasse touched her cheek and smiled at her lovingly. "Ah, they're not so bad," he said expansively.

"Are you out of your mind?"

"I bet if we got to know them we'd find they're just like everybody else."

"Up yours." Yoka was definite about everything—no half-way stuff with her. It was a good thing she thought he was a Dane and that she couldn't speak Danish. Thank God. Everything she did excited him, and when he kissed her his ears buzzed. The amazing thing was that no one had ever *liked* him before, much less loved him. She loved. She was crazy about him. At first, he hadn't been sure that he wanted anything like that. Who wants to feel owned? He had always realized that he'd had a big edge in life because nobody liked him. No brakes, hit and run. But now that he had a taste of the feeling of being loved—and by the fiercest woman he had ever met—he knew what he had been missing.

"How come you like me so much, Yoka?" he had asked her once.

"I like the way you balance a beret, you little shit," she had said; and she had grabbed him by his buzzing ears and pulled his mouth down to hers and made a meal of it. For her birthday in October—Yoka was a Libra and therefore sensitive to beauty—Strasse had given her a big diamond ring that Fräulein Nortnung had located for him, *plus* all of her police papers from Amsterdam, her entire record. Yoka had been very big-time; she had even been up for armed robbery. He simply could not imagine it—a beautiful, sweet little doll like this and she had the nerve of thirty Wild-West Indians and a strike on her for armed robbery. That was real aristocracy.

Yoka had gazed down at the police papers with awe. "Where the hell did you get these?" she gasped.

He shrugged, so delighted that he wanted to jig. "I gave a man some money and he gave them to me. And they aren't copies—you burn them and there won't be any record left."

"Burn them? Are you crazy? Honey, they came from you. No man in the whole world but you would think of such a wonderful thing. You want to know why I love you, you sick little bastard? This is why I love you. You are so offbeat, you are so absolutely crazy, that I can't get it through my head that you belong to me."

Well, that was the way it was. He had talked to her about getting married. It wasn't something he just said; he thought out every word beforehand so she would understand how

257

difficult it was for him to say such a thing. It made her cry, but it was a helpless, grateful, defenseless, total, ecstatic kind of crying, and it made him feel like a giant. He had done more for her than he had ever done for anyone, and all the while this joy pierced his heart he was crying himself and didn't know it. He cried. He actually cried for the first time in his life that he could remember. Maybe it was the first time in his life he could remember feeling *anything*, because what he had felt for Yoka was nothing compared to what he felt after she had reacted to his asking her to marry him. He had offered her the only important thing he had to give, and she valued it.

They calmed down after a while. The tremendous feeling didn't go away, but they calmed down because nobody could go on that way without snapping a spine. She didn't even answer him for two days; they just stayed in that great big bed. Then late one night she said, "I was married once to a guy who had more wives at one time than both of us have fingers, and I swore—I tell you I even took a razor blade and opened my vein a little bit so I could do it in blood—and I swore that I would never marry another son-of-a-bitch of a man if I lived forever. Oh, honey, oh, honey." She began to cry again and she pressed her face so hard into his shoulder that he thought she would break her nose.

"You won't marry me?" he said hoarsely. His hands and feet felt as cold as death.

"I will, honey. I will because I have to. And I've got to break what I swore. Because I love you, I love you, I love you."

"We'll get married tonight," he said eagerly, thinking at the same instant that he'd have to buy some faked papers from Piocher.

"We get married the day they carry the last dead German out of this town," Yoka said. "Maybe we won't wait until this rotten war is over, but we'll wait that long. Marriage is a holy thing, and I don't want any Germans in the same country when it happens to me."

When he thought it all over later, he realized he should have known better. He had given her his private telephone number in his own quarters at the Avenue Foch, in case there was ever any emergency and she needed him. Nobody was allowed to answer that phone but him. Yoka didn't know where it was; she had never had occasion to use it in over

258

three years because there never had been a situation she couldn't handle. Whatever happened in one of his clubs was all in a night's work to her.

Everything was going so splendidly. He had shipped out a little over six thousand Jews in two weeks, all to Auschwitz. It was a new record. Everybody in Berlin was purring at him. It was a rough time because the increase in the night-club business sometimes kept him up as late as eight in the morning, and then he had to go straight to the office. Too many pills, maybe, but it was the only way he could keep going. He'd been told that Professor Morell had said that a man had to go very easy with those pills, but he had such fatigue. The God-damn Jews. How could he keep the shipments moving out without the pills? But sometimes he would lose all the colors of everything for fifteen or twenty minutes at a time. No color—what a world that would be! And sometimes all the thoughts in his head would go way up to the top of his skull and then slide down at him in a crazy tilt, picking up enormous speed and threatening to slide down on him like a runaway piano on the deck of a ship in a storm. And the music he heard! If he had the skill to write it down he wouldn't do it. Even if he did, no instrument could play it. It would have to be sung by screaming people whose feet were on fire. Horrible music.

"Have you heard the way people scream when their feet are on fire?" he said to the French police inspector across the desk from him.

The policeman stared at him blankly and said, "Now these lists of convalescent homes. What is your feeling about that?"

"What do you mean?"

"I mean they are sick people, mostly old people, so I suggest we jump over this list and go on to the next. No need to—"

Strasse hit the desk with his fist so hard that everything on it jumped. Here it was, almost one in the morning, and he hadn't been able to visit one of his clubs that evening, and these idiots were still splitting hairs about Jews. "Don't you people ever learn anything?" he screamed. "You've been working with me for three years and eating pretty well. You've got a few deals on the side, so maybe you are even a rich man by now. And I did it for you. But when I try to teach you the way you have to learn to think, you just can't do it." The shifting liquid heat started inside his head and ran like molten gold across the top of his forehead, dropped imperceptibly, like a linotype machine, then started to burn its way back to the other side where it dropped and started again. "They're Jews, aren't they? It is that simple. They will be dead in exactly four days, won't they? What difference does it make how old they are or whether they have a bad cold? Jews, Jews! We are here to kill Jews. Will you ever, ever learn that?" Then the private telephone rang, and Strasse picked it up wearily. It seemed to weigh sixty-eight pounds.

"Strasse," he said into the telephone.

"Baby? Yoka. We got trouble." He sat up very straight.

"Who? Where?"

"The Casino Latino. I've locked myself in the office. It's the fucking SS fighting the fucking Milice. They're wrecking the joint, and I can't raise any cops."

"Stay locked in there, you hear?" he said frantically. "I'll be right there." He hung up. "Come on," he said to the four policemen. "And bring a few loaded sticks. They're breaking up one of my night clubs." They all charged out of the room, and in less than eight minutes they were at the Casino Latino. A full-scale free-for-all was going on, but when one of the inspectors blew a whistle the fighters paused as though a motion picture projector had stopped in mid-reel. Slowly eyes were raised to the small balcony where Strasse, with the Totenkorps Death's Heads shining on his uniform, stood with the four cops.

"Gestapo!" he screamed at them.

The fighting stopped cold. They were all blind drunk.

"You will line up in two files—SS to the right, Milice to the left." He snapped his fingers and pointed. "You will give names, ranks, and serial numbers. Whatever the damages are to this place you will pay double, and whatever labor is required you will provide yourselves. Line up!"

He had seen Yoka open the door of the office at the back and, knowing that she was watching, he began to hyperbolize. "You are filthy swine! You are low, rotten filth!" He turned to the police. "Get them out. March them to the nearest commissariat. I don't want to look at them. Out! Out!"

As the bruised and drunken men moved past him to the door, Strasse walked down the steps to the back of the room where Yoka was standing, waiting to tell him how masterful and wonderful he was. She was deathly pale, but of course it had been a frightening experience to be trapped in a cellar with wild men. Well, he had shown her how such matters were handled.

"What is that uniform?" she asked in a shaking voice. He blinked, confused, then collected himself and looked down. He was wearing his uniform. Those damned pills! My God. Well, what the hell, it had to happen sooner or later. "Listen, Yoka. Maybe I should have told you. But who had the time, correct? I am not really a Dane. You know what I mean—I am a German, I am with the Gestapo. I am a German, you know?"

She stared at him in horror. Her expression was so different that it upset him. "What's the matter?" he said. She did not answer. "Yoka! Stop looking at me like that! I admit it, I should have told you. But you liked me to be Danish. You liked the beret. You said it many times. You like night clubs. You like night clubs as much as I do. Where do you think I got the night clubs?" She stuffed her shaking hand into her mouth. "Yoka! Answer me! I am the same man. Nothing has changed but the suit I wear. Nothing else. You are the same and I am the same." Her legs gave away, and she sank as slowly as a fog, toppling sideways into a chair, still staring up at him with a look of the most unbelieving horror; and a terrible thought came to Strasse as he looked at her, a terrible, terrible thought.

"Are you a Jew?" The sentence exploded out of him before he even knew what he had been thinking. "Is that why you always cursed Germans? Is that why you are looking at me like that? Yoka! Answer me! Tell me! Are you a Jew?" He leaned over and pulled her to her feet; when he shook her he could hear her teeth strike against each other. "Tell me! I won't be angry. It is all right. There are ways to make it all right if you are a Jew. It has been done, Yoka. But you must tell me. Are you a Jew? I must know that. Are you a Jew? I have to know that." She did not answer him with words, but from far back in her throat she spat at him. It splattered across his face and he let her go and she fell again into the chair. He wheeled away from her, meaning to walk purposefully, but he found himself running out of the room into the deserted street.

Dawn was beginning to show. He fumbled in his pocket

261

for the pills, and took three instead of one. Within a matter of yards, he felt better. All at once he began to see things more clearly. He walked down the inclined rue de Ponthieu, and his mind formed itself in a perfectly circular pattern, permitting him to see almost all of the known world as though through a remarkable telescope. Then the juice-filled, pain-wild music began in his head, and he stood on the corner of the rue du Colisée and leaned against the building, waiting for it to fade away into giant patterns of black and white herringbone tweed. Then the bubbling-water effects began: churning round domes of red, breaking and then re-forming. Moving mechanically, he walked through empty streets until he reached the Place Beauvau, and Gestapo headquarters for Paris. Like an automaton he saluted the guards and entered the courtyard.

Inside, he sought out the duty officer, who saluted him warily. "Issue a pick-up order for Yoka Karmo," Strasse said. "She will either be at the night club Casino Latino, in the rue de Ponthieu, or at five Boulevard Mistler." The duty officer noted the facts on his form sheet while Strasse rambled on. "I want her interrogated. I want to know if she is a Jew. I want her interrogated until she admits to either being a Jew or not being a Jew. After she makes her statement, I want it checked out in Amsterdam." He stared at the duty officer blankly, trying to remember what he had just said, and then screamed into the man's face. "And I want action, do you hear that?" He pouted. "Get me a car."

Feeling like a ruler of men but slightly tired, Captain Strasse went to his quarters on the Avenue Foch to try to get some sleep. It was four-thirty; he could sleep until nine. He scrawled a do-not-disturb sign, tacked it on the outside of his door, and was asleep, fully dressed, in seconds.

Strasse slept until five forty-five P.M. He thought of chewing out his people for letting him sleep so long, but he knew that he had needed it. He was still so tired that it took him almost five minutes to edge his hand to the table beside the bed and reach the bottle of pills. God bless Professor Morell. He rested for five minutes before unscrewing the cap of the bottle and swallowing a pill.

Exactly eleven minutes later Strasse was prancing from wall to wall under a cold shower, singing the Horst Wessel song at the top of his lungs. God, he felt good. What in God's name did that marvelous Professor Morell put in those pills? If the Fuehrer would only take four of them some morning, the war in the East would be over by nightfall. Well, he had shot a whole day. It was the first workday he had ever missed, rain or shine, in sickness or in health, for richer, for poorer. He was toweling himself when he thought of Yoka. Something about Yoka. What was it? Damn it, what was it? Each time he thought he had it, it would slip away again. Business. No use. He shrugged. It would come to him. He dressed in civilian clothes and a jaunty blue beret.

Yoka wasn't at her apartment and the bed hadn't been slept in. Or maybe she had made the bed. He prowled the room nervously, and when he heard footsteps on the stairs he poked his head out the door. But it was only Mme. Cardozo knocking a broom around on the stairs. "Did Mlle. Karmo go out?" Mme. Cardozo shrugged. "Did she come in?" Mme. Cardozo raised her left eyebrow. She hated Danes. He slammed the door shut and pushed past her down the stairs. Yoka must be at the commissary. But it turned out that she had not been there all day, and by the time he reached the Casino Latino, where they always met for Yoka's breakfast early in the evening, it was not only closed, it was a wreck. Every table in the place had been broken, and the big bar mirror was smashed. His first little joint, ruined. He was outraged. He heard voices in the back and found the porter with the barman, who had a split lip and a big mouse under his right eye. "Where's Yoka?" he asked.

"Jesus, M'sieu Strasse! Jesus, the Gestapo took her," the porter said excitedly. "They came maybe half an hour after you left." Both men had jumped to their feet deferentially when he came in and now they were looking at him apprehensively. "The Gestapo?" he said with some confusion. "The *Gestapo?*"

Neither man answered him. "After I left?" he asked blankly. The two men glanced at each other quickly, and then the porter shrugged. They had been working for him for three years, so why should it be different now? "There was a riot, boss. SS and the Milice. Yoka called you. You came in with four cops and stopped everything." He paused. He almost didn't say it, but then he took a deep breath. "You were in uniform."

263

It all began to come back. As Strasse stumbled toward the front door he saw something red on the floor and bent over to pick it up. It was silk. It was the collar of Yoka's silk dress. He ran out the door and down the hill. At the bottom he stopped short, took the bottle out of his pocket, shook the last pill from it and swallowed it. He waited, leaning against the building for a few minutes, and then walked back to the club and into the office to telephone. "Get out there and clean up that mess," he said to the two men as he passed them. They leaped to their feet.

He called Gestapo Paris headquarters and asked for his office. When the girl came on he said, "I am at Anjou forty-five ninety. I want information immediately on an arrest made this morning in the rue de Ponthieu at about four-fifteen. Name of Yoka Karmo. Call right back." He lit a cigarette and considered things anew through the Morell space viewer. A girl like Yoka. Well, it was convictions plus principles. He had done the right thing instinctively. She wasn't a Jew, of course. He could spot a Jew at a thousand yards, upwind and in the dark. But for some reason he hated Germans. So what? He hated Jews. Mme. Cardozo hated Danes. The French hated everybody. Well, now she knew that he was a German and he must get her back. Must. They would cross-examine her and she would make a statement that she was not a Jew—which could easily be checked by telephoning Amsterdam, anyway. And it would probably turn out that the interrogation had been a very good thing. If she hated Germans, maybe she had to learn to be afraid of them so that she would need him to protect her. Everything was going to be all right.

The telephone rang. "Strasse."

"We have no conclusive report here, Captain Strasse, but we have a call in to Major Rau in Amsterdam."

"Where is the woman now?"

"They were full up here, Captain, so she was taken to the rue Lauriston." Strasse shuddered involuntarily. "Send me a car, please," he said. "Thirty-six rue de Ponthieu." As he hung up he was feeling terribly nervous. The rue Lauriston was Gestapo-France headquarters, and the interrogators there were called the merry convicts. The pill bottle was empty and he flung it into the corner of the room. How could he let himself run this low? More pills would have arrived at Avenue Foch by now.

Strasse did not reach rue Lauriston until eight fifty-five P.M. and he went directly to Lafont's office, sweating hard; that damned woman was so stubborn that she could get herself into trouble. She was too damned independent. These convicts of Lafont's weren't Germans; they didn't care about the book of instructions for interrogations. He wished that Yoka had been interrogated at the rue des Saussaies.

Lafont was always glad to see him, for Strasse was his principal source of supply of customers. They greeted each other, and then Strasse asked about Yoka. Lafont called for the booking sheets and ran his finger down the list. "Here she is. We booked her at four forty-two this morning. A tough customer."

"Did she make her statement? Is she a Jew?"

"I think she was a Jew," Lafont said. "But Cassamondu is positive she wasn't."

"Never mind opinions. What was her statement?"

"She refused to make a statement."

"You mean they're still interrogating her? Seventeen hours?"

"Oh, no," Lafont said. "That's all done. She died at"—he bent over the sheet again—"at five forty-one P.M." He shook his head with admiration. "She was a tough customer, that girl."

The mangling music started inside him and the gold line began to burn across his head, then down a space, then across again. The thoughts climbed to the top of the high ledge just behind his forehead, then chuted downward on a jagged course, gathering enormous weight and speed, and there was no place he could go to get away from it.

An axe clove him in two and the two halves went stumbling along the rue Lauriston down the hill toward the Etoile while the Gestapo car trailed after the two halves. He had become two men. One had committed *Rassenschande*, the most obscene act of which a human was capable. He had defiled his race, he had defiled the Corps, he had smeared filth over his honor and the honor of the SS. There was only one penalty. He would write a formal confession to the Reichsfuehrer SS that he had entered the unclean body of a Jew. He would only be shot when he deserved disemboweling.

Reeling along beside this ruined SS officer was the other half—the lost half. Yoka was dead. Yoka. How could he

live? What was living? Stale bread and the smell of sweat
in his night clubs, those filthy rat holes. Chasing after Jews
as though they thought they could ever kill every one of
them. There would always be more. Why should he live
without Yoka? No one wanted him. She had wanted him,
but she was dead. A Jew. How could there be a God who
would send him such a woman after making her a Jew?
She had to be a Jew; if she had been racially pure she
would have shouted it out to the skies. She would have
been defiant, but she would have told Lafont's men in the
rue Lauriston before they . . . before . . . He could not
bear to see it, but it came tumbling over the white-hot
ledge behind his forehead and roared straight at him. He
saw what they were doing to Yoka and he began to run,
screaming steadily as he ran. He had to get to the pills, he
must get the pills.

The Gestapo driver raced ahead, then jumped out of the
car and caught Captain Strasse in his arms just before he
reached the corner of the rue de Presbourg. He pushed
the Captain onto the floor in the back, got in again and
drove quickly to 31 bis Avenue Foch.

The pills had not arrived; transport had been delayed because of sabotage. The cramps started, and Strasse began to
vomit steadily.

At eleven forty-eight P.M. Fräulein Franzblau called
from the rue des Saussaies and he made himself take the
call. "Strasse."

"Captain Strasse, Major Rau in Amsterdam has just called
us back. The Karmo birth records were available on parents,
grandparents and great-grandparents. Karmo is not a Jew.
She is one hundred percent racially pure, I am happy to say."

Twenty

✠

THE ALLIED ARMIES were advancing across France. All freight
and railroad stations in and around Paris had been de-

stroyed by bomber attacks and by the persistent sabotage of railroad workers. The problems of food, power, and water supply were close to insoluble. The power supply from the Massif Central had been cut off, and Paris had to depend for light and power on a switchover from the Kembs power station on the upper Rhine. The city depended for food upon the black market, and over eighty percent of the population was starving on less than minimum subsistence levels.

Fräulein Nortnung wasn't hungry, but she was very depressed when she reached the flat at midday on July 20th. The office of the BdS has been closed for half a day. Piocher took her shoes off and rubbed her feet while she drank twenty-five-year-old Scotch whiskey. "Why do you rub my feet?" she asked listlessly. "I am hardly ever on my feet. I sit down all the time. You should rub my ass."

"Gets the circulation going all over," Piocher said. "You're very down tonight, *liebchen*. What's the matter?"

"You know why I'm home?"

"No."

"The office is closed for half a day."

"Really?"

"You know why it's closed for half a day? Remember that sweet little guy, the four-four-b fellow, Captain Strasse?"

"A sweet little guy?"

"Yes, you know the one."

"If he's a sweet little guy, what would you call Caligula?"

"I don't know him."

"All right. What about Strasse?"

"I can't get it through my head. He killed himself."

"Ah?"

"What a tragedy."

"Why?"

"Why? Should I say it was a cute thing? That's what you say when people shoot themselves. What a tragedy."

"I meant why did he kill himself?"

"Who knows? Did you ever see anyone with more to live for? He would have made Standartenfuehrer for sure. He was only about twenty-seven years old and he was marvelous at his job."

"Go in and run a tub for yourself."

"Why?" He stared at her with his hard eyes. "All right, Carlie. I'll run the tub."

"Best thing for you. I'll be away all night and before I go—" She jumped up at once.

"I'll run the tub right now." She thundered out of the room on her gorgeous and substantial legs. He waited until he heard the bath water running, and then telephoned Military Headquarters.

At twelve forty-seven P.M. on July 20, 1944, Piocher picked Veelee up in his car at the Place de l'Alma and then drove slowly along the *quai.*

"The St. Quentin *reseau* has checked out your information and it is quite accurate," Piocher said. "We will make the strikes tonight."

"Very good. Give me the names of the two men."

"All the locomotive shops and the tank assembly plants will go up. No bombers have ever been able to get in, but we'll make it on foot and make it stick, thanks to you."

Veelee said nothing.

"There are no longer two men, General. The second man, the man who gave the order to the police to arrest your son, killed himself last night. He was Captain Strasse, head of Gestapo Section four-four-b." Veelee moaned softly. "The first man, the man who had Strasse issue the order to arrest your son, is the BdS, SS Standartenfuehrer Eberhard Drayst."

"Do you know why, Piocher? Does anyone know why?"

Piocher coughed, then pursed his lips as he stared carefully at the road ahead. "Drayst is somewhat unbalanced about your wife," he answered. "He tried to rape her in Berlin during the November pogroms in thirty-eight." Veelee grunted heavily, then turned to Piocher, his monocle glittering. "Your wife will confirm it, General," Piocher said reassuringly. It began to rain lightly, and he started the windshield wiper. "If I can be of any help to you, General—"

"We have our own plans," Veelee said, "but there are things I will need. Civilian clothes, for one."

"Size?"

"For Drayst, and some bandages." He spoke on in detail; he would need everything before six o'clock.

"Drayst has shut down his office for half a day. He will be alone. He is working on a report and there will be no one else on his floor."

"Thank you." They did not speak again. The car left Veelee at the Etoile at the head of Avenue Kléber, and he hurried toward the Hôtel Majestic.

For ten days the men who had plotted the Fuehrer's assassination waited uneasily and uncertainly in the Bendlerstrasse. The attempt was to have been made on July 11th, then on July 15th. By the 20th, they all knew that they could not wait because it would be impossible to keep the secret any longer.

The Fuehrer's headquarters at Rastenburg in East Prussia, called the Wolf's Lair, was in a dark forest, deep in perpetual twilight under the camouflage of heavy trees. Guns, bayonets, electric fences, barbed-wire gates, and abnormal suspicion kept the world out. Not even Keitel and Jodl, who had been sentenced to stand beside the Fuehrer for the rest of his life, could be passed into the Wolf's Lair without being checked and rechecked at each of the series of entrances.

At eight-ten in the morning of July 20th, Lieutenant-Colonel Claus von Stauffenberg was passed through the entrances carrying a two-pound bomb wrapped in a shirt in his briefcase. At noon, after breakfast with the Headquarters Commandant, Lieutenant-Colonel Streve, a fellow conspirator, Stauffenberg was received by Keitel.

Von Stauffenberg had lost parts of both hands in the war, so before leaving Keitel's office for the Fuehrer's briefing room he excused himself, went into a toilet and, using special tongs, broke the acid capsule which would set the fuse of the bomb. Then he rejoined Keitel and they walked sedately into the night world of the Teutonic forest to the *Gaestebaracke*, where the day's briefings were to be held. As they entered the room, General Heusinger, Director of Military Operations, had already begun his report to the Fuehrer on conditions on the Eastern front. Stauffenberg moved to the right-hand corner of the map-strewn table which held the Fuehrer's attention, slid the briefcase under it, to the right of the officer sitting there, and then left the room. The officer was Colonel Brandt, unable to escape destiny, the ever unknowing accomplice who as a favor to Veelee had so willingly and guilelessly transported the bomb package into the Fuehrer's plane. The briefcase was in Colonel Brandt's way, so he pushed it against the heavy table leg on the side farthest from the Fuehrer. General Heusinger had reached the final section of his report—*"Wenn jetzt nicht endlich die Heeresgruppe vom Peipussee zuruechgenommen wird, dann wückrden wir eine Katastrophe"*—when the bomb exploded, at twelve-fifty P.M.

In Berlin the revolutionaries waited for word that the bomb had been exploded, but the chief signals officer of Rastenburg, General Fellgiebel, in command of the Communications Center, panicked when he saw the wavering line of wounded men, their faces smudged and some of them in shock, as they stumbled out of the *Gaestebaracke*. The Fuehrer, who was in the lead, was supported by Keitel. Fellgiebel did not notify his fellow conspirators at the Bendlerstrasse, nor, most importantly, did he blow up the communications installation as planned. He was to be executed by the Fuehrer for treason just the same.

General Olbricht, Chief of Staff of the Home Army, had alerted the Commandant of Berlin and the unit commanders at the camps at Doeberitz, Jueterbog, Krampnitz, and Wuensdorf to stand by for instant assignment. General Hoepner, who had been publicly cashiered by the Fuehrer and forbidden to wear his uniform, brought it to the Bendlerstrasse in a suitcase and changed into it in a lavatory next to Olbricht's office. General Beck wore a rumpled brown tweed suit. The plotters assembled one by one in serried ranks from Field Marshal von Witzleben down to Lieutenant von Hammerstein. By two o'clock they had become apprehensive. At three-twelve P.M. General Thiele of Olbricht's staff got through to Rastenburg and received an inconclusive report that there had been an explosion in which many had been killed and wounded. At three thirty-seven P.M. Stauffenberg's adjutant, calling from the military airfield at Rangsdorf to ask irritatedly why no car had been sent to meet them, told Olbricht's chief of staff, who took the call, "The Fuehrer is dead."

At four-ten von Stauffenberg was on the telephone to all field commanders who were part of the conspiracy. He reached General von Stuelpnagel in Paris at four twenty-seven and repeated his prepared message in staccato fashion: "Hitler is dead. You must seize all wireless stations and information centers. If there is SS opposition it must be broken."

Count von Stauffenberg had a light and pleasant voice and none of the happy tenor of it changed under the pressure of the excitement, then or later. "It is entirely likely that Hitler's headquarters will issue counterorders. They may have already done so, but they are not to be obeyed. They are not authentic. Field Marshal von Witzleben and the Wehrmacht have taken over all executive power. The Reich is in danger, and as always in its greatest need, the army takes over."

General von Stuelpnagel had actually received word of the assassination before the leaders of the revolt at the Bendlerstrasse. His Commander in Chief for Gross-Paris, General Baron von Boineburg-Langsfeld, had gotten a call at two thirty-five P.M. from a Swedish countess who told him that the Swedish radio had reported that an attempt had been made on Hitler's life. General Boineburg had advised von Stuelpnagel, from the Hôtel Méance, and then had asked if any such word had come through the regular communications channels. Veelee was with the Military Governor when von Stauffenberg called.

When General von Stuelpnagel rang off he looked up at Veelee, swallowed hard, and blinked. "Hitler is dead, thank God," he said, and Veelee sat down slowly as though to conserve himself. "Kluge has been notified," Stuelpnagel added in a worried voice.

"To have everything depend upon Field Marshal Kluge makes it seem as though Germany were cursed," Veelee said intently.

"Kluge will hold fast this time."

"No, sir."

"Kluge hated Hitler and he guaranteed to General Beck that if Hitler were removed he would surrender the armies."

"If I may say so, sir, Field Marshal Kluge will need to see the corpse and feel its coldness. Unless he is forced, the Field Marshal cannot make such a decision. He feeds on fright, sir. He will have to be forced."

"Force?" The idea amused Stuelpnagel. "How do we force the Field Marshal who is now Commander in Chief of the armies of the West?"

"We must arrest the SS, sir."

"Rhode!"

"When the SS is in jail, when we line them up against a

wall at Fresnes and shoot them, Kluge will then realize that the Fuehrer is really dead."

Stuelpnagel turned in his chair, picked up the telephone, and spoke with his secretary. "I want to talk to the Military Commander for Gross-Paris, please." He reconsidered. "No, change that. Ask the Military Commander to come to this office, please. And the Chief, and von Teuchert, von Bargotsky, and von Falkenhausen. You too. I want to dictate an order." Veelee was on his feet, his monocle glittering, staring fixedly through his one eye. "Since this was your idea, Rhode, is it your intention to wish to engage in the operation?"

"Yes, sir. I request permission to arrest SS Standartenfuehrer Drayst, sir." Stuelpnagel nodded as his secretary, Countess Podewills, entered. In a firm voice he dictated: "From Military Commander, France, to Military Commander for Gross-Paris. Order: SS and SD have made a *putsch* in the Reich aiming at the liquidation of the Fuehrer. Arrest immediately the SS and SD and disarm them, as well as the SS chief for France, General Koltrastt, with his staff. Secure all office papers. In case of resistance, force is to be applied without consideration." He smiled wryly at Veelee. "This arrest is going to be hard on Boineburg—Koltrastt has some secret source for obtaining an unlimited supply of *Importens*, Boineburg's favorite cigars."

The meeting convened at five-o-three P.M., and Stuelpnagel read his order to the assembled officers. There was no comment except from General Boineburg. "I suggest, sir, that inasmuch as the SD headquarters are on a main traffic artery and the sight of Germans fighting Germans might not be the best thing for the French to see, it would be better to conduct the operation later on in the evening."

"Very good. When?"

"Ten-thirty? The SS would all be in their quarters ready for the plucking."

"Ten-thirty it is, then." Von Stuelpnagel nodded to Colonel von Linstow, his Chief of Staff, to take over. In turn, Linstow bowed gracefully to General von Boineburg. "Your show, sir," he said.

"We'll use the Second Battalion of the Motorized Rifles of the First Security Regiment and reinforce them with armored cars," von Boineburg said. "They are just over the river at the Ecole Militaire. They'll be formed at ten-fifteen in front of the Porte Dauphine at the foot of Avenue Foch and at the end of the Boulevard Lannes, where General Koltrastt has his headquarters. This is only two streets from HSPF headquarters and four streets from the BdS. Other units of the First will overpower and arrest all Gestapo posts and those assigned SS resistance pockets which are a part of the preparation for the defense of the city."

"For the sake of protocol, which will concern the Field Marshal more than anyone else," Stuelpnagel said laconically, "I would suggest that the arrests of the HSPF and the BdS be made by general officers. If you have no objections, General von Boineburg, I will assign the arrest of the BdS to General Rhode."

"Very good, sir," Boineburg said. "My aide, General Brehmer, the ZGV, will arrest the HSPF, and I'll assign Colonel von Kraewel to General von Rhode for the BdS. We will take both of them in custody, with their staffs, to the Hôtel Continental next to my headquarters. All remaining officers will be transported in custody to the Fresnes-Wehrmacht prison. The enlisted men will go to the Fort de l'Est."

"Move fast, please," von Stuelpnagel said. "They are two thousand heavily armed men and it is quite possible that the navy and the Luftwaffe ground units might try to resist the arrests with arms. Thank you, gentlemen, and good luck."

Six minutes after the officers had left, General Beck telephoned from the Bendlerstrasse.

"Stuelpnagel, I call to tell you that contrary to a previous report, the attempt on the life of Hitler has failed."

"Failed?"

"We cannot stop now. We have lost the fifty-one percent chance to bring it off, but we can still do it. Are you with us?"

"I have ordered the arrest of the SS here."

There was a pause while Beck considered all that this meant. His voice shook. "Germany will never forget you for that."

Stuelpnagel rolled his eyes to the ceiling. "What about von Kluge?"

"Have you talked to him?"

"Not yet."

"I will call him now," General Beck said. "And this time he must stand with us."

"I will have your call put through from here." Von Stuelpnagel picked up the other telephone, gave the order for the

273

call, and when Kluge picked up his telephone Stuelpnagel advised him that he was on the line. For a few minutes he listened while General Beck spoke to the Field Marshal and then he hung up slowly, his eyes clouded with dread and doubt. He stared blankly out of the window for some time until Countess Podewills came in with two teletyped dispatches. He read them and then telephoned Veelee. "An order has come through from Field Marshal von Witzleben," he said. "It says: 'The elimination of SS and SD resistance is to be undertaken ruthlessly.' I wanted you to know that you had made your excellent suggestion first."

"Thank you, sir."

"There are two other bits of news. I have been invited to dinner with Field Marshal von Kluge at La Roche Guyon." He paused, closing his eyes for a moment. "And Hitler is still alive."

Twenty-One

✠

Von Kluge, who had taken over the command of Army Group B from General Rommel, had left his headquarters in St. Germain, where he was Commander of the Armies in the West, to his Chief of Staff, General Gunther von Blumentritt, and had retained Rommel's Chief of Staff, General Dr. Hans Speidel, at La Roche Guyon. When Kluge had taken over the command of the West from Rundstedt on July 6th, he had immediately sent word to General Beck that if the Fuehrer died he would support the army *putsch*. This had also been conveyed to Rommel, but he neither trusted nor respected Kluge and informed Stuelpnagel that he was going to take independent action if Kluge failed to keep his word. Unfortunately, on July 17th Rommel was severely injured in an automobile accident, and Kluge took over his group.

Army Group B headquarters was in a château built against the cliffs on the north bank of the Seine, between Mantes la Jolie and Vernon. Rommel had fashioned himself a modest apartment on the ground floor, adjoining a rose garden. His study was a recreation of French culture; it had splendid tapestries and an inlaid Renaissance desk on which Louvois had signed the revocation of the Edict of Nantes in 1685. The Field Marshal's staff was purposely kept small: eleven officers, including two historians. Contrary to regulations, there was no National Socialist political officer—a position which had been introduced into the Wehrmacht in 1943 to whip discontented spirits into line.

Early on the morning of July 20th, at eight-ten A.M., Field Marshal von Kluge was driven to the Fifth Panzer Army headquarters where he ordered all army and corps commanders to meet him. The briefing was to make clear the Field Marshal's instructions concerning the battle then being waged in the critical Caen and St. Lô areas. No political matters were discussed.

At five-o-three P.M. General Blumentritt reached the Field Marshal by telephone to tell him that the Fuehrer was dead. One hour later, when von Kluge had returned to La Roche Guyon, the radio was announcing that the assassination attempt had failed, and that the Fuehrer himself would broadcast later that evening. As Kluge shifted this information from hand to hand like a hot bullet, General Beck telephoned from Berlin.

"You have the news, Kluge, that Hitler is still alive?"

"Yes. Quite a surprise."

"Nonetheless, Kluge—" Beck's tone was grim and ominous.

"My God, Beck! I have orders pouring in from the Bendlerstrasse and from Fuehrer headquarters, and each tell different stories."

"Listen to me. So much depends on you. So much. There is still a very good chance that we will carry the day."

"Things are happening too fast, Beck. I need time to think."

"You must proceed as we have agreed."

"What is the position of the navy?"

"If you contact General Eisenhower instantly, they will come along with us. We are the leaders. What is your answer?"

"How badly hurt is Hitler, Beck?"

"Kluge, I am going to put this question to you plainly. Do you approve of what has happened here and are you ready to place yourself under my command?"

Kluge did not answer.

"Kluge! We must go forward now whatever happens! Let us be firm at this moment. Let us be strong for Germany!"

"I am perfectly aware of all of our conversations and agreements, Beck. However, they were concerned with a situation which greatly differs from this one. The Fuehrer is still alive. That presents an unforeseen circumstance, and it calls for renewed conversations with my staff officers."

"Renewed conversations? How much time do you think has been given to us?"

"I—I'm sorry, Beck. I will call you back in a half-hour." Kluge put down the telephone.

It was all slipping away from them by seven P.M. Fellgiebel had failed to cut off the Fuehrer's headquarters from the outside world; other plotters had failed to take possession of the radio facilities in Berlin and other major cities; the conspirators' maps of the SS disposition in Berlin were faulty; the Panzer units on which so much reliance had been placed had not appeared; the crack guards regiment, Wachtbataillon Grossdeutschland, had been persuaded by Dr. Goebbels to sign operations to capture the conspirators' headquarters at the Bendlerstrasse, where they had not even posted a sentry to warn them against attack. The conspiracy had been corrupted by corrosive fear of the Fuehrer and of his supreme authority.

General von Stuelpnagel arrived at Kluge's headquarters at La Roche Guyon at seven twenty-eight P.M. in the company of Veelee and his aide-de-camp, Lieutenant-Colonel von Hafacker, a tall calm man who had been a hero of the resistance movement.

The three men met Kluge briefly in his office. "In such a short time everything has changed, has it not, gentlemen?" the Field Marshal said.

"It may seem that way, sir," Stuelpnagel answered blandly, "but nothing has changed much. One man who was supposed to be dead is still alive. One man. You hold all the cards. You are the hero of this great victory."

"Hero?" the Field Marshal said with asperity. "Victory?"

"As soon as you surrender to the enemy commanders, Hitler will fall."

"No, no. The Fuehrer is still alive, sir. That changes everything."

"Kluge, do you or do you not want to save the Reich and to save the army? Only you can do it. The Allies will not deal with him. They *will* deal with you. Surrender to them, Kluge. Now—tonight."

"The attempt has failed. Everything is over. Why, if the Fuehrer knew that I—"

"You must act. You have given your word. This must be done. *It must be done.* To help you make up your mind, I should tell you, sir, that before I left Paris to meet you here I issued an order for the arrest of the SS and SD."

Von Kluge stared at him, the jaw in his weak face dropping. He reached for the telephone and asked for General von Blumentritt, staring steadily and unseeingly at Stuelpnagel as his tongue licked his lips.

"Blumentritt? General von Stuelpnagel has just reported to me an unparalleled act of insubordination. He has ordered the arrest of the SS in Paris without consulting me. You will telephone von Linstow at once and order him, in my name, to stop the action immediately." He hung up. He glared at Veelee and von Hafacker.

"It cannot be stopped, sir," Stuelpnagel said silkily. "It is too late. And when I made the decision to do it, so much became clear. The revolt in Berlin was unnecessary, and so was the attempt on Hitler's life. We won the revolt, in Paris, when the order was given to arrest the SS. Kluge, I hand victory to you on a golden platter. Make the telephone call to General Eisenhower's headquarters now and you will be the savior of Germany and the German Army. Establish the liaison. Act, Kluge!"

Kluge hesitated. He gripped the desk and for an instant half turned and faced in the direction of the Wolf's Lair, his head cocked, as if he were listening to that terrible voice. His frightened face was green and silver in the half-light as he looked over at Stuelpnagel and then at Veelee.

Veelee drew himself up to his great height and put the monocle firmly in his right eye socket. His stare radiated arrogance and contempt for von Kluge. Though Veelee was fifteen years younger than either man, his silver hair and paralyzed face made him seem their contemporary. In his hereditary allegiance to the German Army he was two hundred years older than either of them, and his voice had the force of a mace. "Our major cities are all destroyed, sir," he said to von Kluge slowly, "and all of the genius of Germany has been destroyed. And what this upstart politician has done has changed Germany from a nation of poets, builders, and thinkers into a den of murderers and hangmen. The army has never been in greater peril. Count our dead, sir, as if that could be done. One million, two million or five million —all wasted by a guttersnipe. Why did it happen, sir? It happened because of the cowardice of people like us, the opportunism of people like us. We, the German Army could have struck him down in any twenty-minute period of any hour of the clock from 1933 until this day, sir. Hear the dead! Deliver our country and our army. Pull him down, sir!"

Von Kluge's face had grown colder and colder as he had listened. "You must shoulder your own responsibility," he said, "but I should advise the three of you to change into civilian clothes and go into hiding."

Twenty-Two

✠

COLONEL DRAYST was wearing nothing but a light silk dressing gown. He had finished the draft of his general order, and now he sat under the green reading light at the large desk in his commodious suite at the Avenue Foch headquarters, re-reading what he had written and filled with resentment at Strasse for having left such an enormous job undone.

20 July, 1944
    To: IV4b   SECRET! ! ! !
MEMORANDUM: on the increase in arrests of Jews in France.
1: JEWISH PERSONALITIES TO BE ARRESTED
(a) All persons who are Jews to be arrested without regard to nationality or other circumstances . . .

At nine-twelve P.M. Drayst was interrupted by the ringing of his private telephone. He lifted it apprehensively.

"Colonel Drayst?" The voice was intimate and inviting, and he could not believe his ears. It was Frau General von Rhode! It was difficult for him to control his breathing, and he opened his dressing gown with his free hand. The calls he had been making to her had finally taken effect.

"But, lovely lady, how did you get this telephone number?"

She laughed deliciously. "My husband is not the Nachrichtenfuehrer for nothing, Colonel."

"May I help you in some way, beautiful lady?"

"I want to see you." What a feeling it was! What a feeling! "Why?"

"You know why. You have told me why a hundred times on this telephone. Don't you . . . want to any more?"

"Oh, wonderful lady! But what made you change your mind?"

"My mind keeps going, and I cannot sleep. I keep making wonderful pictures of you. Of us." All she heard was his labored breathing. "I want to see you tonight," she pleaded.

"Yes!"

"At ten-fifteen?"

"Where?"

"Your quarters is the only place that is possible."

"Yes, yes. Ten-fifteen." He began to babble obscenities, but after a few minutes he realized that she had hung up.

The troops of the First Security Regiment diverted all traffic away from the Avenue Foch, but even during the day there were few French pedestrians in the sixteenth arrondissement. The troops who had been formed under the trees at the convergence of the Avenue Foch and the Boulevard Lannes were so quiet and unobtrusive that the officers and men working in the lighted windows at the SS headquarters building at No. 57 were completely unaware of them. At ten-seventeen P.M. General von Boineburg drove up in high spirits. In both directions he was able to see the sentries at the SS and the SD buildings. These men, called Hiwis, were the shop jokes of the SS, for they were Lithuanian volunteers who spoke German with an hilarious accent.

After a short conference with his chief of staff, General Brehmer, and with General von Rhode and the regimental commander, Colonel von Kraewel, General von Boineburg gave the order to advance at ten twenty-nine P.M. At a single whistle blast the men ran out from under the trees and into the waiting trucks. The trucks peeled off in two directions, those going to the left making a short run into the Boulevard Lannes and those to the right grinding up the fifteen-hundred-yard incline of the Avenue Foch toward SD headquarters.

As the trucks came abreast of SS headquarters there was another whistle blast and the troops hit the street, officers with drawn revolvers and men with machine rifles. The sentries offered no resistance, and in a few minutes all the SS troops had been mustered out into the yard, searched, and loaded into trucks. All files were secured and removed and the armories were emptied. With pistols to their heads, SS officers sat at telephones and sent out the standard SS emergency call which would bring in all officers and men not on the post. Female employees were taken into custody in separate trucks. An SS Sturmbannfuehrer asked a sergeant-major if he had thought of the consequences of such an outrage; the sergeant-major replied that if there was any thinking to be done it would be by the Sturmbannfuehrer, for he was going to be lined up with the others and shot the next morning at Fresnes. General Brehmer arrested the astonished General Koltrastt who was chatting on the telephone in his shirtsleeves with Otto Abetz, the German political commissar.

The fearful SS, which had pledged to fight to the last man, fell with only one shot fired—a rifle that went off when one of the Hiwi sentries did his comical best to cut a smart salute for General Brehmer.

The other group of trucks rolled to a halt in front of 72-84 Avenue Foch, and at the whistle the troops piled out and raced into the building, the first men in actually taking a Hiwi sentry salute. General von Rhode led the way, directly ahead of the lieutenant in command of the battalion of troops. They separated at the main floor. Veelee grabbed the rifle of an astonished SS guard already in custody, and took the lift to the fifth floor.

Paule was waiting for him in the corridor, her eyes burning, her face bloodless. She carried a suitcase. They stood there together quietly for an instant, and Veelee kissed her cheek. Then she led the way to the large double door at the end of the hall and knocked on it softly.

"Come in, lovely lady, come in," Drayst's voice said, and

the door began to open. As Veelee crossed the threshold Drayst was smiling. Veelee drove the butt of the rifle directly into Drayst's mouth with all the force of his single powerful arm. Teeth scattered on the floor and Drayst was driven backward almost fifteen feet before he fell unconscious on the floor. Veelee moved forward and stood over him, holding the rifle over the body like a pile driver. As Paule shut the door and entered the room, he drove the rifle butt downward, then lifted it, and struck the gaping, bleeding mouth again. Paule moaned and spun away, turning her back on the gaping face. The rifle butt removed every one of Drayst's teeth as Veelee turned the head with his boot to reach all of them. When he tossed the rifle on the bed Paule turned around, but she could not look at the body on the floor or at Veelee. She swayed for a moment, and then she lifted the suitcase and crossed the room with it to Drayst. Kneeling beside him and forcing herself to look down at his broken toothless face, she began to sob. She poured styptic collodion over him, turning his head to one side so that neither the astringent nor the blood could choke him. Her tears fell on him as she handled him tenderly. Then she opened a can of penicillin powder and sprinkled it liberally into what had once been the shape of a human mouth. An extraordinary swelling of the tongue, gums, and lips had started. Drayst would not have been able to talk comprehensively for many weeks even if he was going to live that long, and his face was no longer recognizable.

Paule took a large roll of bandage from the suitcase and, sitting on the carpet beside Drayst's head, began to bandage him carefully, attaching gauze tampons to the bandage so that they would absorb the blood. While she bandaged, Veelee struggled with his one arm to put the civilian clothes on Drayst: a bright pink shirt and a clip-on bow tie, socks and yellow shoes, a loudly checked suit with padded shoulders, and a checked cloth cap. When Paule finished bandaging she took over, and in a few minutes the disguise was complete. Together they lifted Drayst to his feet. His legs would not support him, so they dragged him to the door, Paule carrying the suitcase, down the corridor and into the lift.

The building was silent; the battalion had done its work. Drayst lay on the floor of the elevator as limp as a scarecrow, hat jaunty over his bandages which gave him a widely outlined clown's mouth in wet red. On the street floor they left him crumpled while they checked the location of the staff car. It had been parked exactly where Veelee had ordered. They returned and dragged the former Colonel Drayst across the marble floors, rolled him down the steps, and threw him onto the floor in the back of the car. The shattered face was trying to talk, but the sounds which came out were hardly human, and certainly not words.

The car flew Veelee's pennant, and Paule moved it across the deserted city at high speed.

"I have civilian clothes in the boot of the car for you," she said.

"No. I thank you, but I cannot."

"You wanted Kluge to give all of you up to the enemy, so why won't you do that yourself? You must act as the symbol of the army. You must surrender—symbolically—for your comrades."

"That is not possible."

"Then what will happen?"

"I don't know."

"They will arrest you. You will be shot."

"Perhaps. That is a hazard of my family's profession, my dear Paule. But so many officers are involved that even he cannot shoot them all."

"He can, Veelee. He will, dearest!"

"I think not. But there are no more battles for me." He sighed. "What will you do after tonight, my darling?"

"I don't know. If you go, I will have nothing."

"You could go to Spain . . . to—"

"No."

"I want you to be safe."

"I am yours, Veelee. I belong to you. It was never meant to be any other way."

He lifted her hand and kissed it. "I will love you forever," he said.

The car climbed the rue Lafayette. It slowed down at the check point in the Porte de Pantin and Veelee leaned forward into the searchlights. The sergeant of police waved them on and the car moved out into the rue de Paris."

"I am frightened," Paule said, staring at the road.

"Why not? Hitler is still alive."

"Not that. No more." She shuddered. "I know I don't understand yet what we are doing tonight—but I am frightened of what will happen when I do."

Veelee's voice became hard. "We accomplished what we had pledged our honor to do."

"When Papa was alive it was so good to live," Paule said. "If we could only get back to that time."

"Drancy ahead," Veelee said. When the car stopped at the gate he ordered the duty sergeant to take them to the Officer of the Day.

The French police had long since been replaced by SS troops. Drancy was now run by Totenkopf battalions. The Officer of the Day was an SS Sturmbannfuehrer whom Veelee addressed by the army rank of major, which made the man stand taller. Between them the duty sergeant and Veelee manhandled and dragged Drayst into the orderly room and dumped him into a chair. Paule entered behind them and sat in a chair on the other side of the room, ignoring the major and staring at Drayst with desperate gratitude. Drayst was making mewing sounds at the Sturmbannfuehrer, a man whom he had known for almost ten years. His eyes were alive with a terror that demanded to be understood, but no one except Paule even looked in his direction. He reached up and pulled at the sergeant's tunic with his left hand and almost had his wrist broken by a downward slash of the sergeant's hand.

"Here is a very, very special Jew, Major," Veelee said. "He is a very special guest who is now in your hands at the personal order of the Military Governor."

"Yes, my General!" The Sturmbannfuehrer had never seen a combat general before. Veelee unbuttoned his left breast pocket under the dazzling rows of combat ribbons and removed the splendidly authenticated papers for Drayst which Piocher had asked Fräulein Nortnung to make up for him as a special favor, and which had been signed that morning by SS Colonel Drayst himself. "His papers," Veelee said, and handed them with a bow to the Sturmbannfuehrer.

"Yes, my General."

"When does the next train leave for the East?" Veelee knew the answer because Piocher had told him, but he wanted to have it confirmed. "Where does it go?"

"At thirteen-eleven, my General." The Sturmbannfuehrer looked at his watch. "In forty-nine minutes, to Auschwitz." The check-suited, bandaged figure on the chair made a series

283

of disgusting sounds, and the sergeant cuffed it with a heavy backhand. "It will leave from Bobigny, which is directly adjacent, as you may know."

"When does it reach Auschwitz?"

"Between sixty hours and four days, sir. Depending. This train has been routed through Nancy and Strasbourg into Stuttgart and Nuremberg, then to Dresden, Breslau, and Kattowitz to Auschwitz. It is a very heavy, extremely crowded train." The major smiled down at Drayst. "He will just fit into it." Drayst made more noises. "He sounds like a drowning duck," the Sturmbannfuehrer said. "You may be sure, my General, that he will travel with the first selection and that there will be no delays about his personal final solution at Auschwitz."

"The Military Governor asked me to see him actually put on the train," Veelee said.

"Very good, my General." The Sturmbannfuehrer made a ceremony of selecting exactly the right seal for the papers, then stamped each of the copies smartly and, keeping one copy, handed the others to the sergeant. "Load him," he said. The sergeant saluted and grabbed Drayst and half lifted and half carried him to the door. The Sturmbannfuehrer clicked his heels loudly and made a slight bow to Veelee.

As Paule reached the door, Veelee behind her, the radio in the room suddenly crackled and the Sturmbannfuehrer turned up the volume in anticipation of an announcement.

"Attention, please! In just a few moments the Fuehrer will be on the air." On the threshold the sergeant, still dragging Drayst, stopped and turned. Paule and Veelee came back into the room to listen, and the sergeant pulled the prisoner backward and dropped him on a chair. When Drayst began to make his awful noises again, the sergeant pulled his pistol out and turned it in his hand, making its butt a club. He stared down at Drayst and the mewing, gagging sounds stopped.

Like a sudden, terrible blow, the Fuehrer's iron, saber-toothed voice exploded out of the loudspeaker at them.

"My German comrades!

If I speak to you today it is first in order that you should hear my voice and should know that I am unhurt and well, and secondly, that you should know of a crime unparalleled in German history. A very small

284

clique of ambitious, irresponsible and, at the same time, senseless and stupid officers had concocted a plot to eliminate me and, with me, the staff of the High Command of the Wehrmacht. The bomb planted by Colonel Count von Stauffenberg exploded two meters to the right of me. It seriously wounded a number of my true and loyal collaborators, one of whom has died. I myself am entirely unhurt, aside from some very minor scratches, bruises, and burns."

Veelee held Paule's shoulders tightly, as though to protect her from the attack of that voice. He thought of von Stuelpnagel and of the fact that they were now as good as dead. From every ten conspirators the Gestapo would extract the names of a hundred more, until German ground was hot and soft with running German blood.

"I regard this as a confirmation of the task imposed upon me by Providence.

The circle of usurpers is very small and has nothing in common with the spirit of the German Wehrmacht and, above all, none with the German people. It is a gang of criminal elements which will be destroyed without mercy."

The Fuehrer's voice rose hysterically.

"We will not again be stabbed in the back as in 1918. I will root out these traitors and destroy them, and their women, and their children. I, your Fuehrer, will live on to change the world, while these betrayers, to the last man and child, will be killed like cattle, unworthy of my greatness."

There was a threatening pause while they stared at the radio, and then the Reichsmarschall's voice was heard. The little unit of listeners dispersed: the sergeant pulled Drayst to his feet and flung him out of the room; Veelee nodded his good night to the Sturmbannfuehrer; the officer clicked his heels and bowed as they left the shack.

The Sturmbannfuehrer made notations in his charge book, recorded Veelee's instructions, and then turned to the orderly typing at the back of the room and shouted that he wanted to send a telegram.

As the Sturmbannfuehrer spoke, the orderly typed:

RF   SS

SICHERHEITSDIENST

21ST JULY 1944

IV J 225A

NO. 7

TO: REICHSSICHERHEITSHAUPTAMT REFERAT IV4B HERRN OBERSTURMBANNFUEHRER EICHMANN (OR DEPUTY IN CASE OF ABSENCE)

BERLIN

ALSO:

TO: THE INSPECTOR OF THE ORANIENBURG CONCENTRATION CAMP

TO: THE CONCENTRATION CAMP AUSCHWITZ

ON 21 JULY 1944 TRANSPORTATION TRAIN NO. 1901/ 31 HAS LEFT THE DEPARTURE STATION LE BOURGET DRANCY IN THE AUSCHWITZ DIRECTION WITH 1224 JEWS.

THE PERSONS AFFECTED ARE IN ACCORDANCE WITH DIRECTIVES.

THE LEADER OF THE TRANSPORT IS SERGEANT-MAJOR GELDWASSER WHO HAS BEEN GIVEN THE LIST OF NAMES IN DUPLICATE.

RATIONS AS USUAL ISSUED FOR SEVEN DAYS PER JEW.

URGENT: PROCESSING OF JEW 563872 CAR 1184 MUST BE EXPEDITED AT EARLIEST BY SPECIAL ORDER, MILITARY GOVERNOR FOR FRANCE, AND EXPEDITION CONFIRMED TO UNDERSIGNED.

JOACHIM NOLANDER

SS STURMBANNFUEHRER

Paule and Veelee held each other's hands as they watched Drayst being dragged out of the truck at the railroad siding. Drayst struggled violently as he caught sight of them and screamed through his bandages at them, his hands and arms outstretched and shuddering. The two SS men opened the padlocks of Car 1184 and rolled the door back. Under the single electric bulb on the siding scores of pale faces stared

286

ut of the freight car at them. None of them spoke or made
sound, but their eyes accused God.

"No!" Paule cried out. "No! No!" The sergeant dragged
rayst toward the open train as Paule ran toward them.
sing all of her strength, she tried to pull Drayst and the
ergeant back with her, begging them to stop. As the ser-
eant rammed Drayst into the mass of bodies Drayst spun,
is eyes pleading with Paule. A bleating cry exploded from
is throat, but the sound was muffled as the door was
ammed shut. She could still hear him as the two SS men
napped the padlocks.

Paule ran to Veelee and held his shoulders, shaking him.
What will we do?" she sobbed. "For the rest of our
ves, what will we do?"

He stared at her stolidly, unable to comprehend her
hange. "We have killed a monster," he said at last.

Her eyes were deadened. "We have become the monster,"
he said as the train began to move and Drayst's sounds
nelted into the noises of furious steam. She turned away,
obbing helplessly, and began to run toward the retreating
ght on the last car of the train. "Papa! Help me! Please,
apa, help me!" She ran faster and shouted after the train.
Franz! Set to!" she pleaded. "Franz! Set to!"

BOOK EXCHANGE
472 S. Citrus
Azusa, Ca. 91702

CREST BOOKS

ON TOP WITH
THE BIG BESTSELLERS

A FLAG FULL OF STARS by Don Robertson (m838) 95¢

THIS ROUGH MAGIC by Mary Stewart (t837) 75¢

THE MAN by Irving Wallace (M841) 95¢

THE I HATE TO HOUSEKEEP BOOK
by Peg Bracken (d830) 50¢

IN VIVO by Mildred Savage (m824) 95¢

THE GREAT WORLD AND TIMOTHY COLT
by Louis Auchincloss (R825) 60¢

MASTER OF FALCONHURST by Kyle Onstott (M805) 95¢

THE THIRD DAY by Joseph Hayes (T816) 75¢

THE IPCRESS FILE by Len Deighton (R807) 60¢

THE PILGRIM PROJECT by Hank Searls (R798) 60¢

THE KEEPERS OF THE HOUSE
by Shirley Ann Grau (R799) 60¢

THE NIGHT IN LISBON by Erich Maria Remarque (R794) 60¢

LOOKING FOR THE GENERAL by Warren Miller (R793) 60¢

THE I HATE TO COOK BOOK by Peg Bracken (D777) 50¢

THE ADVENTURES OF AUGIE MARCH
by Saul Bellow (M780) 95¢

DR. SPOCK TALKS WITH MOTHERS
by Benjamin Spock, M.D. (R759) 60¢

THE VENETIAN AFFAIR by Helen MacInnes (T746) 75¢

THE TIN DRUM by Günter Grass (M691) 95¢

Wherever Paperbacks Are Sold
FAWCETT WORLD LIBRARY

If your dealer is sold out, send only cover price plus 10¢ each for postage and handling to Crest Books, Fawcett Publications, Inc., Greenwich, Conn. Please order by number and title. If five or more books are ordered, no postage or handling charge is necessary. No Canadian orders. Catalogue available on request.